THE
PLOTTERS

THE
PLOTTERS
UN-SU KIM

Translated from the Korean
by Sora Kim-Russell

4th ESTATE • *London*

4th Estate
An imprint of HarperCollins *Publishers*
1 London Bridge Street
London SE1 9GF

www.4thEstate.co.uk

Originally published in Korea as 설계자들 by Munhakdongne Publishing Corporation in 2010
First published in English by The Text Publishing Company in 2018
First published in Great Britain by 4th Estate in 2019

1

This book is published with the support of the
Literature Translation Institute of Korea (LTI Korea).

This translation originally published in Australia,
in slightly different form, by The Text Publishing Company.

A catalogue record for this book is
available from the British Library

ISBN 978-0-00-831576-4 (hardback)
ISBN 978-0-00-831577-1 (trade paperback)

Printed and bound in Great Britain by
CPI Group (UK) Ltd, Croydon, CR0 4YY

MIX
Paper from
responsible sources
FSC www.fsc.org FSC™ C007454

This book is produced from independently certified FSC paper
to ensure responsible forest management.

For more information visit: www.harpercollins.co.uk/green

CONTENTS

ON HOSPITALITY

The old man came out to the garden.

Reseng tightened the focus on the telescopic sight and pulled back the charging handle. The bullet clicked loudly into the chamber. He glanced around. Other than the tall fir trees reaching for the sky, nothing moved. The forest was silent. No birds took flight, no bugs chirred. Given how still it was out here, the noise of a gunshot would travel a long way. And if people heard it and rushed over? He brushed aside the thought. No point in worrying about that. Gunshots were common out here. They would assume it was poachers hunting wild boar. Who would waste their time hiking this deep into the forest just to investigate a single gunshot? Reseng studied the mountain to the west. The sun was one hand above the ridgeline. He still had time.

The old man started watering the flowers. Some received a gulp, some just a sip. He tipped the watering can with great ceremony, as if he were serving them tea. Now and then he did a little shoulder shimmy, as if dancing, and gave a petal a brief caress. He gestured at one of the flowers and chuckled. It looked like they were having a conversation. Reseng adjusted the focus again and studied the flower the old man was talking to. It looked familiar. He must have seen it before, but he couldn't remember what it was called. He tried to recall which flower bloomed in October—cosmos? zinnia? chrysanthemum?—but none of the names matched the one he was looking at. Why couldn't he remember? He furrowed his brow and struggled to come up with the name but soon brushed aside that thought, too. It was just a flower—what did it matter?

A huge black dog strolled over from the other end of the garden and rubbed its head against the old man's thigh. A mastiff, purebred. The same beast Julius Caesar had brought back from his conquest of Britain. The dog the ancient Romans had used to hunt lions and round up wild horses. As the old man gave the dog a pat, it wagged its tail and wound around his legs, getting in his way as he tried to continue his watering. He threw a deflated soccer ball across the garden, and the dog raced after it, tail wagging, while the old man returned to his flowers. Just as before, he gestured at them, greeted them, talked to them. The dog came back immediately, the flattened soccer ball between its teeth. The old man threw the ball farther this time, and the dog raced after it again. The ferocious mastiff that had once hunted lions had been reduced to a clown. And yet the old man and the dog seemed well suited to each other. They repeated the game over and over. Far from getting bored, they looked like they were enjoying it.

The old man finished his watering and stood up straight, stretching and smiling with satisfaction. Then he turned and looked halfway up the mountain, as if he knew Reseng was there. The old man's smiling face entered Reseng's crosshairs. Did he know the sun was less than a hand above the horizon now? Did he know he would be dead before it dipped below the mountain? Was that why he was smiling? Or maybe he wasn't actually smiling. The old man's face seemed fixed in a permanent grin, like a carved wooden Hahoe mask. Some people just had faces like that—people whose inner feelings you could never guess at, who smiled constantly, even when they were sad or angry.

Should he pull the trigger now? If he pulled it, he could be back in the city before midnight. He'd take a hot bath, down a few beers until he was good and drunk, or put an old Beatles record on the turntable and think about the fun he'd soon have with the money on its way into his bank account. Maybe, after this final job, he could change his life. He could open a pizza shop across from a high school, or sell cotton candy in the park. Reseng pictured himself handing armfuls of balloons and cotton candy to children and dozing off under the sun. He really could live that life, couldn't he? The idea of it suddenly seemed so wonderful. But he had to save that thought for after he pulled the trigger. The old man was still alive, and the money was not yet in his account.

The mountain was swiftly casting its shadow over the old man and his cabin. If Reseng was going to pull the trigger, he had to do it now. The old man had finished watering and would be going back inside any second. The job would get much harder then. Why complicate it? Pull the trigger. Pull it now and get out of here.

The old man was smiling, and the black dog was running with the soccer ball in its mouth. The old man's face was crystal clear in the crosshairs. He had three deep wrinkles across his forehead, a wart above his right eyebrow, and liver spots on his left cheek. Reseng gazed at where his heart would soon be pierced by a bullet. The old man's sweater looked hand-knit, not factory-made, and was about to be drenched in blood. All he had to do was squeeze the trigger just the tiniest bit, and the firing pin would strike the primer on the 7.62 mm cartridge, igniting the gunpowder inside the brass casing. The explosion would propel the bullet forward along the grooves inside the bore and send it spinning through the air, straight toward the old man's heart. With the high speed and destructive force of the bullet, the old man's mangled organs would explode out the exit wound in his lower back. Just the thought of it made the fine hairs all over Reseng's body stand on end. Holding the life of another human being in the palm of his hand always left him with a funny feeling.

Pull it.

Pull it now.

And yet for some reason, Reseng did not pull the trigger and instead set the rifle down on the ground.

"Now's not the right time," he muttered.

He wasn't sure why it wasn't the right time. Only that there was a right time for everything. A right time for eating ice cream. A right time for going in for a kiss. And maybe it sounded stupid, but there was also a right time for pulling a trigger and a right time for a bullet to the heart. Why wouldn't there be? And if Reseng's bullet happened to be sailing straight through the air toward the old man's heart just as the right moment fortuitously presented itself to him? That would be magnificent. Not that he was waiting for the best possible moment, of course. That auspicious moment might never come. Or it could pass by right under his nose. It occurred to him that he simply didn't want to pull the trigger yet. He didn't know why, but he just didn't. He lit a cigarette. The shadow of the mountain was creeping past the old man's cottage.

When it turned dark, the old man took the dog inside. The cottage must not have had electricity, because it looked even darker in there. A single candle glowed in the living room, but Reseng couldn't make out the interior well enough through the scope. The shadows of the man and his dog loomed large against a brick wall and disappeared. Now the only way Reseng could kill him from his current position would be if the old man happened to stand directly in the window with the candle in his hand.

As the sun sank below the ridge, darkness descended on the forest. There was no moon; even objects close at hand were hard to make out. There was only the glimmer of candlelight from the old man's cottage. The darkness was so dense that it made the air seem damp and heavy. Why didn't Reseng just leave? Why linger there in the dark? He wasn't sure. Wait for daybreak, he decided. Once the sun came up, he'd fire off a single round—no different from firing at the wooden target he'd practiced with for years—and then go home. He put his cigarette butt in his pocket and crawled into the tent. Since there was nothing else to do to pass the time, he ate a packet of army crackers and fell asleep wrapped up in his sleeping bag.

Reseng was awakened abruptly about two hours later by heavy footsteps in the grass. They were coming straight toward his tent. Three or four irregular thuds. A torso sweeping through tall grass. He couldn't decipher what was coming his way. Could be a wild boar. Or a wildcat. Reseng disengaged the safety and pointed his rifle at the darkness, toward the approaching sound. He couldn't pull the trigger yet. Mercenaries lying in wait had been known to fire into the dark out of fear, without checking their targets, only to discover that they'd hit a deer or a police dog or, worse, one of their fellow soldiers lost in the forest while out scouting. They would sob next to the corpse of a brother in arms felled by friendly fire, their beefy, tattooed bodies shaking like a little girl's as they told their commanding officers, "I didn't *mean* to kill him, I swear." And maybe they really hadn't meant to. Since they'd never before had to face their fear of things going bump in the night, the only thing someone with muscles for brains knew how to do was point and shoot into the dark. Reseng waited calmly for whatever was out there to reveal itself. To his surprise, what emerged was the old man and his dog.

"What are you doing out here?" the old man asked.

Now, this was funny. As funny as if the bull's-eye at the firing range had walked right up to him and said, *Why haven't you shot me yet?*

"What're *you* doing out here? I could've shot you," Reseng said, his voice trembling.

"Shot *me*? How's that for turning the tables?" the old man said with a smile. "This is my land. You're the one who doesn't belong, crashing on someone else's property." He looked relaxed. The situation was unusual, to say the least, and yet he didn't seem at all taken aback. Instead, the one taken aback was Reseng.

"You startled me. I thought you were a wild animal."

"You're a hunter?" the old man asked, looking pointedly at Reseng's rifle.

"Yes."

"That's a Dragunov. You only see those in museums. So poachers these days hunt with Vietnam War rifles?"

"I don't care how old the gun is as long as it can take down a boar." Reseng tried to sound nonchalant.

"True. If it stops a boar, then it doesn't matter what gun you use. Hell, if you can stop a boar with chopsticks—or a toothpick, for that matter—you can skip the gun altogether."

The old man laughed. The dog waited patiently at his side. It was much bigger than it had looked through the scope. And much more intimidating than when it was chasing after a deflated soccer ball.

"That's a nice dog," Reseng said. The old man looked down at the dog and stroked its head.

"He *is* a nice dog. He's the one who sniffed you out. But he's old now."

The dog never took its eyes off of Reseng. It didn't growl or bare its teeth, but it wasn't exactly friendly, either. The old man gave the dog's head another pat.

"Since you insist on staying the night, don't catch cold out here. Come to the house."

"Thank you for the offer, but I wouldn't want to trouble you."

"It's no trouble."

The old man turned and strode back down the slope, the dog at his heels. He didn't have a flashlight, but he seemed to have no trouble finding his way through the dark. Reseng's mind was in a whirl. His rifle was charged and ready, and his target was only five meters away. He watched the old man disappear into the darkness. A second later, he shouldered the rifle and headed down after him.

The cottage was warm. A fire blazed in the redbrick fireplace. There were no furnishings or decorations, save for a threadbare rug and small table in front of the fire and a few photos on the mantelpiece. The photos were all of the old man, sitting or standing with others, always at the center of the group, the people at his sides smiling stiffly, as if honored to be photographed with him. None of the photos seemed to be of family.

"Kind of early in the year for a fire," Reseng said.

"The older you get, the more you feel the cold. And I'm feeling it more than ever this year."

The old man stuffed a few pieces of dry wood into the fire, the flames balking briefly at the new addition. Reseng unslung his rifle from his shoulder and leaned it against the doorjamb. The old man stole a glance at the gun.

"Isn't October closed season for hunting?"

There was a twinkle in his eye. He'd been using banmal, the familiar form of speech, as if he and Reseng were old friends, but it didn't bother Reseng.

"A man could starve to death trying to follow every law."

"True, not all laws need to be followed," the old man murmured. "You'd be stupid to try."

As he stirred the logs with a metal poker, the flames rose and licked at a piece of wood that had not yet caught fire.

"Well, I've got booze and I've got tea, so pick your poison."

"Tea sounds good."

"You don't want something stronger? You must've been freezing."

"I don't usually drink when I'm hunting. Besides, it's dangerous to drink if you're going to sleep outdoors."

"Then indulge tonight," the old man said with a smile. "Not much chance of freezing to death in here."

He went to the kitchen and returned with two tin cups and a bottle of whiskey, then used a pair of tongs to carefully retrieve a kettle of black tea from inside the fireplace. He poured tea into one of the cups. His movements were smooth and measured. He handed the cup to Reseng and filled his own, then surprised Reseng by topping it off with whiskey.

"If you're not warmed up yet, a touch of whiskey'll get you the rest of the way. You can't go hunting until daybreak anyway."

"Does tea go with whiskey?" Reseng asked.

"Why not? It's all the same going down."

The old man wrinkled his eyes at him. He had a handsome face. He looked like he would have received a lot of compliments in his younger days. His chiseled features made him seem somehow tough and warm at the same time. As if the years had gently filed down his rough edges and softened him. Reseng held out his cup as the old man tipped a little whiskey into it. The scent of alcohol wafted up from the warm tea. It smelled good. The dog sauntered over from the other end of the living room and lay down next to Reseng.

"You're a good person."

"Pardon?"

"Santa likes you," the old man said, gesturing at the dog. "Dogs know good people from bad right away."

Up close, the dog's eyes were surprisingly gentle.

"Maybe it's just stupid," Reseng said.

"Drink your tea."

The old man smiled. He took a sip of his spiked tea, and Reseng followed suit.

"Not bad," Reseng said.

"Surprising, huh? Tastes good in coffee, too, but black tea is better. Warms your stomach and your heart. Like wrapping your arms around a good woman," he added with a childish giggle.

"If you've got a good woman, why stop at hugging?" Reseng scoffed. "A good woman is always better than some boozy tea."

The old man nodded. "I suppose you're right. No tea compares to a good woman."

"But the taste is memorable, I'll give you that."

"Black tea is steeped in imperialism. That's what gives it its flavor. Anything this flavorful has to be hiding an incredible amount of carnage."

"Interesting theory."

"I've got some pork and potatoes. Care for some?"

"Sure."

The old man went outside and came back with a blackened lump of meat and a handful of potatoes. The meat looked awful. It was covered in dirt and dust and still had patches of hair, but even worse was the rancid smell. He shoved the pork into the hot ash at the bottom of the fireplace until it was completely coated, then skewered it on an iron spit and propped it over the fire. He stirred the flames with the poker and tucked the potatoes into the ash.

"I can't say that looks all that appetizing," Reseng said.

"I lived in Peru for a while. Learned this method from the Indians. Doesn't look clean but tastes great."

"Frankly, it looks pretty terrible, but if it's a secret native recipe, then I guess there must be something to it."

The old man grinned at Reseng.

"Just a few days ago, I discovered something else I have in common with the native Peruvians."

"What's that?"

"No refrigerator."

The old man turned the meat. His face looked earnest in the glow of the fire. As he pricked the potatoes with a skewer, he murmured at them, "You'd better make yourselves delicious for our important guest." While the meat cooked, the old man finished off his spiked tea and refilled his cup with just whiskey, then offered more to Reseng.

Reseng held out his cup. He liked how the whiskey burned on its way down his throat and radiated smoothly up from his empty stomach. The alcohol spread pleasantly through his body. For a moment, everything felt unreal. He would never have imagined it: a sniper and his target sitting in front of a roaring fire, pretending to be best friends. . . . Each time the old man turned the meat, a delicious aroma wafted toward him. The dog moved closer to the fireplace to sniff at the meat, but he hung back at the last moment and grumbled instead, as if afraid of the fire.

"There, there, Santa. Don't worry," the old man said, patting the dog. "You'll get your share."

"The dog's name is Santa?"

"I met this fellow on Christmas Day. That day, he lost his owner and I lost my leg."

The old man lifted the hem of his left pant leg to reveal a prosthesis.

"He saved me. Dragged me over nearly five kilometers of snow-covered road."

"That's a hell of a way to meet."

"Best Christmas gift I ever got."

The old man continued to stroke the dog's head.

"He's very gentle for his size."

"Not exactly. I used to have to keep him leashed all the time. One glimpse of a stranger and he'd attack. But now that he's old, he's gone soft. It's odd. I can't get used to the idea of an animal being this friendly with people."

The meat smelled cooked. The old man poked at it with the skewer and took it off the fire. Using a serrated knife, he carved the meat into thick slices. He gave a piece to Reseng, a piece to himself, and a piece to Santa. Reseng brushed off the ash and took a bite.

"What an unusual flavor. Doesn't really taste like pork."

"Good, yeah?"

"It is. But do you have any salt?"

"Nope."

"No fridge, no salt—that's quite a way to live. Do the native Peruvians also live without salt?"

"No, no," the old man said sheepishly. "I ran out a few days ago."

"Do you hunt?"

"Not anymore. About a month ago, I found a wild boar stuck in a poacher's trap. Still alive. I watched it gasp for breath and thought to myself, Do I kill it now or wait for it to die? If I waited for it to die, then I could blame its death on the poacher who left that trap out, but if I killed it, then I'd be responsible for its death. What would you have done?"

The old man's smile was inscrutable. Reseng gave the tin cup a swirl before polishing off the alcohol.

"Hard to say. I don't think it really matters *who* killed the boar."

The old man seemed to ponder this for a moment before responding.

"I guess you're right. When you really think about it, it doesn't matter who killed it. Either way, here we are enjoying some Peruvian-style roasted boar."

The old man laughed loudly. Reseng laughed, too. It wasn't much of a joke, but the old man kept laughing, and Reseng followed suit with a loud laugh of his own.

The old man was in high spirits. He filled Reseng's cup with whiskey until it was nearly overflowing, then filled his own and raised it in a toast. They downed their drinks in one gulp. The old man picked up the skewer and fished a couple of potatoes from the hot ashes. After taking a bite of one, he pronounced it delicious and gave the other to Reseng. Reseng brushed off the ashes and took a bite. "That *is* delicious," he said.

"There's nothing better than a roasted potato on a cold winter's day," the old man said.

"Potatoes always remind me of someone. . . ." Reseng started to babble. His face was red from the alcohol and the glow of the fire.

"I'm guessing this story doesn't have a happy ending," the old man said.

"It doesn't."

"Is that someone alive or dead?"

"Long dead. I was in Africa at the time, and we got an emergency call in the middle of the night. We jumped in a truck and headed off. It turned out that a rebel soldier who'd escaped camp had taken an old woman hostage. He was just a kid—still had his baby fat. Must've been fifteen, maybe even fourteen? From what I saw, he was worked up and scared out of his wits, but not an actual threat. The old woman kept saying something to him. Meanwhile, he was pointing an AK-47 at her head with one hand and cramming a potato into his mouth with the other. We all knew he wasn't going to do anything, but then the order came over the walkie-talkie to take him out. Someone pulled the trigger. We ran over to take a closer look. Half of the kid's head was blown away, and in his mouth was the mashed-up potato that he never got the chance to swallow."

"The poor thing. He must've been starving."

"It felt so strange to look into the mouth of a boy with half his head missing. What would've happened if we'd waited just ten more seconds? All I could think was, If we had waited, he would've been able to swallow the potato before he died."

"Not like anything would've changed for that poor boy if he had swallowed it."

"No, of course not." Reseng's voice wavered. "But it still felt weird to think about that chewed-up potato in his mouth."

The old man finished the rest of his whiskey and poked around in the ashes with the skewer to see if there were any more potatoes. He found one in the corner and offered it to Reseng, who gazed blankly at it and politely declined. The old man looked at the potato; his face darkened and he tossed it back into the ashes.

"I've got another bottle of whiskey. What do you say?" the old man asked.

Reseng thought about it for a moment. "Your call," he said.

The old man brought another bottle from the kitchen and poured some for him. They sipped in silence as they watched the flames dance in the fireplace. As Reseng grew tipsy, a feeling of profound unreality washed over him. The old man's eyes never left the fire.

"Fire is so beautiful," Reseng said.

"Ash is more beautiful once you get to know it."

The old man slowly swirled his cup as he gazed into the flames. He smiled then, as if recalling something funny.

"My grandfather was a whaler. This was back before they outlawed whaling. He didn't grow up anywhere near the ocean—he was actually from inland Hamgyong Province, but he went down south to Jangsaengpo harbor for work and ended up becoming the best harpooner in the country. During one of the whaling trips, he got dragged under by a sperm whale. Really deep under. What happened was, he threw the harpoon into the whale's back, but the rope tangled around his foot and pulled him overboard. Those flimsy colonial-era whaling boats and shoddy harpoons were no match for an animal that big. A male sperm whale can grow up to eighteen meters long and weigh up to sixty tons. Think about it. That's like fifteen adult African elephants. I don't care if it were just a balloon animal—I would never want to mess with anything that big. No way, no how. But not my grandfather. He stuck his harpoon right in that giant whale."

"What happened next?" Reseng asked.

"Utter havoc, of course. He said the shock of falling off the bow made him woozy, and he couldn't tell if he was dreaming or hallucinating. Meanwhile, he was being dragged helplessly into the dark depths of the ocean by a very angry whale. He said the first thing he saw when he finally snapped out of his daze was a blue light coming off the sperm whale's fins. As he stared at the light, he forgot all about the danger he was in. When he told me the story, he kept going on about how mysterious and tranquil and beautiful it was. An eighteen-meter-long behemoth coursing through the pitch-black ocean with glowing blue fins. I tried to break it to him gently—he was practically in tears just recalling it—that since whales are not bioluminescent, there was no way its fins could have glowed like that. He threw his chamber pot at my head. Ha! What a hothead! He told the story to everyone he met. I told him everyone thought he was lying because of the part about the fins. But all he said to that was, 'Everything people say about whales is a lie. Because everything they say comes from a book. But whales don't live in books, they live in the ocean.' Anyway, after the whale dragged him under, he passed out."

The old man refilled his cup halfway and took a sip.

"He said that when he came to, there was a big full moon hanging in the night sky, and waves were lapping at his ear. He thought luck was on his side and the waves had pushed him onto a reef. But it turned out he was on top of the whale's head. Incredible, wouldn't you say? There he was, lying across a whale, staring at a buoy, a growing pool of the whale's slick red blood all around him, and the whale itself, propping him up out of the water with its head, that harpoon still sticking out of its back. Can you imagine anything stranger or more incomprehensible? I've heard of whales lifting an injured companion or a newborn calf out of the water so they can breathe. But this wasn't a companion or a baby whale, or even a seal or a penguin. It was my grandfather, a human being, and the same person who'd shoved a harpoon in its back! I honestly don't understand why the whale saved him."

"No, it doesn't make any sense," Reseng said, taking a sip of whiskey. "You'd think that whale would have torn him apart."

"He just lay there on the whale's head for a long time, even after he'd regained consciousness. It was awkward, to say the least. What can you do when you're stuck on top of a whale? There was nothing out there but the silvery moon, the dark waves, a sperm whale spilling buckets of blood, and him—well and truly up shit creek. My grandfather said the sight of all that blood in the moonlight made him apologize to the whale. It was the least he could do, you know? He wanted to pull out the harpoon, too, but easier said than done. Throwing a harpoon is like making a bad life decision: so easy to do, but so impossible to take back once the damage is done. Instead, he cut the line with the knife he kept on his belt. The moment he cut it, the whale dove and resurfaced some distance away, then headed straight back to where my grandfather was clinging to the buoy, struggling to stay afloat. He said it watched as he flailed pathetically, filled with shame, all tangled up in the line from the harpoon he himself had thrown. According to my grandfather, the beast came right up and gazed at him with one enormous dark eye, a look of innocent curiosity that seemed to say, *How did such a little scaredy-cat like you manage to stick a harpoon in the likes of me? You're braver than you look!* Then, he said, it gave him a playful shove, as if to say, *Hey, kid, that was pretty naughty. Better not pull another dangerous stunt like that!* All the blood it had lost was turning the water murky, and yet it seemed to brush off the whole matter of my grandfather stabbing it in the back. Each time my grandfather got to this part of the story, he used to slap his knee and shout, 'That monster's heart was as big as its body! Completely different from us small-minded humans.' He said the whale stayed by his side all night, until the whaleboat caught up to them. The other whalers had been tracking the buoys in search of my grandfather. As soon as the ship appeared in the distance, the whale swam in a circle around him, as if it were saying good-bye, and then dove again, even deeper than before, the harpoon with my grandfather's name carved into it still quivering in its back. Incredible, huh?"

"Yeah, that's quite a story," Reseng said.

"I guess that after that narrow escape from a watery death, my grandfather had some serious second thoughts about whaling. He told my grandmother he didn't want to go back. My grandmother was a very kind and patient woman. She hugged him and said if he hated catching whales that much, then he should stop. He said he sobbed like a baby in her arms and told her, 'I felt so scared, so terribly scared!' And then he really did keep his distance from whaling for a while. But those crybaby days of his didn't last long. They were poor, there were too many mouths to feed, and whaling was the only trade he'd ever learned. He didn't know how else to provide for all those hungry children squawking at him like baby sparrows. So he went back to work and launched his harpoon at every whale he saw in the East Sea until he retired at the age of seventy. But there was one more funny thing that happened: In 1959, he ran into the same sperm whale again. Exactly thirty years after his miraculous survival. His rusted old harpoon was still stuck in its back, but the whale was just swimming along, all gallant and free, as if that harpoon had always been there and were simply a part of its body. Actually, it's not uncommon to hear about whales surviving long after a harpoon attack. They even say that once, in the nineteenth century, a whale was caught with an eighteenth-century harpoon still stuck in it. Anyway, the whale didn't swim off when it saw the whaling ship; in fact, it cruised right up to my grandfather's boat, the harpoon sticking straight up like a periscope, and slowly circled it. As if it were saying, *Hey! Long time no see, old friend! But what's this? Still hunting whales? You really don't know when to quit, do you?*" The old man laughed.

"Your grandfather must have felt pretty embarrassed," Reseng said.

"You bet he did. The sailors said my grandfather took one look at that sperm whale and dropped to his knees. He threw himself on the deck and let out a howl. He wept and called out, "Whale, forgive me! I'm so sorry! How awful for you, swimming all those years with a harpoon stuck in your back! After we said good-bye, I wanted to stop, I swear. You probably don't know this, since you live in the sea, but things have been really tough up on land. I'm still living in a rental, and my brats eat so much, you'd be shocked at what it costs to feed them. I had to come back because I could barely make ends meet. Forgive me! Let's meet again and have a drink together. I'll bring the booze if you catch us a giant squid to snack on. Ten crates of soju and one grilled giant squid should do it. I'm so sorry, Whale. I'm sorry I stabbed you in the back with a harpoon. I'm sorry I'm such a fool. Boo-hoo-hoo!'"

"Did he really yell all of that at the whale?" Reseng asked.

"They say he really did."

"He was a funny guy, your grandfather."

"He was indeed. Anyway, after that, he gave up whaling and left

Jangsaengpo harbor for good. He came up to Seoul and spent all his time drinking. I imagine he felt pretty trapped, given that he couldn't go out to sea anymore, and with barbed wire strung all across the thirty-eighth parallel, he couldn't go back north to his hometown, either. So whenever he got drunk, he latched on to people and started up with that same boring old whale tale. He told it over and over, even though everyone had already heard it hundreds of times and no one wanted to hear it again. But he wasn't doing it to brag about his adventures on the high seas. He believed that people should emulate whales. He said that people had grown as small and crafty as rats, and that the days of taking slow, huge, beautiful strides had vanished. The age of giants was over."

The old man swigged his whiskey. Reseng refilled his cup and took a sip.

"Toward the end, he found out he was in the final stages of liver cancer. It wasn't exactly a surprise. As a sailor, he'd been guzzling booze from the age of sixteen to the age of eighty-two. But I guess the news meant nothing at all to him, because no sooner did he return from seeing the doctor than he hit the bottle again. He gathered his kids together and told them, 'I'm not going to any hospital. Whales accept it when their time comes.' And he never did go back to the doctor. After about a month, my grandfather put on his best clothes and returned to Jangsaengpo harbor. According to the sailors there, he loaded a small boat up with ten crates of soju, just like he'd said he would, and rowed until he disappeared over the horizon. And he never came back. His body was never found. Maybe he really did row until he caught the scent of ambergris and tracked down his whale. If he did, then I'm sure he broke open all ten crates of soju that night as they caught up on the years they'd missed, and if he didn't, then he probably drifted around the ocean, drinking alone, until he died. Or maybe he's still out there somewhere."

"That's quite an ending."

"It's a dignified way to go. In my opinion, a man ought to be able to choose a death that gives his life a dignified ending. Only those who truly walk their own path can choose their own death. But not me. I've been a slug my whole life, so I don't deserve a dignified death."

The old man smiled bitterly. Reseng was at a loss for a response. The look on the old man's face was so dark that Reseng felt compelled to say something comforting, but he really couldn't think of what to say. The old man refilled his cup with whiskey and polished it off again. They sat there for a long time. Each time the flames died down, Reseng added more wood to the fire. While Reseng and the old man sipped whiskey in comfortable silence, each new piece caught fire, crackled and flared up hot and ferocious, then slowly burned down to glowing charcoal, and then to white ash.

"I really talked your ear off tonight. They say the older you get, the more you're supposed to keep your purse strings open and your mouth shut."

"Oh, no, I enjoyed it."

The old man shook the whiskey bottle and eyed the bottom. There was only about a cup left.

"Mind if I finish this off?"

"Go right ahead," Reseng said.

The old man poured the rest of the whiskey into his cup and downed it.

"We'd better call it a night. You must be exhausted. I should've let you sleep, but instead I kept talking."

"No, it was a nice evening, thanks to you."

The old man curled up on the floor to the right of the fireplace. Santa sauntered over and lay down next to him. Reseng lay down to the left of the fireplace. The shadows of the two men and the dog danced on the brick wall opposite them. Reseng looked at his rifle propped against the door.

"Have some breakfast before you leave tomorrow," the old man said, rolling onto his side. "You don't want to hunt on an empty stomach."

Reseng hesitated before saying, "Of course, I'll do that."

The crackling fire and the dog's steady breaths sounded unusually loud. The old man didn't say another word. Reseng listened for a long time to the old man and the dog breathing in their sleep before he finally joined them. It was a peaceful sleep.

When he awoke, the old man was preparing breakfast. A simple meal of white rice, radish kimchi, and doenjang soup made with sliced potatoes. The old man didn't say much. They ate in silence. After breakfast, Reseng hurried to leave. As he stepped out the door, the old man handed him six boiled potatoes wrapped in a cloth. Reseng took the bundle and bade him a polite farewell. The potatoes were warm.

By the time Reseng returned to his tent, the old man was watering the flowers again. Just as before, he tipped the watering can with care, as if pouring tea. Then, just as before, he spoke to the flowers and trees and gestured at them. Reseng made a minor adjustment to the scope. The familiar-looking flower grew sharp and distinct in the lens and blurred again. He still could not remember its name. He should have asked the old man.

It was a nice garden. Two persimmon trees stood nonchalantly in the courtyard, while the flowers in the garden beds waited patiently for their season to come. Santa went up to the man and rubbed his head against the man's thigh. The old man gave the dog a pat. They suited each other. The old man threw the deflated soccer ball across the garden. While Santa ran to fetch it, the old man watered more flowers. What was he saying to them? On closer inspection, he did indeed have a slight limp. If only Reseng had asked him what had happened to his left leg. Not that it makes any difference, he thought. Santa came back with the ball. This time, the old man threw it farther. Santa seemed to be in a good mood, because he ran around in circles before racing off to the end of the garden to fetch the ball. The old man looked like he had finished watering. He put down the watering can and smiled brightly. Was he laughing? Was that carved wooden mask of a face really laughing?

Reseng fixed the crosshairs on the old man's chest and pulled the trigger.

ACHILLES' HEEL

Reseng was found in a garbage can. Or, who knows, maybe he was born in that garbage can.

Old Raccoon, who had served as Reseng's foster father for the last twenty-eight years, liked to tease Reseng about his origins whenever he got to drinking. "You were found in a garbage can in front of a nunnery. Or maybe that garbage can was your mother. Hard to say. Either way, it's pretty pathetic. But look on the bright side. A garbage can used by nuns is bound to be the cleanest garbage can around."

Reseng wasn't bothered by Old Raccoon's teasing. He decided that being born from a clean garbage can had to be better than being born to the type of parents who'd dump their baby in the garbage.

Reseng lived in the orphanage run by the convent until he was four, after which he was adopted by Old Raccoon and lived in his library. Had Reseng continued to grow up in the orphanage, where divine blessings showered down like spring sunshine and kindly nuns devoted themselves to the careful raising of orphans, his life might have turned out very differently. Instead, he grew up in a library crawling with assassins, hired guns, and bounty hunters. Just as a plant grows wherever it sets down roots, so all your life's tragedies spring from wherever you first set your feet. And Reseng was far too young to leave the place where he'd set down roots.

The day he turned nine, Reseng was snuggled up in Old Raccoon's rattan rocking chair, reading *The Tales of Homer*. Paris, the idiot prince of Troy, was right in the middle of pulling back his bowstring to sink an arrow into the heel of Achilles, the hero whom Reseng had come to love over the course of the book. As everyone knows, this was a very tense moment, and so Reseng was completely unaware that Old Raccoon had been standing behind him for a while, watching him read. Old Raccoon looked angry.

"Who taught you to read?"

Old Raccoon had never sent Reseng to school. Whenever Reseng asked, "How come I don't go to school like the other kids?" Old Raccoon had retorted, "Because school doesn't teach you anything about life." Old Raccoon was right on that point. Reseng never attended school, and yet in all of his thirty-two years, it had not once caused him any problems. Problems? Ha! What kind of problems would he have had anyway? And so Old Raccoon looked gobsmacked to discover Reseng, who hadn't spent a single day in school, reading a book. Worse, the look on his face said he felt betrayed to learn that Reseng knew how to read.

As Reseng stared up at him without answering, Old Raccoon switched to the low, deep voice he used to intimidate people.

"I *said*, Who. Taught. You. To. Read?"

His voice was menacing, as if he was going to catch the person who had taught Reseng how to read and do something to them right then and there. In a small, quavering voice, Reseng said that no one had taught him. Old Raccoon still had his scary face on; it was clear he didn't believe a word of it, and so Reseng explained that he'd taught himself how to read from picture books. Old Raccoon smacked Reseng hard across the face.

As Reseng struggled to stifle his sobs, he swore that he really had learned to read from picture books. It was true. After he'd managed to dig through the 200,000 books crammed on the shelves of Old Raccoon's gloomy, labyrinthine library to find the few books worth looking at (a comic book adaptation about American slavery, a cheap adult magazine, and a dog-eared picture book filled with giraffes and rhinoceroses), he'd deciphered how the Korean alphabet worked by matching pictures to words. Reseng pointed to his stash of picture books in the corner of the study. Old Raccoon hobbled over on his lame leg and examined each one. He looked dumbfounded; he was clearly wondering how on earth those shoddy books had found their way into *his* library. Hobbling back, he stared hard at Reseng, his eyes still filled with suspicion, and yanked the hardback copy of *The Tales of Homer* from his hands. He looked back and forth between the book and Reseng for the longest time.

"Reading books will doom you to a life of fear and shame. So, do you still feel like reading?"

Reseng stared blankly at him—staring blankly was all he *could* do, as he had no idea what Old Raccoon was talking about. Fear and shame? As if a mere nine-year-old could comprehend such a life! The only life a boy who'd just turned nine could imagine was complaining about a dinner that someone else had prepared. A life in which random events just kept happening to you, as impossible to stop as a piece of onion that keeps slipping out of your sandwich. What Old Raccoon said sounded less like a choice and more like a threat, or a curse being put on him. It was like God saying to Adam and Eve, "If you eat this fruit, you'll be cast out of Paradise, so do you still want to eat it?" Reseng was afraid. He had no idea what this choice meant. But Old Raccoon was staring him down and waiting for an answer. Would he eat the apple or not?

At last, Reseng stiffly raised his head and composed himself, fists clenched, his face a picture of determination, and said, "I will read. Now, give me back my book." Old Raccoon gazed down at the boy, who was gritting his teeth, barely containing his tears, and handed back *The Tales of Homer*.

Reseng's demand to retrieve his book did not come from an actual desire to read or to defy Old Raccoon. It was because he was clueless about this whole "life of fear and shame" thing.

After Old Raccoon left the room, Reseng wiped away the tears that had only then begun to spill, and curled up into a ball on the rattan rocker. He looked around at Old Raccoon's dim study, which grew dark early because the windows faced northwest, at the books stacked to the ceiling in some complex and incomprehensible order, at the maze of shelves quietly staked out by dust, and wondered why Old Raccoon was so upset about him reading. Even now, at the age of thirty-two, whenever he pictured Old Raccoon, who had spent most of his life sitting in the corner of the library with a book in his hands, he couldn't wrap his head around it. For that nine-year-old, the whole incident had felt as awful as if one of his buddies with a pocketful of sweets had stolen Reseng's single sweet from his mouth.

"Stupid old fart, I hope you get the shits!"

Reseng put his curse on Old Raccoon and wiped the last of his tears with the back of his hand. Then he reopened the book. How could he not? Reading was no longer just some simple way to pass the time. It was now this boy's Great and Inherent Right, a right won with much difficulty, even if it meant being hit and cursed to live a Life of Fear and Shame. Reseng returned to the scene in *The Tales of Homer* where the idiot prince of Troy pulls back his bowstring. The scene where the arrow leaves the string and hurtles toward his hero, Achilles. The scene where that cursed arrow pierces Achilles' heel.

Reseng trembled as Achilles bled to death at the top of Hisarlik Hill. He had been certain his hero would easily pluck that damn arrow from his heel and immediately run his spear through Paris's heart. But the unthinkable had happened. What had gone wrong? How could the son of a god die? How could a hero with an immortal body, unfellable by any arrow, unpierceable by any spear, be undone by an imbecile like Paris, and, worse, *die* like an imbecile because he hadn't protected his one, tiny, no-bigger-than-the-palm-of-his-hand weak spot? Reseng reread Achilles' death scene over and over. But he could not find a line about Achilles' coming back to life.

Oh, no! That stupid Paris really did kill Achilles!

Reseng sat lost in thought until Old Raccoon's study was pitch-black. He couldn't yell, he couldn't move. Now and then the rocking chair creaked. The books were submerged in darkness, and the pages rustled like dry leaves. All he had to do was stick his hand out to reach the light switch, but it didn't occur to Reseng to turn on the light. He trembled in the dark like a child trapped in a cave teeming with insects. Life made no sense. Why had Achilles bothered to cover his torso in armor, when he should have protected his left heel, his one and only mortal weakness? Stupid idiot, even nine-year-olds knew better. It burned Reseng up to think that

Achilles had failed to protect his fatal weak spot. He couldn't forgive his hero for dying like that.

Reseng wept in the dark. On every page of the sea of library books that he was either itching to read or would eventually get bored enough to read, heroes and beautiful, charming women, countless people struggling to overcome hardship and frustration and achieve their goals, all died at the arrows of idiots because they failed to protect their one tiny weakness. Reseng was shocked at how treacherous life was. It didn't matter how high you rose, how invincible your body was, or how firmly you clung to greatness, because all of it could vanish with a tiny, split-second mistake.

An overwhelming distrust in life overcame him. He might fall at any moment into any number of traps lying in wait. His tender life could one day be struck by luck so bad, it would leave him in utter turmoil; he would be gripped by terror he couldn't shake off no matter how hard he fought. Reseng was possessed by the strange and unfamiliar conviction that everything he held dear would one day crumble in an instant. He felt empty, sad, and completely alone.

That night, Reseng sat in Old Raccoon's library for a very long time. The tears kept falling, and he cried himself to sleep on Old Raccoon's rocking chair.

BEAR'S PET CREMATORIUM

"If things don't pick up, I'm in deep shit. Business has been so slow, I'm stuck cremating dogs all day."

Bear flicked his cigarette to the ground. He was squatting down, and the seat of his pants threatened to rip open under his hundred-plus-kilogram frame. Reseng wordlessly pulled on a pair of cotton work gloves. Bear heaved himself up, brushing off his backside.

"Do you know some people are such morons, they're actually dumping bodies in the forest? Your job doesn't end when the target's dead; you also have to clean up after yourself. I mean, what day and age is this? Dumping bodies in the forest? You wouldn't even bury a dog out there. Nowadays, if you so much as tap a mountain with a bulldozer, bodies come pouring out. No one takes their job seriously anymore, I swear. No integrity! Stabbing someone in the gut and walking away? That's for hired goons, not professional assassins! And anyway, it's not like it's easy to bury a body in the woods. A bunch of idiots from Incheon got caught dragging a huge suitcase up a mountain a few days ago."

"They were arrested?" Reseng asked.

"Of course. It was pretty obvious. Three big guys carrying shovels and dragging a giant suitcase into the forest. You think people living nearby saw them and thought, Ah, they're taking a trip, in the dead of night, to the other side of the mountain? Stupid! So my point is, instead of dumping bodies in the mountains, why not cremate them here? It's safe, it's clean, and it's better for the environment. Business is so slow, I'm dying!"

Bear pulled on work gloves as he grumbled. He always grumbled. And yet this grumbling, orangutan-size man seemed as harmless as Winnie-the-Pooh. That might have been because he looked like

Winnie-the-Pooh. Or maybe Pooh looked like Bear. Bear provided a corpse-disposal service, albeit an illegal one. Pets, of course, were legal. He was licensed to cremate cats and dogs. The human bodies were done on the sly. He was surprisingly cuddly-looking for someone who burned corpses for a living.

"I swear, you wouldn't believe the things I've seen. Not long ago, this couple came in with an iguana. Had a name like Andrew or André. What kind of a name is that for an iguana? Why not something simpler, something that rolls off the tongue, like Iggy or Spiny? Anyway, it's ridiculous the names people come up with. So this stupid iguana died, and this young couple kept hugging each other and crying and carrying on: 'We're so sorry, Andrew, we should have fed you on time, it's all our fault, Andrew.' I was dying of embarrassment for them."

Bear was on a roll. Reseng opened the warehouse door, half-listening to his rant.

"Which cart?" he asked.

Bear took a look inside and pointed to a hand cart.

"Is it big enough?" Reseng asked.

Bear sized it up and nodded.

"You're not moving a cow. Where'd you park?"

"Behind the building."

"Why so far away? And it's uphill."

Bear manned the cart. He had an easy, optimistic stride that belied his penchant for grumbling. Reseng envied him. Bear didn't have a greedy bone in his body. He wasn't one to run himself into the ground trying to drum up more business. He got by on what he made from his small pet crematorium and had even raised two daughters by himself. His eldest was now at college. "I stick to light meals," he liked to claim. "To stretch my food bill. I just have to hold out for a few more years, until my girls are on their own." Bear spooked easily. He never took on anything suspicious, even if he needed the money. And so, in a business where the average life span was ridiculously short, Bear had lasted a long, long time.

Reseng popped open the trunk. Bear tilted his head quizzically at the two black body bags inside.

"Two? Old Raccoon said there'd be only one package."

"One man, one dog," Reseng said.

"Is that the dog?" Bear asked, pointing at the smaller of the bags.

"That's the man. The big one's the dog."

"What kind of dog is bigger than a man?"

Bear opened the bag in disbelief. Inside was Santa. His long tongue flopped out of the open zipper.

"Holy shit! Now I've seen it all. Why'd you kill the dog? What'd it do, bite your balls?"

"I just thought it was too old to get used to a new master."

"Well, look at you, meddling with the instructions you were given," Bear said with a snigger. "You need to watch your step. Don't get tripped up worrying over some dog."

Reseng zipped the bag back up and paused. Why *had* he killed the dog? When he'd gone back to collect the old man's body, the dog had been quietly standing watch. With his back to the sun, Reseng had looked down at the sunlight spilling into the dog's cloudy brown eyes. The dog hadn't growled. It was probably wondering why its master wasn't moving. Reseng had stared at the dog, which was now too old to learn any new tricks. No one's left in this quiet, beautiful forest to feed you, he thought. And you're too old to go bounding through the forest in search of food. Do you understand what I'm saying? The late autumn sun cast its weak rays over the crown of the dog's head. It had gazed up at him with those cloudy brown eyes as Reseng stroked its neck. Then he had raised his rifle and shot the dog in the head.

"Pretty heavy for an old man," Bear said as he grabbed one end of the body bag.

"I told you, this one's the dog," Reseng grumbled. "That one's the old man."

Bear looked back and forth at the bags in confusion.

"This damn dog is heavy."

After loading the bodies onto the cart, Bear looked around. The pet crematorium was a quiet place at two in the morning. Of course it was. No one would be coming to cremate a pet at this hour.

Bear opened up the gas valve and lit the furnace. The flames rose, peeling the black vinyl bag away from the two bodies like snakeskin being shed. The old man was stretched out flat, with the dog's head resting on his stomach. As the furnace filled with heat, their sinews tightened and shrank, and the old man's body began to squirm. It was a sad sight, as if he were still clinging to the world of the living. Was there even anything left for him to cling to? It didn't matter. It was over. In two hours, he'd be nothing but dust. You can't cling to anything when you're dust.

Reseng stared at the contorted body. The old man had been a general. Throughout the three long decades of military rule in South Korea, he had been working behind the scenes, in the shadow of the dictator, drawing up lists of targets and orchestrating their assassinations. How had he pulled it off? It wasn't easy back then for former members of the North Korean army to succeed in the South Korean army and harder still to earn a spot in the Korean Central Intelligence Agency. But he'd survived. He'd made it through the first dictator's twenty years of ironfisted rule, the toppling of the regime, the coup d'etat that followed, and the next ten years under a new military regime. He'd survived the political monkey business and the unrelenting suspicion directed at former North Korean soldiers, and became a general. Whenever someone fell into disfavor with the dictator, this general with two shiny stars on his cap would seek out Old Raccoon's library. He'd hand over the list with the target's name on it and, most brazenly of all, use the people's tax money to settle the bill.

But in the end, his own name had made it onto the list. That's how it went. The good times came to an end sooner or later and, in order to survive, those who found themselves dethroned had to sort out what they'd done and sweep up the scraps. As always, time had a way of circling around and biting you on the ass.

Once, when Reseng was twelve, the old man had come to the library dressed in uniform. It was a fine uniform. The old man came right up to Reseng.

"What're you reading, boy?"

"Sophocles."

"Is it fun?"

"I don't have a dad, so I can't really understand it."

"Where's your dad?"

"In the garbage can in front of the nunnery."

The general grinned, stars sparkling, and ruffled Reseng's hair. That was twenty years ago. The little boy remembered that moment, but the old man had probably forgotten.

Reseng took out a cigarette. Bear lit it for him, took out one of his own, and started whistling birdcalls through a cloud of smoke. On his way out, Bear checked their surroundings again, as if expecting someone to appear suddenly. Reseng watched the bodies of the old man and the dog meld together in the heat.

A surprising number of idiots mistakenly thought they could pull off a perfect crime only if they personally disposed of the evidence. They would lug a can of gasoline to a deserted field and try to burn the body themselves. But cremation was never as easy as people thought. After messing around with trying to set the body on fire, they ended up with a huge, steaming lump of foul-smelling meat. Joke was on them. Any decent forensic scientist could take one look at that barbecue gone wrong and figure out the corpse's age, sex, height, face, shape, and dentition. A body had to burn for at least two hours at temperatures well above thirteen hundred degrees inside a closed oven in order to be completely incinerated. Other than crematoriums, pottery or charcoal kilns, or a blast furnace in a smelting factory, it was very difficult to produce that kind of heat. That was why Bear's Pet Crematorium stayed in business. The next important step was to grind the bones. Forensic scientists can determine age, sex, height, and cause of death from just three fragments of a pelvis. So any remaining bone or teeth had to be completely destroyed. Even the most finely ground bones still hold clues, and teeth maintain their original shape even under extreme conditions, including fire. So the teeth had to be pulverized with a hammer and the bone ash safely scattered. It was the only way to disappear your victim.

Reseng took out another cigarette and checked the time. Ten past two. Once the sun came up, he'd be able to finish work and head home. Sudden fatigue settled over his neck and shoulders. One night on the road, one night at the old man's place, and now one night at Bear's Pet Crematorium. He'd been away from home for three nights. His cats had probably run out of food. . . . Reseng pictured his darkened apartment, the two Siamese yowling in hunger. Desk and Lampshade. Crazily enough, they were starting to take after their names. Desk liked to hunch over into a square, like a slice of bread, and stare quietly at a scrap of paper on the floor, while Lampshade liked to crane her neck and stare out the window.

Bear brought out a basket of boiled potatoes and offered one to Reseng. Just his luck—more potatoes. The six the old man had given him that morning were still in the car. Reseng was hungry, but he shook his head. "Why aren't you eating? Don't you know how tasty Gangwon Province potatoes are?" Bear looked puzzled. Why would anyone refuse something so delicious? He shoved an entire potato into his mouth and swigged a good half of the bottle of soju he'd brought out, as well.

"I cremated Mr. Kim here a while back," Bear said, wiping his mouth with the back of his hand.

"Mr. Kim from the meat market?"

"Yup."

"Who took him out?"

"I think Duho hired some young Vietnamese guys. That's who's taking all the jobs these days. They work for peanuts. Everywhere you look, it's nothing but Vietnamese. Well, of course, there are also some Chinese, some defectors from the North Korean special forces, and even a few Filipinos. I swear, there are guys who'll take someone out for a measly five hundred thousand won. Nowadays, assassinations cost practically nothing. That's why they're all at each other's throats. Once Mr. Kim's name made the list, he didn't stand a chance."

Reseng exhaled a long plume of smoke. Bear had no reason to lament the plummeting cost of assassinations. The more bodies there were, the better Bear fared, regardless of who carried out the killings. He was just humoring Reseng. Bear took another bite of potato and another swig of soju. Then he seemed to remember something.

"By the way, the strangest thing happened. After I had finished cremating Mr. Kim, I found these shiny pearl-like objects in his ashes. I picked them up to take a closer look, and what do you know? Śarīra. Thirteen of them, each no bigger than a bean. Crazy!"

"What are you talking about?" Reseng said in shock. "Those are only supposed to come out of the ashes of Buddhist masters. How could they come out of Mr. Kim?"

"It's true, I swear. Want me to show you?"

"Forget it." Reseng waved his hand in annoyance.

"I'm telling you, they're real. I didn't believe it at first, either. Mr. Kim—what'd everyone call him again? 'The Lech'? Because he'd guzzle all those health tonics and stuff to increase his virility, then bang anything that moved? That's what killed him, you know. Anyway, how could something as precious as śarīra come out of someone as rotten as he was? And thirteen, no less! They're supposed to mean you've achieved enlightenment, but from what I see, it's got nothing to do with meditating all the time, or avoiding sex, or practicing moderation. It's more like dumb luck."

"You're sure they're real?" Reseng still wasn't convinced.

"They're real!" Bear punctuated his words with an exaggerated shrug. "I showed them to Hyecho, up at Weoljeongam Temple. He stared at them for the longest time, with his hands clasped behind his back like this, and then he slowly licked his lips and told me to sell them to him."

"What would Hyecho want with Mr. Kim's śarīra?"

"You know he's always chasing skirt, gambling and boozing it up. But that dirty monk's got an itchy palm. He's secretly worried what people will say about him if they don't find śarīra among his ashes when he's cremated. That's why he's got his eye on Mr. Kim's. If he swallows them right before he dies, then it's guaranteed they'll find at least thirteen, right?"

Reseng chuckled. Bear shoved another potato in his mouth. He took a swig of soju and then offered Reseng a potato, as if embarrassed to be eating them all himself. Reseng looked at the potato in Bear's paw and suddenly pictured the way the old man had talked to the dog, to the pork roasting over the fire, even to the potatoes buried under the ashes. *You'd better make yourselves delicious for our important guest.* That low, hypnotic voice. It struck him then that the old man must have been lonely. As lonely as a tree in winter, every last leaf shed, nothing but bare branches snaking against the sky like veins. Bear was still holding out the potato. Reseng was suddenly famished. He accepted the potato and took a bite. As he chewed, he stared quietly at the flames inside the furnace. Between the fire and the smoke, he could no longer tell what was old man and what was dog.

"Tasty, huh?" Bear asked.

"Tasty," Reseng said.

"Not to change the subject, but why the hell is tuition so expensive now? My older daughter just started university. I'll need to burn at least five more bodies to afford her tuition and rent. But where am I going to find five bodies in this climate? I don't know if it's just that the economy's bad or if the world's become a more wholesome place, but it's definitely not like the old days. How am I supposed to get by now?"

Bear frowned, as if he couldn't stand the thought of a wholesome world.

"Maybe you should think about those pretty daughters of yours and go straight," Reseng said. "Stick to cremating cats and dogs instead, you know, more wholesome like."

"Are you kidding? Cats and dogs would have to get a lot more profitable first. I charge by the kilo for cremating pets, and nowadays everyone's into those tiny ratlike dogs. Don't get me started. After I pay my gas, electricity, taxes, and this, that, and everything else, what's left? If only people would start keeping giraffes or elephants as pets. Then maybe Bear would be rich."

Bear shook the soju bottle and emptied what was left into his mouth. He stretched. He looked worn-out. "So should I sell them?" he asked abruptly.

"Sell what?"

"C'mon, I already told you! Mr. Kim's śarīra."

"May as well," Reseng said irritably. "What's the point of holding on to them?"

"That so-called monk offered me three hundred thousand won for them, but I feel like I'm getting ripped off. Even if they did come out of Mr. Kim's garbage can of a body, they're still bona fide śarīras."

"Listen to you," Reseng said. "Going on as if they're actually sacred."

"Should I ask him to bump it up to five hundred thousand?"

Reseng didn't respond. He was tired, and he wasn't in the mood to joke anymore. He stared wordlessly into the fire until Bear got the hint. Bear gave his empty soju bottle another shake, then went to get a fresh one.

White smoke spewed out of the chimney. Every time he dropped off a body for cremation, Reseng got the ridiculous notion that the souls of those once-hectic lives were exiting through the chimney. A great many assassins had been cremated there. It was the final resting place for discarded hit men. Hit men who'd messed up, hit men tracked down by cops, hit men who ended up on the death list for reasons no one knew, and assassins who'd grown too old—they were all cremated in that furnace.

To the plotters, mercenaries and assassins were like disposable batteries. After all, what use would they have for old assassins? An old assassin was like an annoying blister bursting with incriminating information and evidence. The more you thought about it, the more sense it made. Why would anyone hold on to a used-up battery?

Reseng's old friend, Chu, had been cremated in this same furnace. Chu was eight years older, but the two of them had been like family. With Chu's death, Reseng had sensed that his life had begun to change. Familiar things suddenly became unfamiliar. A certain strangeness came between him and his table, his flower vase, his car, his fake driver's license. The timing of it all was uncanny. He had once looked up the man whose name was on his stolen driver's licence. A devoted father of three and a hardworking and talented welder, according to everyone who knew him, the man had been missing for eight years. Maybe he had ended up on a hit list. His body might have been buried in the forest or sealed inside a barrel at the bottom of the ocean. Or maybe he had even been cremated right here in Bear's furnace. Eight years on, the family was still waiting for him to come home. Every time he drove, Reseng joked to himself: This car is being driven by a dead man. He felt that he lived like a dead man, a zombie. It only made sense that he was a stranger in his own life.

Two years had passed since Chu's death. He'd been an assassin, like Reseng. But unlike Reseng, Chu hadn't belonged to any particular outfit; instead, he'd drifted from place to place, taking on short gigs. The Mafia had a saying: The most dangerous adversary was a pazzo, a madman. A person who thought they had nothing to lose, who wanted nothing from others and asked nothing of him- or herself, who behaved in ways that defied common sense, who quietly followed her or his own strange principles and stubborn convictions, which were both inconceivable and unbelievable. A person like that would not be cowed by any formidable power. Chu had been that kind of person.

On the other hand, it was easy to deal with adversaries who were backed into a corner and desperate not to lose what they had. They were the plotters' favorite prey. It was obvious where they were headed. They ended up dead because they refused to acknowledge, right up to the very end, that they could not hold on to whatever it was they were trying to hold on to. But not Chu. Chu had been out to prove that this ferocious world with its boundless power could not stop him as long as he desired nothing.

Chu had been prickly, but his work was so clean and immaculate that Old Raccoon had usually given him the difficult assignments. He'd wanted to make Chu an official member of the library and had warned him, "Even a lion becomes a target for wild dogs when it's away from its pride." Each time, Chu had sneered and said, "I don't plan on living long enough to turn into a cripple like you."

Despite not belonging to any one outfit, Chu had lasted for twenty years as an assassin. He'd done all sorts of dirty work, taken government jobs, corporate jobs, jobs from third-tier meat-market contractors, no questions asked. Twenty years—it was an impressive run for an assassin.

But then one day four years ago, Chu's clock had stopped. No one knew why. Even Chu had confessed to Reseng that he didn't understand why it had happened, why his clock had suddenly stopped after running so faithfully for twenty years. What led up to it was that Chu decided to let one of his targets go. She was no one special, just another twenty-one-year-old high-priced escort. Shortly after, a news story came out about a certain national assemblyman who had leaped to his death. He'd been hounded by accusations of bribery, corruption, and a sex scandal involving a middle schooler. There was no way that a lowlife like him who enjoyed sex with middle school girls had committed suicide to preserve his honor, which he'd long since done a great job of destroying on his own. Every plotter who saw the news must have instantly thought of Chu. And Chu didn't stop there. He also went after the plotter who'd put out the contract on the escort. But he failed to track the plotter down. Not even the great Chu could pull that off. By then, Chu was a wanted man. It has to be said that plotters spend more time on finding safe hideouts for themselves and ensuring their own quick exits than on planning hits.

The plotters' world was one big cartel. They had to take out Chu, but not for anything as flimsy as pride. There was no such thing as pride in this business. They had to take him out so as not to lose customers. Like any other society, their world had its own strict rules and order. Those rules and order formed the foundation on which the market took shape, and then in streamed the customers. If order fell, the market fell, and if the market fell, bye-bye customers. Chu had to have known that. The moment he made up his mind to save the woman, he signed his own death warrant. Chu risked everything to save one unlucky prostitute.

It took the meat market's trackers less than two months to find her. She was hiding in a small port city. The high-class call girl who'd once entertained only VIP clients in four-star hotels was now selling herself to sailors in musty flophouses. If she'd holed up quietly in a factory instead of going to the red-light district, she might have dodged the trackers a little longer. But she'd ended up on the stinking, filthy streets instead. Maybe she'd run out of money. Since she'd had to leave Seoul in a hurry, she would've had no change of clothes and nowhere to sleep. Plus, it was winter. Cold and hunger have a way of numbing people to abstract fears. She might have thought she was going to die anyway, and so what difference did it make? It's hard to say whether it was stupid of her to think like that. She couldn't possibly have enjoyed whoring herself out in a port city on the outskirts of civilization, sucking drunk sailor dick for a pittance. But she would've felt she had no other choice. All you had to do was look at her hands to understand why. She had slender, lovely hands. Hands that had never once imagined a life spent standing in front of a conveyer belt tightening screws for ten hours a day, or picking seaweed or oysters from the sea in the dead of winter. Had she been born to a good family, those hands would have belonged to a pianist. But her family wasn't all that good, and so she'd been whoring herself out since the age of fifteen.

She must have known that returning to the red-light district meant she wouldn't last long. But she went back anyway. In the end, none of us can leave the place we know best, no matter how dirty and disgusting it is. Having no money and no other means of survival is part of the reason, but it's never the whole reason. We go back to our own filthy origins because it's a filth we know. Putting up with that filth is easier than facing the fear of being tossed into the wider world, and the loneliness that is as deep and wide as that fear.

Old Raccoon had summoned Reseng as soon as the plotter's file arrived. Reseng found him sitting at his desk in his study, leafing through the document. He assumed it contained the woman's photo, her address, her hobbies, her weight, her movements, and the names of all the people related to or involved with her in any way—in other words, all the information needed to kill her. It would also state the designated manner of her death and the method of disposal of the body.

"I don't know why they're wasting money on this. Says she's only thirty-eight kilos. Break her neck. It'll be as easy as stepping on a frog."

Old Raccoon thrust the file at Reseng without looking at him. Reseng raised an eyebrow. Was stepping on a frog that easy? Old Raccoon had a habit of making cynical jokes to hide his discomfort. But Reseng wasn't sure whether what bothered Old Raccoon was having to kill a twenty-one-year-old girl—and one who weighed only thirty-eight kilos, at that—or if his pride was hurt at having to accept a low-paying contract, though he knew full well the library needed the business.

Reseng flipped through the file. The woman in the picture looked like a Japanese pop star. It said she was twenty-one, but she didn't look a day over fifteen. Reseng had never killed a woman before. It wasn't that he had some special rule against killing women and children; it was simply that his turn hadn't come around yet. Reseng had no rules. Not having rules was his only rule.

"What do I do with the body?" Reseng asked.

"Take it to Bear's, of course," Old Raccoon said irritably. "What else would you do? String her up at the Gwanghwamun intersection?"

"It's a long way from where she is to Bear's place. What if I get pulled over while she's in the trunk?"

"So lay off the booze and drive like a kitten. It's not like the cops are going to force you to pull over and claim you shot at them. They've got better things to do."

His voice dripped with sarcasm. That was also his way of disguising anger. Reseng just stood there, not saying a word. Old Raccoon flicked his wrist to tell him to get lost, then got up, pulled a volume of his first-edition *Brockhaus Enzyklopädie* from the shelf, set it on a book stand, and began reading out loud, mumbling the words under his breath, completely indifferent to Reseng, who was still standing in front of him. He had been rereading it recently. When he finished, he would reread the English edition of the *Encyclopædia Britannica*. Old Raccoon's awkward, self-taught German filled the room. As Reseng opened the door and stepped out, he muttered, "No real German would understand a word of that."

Old Raccoon had long ago stopped stocking his personal shelves with anything that wasn't a dictionary or an encyclopedia. As far as Reseng could remember, he'd refused to read anything else for the last ten years. "Dictionaries are great," he'd explained. "No mushiness, no bitching, no preachiness, and, best of all, none of that high-and-mighty crap that writers try to pull."

The port city where the woman was hiding looked as run-down as a diseased chicken. The once-bustling city that had kept the Japanese imperial forces supplied with war munitions had been in decline ever since liberation. Now it seemed nothing could turn it around. Reseng got off the express bus and headed for the parking lot, where he looked for a license plate ending in 2847. At the very end of the lot was an old Musso SUV. He took the keys out of his pocket, opened the door, and got in. As soon as he started the ignition, the low fuel warning light blinked on.

"Son of a bitch left the tank empty," Reseng muttered in irritation at the stupid plotter, wherever and whoever he was.

He parked in the motel's underground parking garage. The plotter had instructed him to use the third space away from the emergency stairs, but a big luxury sedan was already parked there. Reseng checked his watch: 1:20 p.m. The owner of the sedan had either arrived the night before and hadn't left yet or he was treating himself to a leisurely lunch with his mistress. Reseng had no choice but to park next to the wall. He got out and checked the walls and ceiling. The motel was too old and shabby to have security cameras. Reseng opened the trunk and took out the oversize duffel bag and body bag that had been left there for him.

As indicated in the file, the motel counter was unstaffed. The clock on the wall pointed to 1:28. Reseng took the key for room 303 from its pigeonhole and went up the stairs. Before opening the door, he pulled on a pair of black leather gloves.

The motel room had seen better days. On the bed was a dirty quilt that he could tell at once hadn't been washed in years, and on a shelf was half a roll of toilet paper, a metal ashtray, and an old eight-sided box of safety matches. The wallpaper was so faded that he couldn't tell what color it had once been, and sticking out of the window was an air conditioner shaped like a German tube radio that had to be at least thirty years old; it looked like something awful would spew out of it if he were to turn it on. Glued to a discarded semen-encrusted condom stuck between the mattress and the bed frame was a single pubic hair that could have belonged to either a man or a woman. The glow of the overhead fluorescent was dimmed by a thick layer of dust and long-dead insects trapped inside the light cover. The room looked like a scene from a black-and-white movie in the 1930s.

"How depressing," Reseng muttered as he set the duffel bag and the black Samsonite attaché case he'd brought with him from Seoul in the corner and sat on the edge of the bed. It was so filthy, he could practically hear the cheers of a billion germs thinking they had just gone to heaven. He put a cigarette in his mouth and took a match from the eight-sided box. They still make these? he thought as he struck the match against the side.

At exactly two o'clock, Reseng called the phone number in the file.

"I'm inside. Room three oh three."

The man on the other end said nothing for several long seconds. All Reseng heard was the unpleasant sound of the man breathing into the phone, then the dial tone. Reseng stared at the receiver. "Prick," he muttered. He opened the window, looked out at the narrow alleys winding behind the train station, and lit another cigarette. The red-light district was a quiet place at two in the afternoon.

It took the woman over two hours to show up. As soon as she

entered, she glanced indifferently at Reseng and said hello. She had the careless, conceited air typical of women who knew they were beautiful, along with a baby face, a tight little body, the kind of looks that would turn any man's head, and something in her expression that was hard to pin down, like a faint, gloomy shadow hanging over her, which brought to his mind a picture on a calendar of a fallen ginkgo leaf.

"Take your clothes off," she said.

She took off hers. It took her less than five seconds to strip off her dress, bra, and panties and stand naked in front of Reseng. He gawked at her. Her unusually large breasts on such a bony torso reminded him of the girls in Japanese porn comics. Her skin looked baby-soft.

He had no idea what had gone down inside the assemblyman's room. But he couldn't imagine that she'd actually had anything to do with his death. Her only crime was sucking the clammy, flaccid dicks of aging tycoons with a thing for underage girls. And there was no way she'd made much money from it. The old men would have shelled out a ton of cash to bed her, but the lion's share would've gone to her pimp. She simply had bad luck. But in the end, even bad luck is just another part of life.

"Aren't you going to get undressed?" she asked.

Reseng kept staring, saying nothing.

"Hurry up already. I've got places to be," she said, clearly irritated.

She looked as arrogant as ever, despite her whiny voice. Without taking his eyes off of her, Reseng slowly slipped his hand inside his leather jacket. Which should he choose, the gun or the knife? Which one was less likely to startle her and make her scream or fly into a panic? When asked, most people said they were more afraid of knives than guns, which made no sense to him. But then, fear is never rational. Reseng chose the gun. Before he could pull it out, the woman's face stiffened.

"May I put my clothes back on?" Her voice trembled.

"Why?"

"I don't want to die naked."

Her eyes met his. They held no trace of anger or hatred. Her weary eyes simply said that she'd learned too much about the world in too short a time; her vacant pupils said she was tired of feeling afraid and didn't want to see anything anymore.

"You're not going to die naked," Reseng said.

But the woman didn't move.

Reseng softened his tone. "Get dressed, please."

She picked up her clothes from the floor, her hands shaking as she pulled up her dainty Mickey Mouse panties. When she was dressed, Reseng guided her to the bed by her shoulder and locked the door. The woman took a pack of Virginia Slims from her bag and tried to light one, but her hands shook so hard that she couldn't get the lighter to work. Reseng pulled his Zippo from his pocket and lit it for her. She gave him a slight nod of thanks and took a deep drag, then turned her head and exhaled a plume of smoke in what seemed like an infinitely long sigh. He could tell she was making an effort to stay calm, as if she'd been practicing for this moment, but her thin shoulders were already trembling.

"I hate having marks on my body. Could you avoid leaving any?" she asked quietly.

She wasn't begging for mercy. All she wanted was to die without any cuts or bruises. He suddenly wondered about Chu. What was it about this woman that had stopped Chu's clock? Had her frail body filled him with sympathy? Had she reminded him too much of a girl in a Japanese porn video? Had the mysterious melancholy clouding her features aroused in him a misplaced sense of guilt? No. That'd be ridiculous. Chu wasn't the kind of guy who would fuck up his life because of some cheap romantic notion.

"You hate having marks . . ."

Reseng slowly echoed her. The woman's eyes flickered nervously. He found it hard to believe that she was more afraid of having marks on her body than of dying. Reseng gazed down at the floor for a moment before raising his head.

"You won't have any marks." He tried to keep his voice as level as possible.

A startled look came over her face. She seemed to have just figured out what the oversize bag in the corner was for. She must have pictured it, because her entire body began to shake.

"Are you putting me in that?"

Her voice had a nervous tremor, but she managed not to stutter. Reseng nodded.

"Where will you take me? Are you going to leave my body at a garbage dump or in the forest?"

For a moment, Reseng wondered if he really had to tell her. He didn't. But whether he did or not, it changed nothing.

"You won't be buried in the forest or dumped in a landfill. You'll be cremated at a facility. Though not, strictly speaking, legally."

"Then no one will know I'm dead. There won't be a funeral."

Reseng nodded again. She'd toughed everything else out, but for some reason that made her burst into tears. Why make such a fuss about what'll happen to your corpse when you're facing imminent death? She seemed more worried about what she would look like after death than about the death itself. What a thing for someone her age to worry herself over.

She gritted her teeth and wiped her eyes with her palm. Then she fixed Reseng with a look that said she was not going to beg for her life or waste any more tears on someone like him.

"How are you going to kill me?"

Reseng was taken aback. Fifteen years as an assassin, and he had never once been asked that.

"Are you serious?"

"Yes," she said flatly.

As per the plotter's orders, he was going to break her neck. Snapping the slender neck of a woman who weighed no more than thirty-eight kilos would be a piece of cake. As long as she didn't put up a fight, it would be quicker and less painful than might be imagined. But if she did struggle, she could end up with a broken vertebra jutting through the skin. Or writhing in agony for several long minutes until she finally suffocated from a blocked airway, fully conscious the whole time.

"How would you like to die?"

As soon as the question was out, Reseng felt like an ass. What kind of question was that? How would you like to *die*? It sounded like he was a waiter asking how she'd like her steak cooked. She lowered her head in thought. He could tell she wasn't actually choosing right then and there, but was instead confirming a decision she had already made for herself.

"I have poison," she said.

Reseng didn't get it at first, and he repeated the words to himself: *I. Have. Poison.* So she'd already thought about suicide. And she'd chosen poison as her way out. He wasn't surprised. Statistically, men usually chose guns or jumping to their deaths, whereas women preferred pills or hanging. Women tended to prefer a means of death that left their bodies undamaged. But, contrary to what they imagined, the kinds of poisons that were easy to purchase, like pesticides or hydrochloric acid, resulted in very long, very painful deaths, and had high rates of failure.

"It's the least you could do," she said, her eyes pleading.

Reseng avoided the woman's gaze. Break her neck, stuff her in the bag, and get to Bear's. That was his job. Plotters hated it when lowly assassins took it upon themselves to change the plot. It wasn't about pride. The problem was that if the plot changed, then the people waiting at their various posts would need new cues, and everyone's roles would get out of sync. If incriminating evidence got left behind or if things went sour, then someone else would have to die in order to cover it up. And sometimes that someone was you. Changing the assigned plot was not just a headache but a potential death sentence.

Reseng looked at the woman. She was still gazing at him, pleading—not for her life, but for this one last thing. Could he grant it to her? Should he? Reseng furrowed his brow.

If she took poison, it would remain in the ashes even after cremation. And if traces of her DNA were found in his car or on his clothes and poison was detected in a sample of her ashes, there would be compelling evidence of foul play. But that sort of thing happened only in the movies, and was rare in real life. Plotters weren't perfectionists, they were just pricks. Poison, broken neck—it made no difference. The woman would be cremated either way, and her ashes would sink quietly to the bottom of a river.

"What kind of poison?" Reseng asked.

She took a packet from her purse. He held out his hand. She hesitated before giving it to him. He gave the cellophane packet a gentle shake and held it up to the light. There was a loose white powder inside.

"Cyanide?"

She nodded, her eyes never once leaving his.

"How much do you know about cyanide?"

She tipped her head to one side, as if she didn't understand the question.

"I know you die if you swallow it." Her voice sounded half daring and half annoyed. "What else is there to know?"

"Where'd you get it?"

"I stole it from a friend of mine who was planning to kill herself."

Reseng smiled. To her, it probably looked like a smirk, but in truth it was closer to pity. His lips tended to curl whenever he didn't know quite what to say.

"If this friend of yours bought it off the Internet or from a drug dealer, then there's a good chance it's fake. And if it is, you could have a real problem on your hands. But even if it is real, death by cyanide is not the romantic death you think it is. Nor will you die in seconds. I'm guessing you think this is one of those suicide pills that spies take to die instantly, but those contain liquid cyanide, not this solid stuff."

Reseng flicked the cellophane packet onto the floor like a cigarette butt. She scrambled for it, panicked, as if it were precious to her, then looked up at him dubiously.

"It won't kill me?"

"Two hundred and fifty milligrams is enough to kill most people. But it's extremely painful. Your muscles get paralyzed, your tongue and throat burn, your organs melt, and it can take anywhere from minutes to hours until you eventually die of asphyxiation. Some people take longer, and some actually survive. Not only that, you don't leave a very pretty corpse behind."

The woman's shoulders slumped. Her face filled with despair. She turned to the window; she'd stopped crying or even shaking. She just stared blankly at the sky, her eyes unfocused. Reseng checked his watch: 4:30. He had to get out of there before it got dark. Once the sun went down, the alleys would be crawling with prostitutes, their faces freshly painted, and johns drunk on booze and lust.

"Lucky for you, I have the perfect thing."

Reseng gestured at the attaché case. The woman turned to look.

"Barbituric acid. Peaceful way to go. Doesn't hurt like cyanide or rat poison, and won't leave you looking messed up or ugly. It'll be just like falling asleep. A scientist back in the mid-nineteenth century, Adolf von Baeyer, came up with barbiturates while working on sedatives and sleeping pills. He named it after his friend Barbara. It's still used as a sedative. It's also been used for hypnosis, as a tranquilizer, and even has hallucinogenic properties. Other drugs, like barbital and ruminol, were based on it. It's used for euthanasia all over the world."

The woman made a face at his long-winded explanation, but she nodded.

"I'll give it to you if you answer something for me," Reseng added. "Then you'll get the peaceful death you want."

She nodded again.

"Do you remember a tall man who was hired to kill you?"

"Yes."

"Why did he let you live?"

She shifted her weight from side to side and pressed her hand to her forehead. As she recalled the events of that day, her expression kept changing from wonder to horror and back again.

"I honestly don't know. He stared at me for almost half an hour and then left."

"That's it?"

"Yes. He just sat there quietly and looked at me."

"He didn't say anything?"

"He said, 'Stay away from your regular places. Don't go back. If you're really lucky, you might just survive.' That's what he told me."

Reseng nodded.

"Is he dead?" she asked.

"He's still alive, but probably not for long. Once you're on the list, your chances are shot."

"Is he going to die because of me?"

"Maybe. But not *only* because of you."

Reseng checked his watch again. He gave the woman a look to indicate that time was up. She didn't react. He opened the briefcase and took out a pill bottle and a bottle of Jack Daniel's.

She watched him silently, then asked, "If you cremate me in secret, no one will know I'm dead, right? My mother will spend the rest of her life waiting for me to come home."

Reseng paused in the middle of taking the pills out of the bottle. The woman started crying. He was relieved she wasn't crying loudly. He waited for her tears to stop. Was it her quiet weeping that had stopped Chu's clock? After five minutes, he rested his hand on the woman's shoulder to tell her they couldn't delay any longer. She brushed his hand away in irritation.

"Can I write my mother a letter?"

Reseng gave her a pained look.

She added, "It doesn't matter if she never gets it."

Her eyes were still brimming with tears. Reseng checked his watch again and nodded. She took a pen and a small appointment book out of her bag and began to write on one of the pages.

Dear Mom,

I'm sorry. I'm sorry to Dad in heaven, too. I meant to save up money and go to school and get married, but it didn't work out. I'm sorry I died before you. Don't worry about me. Dying this way isn't so bad. The world's a rotten place anyway.

A tear fell on the word *heaven,* blurring the ink. She signed it, then tore the page out and handed it to Reseng.

"Pretty handwriting," he said.

What a dumb thing to say. Reseng had no idea why he'd said it. The woman put the appointment book back into her bag. He assumed she was reaching for a handkerchief next to wipe away her tears, but to his surprise she took out a makeup pouch. She gave him another look to indicate that she needed a little more time. He raised his hand to tell her to go ahead. During the more than ten minutes she spent carefully reapplying her makeup, Reseng stood and stared, one eyebrow raised. What sort of vanity was this? She finished touching up her face and put her makeup away. The click of the bag closing sounded unusually loud.

"Will you stay with me until I'm gone? I'm a little scared," she said with a smile.

Reseng nodded and offered her the pills. She stared at them for several seconds before taking them from his palm and swallowing them with the glass of whiskey he poured for her.

Reseng tried to help her to lie down, but she pushed him away and stretched out on the bed by herself. She rested her hands on her chest and stared up at the ceiling. It didn't take long for the hallucinations to start.

"I see a red wind. And a blue lion. Right next to it is a cute rainbow-colored polar bear. Is that heaven?"

"Yeah, sure, that's heaven. You're on your way there now."

"Thanks for saying that. You're going to hell."

"Then I guess we won't be seeing each other again. Because you're definitely going to heaven, and I'm definitely going to hell."

She let out a small laugh. A single tear spilled from her smiling eyes.

Chu held out another two years after the woman died.

Like the sly jackal that he was, like the insane thorn in the side of the plotters that he was, Chu stayed one step ahead of the frenzied, persistent hunt. Rumors spread about trackers and assassins falling prey to Chu, too blinded by the promise of reward money to watch their own tails while tailing him, and those same rumors got twisted up and blown out of proportion and kept the denizens of the meat market entertained for some time. Reseng wasn't surprised. Those third-rate hired guns and aging bounty hunters accustomed to nothing more challenging than chasing down runaway prostitutes were no match for Chu and never had been. But there was no way of knowing whether any of the rumors floating like wayward soap bubbles around the meat market were true. Most deaths in their world, of trackers and assassins alike, never surfaced. At any rate, maybe the rumors *were* true, because Chu could not be caught.

About a year after he'd gone underground, Chu went on the offensive. He hunted down several plotters and killed them, along with several contractors and brokers. At one point, he sauntered right into the midst of the meat market and smashed up a contractor's office. But the plotters he targeted had nothing to do with the botched call girl job. In fact, they were closer to amateurs— low-rate plotters hired by cheap contractors for onetime gigs. No one understood why Chu picked them, other than the fact that he stood no chance of getting anywhere near the people who actually operated the gears of the plotting world.

After Chu trashed the office and stole a ledger that he couldn't possibly have had any use for, a group of men turned up in Old Raccoon's library. One of the men was Hanja. Though he looked like any other boss of a security company, he ran a corporate-style contracting firm, making money not only from government agencies and corporations but also from whatever he could gain from the black market. The meat-market dealers were nothing but small-time hoodlums to Hanja, so the fact that they were at the same meeting showed just how rattled and pissed off Chu had made everyone. Hanja sat on the couch, looking like he'd just taken a bite out of a giant turd.

When Old Raccoon took his seat, the meat-market dealers all started talking at once.

"I'm losing it, I tell you. What the fuck does Chu want anyway? We have to know what he wants if we're going to sweet-talk him, or trick him out into the open. Either way, let's do *something,* dammit."

"That's what I've been saying. Why isn't that lunatic talking? Someone cut out his tongue or what? If it's cash he wants, he should say he wants cash. If his feelings got hurt, he should say so.

If he's angry, he should say he's angry. But he's gotta say something. He can't just bust in, smash everything to shit, and leave."

"I swear, he's cost me an arm and a leg. He's killed three of my guys already. And it doesn't stop there! I had to pay to get rid of their bodies, as well. Fuck, man. Bear's the only one benefiting from this. But why is Chu only going after my guys? There are way worse guys here than me."

"Look in a mirror lately? Who here is worse than you?"

"Hey, did any of you write him an IOU? You have to pay cash. Cash! Chu hates IOUs!"

Old Raccoon sat in the middle, looking amused. Why? Especially considering that Chu could walk in at any moment and shove a knife in his stomach.

"The scholars of the Joseon dynasty had a saying," Old Raccoon said with a smile. "'There's no telling which way a frog or King Heungseon will leap.' They could just as easily have been speaking of our predicament."

"What do you think Chu is up to?" Choi the Butcher asked. Choi hired out illegal Chinese immigrants of Korean descent as cheap labor.

"How would I know what that lunatic is thinking? Maybe he wants to slit my throat. Or yours."

"Let's offer a reward." Hanja, who'd been sitting quietly in the corner, finally spoke up. "To whoever provides information to help us find him. That'll get people moving. Detectives will want a piece of the action, too."

"Money? Are we all pitching in equally?" Choi asked.

"Fuck no." Minari Pak, whose office had been trashed by Chu, gave Hanja a sidelong glance and grumbled. "Some people in this room do a hell of a lot more business than the rest, so what's this crap about equal? Don't you know how much damage he did to my place."

Hanja silenced them with two words.

"I'll pay."

He wasn't showing off. He just wanted to put an end to the

meeting. The other men looked annoyed at Hanja's cockiness, but it was obvious they were relieved.

"The saying goes that kindness starts with having a full larder, and that must certainly be true of our generous and wealthy friend here." The sarcasm in Old Raccoon's voice was unmistakable as he looked at Hanja.

Hanja smiled broadly at Old Raccoon and said, "What can I say? Unlike you, I'm not picky. If you ask me to do a job, I do it. I work hard. In earnest. And in silence."

Ironically, the overthrow of three decades of military dictatorship, a return to democratically elected civilian presidencies, and the brisk advent of democratization led to a major boom in the assassination industry. During the era of dictatorship, assassinations were clandestine operations carried out by a small number of plotters, hit men expertly trained by the government or the military, and highly experienced and trustworthy contractors. In fact, there wasn't even enough action to call it an industry. Those who knew about the plotting world or were involved in it were few, and there was never that much work. The military, for the most part, had no interest in plotters. Those were untroubled and unenlightened times when you could pack a troublemaker into your jeep with their whole family watching, lock them away in the basement of a building on Namsan Mountain, beat them until they were half-crippled, and send them back home, without hearing a peep out of anyone. Why bother with a highly skilled plotter?

What sped up the assassination industry was the new regime of democratically elected civilian administrations that sought the trappings of morality. Maybe they thought that by stamping their foreheads with the words *It's okay, we're not the military,* they could fool the people. But power is all the same deep down, no matter what it looks like. As Deng Xiaoping once said, "It doesn't matter whether a cat is white or black as long as it catches mice." The problem was that the newly democratic government couldn't use that basement on Namsan to beat the crap out of loudmouthed pains in the ass. And so, in order to avoid the eyes of the people and the press, to avoid generating evidence of their own complex chain of command and execution, and to avoid any future responsibility, they started doing business on the sly with contractors. And thus began the age of outsourcing. It was cheaper and simpler than taking care of it themselves, but best of all, there was less cleanup. On the rare occasion that the shit did hit the fan, the government was safe and clear of it. While contractors were being hauled off to jail, all they had to do was look shocked and appalled in front of the news cameras and say things like "What a terrible and unfortunate tragedy!"

The boom really took off when corporations followed the state's lead in outsourcing to plotters. Corporations generated far more work than the state, and the contractors' primary clientele shifted from public to private. As the jobs increased, small, lesser-known start-ups began to crowd in, and washed-up assassins, gangsters, retired servicemen, and former homicide detectives, who were tired of working for peanuts, swarmed to the meat market. And, like an alligator, Hanja waited just below the surface, eyeing the scene closely and observing the changes, biding his time. While Old Raccoon faded out of relevance, unable to perceive the shifting tides, this dandy with a Stanford MBA secretly cultivated his own team of plotters and mercenaries under the cover of a perfectly legal security company.

The principles of the market hadn't changed since it first sprang into being. Whoever provided a better service at a lower price was the winner. Hanja knew that. While Old Raccoon was cooped up in his library, reading encyclopedias and reminiscing about all the goodies that had fallen into his lap back in the days of dictatorship, and the meat market's third-rate contractors were too blind with greed over the scraps to do their work properly and were being hauled off to prison, Hanja was building his modern network of businessmen and officials, recruiting experts from every field, and employing high-quality plotters. He transformed the once-messy, free-for-all plotting world into a clean, convenient supermarket. You half-expected to be beckoned inside by beautiful models hired to wave and smile and say "Right this way!" and "Who can we kill for you today?" So, no matter how big a stink the meat-market dealers made, Hanja now ruled this world.

The long, boring meeting ground on with no decisions made other than to offer a bounty. It was less a meeting than a gripe session about Chu. Reseng stepped outside to have a smoke. As he was taking a deep drag, Hanja joined him.

Reseng offered him a cigarette.

"I quit. I can't stand things that stink anymore."

Reseng raised an eyebrow in amusement.

Hanja took a gold-plated case out of his suit pocket and offered him a business card.

"Call me. Let's have dinner sometime. We're family, after all."

Reseng stared at Hanja's long, pale fingers before taking the card. Hanja left without rejoining the meeting. Why did Hanja say they were family, when they didn't share a single drop of blood between them? There was just the fact that they'd both grown up in Old Raccoon's library. But they'd never lived there at the same time. By the time Reseng had arrived at the library, Hanja was attending university in the United States.

The bounty was posted, but still Chu hadn't been caught. More rumors sprang up, swirling through the air like falling leaves and disappearing underfoot. Old Raccoon refused to join the hunt. He stayed in his study all day, reading his encyclopedias. So Reseng did nothing, either. The thought of going up against a man like Chu was too much. He had recurring nightmares of running into him. It was always a narrow dead-end street, Reseng trembling at one end and Chu, the brutal assassin, blocking his escape at the other. Reseng knew he was no match for Chu—not in his dreams or in his waking life. The only way someone like him could ever defeat Chu would be by chucking a dagger at him from behind, like the idiot prince Paris.

That summer the rain was incessant. People joked that the

monsoonal front had hunkered down right in the middle of the peninsula and was going on a bender. As with any slack season, Reseng passed the time by starting his mornings with a can of beer, listening to music, staring out the window, and playing with Desk and Lampshade. When the cats fell asleep, their heads resting on each other's bodies, Reseng lay down in bed to read. Books about the rise and fall of the Roman Empire, books about the once-powerful descendants of Genghis Khan who'd roamed freely over the steppes but went into a sudden rapid decline when they settled behind fortress walls, and books about the history of coffee, syphilis, typewriters. When he grew bored of thumbing through pages dampened by the humid air, he tossed the book to the other side of the bed, knocked back another can of beer, and fell asleep. Just another ordinary summer.

On the last day of September, during a heavy rainfall, there was a knock on Reseng's door. When he opened it, Chu was standing there, drenched. He was so tall that the beads of water dripping off the brim of his cap seemed to hang in the air for a long time. He had a large camping backpack, a rolled-up sleeping bag, and a shopping bag filled with beer and whiskey.

"Having a drink with you was next on my bucket list," Chu said.

"Come on in."

Chu stepped through the door, shedding drops of rain and star- tling Desk and Lampshade, who scrambled to the very top of their cat tower and huddled inside. Chu had lost a lot of weight. Lanky to begin with, he was now just skin and bone.

Reseng offered him two hand towels. Chu took off his cap and set his backpack on the floor. He dried his face and hair and brushed the water from his leather jacket.

"No money for an umbrella?" Reseng asked.

"Accidentally left mine on the subway. Didn't want to waste money on another."

"Since when do dead men worry about money?"

"Good point," Chu said with a light laugh. "Dead man or not, I still don't want to waste money on an umbrella."

"You want a change of clothes?"

"No, I'm fine. I'll dry off soon enough. Besides, I doubt your clothes would fit me. You're too short."

"I'm average. You're just tall."

Reseng took out a space heater and put on a pot of coffee. Chu turned on the heater and warmed his hands over it. The cats, unable to resist their curiosity, poked their heads out to inspect Chu. He wiggled his fingers at them. The cats seemed intrigued but didn't leave the tower.

"They won't play with me." Chu looked disappointed.

"I told them never to play with bad guys."

Reseng handed Chu a cup of coffee. Chu gulped it down. Then he put the damp towels on the floor and shivered. Reseng refilled the cup.

"How much is my bounty?" Chu asked.

"Hundred million."

"You could buy a Benz with that. Hey, I'm gifting you a Benz."

Reseng snorted. "What an honor. If I kill you, I get cash *and* glory. For taking down the world's greatest assassin."

"Who cares about glory? Cash is all that matters."

"Why not die quietly on your own terms?"

Chu paused briefly in the middle of emptying the shopping bag. "What's the point? It's easy money; you should take it. Besides, I never did anything nice for you."

"That's true," Reseng said. "You never did."

Chu looked disappointed. "But I paid for more meals than you."

"Did you? How come I don't remember any of those meals?"

"So unfair."

Reseng got ice cubes, whiskey glasses, and some beef jerky from the kitchen while Chu placed the bottles on the table. There were two six-packs of Heineken, two bottles of Jack Daniel's, a fifth of Johnnie Walker Blue, and five bottles of soju.

"That's an odd combo. You drinking all of that?"

"It's my first drink since going on the run."

Chu lined the cans and bottles up neatly.

"If I were you, I would've gotten drunk every day. Must get boring having to stay hidden."

Chu smiled. He filled a whiskey glass with Jack Daniel's and knocked it back. His large Adam's apple bobbed up and down with each swallow.

"Oh yeah, it's been too long," he said, wiping his lips. He looked like he had just reunited with an old friend.

He added two ice cubes to his glass and filled it halfway, then stared at the ice for the longest time before smiling mysteriously.

"I was too scared to drink," he said, his thick eyebrows quivering.

"I didn't know guys like you got scared," Reseng said as he opened a Heineken.

"It's a dumb move to get drunk without someone to watch your back."

Chu emptied the glass and chewed on an ice cube. The sound of the ice grinding and cracking between his teeth put Reseng's nerves on edge. Suddenly, Chu shoved the glass into Reseng's hand. Reseng hurriedly set down his Heineken. Chu filled the glass two-thirds full with Jack Daniel's and added two more ice cubes. The alcohol sloshed as he tossed the ice in.

"Drink up," Chu said, gazing at him. "Jack is a real man's drink."

Chu's commanding tone got on Reseng's nerves.

"Alcohol companies made that up to sell alcohol to fake men like you."

Chu didn't laugh at the joke. Instead, he kept staring at Reseng as if he wanted him to hurry up and drink. Reseng stared down at the glass. It was a lot of alcohol to swallow in one shot. He fished the ice cubes out and dumped them on the tray. Then he gulped the whiskey down.

Chu looked satisfied. He stood up, looked around the room, and went over to the cat tower. Timid Lampshade went back inside and refused to come out, but curious Desk tiptoed closer to Chu and sniffed at his hand. Chu gave the cat a scratch behind the ears. Desk seemed to like it; she lowered her head and purred.

Chu played with the cat for a while before coming back to the table, picking up his glass, and sitting on the edge of the bed. He flipped through the books strewn around on the bedspread.

"Did you know I didn't like you at first? Every time I went to Old Raccoon's library, you were reading. That annoyed me. I'm not sure why. Maybe I was jealous. You seemed different from the rest of us."

"I never read. I was only pretending to when you were there. So I'd look different."

"Well, you did. You looked—how should I put it? Kind of soft."

"You were in the library a lot, too. I bet you read as much as I did."

"I hated reading. But I bet even I could handle this one."

Chu was holding *The History of Syphilis*.

"That's not what you think."

Chu flipped through a few pages and laughed. "You're right. It's not my speed. Why are there no damn pictures?" He tossed it back on the bed and picked up the one next to it, called *The Blue Wolves*. "Wolves? You planning to quit and raise wolves instead?"

Reseng smirked. "It's the story of eight of Genghis Khan's warriors. Plenty of animals like you in that book. It took the Blue Wolves just ten years to build the largest empire in the world."

"What happened to them after?"

"They moved into a fortress and turned into dogs."

Chu looked intrigued as he flipped through a few pages of *The Blue Wolves,* but he seemed to struggle to understand the sentences and soon lost interest. *The Blue Wolves* landed with a thunk on top of *The History of Syphilis*.

"So what's this I hear about you killing the girl?" Chu asked.

Reseng's earlobes turned hot, and he didn't respond. Instead, he picked up the bottle and filled a glass a third of the way with Jack Daniel's. Chu's eyes followed him closely. Reseng gazed at the glass for a moment before drinking. It tasted sweeter than the first glass.

"Where'd you hear that?" Reseng asked. His voice was calm.

"Here and there."

"If you heard it while on the run, then I guess that means everyone knows."

"Lot of crazy rumors in this business." Chu raised an eyebrow, as if to ask why it mattered where he'd heard it.

Reseng looked Chu straight in the eye. "Did Bear tell you?"

"Bear is a lot quieter than he looks."

Chu was taking care to defend Bear, which almost definitely meant that Bear was the one who'd told. There were plenty of places where word could've gotten out, but Bear had no reason to take risks for Reseng's sake. Around here, no one took foolish risks or went out of their way when it came to Chu. Least of all Bear, with his two daughters, whom he'd struggled to raise on his own. Reseng understood. Had it been a detective sniffing around, Bear would have taken it to the grave. All the same, he couldn't help feeling annoyed. When word leaks out, it doesn't have to travel far before you end up in a plotter's crosshairs.

"Did you really think you could save her?" Reseng asked, not backing down.

"No, of course not. I'm not the type to save anyone. I'm too busy trying to keep myself alive."

"So there's nothing strange about what I did. You're the strange one."

"You're right. I'm the strange one. You did what was expected of you."

What was expected . . . Those words made Reseng feel both relieved and insulted. Chu moved over to the table and poured more alcohol. The bottle was already almost empty. Chu emptied his glass again, opened the second bottle, and poured himself another glass. He gulped that one down, as well.

"I wanted to ask you something," Reseng said. "Did you ever go back to see her?"

"Nope."

"Then why let her live? Did you think the plotters would pat you on the shoulder and say 'It happens to all of us'?"

"To be honest, I have no idea."

Chu drank another glass of whiskey. For someone who had gone without any alcohol for two years, he was having no trouble consuming an entire bottle all by himself in less than twenty minutes. His face was turning red. Did he really think he was safe in Reseng's apartment?

Chu asked, "Have you ever met any of the plotters who've given you orders?"

"Not once in fifteen years."

"Don't you wonder?" Chu asked. "Who's telling you what to do, I mean. Who decides when you use the turn signal, when you step on the brake, when you step on the gas, when to turn left, when to turn right, when to shut up and when to speak."

"Why are you wondering that all of a sudden?"

"I was standing there, looking at this girl who was just skin and bones, and I suddenly wondered who these plotters were anyway. I could have killed her with one finger. She was so scared, she just sat there frozen. When I saw how hard she was shaking, I wanted to find out exactly who was sitting at their desk, twirling their pen, and coming up with this bullshit plan."

"I would never have guessed you were such a romantic."

"It's not about romance or curiosity or anything like that. I mean that I didn't realize until then just what a cowardly prick I'd been." Chu sounded on edge.

"Plotters are just pawns like us," Reseng said. "A request comes in, and they draw up the plans. There's someone above them who tells them what to do. And above that person is another plotter telling them what to do. You know what's there if you keep going all the way to the top? Nothing. Just an empty chair."

"There has to be someone in the chair."

"Nope, it's empty. To put it another way, it's only a chair. Anyone can sit in it. And that chair, which anyone can sit in, decides everything."

"I don't get it."

"It's a system. You think that if you go up there with a knife and stab the person at the very top, that'll fix everything. But no one's there. It's just an empty chair."

"I've been in this business for twenty years. I've killed countless guys, including friends of mine. I even killed my protégé. I gave him baby clothes at his daughter's first birthday party. But if what you say is true, then I've been taking orders from a chair all this time. And you broke a defenseless woman's neck because a chair told you to."

Chu downed another glass. As he caught his breath, he poured more whiskey for Reseng. Reseng ignored it and took a sip of his Heineken. He was tempted to blurt out that he hadn't broken her neck, but he swallowed the words back down with a mouthful of beer.

Instead, Reseng said, "You can't shit in your pants just because the toilet is dirty."

Chu sneered.

"You're sounding more and more like Old Raccoon every day," he said. "That's not good. Smooth talkers will stab a guy in the back every time."

"Whereas you sound more and more like a whiny brat. Do you really think this tantrum you're throwing makes you look cool? It doesn't. No matter what you do, you won't change a thing. Just like you changed nothing for that girl."

Chu unzipped the top of his jacket to reveal the leather gun holster under his arm that had been refashioned into a knife holster. He took out the knife and set it on the table. His movements were calm, not the slightest bit menacing.

"I could kill you very painfully with this knife. Make you shiver in agony for hours, blood gushing, steel scraping against bone, until your guts spill out of your body and hang down to the floor. Do you think you'll still be mouthing off about empty chairs and systems and claiming that nothing has changed? Of course not. Because you're full of shit. Anyone who thinks he's safe is full of shit."

Reseng stared at the knife. It was an ordinary kitchen knife, a German brand, Henckels. The blade was razor-sharp, as if it had just come off the whetstone. The top of the handle was wound tightly with a handkerchief. Chu preferred that brand because it was sturdy, the blade didn't rust easily, and you could buy it anywhere. Other knife men looked down on the brand as a lady's knife that was good only for cooking at home, but in fact it was a good knife. It didn't chip or break easily the way sushi knives did.

Reseng peeled his eyes away from the knife and looked at Chu. Chu was angry. But his eyes lacked their usual venomous glint. The whiskey he'd guzzled must have gotten to him. Reseng thought about his own knife in the drawer. He tried to recall the last time he'd stabbed someone. Had it been six years? Seven? He couldn't remember. Could he even get the knife out fast enough? If he made a move for it, Chu might grab his, too. And if he did manage to get the knife out of the drawer in time, could he hold his own against Chu? Did he have any chance at all of being the victor?

Unlikely. Reseng took out a cigarette and started smoking. Chu held out his hand. Reseng took out another cigarette, lit it, and passed it over to Chu, who inhaled deeply and leaned his head way back to stare at the ceiling. He held the pose for a long time, as if to say, If you're going to stab me, do it now.

When the cigarette had burned halfway down, Chu straightened up and looked at Reseng.

"The whole thing's fucked-up, isn't it? I've got all these goons coming after me, hoping to get a taste of that reward money, and meanwhile I have no idea who to kill or what to do. To be honest, I don't even care if there is anything at the top. It could be an empty chair, like you say, or there could be some prick sitting in it. Won't make any difference either way to a knucklehead like me. I could die and come back in another form and I still wouldn't understand how any of this works."

"Will you go to Hanja?"

"Maybe."

"Don't."

"Then where am I supposed to go instead?"

"Leave the country. Go to Mexico, the United States, France, maybe somewhere in Africa. . . . Lots of places you could go. You can find work in a private military company. They'll protect you."

Chu gave a furtive smile.

"You're giving me the same advice I gave that girl. Am I supposed to thank you now?"

Chu downed his whiskey, refilled it, downed it again, then emptied the rest of the second bottle into his glass.

"Aren't you going to drink with me? It's lonely drinking by myself."

Chu wasn't joking. He really did look lonely sitting there at the table. Reseng drank the glass of whiskey Chu had poured for him. Chu opened the Johnnie Walker Blue and poured Reseng another shot. Then he raised his glass in a toast. Reseng clinked his glass against Chu's.

"Oh, that's much better," Reseng said, sounding impressed. "I like this Johnnie Walker Blue stuff better than that 'real man's,' or whatever, Jack Daniel's."

Chu seemed genuinely amused. He didn't say much as they worked on the rest of the bottle. Reseng didn't have anything to say, either, so they drank in silence. Chu drank far more than Reseng. When the bottle was empty, Chu stumbled into the bathroom. Reseng heard the sound of pissing, then vomiting, then the toilet flushing several times. Twenty minutes passed and still he did not come out of the bathroom. All Reseng heard was the tap running. His eyes never left Chu's knife where it sat in the middle of the table.

When Chu still hadn't come out after thirty minutes, Reseng knocked on the door. It was locked and there was no answer from inside. He got a flat-head screwdriver to pry it open. Chu was asleep on the toilet, hunched over like an old bear, and the bathtub was overflowing onto the floor. Reseng turned off the water and helped him to the bed.

Once he was stretched out flat, Chu started to snore, as if he were getting the first good sleep of his life. His snoring was as loud as he was tall. It was so loud that even Lampshade timidly poked her head out from inside the cat tower, crept down to the bed, and started sniffing at Chu's face and hair. Reseng sat on the couch and drank several more cans of beer, then fell asleep watching Desk and Lampshade enjoying their new game of swatting at Chu's hair and walking across his chest and stomach.

When Reseng awoke in the morning, Chu was gone. His big

backpack was gone, too. All that was left was his kitchen knife with the handkerchief wrapped around the handle, lying in the middle of the table like a present.

A week later, Chu's body arrived at Bear's Pet Crematorium.

By the time Old Raccoon and Reseng got there, it was raining hard, just like on the day of Chu's visit. Bear held an umbrella over Old Raccoon as he got out of the car.

"Is it done?" Old Raccoon asked.

Bear looked surprised at the question. "I haven't started yet."

Chu's body was in a toolshed. Bear had refrigerators for storing bodies, but they were small, meant for cats and dogs. He didn't have anything big enough to fit all six foot three of Chu. Old Raccoon unzipped the body bag. Chu's eyes were closed.

"I counted twenty-seven stab wounds," Bear said with a shiver.

Old Raccoon unbuttoned Chu's tattered shirt and counted the stab marks himself. Other than the one that had entered at the solar plexus and pierced a lung, most of the wounds hadn't proved fatal. The assassin could have killed him easily, but instead he'd taken his sweet time, dancing around the vital spots, playing with Chu like a lion cub toying with an injured squirrel. Chu's right elbow was broken, the bone jutting through the skin, and his left hand was still locked tight around a knife. It was the same style and brand as the kitchen knife he had left on Reseng's table. Reseng tried to remove the knife from Chu's grip.

"I tried, too," Bear said. "It won't come loose."

Old Raccoon gazed quietly at Chu's corpse for a moment before gesturing that he'd seen enough. His raised hand trembled. Bear hurriedly zipped the body bag shut.

"Hanja hired a real beast this time. He's called 'the Barber.' Have you heard of him?" Bear asked.

"Only rumors," Old Raccoon said gravely.

"They say he's a cleaner. And that he's merciless. He specializes in taking out people like us. Pretty scary guy. What's the point of stabbing someone twenty-seven times? Seeing the great Chu taken out this way . . . what chance do the rest of us have?" Bear looked scared.

"We should be grateful to him. For taking out garbage like us," Old Raccoon said in his usual cynical way.

Bear loaded Chu's body onto a cart and trundled it over to the incinerator. Together, Reseng and Bear lifted him onto the stainless-steel tray. Chu's feet stuck out past the end. Bear tried to bend his legs onto the tray, but rigor mortis had already set in.

"Damn it. Why's he got to make my life harder with these long legs of his?"

Bear flopped down onto the ground and burst into tears. Reseng gave him a pat on the shoulder and stepped outside. Old Raccoon stared wordlessly at Chu's body, his face expressionless. Finally, Bear got up. His eyes were bloodshot as he closed the door to the incinerator and turned on the power.

Chu's body was nearly fully cremated by the time Hanja arrived. In addition to the driver, there was a slender man sitting in the black sedan with Hanja. Reseng stared closely at him. He didn't look like he would be the one they called the Barber. He was far too young to be the source of the terrible rumors associated with the name. Besides, the Barber wouldn't have come all the way out here just for this.

Hanja got out of the car and bowed politely to Old Raccoon, who responded with a barely perceptible nod. Even though it was two in the morning and a long way from anywhere, Hanja was clean-shaven and dressed in a suit and tie.

After glancing around distractedly, he walked over to where Reseng was squatting on the ground in front of the incinerator, smoking. The overpowering smell of Hanja's aftershave wafted ahead of him.

"I'm late, but I didn't want to miss sending off a great warrior," Hanja said.

Reseng looked up at him. Hanja gave him a wink to show he was joking.

"I heard Chu stopped by your place before coming to see me."

"That so?" Reseng asked, his voice low.

"I would think you'd have called me."

Reseng took a long drag on his cigarette and didn't respond. Hanja took a silver pill case out of his pocket and popped a few mints in his mouth.

"If you'd called me, you'd've gotten some of the reward money. Didn't I tell you I was giving half to whoever gave us information leading to his capture?" Hanja's voice had a teasing lilt.

"I suddenly forgot your number," Reseng said, stubbing his cigarette out on the ground.

Hanja took a business card out of his gold-plated case, leaned down, and slipped it into Reseng's front pocket.

"Make sure you call next time. We all have to work together."

With that, Hanja walked over to Bear, took a thick envelope out of his jacket pocket, and handed it to him. Bear bowed at a ninety-degree angle as he took the envelope. With each word that Hanja said to him, Bear bowed again and said, "Yes, sir, yes, sir, of course, sir." His business with Bear concluded, Hanja lowered his head and looked into the incinerator for three seconds. Then he bowed politely once more to Old Raccoon, got in the car, and left.

Reseng lit another cigarette. *We all have to work together.* The words echoed in his head. Maybe Hanja was right. Guys like them had to work together. Because, unlike them, real men guzzled Jack on an empty stomach, wailed like cats on the toilet, and died with their hands wrapped around a kitchen knife.

The incinerator light turned off.

Bear opened the door and waited for the heat to dissipate. Smoke billowed out, revealing the white bones of the old man and his dog. They looked as lonely and forsaken as a camel's skeleton in the middle of the desert, eroded by sand and wind.

Bear flicked away his cigarette and got to work. He spread a mat on the ground, placed a small table on top of it, and set the table with a candle, incense, a bottle of rice wine, and a wine cup. Bear checked to see if anything was missing, then looked over at Reseng as if to ask why he wasn't joining him. Reseng waved him off.

"Go ahead and ask for forgiveness so you can go to paradise," Reseng said. "I don't mind going to hell."

Bear lit the incense by himself and filled the cup with wine. He bowed twice, kowtowing before the hot white pile of bones resting inside the incinerator. He closed his eyes in contemplation for several long minutes while mumbling something under his breath—a prayer, perhaps, or an incantation. Then he stuck his finger in the wine cup and flicked the wine evenly into the air around the table and in front of the incinerator. Reseng, who had no idea how Bear had come up with this ritual, sat off to one side and smoked until Bear had completed his ceremony and put away the mat. His insides burned from the cigarette smoke making its way up and down his throat.

Bear used a long metal hook to pull the tray out along the rails. Smoke was still rising from the bones. They looked too bare and insignificant to have belonged to the old man who had been laughing and chatting with the flowers and to the dog that had been running around in the garden only hours earlier. Bear pulled on a fresh pair of white gloves, picked up some tongs, and started carefully collecting the old man's bones.

"What should we do with the dog's bones?" Bear asked.

"Mix them together."

"What? We can't do that. Who mixes human and dog bones . . ." Bear paused and stared at Reseng. "You did disobey orders, didn't you?"

Reseng didn't respond.

"Why would you do that? You know what sticks-in-the-mud those plotters are. They *hate* that sort of thing."

"Like anyone's going to pay that much attention to a bunch of ashes. They'll just end up scattered in a river without a trace."

"I better not be the only one who gets fucked over by this."

Reseng shook his head, as if to dispel Bear's concerns.

"Mixing the ashes will bring you luck. That dog was like a special gift to the old man. And you like things that bring you good luck."

Bear thought it over for a moment and then added Santa's bones to the box with the old man's.

"Back when this gentleman was a general," Bear murmured, "he used to drop by now and then, but never in uniform. He was so dapper. . . ."

He checked the tray carefully for any bone fragments he'd missed and swept the ashes together with a broom.

"When I die, I'm going to cremate my body right here," Bear said mawkishly. "People like us should go the same way they do."

"That would be a good thing."

"Yes, a very good thing."

"But if you die, who'll do the cremating?"

Bear looked stumped.

"Huh, I hadn't thought of that."

Bear put the bone fragments into an iron mortar and began grinding them by hand. He ground them down very fine, careful not to let any of the bone dust fly out. Beads of sweat sprang up on his forehead. Even after the bones looked fully pulverized, he ran his fingers through the ash and resumed grinding whenever he felt even the slightest shard.

Finally, after nearly twenty minutes, Bear set down the pestle. He carefully transferred the pulverized bone to a maple-wood box, wrapped it in a cloth, and handed it to Reseng. The ashes were still hot. Reseng put the wooden urn on the passenger seat of his car, took an envelope from his pocket, and gave it to Bear, who took out the bills and counted them twice.

"Would you like a receipt for your taxes?" Bear said with a grin.

"As if I file taxes."

"Drop by more often. That's the only way we'll both make ends meet. I've been dying lately," Bear said with a pout. Reseng smiled weakly.

Reseng got in the car and started the engine. The sun was peeking over the ridge. As the sunlight touched his face, the tension left his body and he felt dizzy. He put his hand on his forehead and rested his head against the window.

When the car still hadn't moved, Bear came over and tapped on the glass.

"You okay?"

Startled, Reseng looked up at Bear through sunken eyes.

"If you're tired, take a nap before you leave." Bear looked worried.

Reseng shook his head. "I have to get going."

He gave Bear a nod to show he was okay, then released the brake and put the car in gear. He made his way down the mountain, toward the highway that would take him back to Seoul. The reflection of Bear waving in the rearview mirror grew smaller and smaller, until it was gone.

THE DOGHOUSE LIBRARY

Of course there weren't any actual dogs there.

Old Raccoon was hardly the type to raise dogs in a library. He'd named his library "The Doghouse" to make fun of people who made a big show of frequenting libraries but never opened any actual books, or possibly to make fun of himself for having spent a good sixty years of his life looking after a library that sat empty of people most of the time. He'd even hung a large signboard engraved with the name THE DOGHOUSE right above the entrance. People visiting the place for the first time usually stared up at it dumbfounded, their heads tilted at a quizzical angle, or laughed. Then, after a second, their faces would turn sour.

"Wait, is he calling *us* dogs? What the fuck?"

What was he thinking when he hung that sign? Reseng attributed it to the cynicism typical of traditional, uptight intellectuals who spent their lives confined to private rooms, the walls padded with books. Unless it was Old Raccoon's way of thumbing his nose at the world that had taken a young librarian leading a simple, happy life with his books, albeit saddled with a limp from a childhood bout with polio, and made him work for years and years as a middleman for plotters and assassins. Whatever the reason, the sign brought him no end of amusement.

Reseng thought it was childish. If this were his library, there was no way he would have hung that sign. But life never goes the way we want it to, and so, if he had found himself forced to hang that sign, through some odd combination of complicated and underhanded stipulations and well-timed blackmail (as if anyone would blackmail someone into doing something so random!), then at least he would, of course, have brought in a few actual dogs. Along with books from all over the world about dogs.

He pictured a young scholar raising his eyebrows at him and asking, "But Mr. Reseng, what kind of name is that for a library? The Doghouse? Are you trying to insult humanity's noble world of the mind?"

Reseng would give the young scholar a polite, dignified smile and say, "Why, of course not, young man. I haven't the slightest intention of flipping the bird at humanity's noble world of the mind. What on earth makes you think that? Perhaps we need to start with your prejudiced notion that books and dogs don't belong together."

He would point to the dogs strolling casually among the crowded shelves.

"Look at these dogs. Aren't they magnificent? And right over here, from D-Eleven to D-Forty-three, are all sorts of books on the subject of dogs. This library has the world's largest collection of books on dogs. We've got books on Chihuahuas, collies, shepherds, greyhounds, Saint Bernards, retrievers. We have books on every single breed of dog in the world. And not only that, this library also has books on dog food, dog breeding, dog lineage, canine interspecies conflict, and a lot more. You might even say this library is the spiritual heart of dogdom—the canine Vatican, if you will."

At last, the young scholar would nod.

"I see, yes. I understand now! Your work is quite impressive!"

"It is a sacred task."

The canine Vatican. Wouldn't that be something? The more he thought about it, the more it seemed like both the dogs and the books would appreciate it and feel elevated by it. But Old Raccoon had not intended any such elegant metaphor. Instead, his choice of the word *doghouse* hinted at the fact that the library (established in the 1920s, right after Imperial Japan had renamed its colonizing strategy from "Martial Rule" to "Cultural Rule") had survived for decades in the shadow of authoritarianism, that it had a shameful and obscene history of its own as the headquarters of every major assassination in South Korea's modern history, and that he was disgusted with himself for being a part of that shameful history.

But Old Raccoon chose that life. Why pick on poor innocent dogs for the choices he'd made? Seriously, what did dogs ever do wrong?

Ten a.m. Reseng entered the Doghouse Library.

It was empty, as usual. The sole employee, a cross-eyed librarian, greeted Reseng, her gaze pointing at some spot he could only guess at.

"Good morning!"

Her cheery voice echoed like a lark's cry from the domed ceiling. That high-pitched voice vexed him every time. It sounded far too bright for a place built during the colonial era by a Japanese master craftsman and left to rot over the next century. He gave the librarian a curt nod and headed straight for Old Raccoon's study.

"He has a visitor," she said, rising from her seat.

Reseng paused. Who would come to the library this early with a job for them?

"A visitor?" Reseng asked. "Who is it?"

"That tall, smart-looking gentleman. The really polite one."

Tall, smart, and polite? Someone with those qualities would have no reason to be skulking around here. Reseng tipped his head in confusion.

Her voice turning impatient, the librarian added, "You know, the guy who wears nice suits and sounds really cool and dignified all the time."

Reseng snorted. She meant Hanja. The cross-eyed librarian thought Hanja was polite and smart and cool and dignified. And all the time, apparently! What on earth had given her that idea? On the other hand, maybe Reseng was the one who had the wrong idea. After all, Hanja was rich, had a fancy degree from Stanford, and was constantly acting the part of a gentleman. Though Reseng could not get on board with the idea that the guy was handsome, he couldn't argue with the fact that Hanja was tall. Reseng nodded and headed again for Old Raccoon's study, but the librarian rushed over and pulled at his arm.

"He told me not to let anyone else in. Not today."

She stressed the words *not today*, as if this day were some once-in-a-lifetime event. She had a tight grip on his arm. He looked pointedly at her hand and then slowly up at her face. She let go.

"Which one of them told you not to let anyone in? Old Raccoon or Hanja?"

She hesitated.

"Hanja. But Mr. Raccoon was standing right next to him when he said it."

Reseng looked at the closed door. Given how early Hanja had rushed over, he must have been pretty angry about how the plot got twisted. Reseng put the maple box containing the ashes of the old man and the dog on the round table in front of the librarian's desk. He sat down and took a pack of cigarettes from his pocket. The second he lit up, the librarian frowned at him.

She sat down at her desk and began to knit; he assumed this meant she'd already completed her tasks for the day. The yarn was red. She hadn't gotten far enough with it yet for him to tell what she was knitting. Reseng had never once seen her read a book. She never even read newspapers or magazines. She just sat by herself at her desk in that deserted library where no books were ever read or checked out and, naturally, were never returned, and passed the time knitting or cross-stitching, or painting her nails every color of the rainbow.

"What is that?" asked the librarian, pausing abruptly in the middle of a row. "Japanese sweets?"

She was looking at the box he'd placed on the table. The maple box was wrapped in a white cloth and looked unmistakably like a wooden urn. Reseng had no idea what made her think it was sweets. "Yeah, they're Japanese sweets. But they're not for you, so keep your paws off 'em."

She stuck her lower lip out at him. It was covered in a thick coat of bright red lipstick. Right above her mouth was a beauty spot that seemed disappointed not to have been born on Marilyn Monroe's face. She'd applied dark red shadow all around her eyes, and her eyebrows were shaved and replaced by two crescent tattoos.

The overall effect made her look odd and simpleminded. That said, other than being cross-eyed, she wasn't bad-looking.

She resumed knitting and seemed to forget all about Reseng sitting in front of her. Her knitting was faster now, but there was still something sloppy and uncertain about her work. She probably had trouble focusing on the stitches.

"You should get surgery," Reseng said.

She looked up at him in confusion.

"I said, 'You should get surgery.'"

"What surgery?"

"For your eyes. To uncross them. They say it's a simple procedure nowadays. Doesn't even cost that much."

She looked taken aback. Her expression seemed to say, Don't you have enough problems, you idiot? Stay out of my business. Or possibly it was saying, I don't care if my eyes are flipping inside out—why should I care what a loser like you thinks?

"It's no one's business what I'm looking at," she said curtly.

She gave him a long, lingering glare. This time, her expression clearly said, Be warned: Your insolence will not be tolerated. You've made me very angry. But with one eye pointing at the ceiling and the other eye pointing at the stacks to the left, that warning came off as more comical than stern. Not that Reseng didn't take her seriously. It's just that it's next to impossible to make a serious threat when you're staring simultaneously at the floor and at the ceiling.

"I'm sorry," he said. "I didn't mean it the way it sounds."

She didn't respond. Instead, she muttered something indecipherable and kept on knitting, her irritation spelled out all over her face. He assumed she'd told him to fuck off under her breath.

Old Raccoon had gone through a lot of librarians. Most of his reasons for firing them were pretty frivolous. He had fired librarians because a book was misshelved, because a two-decades-old book had a tiny tear on the cover and had been left unrepaired for over a month, and because there was too much dust on one of the over nine hundred shelves. He'd even fired one librarian for setting a coffee cup on top of a book. Of course, there were plenty who'd left of their own accord. One left because she said there wasn't enough work to do; another said the place was so dreary that she felt as if she were suffocating; still another said being alone in the constantly empty library made her feel like a character in a horror movie. And one librarian's mysterious reason for leaving was that ever since setting foot in the place, she hadn't been able to read so much as a single sentence.

Reseng had gotten along well with most of the librarians, regardless of how long they lasted. He considered them friends—his only friends, in fact, with whom he could talk about books. With them, he was able to share the thoughts and emotions the books had aroused in him. Which may have been why talking to librarians always left him feeling a certain sense of kinship and peace of mind.

It usually didn't take long for the librarians to wonder about the peculiarities of the library. They would steal a moment when Old Raccoon wasn't around to ask Reseng cautiously what the purpose of the library was and what institution it belonged to. Anyone who found themselves working in that odd place with its crabby owner for longer than a month would naturally start to wonder. Each time he was asked, Reseng explained that it was a members-only library for high-ranking government officials.

They would tilt their heads and say, "But I've never once seen a government official come in to read or check out a book."

And Reseng would say, "That's why our country is so messed up," and laugh.

But the cross-eyed librarian had never, not even once, asked any questions about the place. When she first started the job, she didn't ask where her desk was or what her tasks were. Worse still (or according to the same logic), she didn't ask where the bathroom was or where the broom was stored. It was as if she had no curiosity, interest, or complaints about anything apart from cross-stitching, nail art, and knitting. When Old Raccoon gave her instructions, she listened, with those unsettling eyes of hers aimed any which way, and silently got to work.

So far, she'd lasted a good five years at the Doghouse Library without asking a single question. She had probably been there the longest of all the librarians who'd worked for grumpy, fickle Old Raccoon. She paid no mind whatsoever to what sort of place this library was that stayed empty all year round, or who these people were who came in from time to time with mean, secretive looks on their faces. She just reported for work in the morning, and wiped dust off the books. The rest of the time, she feverishly knit or cross-stitched. But most surprising of all was her unfailing ability to shelve the books so accurately that not even Old Raccoon, who was more exacting than anyone, could find fault with her. Reseng was forever surprised and dubious at how perfectly a librarian who never read could keep books so well organized.

She was, by far, the strangest librarian he'd ever met. Now and then, Reseng would mention a book he was reading, and she would instantly reply in a monotone, chin resting on her hand, "C-Fifty-four has other books like that. Go and have a look." What else could he do, of course, but head straight for C-54, feeling vaguely disconcerted and let down.

Until recently, the library's collection had held steady at 200,000 books. Old Raccoon used to order new books regularly, but he would throw out the same number just as regularly. He claimed he did that because there was no room, but they could have easily stored hundreds of thousands more. The real reason he threw them out was because more books would have meant adding more shelves, and Old Raccoon was loath to move the existing shelves, which he had long ago arranged just so. As far as Reseng could remember, the shelf layout in the Doghouse Library had never once changed. Neither had Old Raccoon's method for sorting the books. Nor did he make room for new categories of books that appeared with the changing times. As a result, books that could not be sorted into one of Old Raccoon's existing categories went straight into the discard pile, even if they were brand-new.

When their time came, Old Raccoon placed a black strip of paper around the discards. It was his own special form of sentencing, a funeral procedure for books that had reached the end of their life. The same way aging assassins were added to a list and eliminated by cleaners when their time came. Of course, a book's life span was determined by Old Raccoon alone, and neither Reseng nor the librarians could understand why certain books had to be tossed.

The books with black bands were gathered by the librarian and stacked in the courtyard to be burned on Sunday afternoons, the librarian's day off. Old Raccoon could have sold them to a second-hand bookshop or even to a recycler, but he insisted on burning them.

Reseng was fond of Old Raccoon's abandoned books. Though he couldn't quite explain why, he felt they deserved his love. And they were the only books he was allowed to take home from the Doghouse. On Sunday mornings, before the books were burned, Reseng would peruse the pile next to the gasoline can and pick out those he liked. After he had finished, the remaining books were left scattered around in the yard, unwanted by either Old Raccoon or Reseng, and looking as pathetic and hopeless as prisoners of war standing before a firing squad.

"You don't have to burn them," Reseng would say. "You could sell them to a secondhand bookshop instead."

Each time, Old Raccoon responded in the same way: "Every book must follow its own destiny."

In other words, the particular destiny of the books that had belonged to this ridiculous, godforsaken place where no one came to read (not even the librarian!) was to be as bored and miserable as court ladies, their untouched virgin bodies wasting away as they pined in sorrow, never once to be loved by the king, until they eventually grew too old and were cast out of the palace.

Reseng was confident in his knowledge that the library would be around for at least as long as people were. He had faith, not in the books, but in the shelves and in the edifice itself that held them. What had sustained the Doghouse all this time were its large wooden bookshelves, carved from the same priceless Chunyang pines used to build palaces during the Joseon dynasty. Books came and went, but those heavy shelves, lovingly crafted by a famous furniture maker during the colonial era and still pristine and unwarped ninety years later, never so much as budged.

The cross-eyed librarian had been knitting for thirty minutes straight. Each time Reseng lit another cigarette, she raised her head and fixed him with a frown. But he kept right on smoking, unfazed. He had no hope of getting anywhere with her anyway. In her mind, Hanja was distinguished and cool and Reseng was a dud.

"What time did Hanja get here?" he asked.

Without looking up, she said, "Nine-thirty."

"When did you get here?"

"Eight."

That was early. The library didn't open until nine, so why had she come an hour early? There was nothing for her to do except clean. He really couldn't understand her. Reseng looked at the door to Old Raccoon's study again. It was still shut. If Hanja had come at nine-thirty, that meant he and Old Raccoon had been talking for over an hour. What on earth about?

Whenever Hanja met with high-ranking government officials or other powers behind the throne, he told them Old Raccoon was "like a father" to him. Sometimes he dropped the word *like* and simply called him his father. The Doghouse Library's gruesome ninety-year history lent Hanja, who was a relative newbie to the assassination business, an air of tradition and authority. Prone to paranoia and easily spooked, the geezers who pulled the strings still trusted Old Raccoon's neat and tidy approach to getting the job done. Now and then, while hearing yet another rumor about Hanja's name-dropping and his riding on Old Raccoon's coattails, Reseng thought maybe he really was his son. After all, a monster like Hanja could only have been sired by another monster.

Reseng was lighting yet another cigarette when he heard shouts coming from Old Raccoon's study. He and the librarian looked up at the same time. More shouts. Old Raccoon's voice. The librarian looked at Reseng in bewilderment. Just then, Hanja came storming out. His face was flushed. He hadn't shaved; even his hair looked uncombed. It was clear he'd rushed directly to the library the second he heard that the plot to kill the old man had been changed. It was the first time Reseng had seen Hanja lose his composure. In fact, it was also the first time he'd heard Old Raccoon yell like a drunken sailor. Old Raccoon's special skill was sarcasm, not volume. As Hanja stomped past, he spotted Reseng and stopped short. His eyes shot back and forth in shock from Reseng's face to the wooden urn wrapped in the white cloth.

"What is that?" Hanja asked angrily.

"Japanese sweets."

Hanja glared at Reseng, biting down hard on his lip, as if he wanted to punch him. But he regained his cool and sneered instead. He started to say something but then turned to the cross-eyed librarian.

"I'm sorry, miss, but would you mind excusing us? I need to have a word with this gentleman."

She looked up at him blankly. He tipped his head ever so slightly to one side. All at once, she leaped up and switched back to the high-pitched, birdlike voice she used whenever she was being polite. "Why, yes, of course, not a problem!" She dropped her knitting needles on the desk. But now that she was out of her chair, she got flustered, obviously unsure about where she was supposed to go, and turned to Hanja again with an awkward smile before rushing outside. After they heard the door click shut behind her, Hanja pulled out a chair and sat across from Reseng.

"Mind giving me one of those?" He gestured to the pack of cigarettes on the table.

"I thought you hated things that stink."

Hanja frowned. He was clearly in no mood for messing around, and he looked haggard, as if he hadn't slept at all. Reseng pushed the cigarette pack and lighter toward him. Hanja tapped one out, lit it, and took a deep drag before exhaling a long plume of smoke into the air.

"It's been so long, it's making me dizzy."

He rubbed his eyes, as if he really was dizzy, or else the smoke was irritating them. They looked bloodshot. Hanja started to take another drag, but he changed his mind and stubbed out the cigarette in the ashtray. He stared for a long time at the wooden urn.

"I specifically asked for the general's body, and you bring me a box of ashes. I can't use ashes." Hanja spoke in a near whisper.

Reseng didn't respond.

"How did such a simple task get so messed up?"

Hanja's voice was soft, placating. Reseng guessed he was sounding him out in order to understand why Old Raccoon had changed the plotter's orders.

"Look," Reseng said. He wanted to show him there was no point in prodding him on this, that nothing would come of it. "I'm just a hit man who works for a daily wage. Minions like me follow the orders we're given, so obviously I have no idea what's going on."

"No idea . . ." Hanja tapped his fingers lightly on the table.

Reseng reached over to retrieve his lighter and cigarettes and lit another.

"How many do you smoke a day?" Hanja asked.

"Two packs."

"Do you not watch the news? Lung cancer is the most lethal form of cancer, and if you smoke, you're fifteen times more likely to get it. For a heavy smoker like you, lung cancer is a given."

"I doubt I'll survive in this business long enough to get lung cancer."

Hanja snorted.

"You're a funny guy. I've always thought that about you," Hanja said. "You're tough to read, but you amuse me. I guess that's why I like you."

Reseng crushed his unfinished cigarette out in the ashtray and lit up another. As Hanja kept on jabbering—"Yeah, a real peach, you are"—Reseng fought the overwhelming urge to punch him right in the mouth.

"That job was worth billions," Hanja said. "That plot was going to be huge, the likes of which a mere day laborer like you could never imagine. But then Old Raccoon blew it before it even began."

"Gee, what a shame. All that money, gone. My heart bleeds for you."

"I'm sure I can salvage it. That is my specialty, after all. But who's going to compensate me for the blow this has struck to my honor and credibility? That nasty Old Raccoon? Or some lowly goon like you?"

Reseng felt disgusted to hear the words *honor* and *credibility* coming out of Hanja's mouth.

"Since when is your stupid honor more important than the general's?"

"What does a corpse need honor for? Leave him be and he'll rot in the ground like he's supposed to."

"I'll be sure to ask your corpse the same question the day Bear cremates you. I'll ask right before you're shoved into the oven."

"See to it that you do. I can assure you that my corpse will give you the same answer I'm giving you now. We're businessmen. Who would do something this stupid when there are billions of won at stake? If you'd just turned over the body like you were told, I could have packaged it into something worth selling by now. The politicians and the press can do whatever they want with it after that. I don't care."

"He was Old Raccoon's only friend!" Reseng shouted. "Not that a loser prick like you would understand that."

Hanja let out an arrogant laugh. He seemed to relish the fact that Reseng had slipped and revealed his true feelings, as if that had been Hanja's intention all along and now he'd gotten what he wanted from him.

"See, I told you you're a funny guy," Hanja said.

Hanja had been planning to get the story out on the nine o'clock news. He wanted the assassination to be front-page, above the crease, in every single newspaper around the country. The death of a general originally from North Korea and a key figure back in the days of the KCIA, before it evolved into the National Intelligence Service! And embedded in his corpse, an unfamiliar 7.62 mm slug that could only have come from a Russian-made AK-47. A suspicious assassination by firearm, positively reeking of foul play.

The day after the body was discovered, yellow police tape would have gone up all around the old man's house, and the normally deserted forest would have been suddenly buzzing with journalists and TV reporters blowing every little thing out of proportion, and bumbling cops who had no idea what they were supposed to be doing. The TV news would have demonstrated how thoroughly scientific the search for clues was by filming the forensics team walking abreast as they noisily sifted through the forest at one-centimeter intervals, starting at the point of impact. The screen would have filled with the giant face of a balding expert, looking extremely serious as he prepared to give an interview. While pointing out exhibits 1, 2, 3, and 4—a shell casing, a chewing-gum wrapper, an empty cookie packet, human feces—found by the forensics team, the giant-faced expert would have spouted endless nonsense about the changing state of international affairs and the movements of the North Korean military. The next day, and the day after that as well, the news would have been full of commentary on the chewing-gum wrapper, the empty cookie packet, the human feces.

What was it that they were hoping to start? In this day and age, when you can book a seat on a small space shuttle, rocket up out of the atmosphere, and stare slack-jawed down at Earth for five long, space-tourist minutes before descending, were they seriously thinking of trying to turn this into another worn-out spy-ring cliché? Not that anyone could have said where the plot originated or what its ultimate goal was. No one ever knew the full truth. In the plotters' world, everyone avoided having any more information than absolutely necessary. The more information you had, the easier it was to become a target. Ignorance was survival. You couldn't just pretend, you had to genuinely not know. Why would anyone bother asking how much you knew when they could simply kill you? That's why everyone stayed inside their own small fence and didn't stick so much as a single toe out of it. Put enough of those small fences together and you got a plot, woven together from ridiculously large and intricate connections and countless stakeholders. Perhaps they'd been planning to blow up a dam, and for budget reasons had forced a turnabout by assassinating a washed-up former general instead.

At any rate, the plot had gone awry: The corpse they were planning to use had been reduced to ash. Just as Hanja had suggested, you can't squeeze a media circus out of a pile of dust.

Hanja checked his watch and stood up. He'd said all he had to say.

"Time to go. Everything's fucked because of you, and I'm the one stuck with the bill."

"Because of me?" Reseng asked wide-eyed.

"If you knew that Old Raccoon had changed the plot, then you should have warned me." Hanja's voice dripped with pity. "You didn't belong on this job in the first place. I don't know why you would butt in and risk taking the fall for him."

Hanja was much calmer and more relaxed now than when he'd burst out of Old Raccoon's study. A consummate realist, he knew how to brush off mistakes. He might even have already thought of his next big stunt.

"And just in case that gave you the wrong idea about yourself," Hanja added, "let me give you some advice: Don't overestimate yourself. You're nothing. That spot you're standing on is all you've got. The second you step outside this library, you're just another washed-up assassin from the meat market, just another disposable needle, used once and thrown away. So watch yourself. And go easy on the cigarettes. If you keep ruining your lungs with those two packs a day of yours, how are you going to be able to run for your life when the time comes?"

Hanja gave him another of his arrogant, hateful smiles. He straightened his jacket as he prepared to leave.

"Oh! Have I given you my card?" he asked, his gestures exaggerated, as if he'd overlooked some critical detail.

Reseng stared at him and did not answer.

Hanja took a card from his gold-plated case and set it in front of Reseng.

"You'll need this. The library won't be open much longer. And you should start thinking about your future, maybe learn to speak more politely. Speaking banmal to your elders doesn't look good. I'm telling you this for your sake," he said with a wink.

"I talk down to anyone and everyone. And you *are* just anyone to me."

Reseng stuck Hanja's business card in the ashtray and stubbed his cigarette out on it. Hanja watched him for a moment and shook his head, then took out another card and this time shoved it into Reseng's jacket pocket. He patted Reseng on the cheek.

"Grow up. How much longer do you think you'll get away with acting cute?"

Hanja strode out of the library, whistling as he went. As the door swung shut, Reseng heard Hanja cheerfully say to the librarian, "Wow, pretty chilly out here! So sorry to make you wait. The conversation just dragged on and on." He heard her response: "Oh, no, it's not that cold!" She sounded giddy.

Reseng took out another cigarette. But he stared at it without lighting up. Hanja was right about one thing: Reseng should never have been assigned to take out the general. Plotters didn't use highly skilled assassins like him when the goal was only to stir up the news. That type of job belonged to washed-up hit men whom no one ever hired anymore, or disposables fresh out of army training, still wet behind the ears and with no clue about how things worked.

Whenever an assassination came to light, the first person the police looked for was the shooter. In the end, all they wanted to know was "Who pulled the trigger?" When they did find whoever had pulled the trigger, they fooled themselves into thinking that everything had been solved. But, when you think about it, the question of who pulled the trigger doesn't matter at all. In fact, it might even be the least important question in an assassination case. What matters is never the shooter, but the person behind the shooter. And yet, in the long history of assassinations, not once has that shadow person been clearly revealed.

People believe Oswald killed Kennedy. But how could a bumbling idiot like Oswald have pulled it off? While the press and the police were busy fingering Oswald, the plotters of assassinations and the pullers of strings who'd orchestrated Kennedy's death slowly and leisurely scattered in different directions and headed back to their nice, safe homes. There, they leaned back in their easy chairs, sipped their champagne, and watched the news. A few days later, when Oswald the clown was eliminated on schedule by another third-rate assassin, the police closed the case, the looks on their faces saying, Well, what can we do now that the key culprit is dead? Life is one big comedy. All the police have to do is find the shooter, and all the plotters have to do is eliminate him.

The police track down a shooter, interrogate him, torture him. This simpleton who pulled a trigger without thinking becomes the media's next hot topic faster than his bullet found its target. Everyone who knows him expresses surprise and alarm to learn he was capable of something so awful. The media digs up everything they can about him, tracks down anyone and everyone who might be even remotely related to him (though, in truth, they are unconnected), pixelate their faces for privacy, and turn the simpleton into a legend. The funniest part is that the idiot who actually pulled the trigger knows next to nothing about what happened. He himself has no idea what he has done. Why on earth would the plotters give such important information to a has-been or a disposable? The plotters' instructions to the assassin are always the same, regardless of country or era: "Who told you to think? Just shut up and pull the trigger."

Reseng lit the cigarette. It occurred to him that if he hadn't cremated the old man, he'd be a corpse, too, right about now. What would Bear's face look like while feeding Reseng's body into the flames? Would that big teddy bear of a man weep hysterically, only to chuckle and bow over and over when Hanja handed him his cash, his tears having mysteriously vanished as he counted the bills twice? Reseng was on his second inhale when the cross-eyed librarian came back in, shivering from the cold. She wrapped the cardigan that she'd left on her chair around her shoulders and crouched under her desk, rubbing her hands over the space heater she kept there. She was down there for a long time before she finally came back up and sat in her chair.

"For fuck's sake, knock it off with the damn smoking already!" she exclaimed, her face livid with contempt.

Reseng stubbed out his cigarette. He looked over at Old Raccoon's study. The door was still closed. Should he go in now? Or should he wait until Old Raccoon had calmed down? He couldn't decide.

"What are you going to do if this place closes?" he asked the librarian.

"The library is closing?" She looked shocked.

"No, I said what *if* it closes."

She hesitated and said, "I'll find a nice guy and get married."

"A nice guy, huh . . ." Reseng chewed over her words and asked, "How about me?"

She looked at him as if he were crazy.

"What's wrong with you? Someone shoot you in the head while I was gone?"

Her voice was so loud that it echoed off the domed ceiling. Reseng laughed. He picked up the urn and walked over to Old Raccoon's study.

When he opened the door, Old Raccoon was reading an encyclopedia out loud, as always; he'd finished the *Brockhaus Enzyklopädie* and was rereading the *Encyclopædia Britannica*. To Reseng's surprise, he looked completely unruffled. He was sitting in the same chair he always sat in, with the same book, reading out loud in the same voice. What was the purpose of reading the same two books over and over? His reading habits made no sense to Reseng. Old Raccoon kept reading until Reseng had shut the study door and set the urn on the coffee table. Though he didn't do it on purpose, the urn clacked loudly against the glass top. At last, Old Raccoon looked up from his book and stared at the urn.

"Why were you gone an extra day?"

He didn't sound angry or accusatory, merely curious.

"The general invited me to stay for dinner."

He thought that would invite follow-up questions, but Old Raccoon nodded. He set his reading glasses on the desk, got up, and came over to the table, then unwrapped the white cloth from the urn and examined the box, briefly caressing the wood with his palm before opening the lid. The old man's and Santa's ashes were neatly wrapped in white paper. Old Raccoon unfolded the paper and ran the ash through his fingers. He could probably tell at once that there were more ashes in the box than there should have been, and that some of it had a different consistency than human cremains. But his face revealed nothing. For all Reseng knew, cowardly Bear might have already called Old Raccoon to confess about the dog, just to cover his own ass.

"Bear ground them really fine." Old Raccoon sounded pleased. That was his only reaction. He folded the paper back, closed the lid, and retied the white cloth. Then he put the urn on his desk.

"Lie low for a few days," he said. "Don't do anything." That meant Reseng was excused.

"Hanja looked pretty angry."

Old Raccoon let out a short laugh. "What's he got to be angry about? He got what he wanted."

"But he was carrying on about us blowing a plot worth billions of won. . . ."

"You really think he'd trust us with something that big? He's thrilled because now he has a reason to run around telling those old government geezers that the Doghouse messed up. Ha! I swear, he's too clever."

Old Raccoon seemed amused. But what on earth was there to laugh about?

"Is the library closing?" Reseng asked.

Old Raccoon looked confused.

"Hanja tried to scare me by saying the library is closing."

Old Raccoon thought about it for a moment. A strange smile came over his face.

"If it closes, it closes," he said flatly. "What's there to be afraid of? Not like there was ever any glory in the library anyway."

But how could that be? How could he close the library that he'd personally overseen for the last sixty years? Old Raccoon's voice was calm and blunt, as if he'd been readying himself for this moment for a long, long time. Perhaps that was why he sounded so determined, as well.

Everyone said that Old Raccoon was born in the library and had lived there his whole life. It wasn't a metaphor. He actually was born in it. He was the son of the handyman who'd lived in a cottage attached to the library and had kept the roof, electricity, and plumbing in working order. After the bout of polio that left him with a permanent limp, Old Raccoon went to work keeping the library clean when he was only six years old. At the age of fifteen, he became a librarian, and at the tender age of twenty-one he became head librarian. It wasn't clear how Old Raccoon, who was not only disabled but hadn't even finished elementary school, was able to beat out the colonial officials who'd graduated from Keijo Imperial University in Seoul or studied abroad in Japan, to become first head librarian and then later director of the library. Perhaps the library was far too quiet and boring a place for smart people to devote their whole lives to. Or perhaps it was just too dangerous.

Old Raccoon was studying the urn closely. After a moment, he seemed to realize Reseng was looking at him and turned his gaze back to the encyclopedia, but it was obvious he wasn't actually reading. He'd forgotten to put his reading glasses back on. As Old Raccoon stared blindly at the page, he suddenly looked much older.

"I'll get going," Reseng said.

Old Raccoon glanced up and nodded.

When Reseng came out of the study, the cross-eyed librarian was gone. He assumed she'd left to eat lunch. He sat down in her chair. To one side of the desk were her knitting needles and a skein of red yarn. A partition concealed a collection of ten or so bottles of nail polish organized by color, a dainty mini vanity, and a makeup bag that looked like the sort of thing professional makeup artists would take with them to a movie set. Next to it was a set of plastic drawers containing office supplies. Each drawer had a name tag stuck to it: PAPER CLIPS, STAPLER, X-ACTO KNIFE, SCISSORS, RULER. Reseng opened the drawer labeled PAPER CLIPS, and sure enough, it contained paper clips. Perched all around the woman's desk were stuffed animals: Mickey Mouse, Winnie-the-Pooh, a panda, a maneki-neko, and a whole lot more. They looked like they'd always been there and were exactly where they were supposed to be. Reseng poked Winnie-the-Pooh, who was wearing a red T-shirt and no underwear, with his belly sticking out, and grinning like an idiot.

The library no longer took in new books. Two years ago, around the time Bear cremated Chu, Old Raccoon had stopped buying any and had even canceled his regular orders. Strictly speaking, the library no longer needed a librarian. All it needed was a secretary, or a janitor. Someone to answer the phone, take out the garbage, and occasionally dust the shelves.

Reseng stood and walked slowly down the rows under the watchful eyes of the old books that hadn't been opened in decades and were so dry that a single match could have set them off like gunpowder. He trailed his fingers along their spines, feeling like he'd returned to an alley he had skipped down as a child.

He stopped and pulled out a book—*The Origin of Everything*. He examined the front and back covers and flipped through the pages. He wasn't actually trying to read it, though he would have back in the old days. He had no interest in the book, nor was there anything in it he hoped to find. He simply flipped through it out of habit. The first line read "The first vegetable ever eaten by human beings was the onion." It wasn't deep, and it wasn't didactic. It simply meant what it said. Listed in the book were other sentences: "The inventor of the reclining chair was Benjamin Franklin." "The first tool ever used was a hammer." Reseng chuckled. Old Raccoon would love this book.

Reseng reshelved the book and looked around at the library. The old wooden shelves glowed in the sunlight filtering down through the slatted windows on the second floor. A library in decline. Its good old days long behind it. Maybe, just as Hanja had said, it was time to close. Everything in it was far too old to handle the changes that had come to the assassination market. The days of youthful recklessness were over. The days of taking on difficult, dangerous assignments without a word of complaint and carrying them off flawlessly. The days when contractors had come from all over in search of Old Raccoon, when the high-paying gigs never stopped coming, when their pockets overflowed with cash. The days when even government officials had to watch themselves around Old Raccoon, and the entire meat market had moved like clockwork at a single word from him. Those days were well and truly over. Just as it got no new books, the big jobs no longer fell to the library.

From the start, Old Raccoon should have been preparing for the day he'd end up an over-the-hill has-been. He should have partnered with a powerful company, or, if that wasn't to his liking, he should have struck a deal with Hanja and handed over his client list. Unless his retirement plan was to get knifed by a bunch of scumbags while limping down a dark alley one night and meet his tragic end as a corpse fished out of the sewer, he should have at least put some money away. Or given some thought to preparing a safe house like others did in someplace like Switzerland or Alaska. But instead, Old Raccoon sat in his crumbling library reading encyclopedias. All he had left were those old books, so old that even a garbage collector would have turned up his nose at them.

Now Old Raccoon's life hung in the balance of Hanja's arithmetic. The only reason he'd survived this long was because Hanja thought there was still some blood to be squeezed out of him. The instant Old Raccoon came up zero in Hanja's calculations, he was dead. Reseng pushed in a book that was sticking out and wondered how *he* fared in Hanja's equations.

"When the library closes, will my life close, too?" He laughed and raised an eyebrow.

He went up to the second floor and checked the corner near the western wall. The tiny desk and chair where he'd read as a child were still there. Since he hadn't gone to school, the Doghouse had been his only education, and, in the absence of any friends, it had been his only playground, as well. He'd spent most of his childhood playing among the shelves or sitting at that tiny desk reading books.

Looking back on it now, Reseng's childhood had been nothing but tedium and apathy. He'd never received so much as a crumb of the adult kindness that was showered on most kids. The bulk of his childhood memories were of the maze of old shelves, the books, the dust, and of Old Raccoon reading day in and day out, his face blank. The librarians he'd worked so hard to befriend had soon left for other places, and the assassins who'd dropped by, trackers hunting down targets, as well as the crafty information traders, all looked gruff and never spoke to him. Of those people, some were still alive, some were long dead, and some were so taciturn and expressionless that he couldn't tell from looking at them whether they were alive or dead.

Old Raccoon had not said another word about Reseng's reading habit after slapping him on his ninth birthday. He did not tell him what to read, nor did he tell him what not to read. He was as uninterested in Reseng as he was in his own life. The library remained empty. And somewhere in that empty library was Reseng's childhood, which had been of no interest to anyone, right along with the books that were no different from a cactus on a shelf or an ornamental stone.

Reseng read purely out of boredom. He didn't read because he liked books; he read because he had to, because otherwise he would get too bored, or too lonely. After figuring out the alphabet on his own at the age of nine, he had stayed in the library until he was seventeen. Growing up in a library meant having no choice but to read. At seventeen, he made his first kill and used the money he earned to move into a small place of his own. His wages for killing a man went toward an electric rice cooker, rice bowls, a table, and silverware. He cooked his own rice for the first time in his new cooker.

Reseng looked down from underneath the second-floor window, where the noon sunshine was spilling in. The librarian had still not returned from lunch, and Old Raccoon's door was still shut. Reseng looked at the bookshelves to the east, the north, the south, and the west in turn. The banks of sleeping books were as still and silent as a fog-covered sea at night. All at once, he found it hard to believe that this quiet place had headquartered a den of assassins for the last ninety years. He marveled at the thought that all those deaths, all those assassinations and unexplained disappearances and faked accidents and imprisonments and kidnappings, had been decided and plotted right here in this building. Who'd chosen this place from which to orchestrate such abominable acts? It was madness. It would have made more sense to set up camp in the office of the National Dry Cleaners Union, or the office of the Organizing Committee to Revitalize Poultry Farming. Why pick a library? Libraries were quiet, book-filled places. What had they ever done to hurt anyone?

BEER WEEK

Reseng cracked open a can of beer.

Seven-thirty in the morning. The alleys lined with four-story redbrick apartment blocks were jammed with people heading off to work. Reseng opened his window and lit a cigarette. The weather was strange. Weak rays of sunlight filtered down from one side of the sky, while a light rain fell from the other. Actually, the rain wasn't so much falling as flying around. The morning commuters in ironed suits scowled up at the sky, unsure whether to open their umbrellas. Reseng took another gulp of beer in honor of those who had to go to work in weather this strange.

You might not think of beer as a breakfast drink, but in fact it's perfect. If knocking back a can of beer after a hard day's work makes you feel refreshed, rewarded, and relaxed, then a can of beer in the morning is about feeling melancholic, fuzzy-headed, improper, and refusing to act like a responsible adult just because the sun's come up. Reseng loved the feeling of irresponsibility that came with drinking beer for breakfast. The same irresponsibility that turned his sarcasm inward as he gazed out his window and thought, Look at all of you, living life to the fullest. As for my life, to hell with it!

Reseng took another swig. Guzzling beer while watching people go to work filled his head with surreal images. He pictured himself lying dead in a coffin and debating what to eat for dinner. Dead in a coffin, but his stomach growling as loudly as ever. How could this be? How on earth could a corpse be hungry? Dead Reseng was starving, but no one brought him any food. The funeral guests were all talking about him. "He really was a piece of shit, wasn't he?" "Yup, a complete asshole." It didn't stop. "I know it's not right to say this in front of the deceased, but honestly, he was such a prick. To hear a kid his age use banmal to people so much older than him! And he never even thanked me for anything I did for him." It was Bear's voice. Reseng wished he could punch Bear in the back of the head for talking shit about him, but he couldn't. He was a corpse.

Reseng finished his cigarette, lit up another, and swallowed an aspirin with a mouthful of beer. Aspirin, cigarette, beer. The inside of his head was heavy and hazy, as if an enormous bank of fog had rolled in. At least once a year, anxiety would swoop down on him for no reason, and his mood would crash. Whenever that happened, Reseng started his mornings with a can of beer. He stayed indoors, turned on some music, curled up on the windowsill like a snail, and drank beer all day.

Reseng drained the can and crumpled it, then tossed it onto his desk, next to the other two he'd finished. Sitting beside the crumpled cans was the bomb he'd found inside his toilet. Reseng picked it up. It was smaller than a box of matches, so dainty that it had filled him with relief, of the "What harm could this little thing do?" variety. But the owner of the meat-market hardware shop had taken one look at it and set him straight.

"Where'd you say the bomb was?"

"In my toilet."

"This would've blown your ass off."

"That tiny thing?"

"The pressure is higher inside a toilet bowl. It's like squeezing a firecracker in your hand when it goes off. Basically, when you sit down to take a shit, your ass forms a seal over the hole, creating the perfect conditions for this bomb to do maximum damage."

"Are you saying it could have killed me?"

"Ever seen anyone survive without an ass?"

"So it wasn't just a threat or a warning."

"Not if it had gone off. But it's hard to say if it would have. I've never seen one of these before. It's waterproofed really well and has a unique chemical fuse that can sense when you take a shit. The amount of explosives is perfectly calculated to take your ass off. But it might be a dud. Hard to say. Though I can tell it was made by an amateur, because pros don't make the wiring this complicated. There's no point."

The owner held the bomb up to the light to examine it again.

"It's really ingenious!" he exclaimed. "Who would make a bomb this cute? None of the guys I know is this creative. I'd love to meet this person."

Reseng scowled. He'd run errands for this shop since he was twelve, which meant he'd known the owner for twenty years. And yet the guy didn't so much as blink an eye at the thought of Reseng dead, with his ass blown off, or at the tragic fact that Reseng might be on a plotter's list. To him, Reseng was no different from his countless other regulars who'd ended up neutralized.

"Anyway, I assume this isn't the work of the government?" Reseng asked.

"Hard to say. Nowadays, there are so many hired guns, companies, and plotters that no one can keep track. What'd you do?"

"I can't count the reasons I should be dead by now. I've been in this business for fifteen years, after all." Reseng held out his hand, meaning the shop owner should shut up and give it back already.

"Well, looks like you survived this one," the owner said, handing back the deactivated bomb.

"Yeah, hooray for constipation."

He'd found the toilet bomb about a week ago. When he stepped into his apartment, the smell was different. His cats, who normally raced straight for the door, had hung back. It was obvious someone had been inside. Reseng stood still for a moment to memorize the unfamiliar smell lingering in the air. Was that perfume? Cosmetics? Could it be body odor? But the smell was so faint, he couldn't quite put his finger on it. At any rate, an intruder who left a smell behind had to be an amateur. Pros never left a smell.

Reseng cautiously opened the shoe cabinet, took out a canister of forensic powder, and sprayed it on the floor in front of the door. An unfamiliar shoe print appeared. A sneaker, about size seven or eight. It belonged to either a woman or a very short man. There were no prints on the living room floor. The intruder had politely removed his or her shoes at the front door before entering.

"How thoughtful," he muttered.

Reseng stepped into the living room and slowly looked around. If someone had been there, things would be either missing or misplaced. At first glance, nothing looked any different. But then he noticed that the books stacked on his desk were in reverse order. Chu's knife, which was always on the third shelf from the bottom, had descended to the second shelf, and the cat toy shaped like a fishing rod, which he kept in the mail organizer, was lying on the table. In the kitchen, a coffee cup was still wet and the tea towel was damp. Reseng picked up the coffee cup, sniffed it, and held it up to the light. He snorted, dumbfounded. What had this person been up to?

The intruder had examined the books in Reseng's reading stack one at a time, starting from the top. What kind of intruder had that much time on their hands? Why go to the trouble of sneaking in just to find out what he was reading? It made no sense. Not only that, the intruder had handled a surprising number of his belongings for no apparent reason. Considering that even the cat toy had been taken out, the intruder must've tried to play with his cats, then gone into the kitchen, made a cup of coffee, *and* washed the cup. What kind of crazy person does that?

Reseng had been gone no more than two hours. At 2:00 p.m. every Monday, Wednesday, and Friday, he was at the swimming pool. He rarely skipped a workout. The intruder probably made sure he was at the pool before breaking and entering. Whoever it was knew his exact movements, which meant that a plotter was behind this. The first thing plotters did was study their targets' movements. After Reseng left that day, the intruder had spent a leisurely two hours inside his home. The intruder had left traces of their presence, not because they were an amateur, but because they just didn't care. It was a message to Reseng: Think long and hard about why I was here.

Reseng stood in the middle of the living room. It took him a moment—it wasn't an easy decision—but once he'd made up his mind, he turned on every light in the place and began ransacking the apartment. He inspected every inch of the wallpaper for tears or knife marks, then did the same for the ceilings and floors. He checked the inside of the stove, the gas lines, the cabinet under the sink, and the insides of the refrigerator and freezer. He upended every drawer, opened every box, and searched the inside of the wardrobe, behind the bookshelf, inside the shoe cabinet and light fixtures, behind the wall clock, and in every corner of the cupboards. Then he examined the bed, the washing machine, the window frames, the curtains. Nothing.

Reseng looked out the window. The sun was going down. What if he was on a plotter's hit list? His mind went blank. The inside of his head filled with smog. He had to think of something, but he felt as if he'd forgotten *how* to think. Someone had come into his home. Not just anyone's home, but the home of an assassin. The intruder wouldn't have done it for fun. The person had either planted a bomb or bugged the place.

Reseng began searching again, still with no clue as to what he was looking for. But this time he was much more thorough. He opened the coffee can, poured out the coffee, and checked the bottom, took apart his Zassenhaus coffee grinder, emptied all of his spice jars and checked the insides, upended his garbage bin and sifted through every piece of garbage. He opened his computer, took out the components, and checked them one by one, took apart his radio and TV set, pulled everything out of the freezer, ripped off the packaging, and even cut open the frozen fish and sliced open every frozen dumpling. He took all the shoes out of the shoe cabinet and turned the pockets of every article of clothing in the closet inside out. He pulled every book from its shelf and opened each one. He even opened every bill and letter, just in case there was something else in one of the envelopes.

Long after the sun had risen, Reseng was still taking things apart. For twenty-one hours straight, he ripped everything open and peeked inside, without stopping to eat or sleep. His apartment looked like a bomb had already gone off, but he refused to stop.

Now and then he wondered if maybe the intruder had left without leaving anything behind. But he didn't care. His face filled with rage, he ripped and pried and wrenched, prodded and probed, and tossed his ruined belongings aside.

After gutting his wall clock, Reseng took a knife to the mattress. The grating of the blade against the metal springs made his skin crawl. He tore out a chunk of foam, checked that there was nothing around it, and then hacked away at the mattress some more and tore out another chunk of foam. He knew he was being stupid, but he kept going.

Sunlight crossed the balcony and illuminated Reseng's face. He was crying. He gazed up at the sun through tear-filled eyes. Shame beamed down over his cheeks in tandem with the sun's warmth. He looked down at his hands. The fingernails were ragged from all that plucking and prying, and the skin was bleeding from where he'd nicked it with the knife. His stomach growled. He'd spent twenty-one hours tearing his home apart nonstop, but now he had no strength left to make any food. He tossed aside the knife and screwdriver, leaned back against his bayoneted sofa, and fell asleep.

He awoke in the afternoon. The sun was still shining. The room was filled with debris. He stared blankly at the mess he'd created. What's wrong with me? he thought. But of the many, many voices inside his head, not a single one gave him an answer.

Reseng grabbed a garbage bag and started filling it with the objects he'd dismantled. Some were old; some were new. Some had sentimental value; others left him wondering how they'd gotten there in the first place. Reseng shoved all of it into the bag regardless. It took two dozen twenty-liter garbage bags to clean up his place. He put the bags in the dumpster in front of the building, and next to it the couch and broken mattress, the springs flopping every which way. If he were a target, then the plotter's hired shadow would be watching right now. The person might even take his garbage bags. But Reseng didn't care. I don't need this stuff anymore, so feel free to shove it up your ass, he thought.

Plotters never moved without a reason. He was certain he was a target. Could he survive this? Probably not. In all the time he'd been in the business, he'd never once seen someone evade the plotters. There were only those who died straightaway and those who managed to hold out slightly longer. But why the fuck am I a target? He sniggered to himself. It was a pretty stupid question. What he should've asked himself was, How did I make it this far? He'd lasted fifteen years in a business where the plotters made a point of regularly cleaning up after themselves. There were too many good reasons for him to be a target. If it weren't for the Doghouse and Old Raccoon, Reseng would've been dead a long time ago. Thirty-two years old. Young compared to the average life span, but a long run for an assassin. His end was overdue. It was time for him to make like Old Orin in *The Ballad of Narayama* and bash his teeth out against a millstone and go into the mountains to die.

The first thing Reseng did when he went back inside was order ten boxes of beer. Whenever he was gripped by anxiety, whenever silent terror rose around him like a river in flood, whenever he found himself sinking into a bottomless swamp of depression, whenever he came home from a killing, and whenever he was confronted by a sticky situation, that old feeling of irresponsibility came over him and Reseng holed up at home and drank beer.

Beer Week. If he was going to drink cool, refreshing beer non-stop, he'd have to do some preparation. Step one: Throw out all the food in the fridge to make room for as many cans of beer as possible. Step two: Order as much beer as he could drink. Step three: Fill the fridge with beer. Step four: Take the peanuts and dried anchovies out of the freezer and keep them handy so he would always be neither full nor hungry. Preparations complete. Now all he had to do was open the fridge, pull out a can of beer, pop the tab, guzzle it, and crush the empty can.

He was a target. Shouldn't he do something about that? The question occasionally crossed his mind mid-swig. But he kept swallowing. All he could do for now was open fridge, take out beer, pop, guzzle, crush. Every now and then he chewed a few peanuts and stared at himself in the mirror while pissing in the toilet. Then he flushed and popped open another beer. Good thing I didn't take apart the fridge, he thought, marveling at his good sense.

He discovered the bomb two days into his bender. He had his head in the toilet, vomiting for the third time. Three or four rounds of vomiting were like a rite of passage for the proper observance of Beer Week. He threw up, drank more beer, threw up again, and drank more beer. Eventually, his body got used to it and the vomiting stopped. The vomit in the toilet bowl consisted solely of yellow gastric fluids, beer, and a few dried anchovy heads. He was in the middle of a dry heave when he spotted something stuck way down inside the hole at the bottom of the bowl. He stared at it for a long time before sticking his hand in and pulling out the object.

It was a tiny ceramic box. White like the rest of the toilet and made from a similar material, it wasn't easy to distinguish at first glance. It reminded him of a hotel soap. He took a closer look. Definitely a bomb. The first thing he felt wasn't shock or fear, but relief. Not because there was anything good about it, but simply because what was supposed to be there finally was.

The phone rang. It was Jeongan, the tracker.

"I asked around. They say these were pretty trendy in Belgium about seven or eight years ago."

"Toilet bombs were trendy?"

"No, stupid! But what a great trend that would've been."

"Then what do you mean?"

"They made pill-size bombs—not big enough to take out a toilet, but enough to set off very tiny explosions inside the body, to look like medical accidents. They say the KGB used them to take out fat Russian politicians with pacemakers or insulin pumps."

"What does that have to do with this bomb?"

"The basic structure is the same. The components are Belgian-made, and the fuse and sensor are both Belgian. Only the explosive is American—you can buy it from any junkyard. But it looks like it was assembled here, because the casing is Chinese. I've never seen such a mishmash. The bomb maker must've ordered the parts from all over. You can't find these on the black market, so they would've had to order it all online. Or they went to Belgium themselves to get it."

"What's your point?" Reseng said, getting irritated.

"My point is that I can't tell just from this who put it in your toilet."

"The parts have serial numbers on them!"

"Hey, imbecile, if a staple had a serial number, would that mean you knew what else had been stapled? This was built from medical supplies!"

"Then find out who built it."

"Do you have any idea how many bomb makers there are? They hide out to avoid the cops. If you say you want to meet them, I'm sure they'll all jump out dancing the cancan, singing 'Here I am!' But why are you so curious about this bomb anyway? It's not like it was in *your* toilet."

"It *was* in my toilet! So keep looking!"

Reseng hung up and took another swig of beer. Jeongan would be turning in soon. He worked at night and slept during the day. Not because he was a night owl, but because most of the people he dealt with were active only at night. While the rest of the city was leaving for work, Jeongan was clocking off. Why did everyone in their line of work have to be so nocturnal? No one was forcing them to. It was exhausting, and the more tired you were, the more tired you got.

Reseng stroked the empty bomb casing. Jeongan had kept the components. He tilted his head and wondered who on earth would use such a silly little bomb. Had they meant for it to go off? Were they really hoping to see a dead man slumped in front of the toilet with his pants and underwear around his ankles and his ass blown off? Such a dainty bomb. It reminded him of the silver pill case Hanja kept in his pocket.

But it couldn't have been Hanja. If Hanja had wanted to get rid of Reseng, he would've hired the Barber. For the past few years, he'd used the Barber every time he neutralized an assassin. The

Barber neutralized them, and Bear cremated them. That was the cleanest method. Eventually, people might ask what had happened to the assassin and assume he was dead.

"What's Froggy been up to these days? He's so talented. Is he taking a break?"

"Hey, you're right. I haven't seen him in forever. Maybe he's dead?"

Assassins went underground every now and then for their own safety, and would resurface after a long break. Sometimes a person you thought was dead would reappear looking perfectly healthy. And sometimes someone you were sure was alive never came back. But dead or alive, no one thought too deeply about it. They didn't mourn, they didn't get sad, and, what's more, they weren't the slightest bit curious.

Anyway, Hanja was simply too busy for a stunt like this. Nor was he witty or fun-loving enough to use such a ridiculous bomb. His sense of humor was shit. It wasn't government spooks, either. They weren't the type to sign off on anything silly. Old-fashioned, they lacked imagination and were not at all flexible. Then who? Who had put this damned bomb in his toilet? He couldn't figure it out.

He took another swig of beer. He needed to think, but his head was a mess. What the hell's wrong with you? he thought. Can't you see your life is at the brink? But finding the bomb had not put a stop to Beer Week. He still had a can in his hand at all times.

He'd been in danger plenty of times before. He screwed up a job badly, left evidence behind. Had a shadow watching his every move for a while. Even got a warning letter from the plotter for disobeying orders. But he'd never once been a target. No one had ever come into his home before. Did Old Raccoon know? Up until a few years ago, a plotter would have needed Old Raccoon's consent to kill Reseng. Was that no longer the case, now that Old Raccoon's position in the industry was slipping? Or were they coming after Reseng and Old Raccoon at the same time?

But why such a ridiculous bomb?

Murder was quiet and simple in the plotting world. There were no huge explosions like in the movies, and rarely any messy car accidents or hails of bullets. It was as silent as snowfall in the night, as secretive as a cat's footsteps. The killings almost never came to light. Since there was no murder case, there was no crime, no suspicion, no investigation. Naturally, there were also no loud news reports, no swarms of reporters, no cops or prosecutors. Only a quiet, melancholy funeral attended by clueless, sniffling family members. Or just a death with no funeral, witnessed by no one.

The rain suddenly grew heavy and splattered on the windowsill. Reseng got up from his chair to close the window. One side of the sky was still sunny. Strange weather. He finished his beer, crushed the can, and set it on his desk. Then he opened a drawer, pulled out a bag of cheap marijuana that Trainer had given him all those years ago, and stared at it. Reseng rolled a joint, but he couldn't bring himself to smoke it. It brought back too many bad memories, and sad ones, and filled him with regret for the mistakes he'd been too stupid to regret at the time. The memories that he tried to keep tucked away would come creeping back like a bad smell, until his whole body reeked of it.

The day that Reseng had decided to try working in a factory, the weather had been as strange as today. That would have been around ten years ago. Raindrops were flying around in an otherwise sunny sky. Reseng was following Old Raccoon's orders and lying low outside the capital. It was a small, provincial manufacturing town belching smoke and lined with tiny factories. Reseng had rented a second-floor studio there and had been looking out the window at laundry on a clothesline. As the clothes whipped around in the wind, taking a beating from the rain and the sun at the same time, they had reminded him of Pierrot the clown: comical yet sad.

The streets were deserted during the day; everyone in that quiet, gloomy town seemed to be employed in the factories. In the early mornings, the streets flooded with bicycles and scooters, like something you'd see in China, and at lunchtime they bustled again with countless workers heading out to eat. The rest of the time the town was desolate, as if the inhabitants had suddenly emigrated to Mars.

Reseng sat at the windowsill and stared at the fake ID that Mun, the forgery expert, had made for him. He was in the middle of memorizing the information he needed to live under his new name: Jang Yimun, male, twenty-four years old. Not much to memorize. It really didn't take much to live under someone else's name in a new town.

As Reseng was reciting his fake resident registration number, a group of laughing factory girls passed under his window. They looked bright and happy. His eye was drawn to the short one in the middle. She had a cute round face, and the most exaggerated body language of the four. She twisted around and wept actual tears as she laughed and said, "Oh, man, that's too funny, that's hilarious!" while slapping the shoulder of the girl next to her. Her laughter echoed from one end of the street to the other. Reseng stuck his head out the window and watched as they went into the factory at the end of the street, laughing the whole way. Because of their bright smiles, he couldn't help thinking that the factory looked as wondrous as Willy Wonka's.

The next day, Reseng applied for a job there. The admin section chief had a face like a crowded balance sheet, as if he'd been born to oversee the administration of a factory. He scrutinized Reseng's résumé and asked, "Geumseong High? So that's, what, a liberal arts high school?"

Reseng nodded.

"If you went to a liberal arts high school, why didn't you go to university? You weren't an activist or anything like that, were you?"

Reseng laughed at the word *activist*. He wanted to say that he hadn't even gone to elementary school, let alone university, but instead he just scratched his head, made a dopey face, and said that his grades were bad.

"How bad?" the admin section chief asked.

"Almost the worst. But not the worst-worst."

"Worst or worst-worst, you still need a brain to work in a factory. Nowadays, you can't do anything without a brain. Hmm . . . Twenty-four . . . Did your army service?"

"I was exempt, sir."

"What? Okay, fine, so you've got no brains and you're some kind of cripple. Then what have you been doing all this time?"

Flustered, Reseng replied, stammering, that after finishing high school he'd worked on some construction sites here and there. The admin section chief narrowed his eyes in suspicion, so Reseng launched into a rambling explanation of how he hadn't wanted to work in a factory and had gone into construction instead, but it hadn't paid as well as he'd thought it would, and he got tired of having to be on the move all the time, and so he'd decided to settle down and learn a skill. He'd broken out into a sweat and was sure he'd made a mess of his story. But the admin section chief nodded and chuckled.

"I swear, those foremen. They keep dragging off all the young guys with their sweet talk about how good construction wages are, but it's bullshit. Every guy thinks he's going to make himself a little nest egg right away, but there's no security, and the cash is just a pipe dream. The monthly pay here may be smaller than what you get at a construction site, but no one's going to bilk you out of a paycheck, you get severance, and the overtime is pretty good. As long as you put in the work, you'll save money. And you don't have to work on Sundays. What more could you want?"

As far as Reseng was concerned, the admin section chief was just bragging about the obvious.

"Work hard!" he said, and he clapped Reseng on the shoulder, looking like the sort of pillar of industry you would've seen on one of those Daehan News newsreels back in the seventies.

"Yes, sir! I'll do my best!" Reseng responded vigorously, feeling like he'd suddenly become a pillar of industry himself.

Reseng was assigned straightaway to Work Team Three, where he did chrome plating. The work didn't require any special skills. All he had to do was dip a die-cast metal frame into a chrome bath for ten seconds, pull it back out, give it a good shake, and let it dry. Despite what the admin section chief had said, it was the kind of work that didn't require the use of a brain at all; even a monkey could have mastered it after ten minutes of instruction. But no one else wanted to do the work because the chrome bath smelled foul, and because it was rumored that it would ruin your skin and leave you in agony for the rest of your life, or else reduce your sperm count and render you sterile.

Reseng worked on chrome plating for two straight months, until a new employee was finally hired and took his place. Chrome plating required him to grip a heavy, unwieldy frame with rubber-gloved hands and teeter forward on his toes, as if he were wringing wet laundry over a bucket, dip the frame carefully into the electroplating solution, and pull it out exactly ten seconds later. What he hated most about the work was how stupid he looked while leaning over the bath. He had to stand with his legs apart and his butt sticking way out—if the God of Chrome Plating himself had come down to Earth, he would have looked just as stupid.

Not long after he'd started, as Reseng was carefully shaking a frame he'd just pulled from the solution, trying to keep the liquid chrome from spattering, the woman with the cute round face who had drawn him to the factory in the first place came over to him. She stood with her hands clasped behind her back, watching him in evident amusement.

"What're you working so hard for? Don't you need to eat?" she asked.

Reseng gave her a befuddled look. She pointed to the clock on the factory wall: 12:20 p.m.

"You don't get overtime for working through lunch," she said.

Her voice was just as cheerful as the day she'd walked past his window, filling the street with her laughter. He took off his gloves.

"Have *you* eaten?" he asked.

"Not yet. I just got back from running an errand for the boss."

"Then, if you don't mind my asking, would you care to have lunch with me?"

She stared at him.

"Why are you talking like that? You sound like a preacher."

The factory was too small to have its own cafeteria. The workers ate at a restaurant down a side street crowded with other tiny factories and small apartment buildings. She gestured to Reseng that they should head out. He nodded and pinned his rubber gloves to a wire and took off his vinyl apron and hung it on a coatrack. Then he lathered his hands with soap and scrubbed them for a full minute. As she watched him scrub, she sighed impatiently.

"You've been here less than a month, right?" she asked as they were leaving.

"About three weeks."

"And you're still on chrome plating?"

He nodded.

"They say it lowers your sperm count if you do it for too long. Each time you dip your hands in, several hundred sperm die. Can you imagine how many are dead after a day's work? I can't even count that high. At that rate, it's practically a massacre. A massacre! I don't know how they can make people do that work."

She looked as if she were talking about an actual genocide she had witnessed. But Reseng figured she wasn't really worried about the number of sperm inside his testicles.

"It's okay," he said. "I've got plenty of sperm. Men produce over four hundred billion sperm over a lifetime. Each time a man ejaculates, something like one hundred and fifty million sperm come shooting out. So that's plenty. No matter how hard I try, I can't have sex three thousand times in a row. But it could be a problem for women. They produce an average of only four hundred eggs total in their lifetime."

She stopped and looked at Reseng in shock.

"Sex? Ejaculation? How dare you talk about that in front of a lady!" She glared at him.

Embarrassed, he nervously held up his hands.

"Truly, I . . . I didn't mean to offend you."

"'Truly'?" She broke into laughter. "Aren't you kind of young to talk like that?"

She started walking ahead. He tagged along behind.

"But is it true that women get only four hundred eggs in their lifetime?" she asked.

"I read it in a book."

"A *book*, huh?" She looked incredulous.

He tilted his head in confusion. He didn't understand the tone of her question.

"What you really mean is you read it in a girlie magazine that you bought at the bus station, right?" she asked with a laugh.

"It's explained in detail in Richard Cardison's *Conquering Infertility*. He's a gynecologist, and according to what he wrote, the number of eggs a woman has is determined by her DNA. Some women have four hundred and twenty-three eggs, some have five hundred, some have three hundred and fifty, you know, and so on."

She stopped again and stared at him, but this time she looked dazed.

"Then how many eggs have I already wasted?" she murmured.

She grew quiet. They continued down the street without speaking. Reseng felt uncomfortable, and she probably felt the same. She was sending him signals that she wanted him to say something, anything, but he couldn't think of what to say. When they were passing the window of his rented room, from where he'd seen her for the first time, he pointed up at it.

"That's where I live."

She looked up. "Isn't it expensive?"

"Not really. Three hundred and fifty thousand won a month, with no deposit."

She stared at him in shock.

"What? How can someone who makes less than a million won a month after taxes say three hundred and fifty thousand isn't expensive? Don't you also have to pay electricity, water and sewerage, gas and other utilities on top of the rent? Do you cook your own food at least?"

"I just moved in. . . ."

"You eat out?"

Reseng nodded.

"Twice a day?"

"Sometimes I have instant noodles at home."

"Have you managed to save *any* money at all? Why are men so immature? They should be saving their hard-earned cash, not burning it with every cigarette they smoke and flushing it away with all the booze they drink. Why do you act like you're living someone else's life? If you keep it up, you'll never own your own home."

She'd turned suddenly furious. Reseng felt like a scolded child, but everything she was saying sounded more or less correct.

"Can I go inside?" she asked, gesturing up at his room with her chin.

Surprised, Reseng asked, "Where? My room?"

"Yes." She looked completely nonchalant.

"Why do you want to go in my room?"

"I want to see how you live."

Before he could say anything, she was bounding up the stairs. He followed without protest. She stopped at his door and looked at him. He stepped in front of it to block her.

"Not today," he said hesitantly. "I mean, how about if I officially invite you over next time?"

"Look, I think you've got the wrong idea. This is not a date. There is no officially inviting each other over. All I'm doing is checking your room, as your factory elder, to see whether or not you're cut out for the factory lifestyle. It might seem like there's nothing to it, but if your daily life isn't shipshape, then you won't do well at work."

The look on her face really was that of a stern factory elder. It was the look of a sergeant inspecting troops for combat readiness, a persnickety dormitory leader preparing for a cleaning inspection. Reseng stared at her in discomfort. She stared right back with a look that said if he knew what was good for him, he'd open that door. He had no choice. He opened the door.

Since he didn't have much in the way of household goods, there was no mess—only the blanket, futon, and pillow he'd bought at the local market, the low table that had been in the room when he moved in, an electric kettle to make ramen and instant coffee, and a single bag of clothes he'd brought from the city. The cabinet under the sink was stacked with instant noodle cups, and next to his pillow and on the table were the books that he'd either brought with him from Seoul or bought at the local bookshop: Albert Camus's

Summer and *The Plague,* Italo Calvino's *The Baron in the Trees,* Martin Monestier's *Suicides,* Andrew Solomon's *The Noonday Demon.*

"What? This place is empty!" She kept looking around.

"I told you I just moved in," he said, plucking a towel from the floor and hanging it up.

"Yeah, but there are still certain basic necessities you have to have. Otherwise, you end up spending more money on little things."

Reseng nodded.

She glanced at the books on his table and asked, "You don't watch TV?"

"No."

She gave herself a quick tour of the room, the bathroom, and the kitchen, as if she were a prospective renter. She even turned on the bathroom tap to check the water pressure and opened every single kitchen drawer. She kept muttering things like "Wow, how do you not have any bowls?" and "This place is hooked up to the city gas line? I guess that's because it's such an expensive neighborhood." As she was doing her inspections, Reseng glanced around and felt satisfied that the room wasn't too dirty. Just then, she let out a shout—more like a scream—from the broom cupboard.

"What *is* all this?"

She was holding up a pair of Reseng's underwear. The cardboard box he'd stuffed full of dirty socks, underwear, T-shirts, and other clothes that needed to be washed was sitting wide open. He rushed over, snatched the underwear from her hand, and shoved it back into the box. While he was hurriedly closing the flaps, she noticed the unopened packages of socks and underwear piled high on the shelf.

"Did you own an underwear shop that went out of business? Why do you have all of this?"

"I don't have a washing machine."

"Then wash it by hand. Are you saying you wear your socks and underwear once and throw them away? Seriously, do you have any brains at all?"

Now she was angry. Of course he wasn't planning to throw the dirty clothes away. But he wasn't exactly planning on squatting in the bathroom and scrubbing it all by hand, either. To tell the truth, he'd been so tired and distracted that he hadn't given any thought at all to what he should do with his dirty underwear.

She glared at him, aghast. He looked up at the ceiling, his face crimson.

"Do you have a woman to wash your underwear for you?" Her voice sounded strange. He looked at her quizzically.

"I'm not saying I'm interested in you. It just burns me up to see someone who doesn't understand the value of money. But I wouldn't want your girlfriend to get the wrong idea."

He had no idea what she meant. "I don't have a woman, but . . ."

She opened the box and started filling a black shopping bag from underneath the shelf with Reseng's dirty underwear. Shocked, he tried to stop her, but she slapped the back of his hand. It stung. He stepped back. She stuffed all his laundry into the bag and stood up.

Pointing her finger in his face, she said, "Keep only two sets of those new socks and underwear and take the rest back for a refund. Got it?"

"I have to have underwear," Reseng said with a pout.

She tapped his face with the laundry bag.

"There's a year's worth of underwear in here as long as you wash it."

By the time they left and headed back to the street, there was only fifteen minutes left of their lunch break.

"I bet you're hungry," she said.

"I'm okay. I can skip a meal now and then."

She disappeared into a corner store and came out with two cartons of banana-flavored milk and a snack cake. She held out the cake and one of the milk cartons. Though it wasn't much, he suddenly felt incredibly indebted to her. He thanked her and accepted the snacks. They sat on a bench in front of the shop to eat.

"Weather's nice," she said, looking up at the sky.

He looked up, too. "Yeah, it is."

"Laundry dries really well on a day like this." She gave the bag of dirty clothes a squeeze.

The next day at the factory, she acted as if she didn't know him.

He tried to wave hello, but she blushed and kept walking to her section. He told himself it was because she was with their coworkers. But even when they bumped into each other in an empty hallway, she merely dipped her head and said nothing. She worked inside on the production line, while Reseng worked outside in a prefab shed where all the plating and painting were done. But in such a small factory, they had plenty of opportunity to bump into each other. Every time, she looked flustered and kept her distance from him, or hurried past, her shoulders hunched.

The next day and the next day, it was the same. He waited outside the gate for her after work, but she came out in a gaggle of coworkers, making it impossible for him to approach her. Even if she had left work alone, he would've had no idea what to say to her. What could he say? Please give back my underwear?

On Friday night, Reseng was lying in bed when there was a knock at his door. He opened it and there she was, holding the shopping bag with both hands, her head bent. When he greeted her, she thrust the bag into his hands without looking at him.

"I gave it a lot of thought and realized I went too far," she said, her head still lowered, her voice soft and trembly. "I'm sorry if I offended you."

"You didn't have to come all this way just to say that. But since you're here, come in and have some tea."

He opened the door wider. She shook her head. He started to step outside, but she shook her hands and stopped him.

"Don't come out. I'll just go."

She turned and went quickly back down the hallway. He watched openmouthed as she rushed away, her small shoulders hunched. What had happened to the feisty, intrepid woman who'd shoved all that dirty underwear into the shopping bag? When he heard her footsteps reach the bottom of the stairs, he went back in and closed the door. He opened the bag. Inside were stacks of neatly folded underwear. He took a pair out and sniffed it. It smelled like a freshly laundered cotton sheet that had dried in the warm afternoon sun. Just then, it hit him: Her kindness was nothing more than genuine compassion for a foolish, pathetic young man who spent half his monthly pay on rent and utilities and the other half on cigarettes, booze, instant noodles, and underwear. He laughed. Oh, so she wasn't hitting on me? But he felt grateful for her compassion. Regardless of whether it was pity or mercy, he'd never received anything like that from a stranger before.

He got up and ran out after her. Five hundred meters down the street, he spotted her. When he caught up to her, he tapped her on the shoulder.

As he gasped for air, he asked, "Want to see a movie this week-end?"

A month later, they moved in together. Reseng didn't have much to move to her place. He'd told the factory he was twenty-four, but in fact he was twenty-two. You didn't have to be a philosopher to know there were millions of reasons for a twenty-two-year-old man and a twenty-one-year-old woman to move in together. They could fall in love while one was bandaging a cut for the other. They could fall for each other while sharing a warm goldfish-shaped pastry from a food cart. They could even find themselves in love while mid-bounce on a pogo stick. So there must have been other couples on this beautiful planet called Earth who'd fallen in love over a bag of dirty underwear and decided to live together.

She turned out to be unimaginably good at housekeeping. Whether it was cooking or cleaning or laundering or ironing or sewing, she did everything quickly and efficiently, and though she seemed to do it all in a halfhearted way, it was always perfect. She would take one look at the clothes Reseng had struggled to fold, the edges never quite lining up, make a face, and refold it all when Reseng stepped away for a second. She would oversleep, and yet even while rushing to wash her hair and get ready for work, she would somehow manage to set the breakfast table with soup, fresh greens, and a grilled fish.

"First we'll save money. Then we'll get married. If you and I both work and save up carefully for twenty years, we'll have enough to buy a nice apartment."

"Twenty years?" he said in shock.

What she was telling him was that in order to escape the tiny studio where they paid monthly rent, to move into another studio with a lump-sum deposit, and then escape that to buy their own apartment, which would still be no bigger than his left nostril, he would have to spend the next twenty years doing that god-awful chrome plating. By then, there wouldn't be a single sperm left in Reseng's testicles.

"Look," he said, "you're barely twenty-one, I'm barely twenty-two. Don't you think we're a little young to be thinking about a life that grim and boring?"

"All I ever think about at the factory is getting married. I imagine married life while I'm tightening screws. I picture having a pretty baby and watching him or her grow up. Seriously, just the thought of it fills my heart with joy and excitement. Otherwise, what's the point of suffering like this? It would be meaningless."

All she ever talked about was married life. Every chance she got, she talked about children, houses, gardens, kitchen appliances. For Reseng, married life sounded like a futuristic world in an animated movie, but she looked so serious and happy that he simply nodded his head and agreed.

After breakfast, they rode their bicycles to work. She had bought his bicycle for him. "Bikes are great. You get good exercise, and you save money. Feel free to use the bus fare you save as spending money." She'd said it as if she were granting him some huge favor. "No man would ride this," he'd said, giving the front tire a kick. "This is a woman's bike. Everyone at the factory will laugh at me." His bike had no gears and an enormous basket—a pink one, at that—big enough to hold twelve kittens.

It turned out it was good exercise. Her place was at the top of a steep hill about a hundred meters off the hilly main road. On market days, she would fill the twelve-kitten-capacity basket with tofu, green onions, radishes, onions, carrots, a sack of rice, fatty slices of pork for kimchi stew, and freshly cleaned and chopped fish. She was so methodical about packing the basket that she could have fitted in a bear cub as well if she had wanted to. While Reseng dripped with sweat trying to pedal his heavily loaded bicycle back up the hill, she licked an ice cream and looked radiant.

"You should've bought me a cart instead," he would grumble.

"I've always wanted to do this," she would say with a huge smile.

The factory folks' reactions to his pink basket were even stronger than he'd expected. When he parked it outside the factory, they crowded around and took turns making fun of him.

"I never would've guessed you had so much flair," the admin section chief said.

His work team leader tapped the basket and said, "Oh, man, if you're riding this to work, how's your mother getting to the market?"

One coworker who'd never once spoken to him suddenly approached him. The man kept starting to say something and then stopping, but finally he looked as if he couldn't control his curiosity any longer.

"Please don't take this the wrong way. I just couldn't help wondering." The look on the man's face was very serious.

"What is it?"

"There's a rumor going around that you're saving up for a sex-change operation. Is it true?"

As the stories spread out of control, even workers at neighboring factories started to talk, until finally the admin section chief asked him, half-jokingly, "Don't you think it's time you did something about it?" Reseng had no choice but to hang a sign on the front of his basket that read, THE RUMORS ARE NOT TRUE. I AM NOT GETTING AN OPERATION. AND I'M ALREADY CIRCUMCISED. He kept it on there for three days straight.

And yet, thanks to the bicycle, he finally became friends with his coworkers. The work got much easier and he started to enjoy himself. His team leader transferred him to the more sophisticated job of drilling holes in copper plates, which paid 200,000 won more per month than chrome plating, and even used his spare time at work to teach Reseng how to trim metal using a lathe. Each time he scraped grease from his hands after work or brushed metal filings off his apron and hung it on the clothesline or laughed as he watched his coworkers play soccer with a paper cup during their breaks, Reseng felt that he had finally become a true member of the factory world. He'd gained a large family overnight.

Now whenever they bumped into each other at the factory, Reseng and the woman shared shy, clandestine smiles. After work they rode home in separate directions so no one would catch on. She took a shortcut, while Reseng went the long way, but he still always arrived first. He would open the door and wait for her. She'd come riding up the hill, dripping with sweat, and he'd take her bike and lock it up for her. Then they would have sex.

Afterward they ate dinner and watched TV. She liked variety shows. Every time someone on TV made a joke, she rolled on the floor laughing and said, "Oh, man, that guy is too funny, that's hilarious!"

Reseng stared straight-faced at the screen and wondered what on earth was so funny.

"Why am I not laughing? Am I too stupid to get it?"

"Yeah, you're too stupid," she said in between laughs.

Reseng thought maybe she was right.

At nine o'clock, she sat at the desk to study.

"I passed the middle school exam last year. Now I need to prepare for the high school one. How far did you get? I only made it to the first year of middle school. My father wouldn't let me keep going."

"On my résumé I put that I finished high school, but I never even went to elementary school."

"Liar," she said, looking askance at him.

While she studied, he lay down and read *Demons* by Dostoyevsky. It was a big book, and a boring one.

'Is that fun to read?" she asked.

"The characters have really long names. For instance, the main character's mother is Varvara Petrovna Stavrogina, and his tutor is Stepan Trofimovich Verkhovensky. Each time a new person appears, it takes well over a line just to say their name. So, no, it's not that fun. Not with this many names to remember."

"Then why read it if it's not fun? You're the only person I know who reads such big books."

"I don't read for any particular reason. It's like you and your TV shows. I just don't know what else to do with my free time."

At eleven, she would start to nod off. Her head dipped lower and lower, until her forehead knocked against the desk. It was sweet. Reseng tapped her on the shoulder and told her to go to bed. She looked at him, confused, and said she wasn't sleeping, that it was just her trick for memorizing the thing she'd just read. She shook her head, saying the test wasn't far off now, opened her eyes wide, and resumed reading. Then about three seconds later, her head started to bob again. When her face was completely buried in the old government-issued textbook, Reseng put down his book and carried her to the futon. He pushed the small desk to one side, turned off the light, climbed under the blanket, and wrapped his arm around her. She wiggled closer and pushed her butt right up against him, took his hand in both of hers and brought it up to her cheek, and then nodded as if all was now as it should be. That was her favorite sleeping position. She told him nothing made her happier than being held by the person she loved, with his hand pressed to her cheek.

"What did you do before this?" she asked, half-asleep.

"I worked on different construction sites for a few years."

"Ha! Liar. You don't have the hands of a construction worker. You're such a shady character. Seriously shady." She sounded as if she were talking in her sleep.

Sometimes he felt a tear slide down her cheek and over the back of his hand. Some nights she cried a lot. He would breathe deeply, as if asleep, and watch the moonlight tiptoe across the room. Eventually she would stop crying, and Reseng would fall asleep, too.

But the next morning, she was always cheerful and full of energy, as if nothing had happened. She would hum as she brushed her teeth and washed her hair and set the breakfast table. After eating, she would say, "I'll take the usual route today. Don't follow me like you did last time," and then jump on her bike and head to work.

Those were the days. Reseng was getting better and better at his job. His team leader asked what he thought about becoming a certified lathe technician. "A man's got to have a skill. With that, you can make a living anywhere. If you pass the written test, I'll personally train you for the practical test."

On Friday evenings, the factory workers split into teams to play pool. Their rule was that the losing team had to pay for both the pool hall and the alcohol, and they were very strict about that rule, which meant that pool on Friday nights was a serious and gripping affair. After the pool hall, they grilled pork skin over coal briquettes and drank soju. When the admin section chief was there, they complained about the boss, and when he wasn't there, they complained about him. He seemed to know that, because he tried his best never to miss either the pool playing or the drinking.

Meanwhile, the job that Reseng had screwed up never made the news. The incident seemed to have been smoothed over, thanks to some easygoing public officials who didn't want to make their jobs more complicated than they had to be. He decided that as long as it never got out and everything slipped silently back to normal, the plotters and their clients wouldn't be too disappointed. But that was just his own opinion. If the plotter decided that he couldn't let someone who did such shoddy work live, then Reseng was a dead man. But half a year had gone by without any contact from Old Raccoon.

Finally, around his eighth month of working at the factory, he received word. He came home to find a letter stuck in the door. It wasn't sent through the mail; someone had delivered it personally. He opened it with trembling hands.

終結, 歸家.

It was Old Raccoon's handwriting. The letter contained only those four words: "It's over. Come home." Reseng wondered what, exactly, was over and where he was supposed to come home to. He couldn't quite imagine having a home somewhere that wasn't here.

The following afternoon, Reseng called Old Raccoon.

"I'd like to stay here a little longer."

After a long silence, Old Raccoon asked, "The factory girl, she's nice?"

Reseng hesitated before saying yes.

"That's fine, then. If you're sure you don't want to return to this line of work, stay there."

He didn't sound critical, cynical, or angry. In fact, it was the first time Reseng had ever heard Old Raccoon sound warm. Reseng stood with the phone to his ear. *Stay there.* He couldn't quite figure out what those words really meant. Factory workers were pouring into the street on their way to lunch. Reseng's woman was with them. She winked at him. One of the guys tapped Reseng on the shoulder as he walked by and asked why he wasn't joining them. Reseng covered the phone with his hand and said, "I'll catch up." She turned to look at him, too, and he smiled and waved for her to go ahead. She smiled back and kept walking. Reseng brought the phone up to his ear again.

"It really is okay if I stay?" he asked.

"Your name there is Jang Yimun?"

"Yes."

"Live by that name. I'll erase the name you had here. That way, you won't have any problems."

With that, he hung up.

Reseng came out of the phone booth and stared at the factory workers in the street. *I'll erase the name you had here. That way, you won't have any problems.* What kind of problems was Old Raccoon talking about? It was April. Cherry trees were in bloom all down the street. He hadn't realized until that moment that they were cherry trees. Not that it mattered. *Sakura, the flower that wilts the moment it blooms.* For some reason, that line of poetry he'd read somewhere was stuck in his head. He looked down at his hands, hardened from eight months of factory work. As he stroked his calluses, he murmured, "My name was Jang Yimun," his voice sounding like he'd just made a great discovery. He stared at the trees and thought about the name Reseng. It had been his for so long, and now it was about to be erased. He wondered what it meant to erase a name. *Sakura, the flower that wilts the moment it blooms.*

He went back to the factory. He did not eat lunch. There was a stack of unfinished work at his station, so he turned on the milling machine and continued drilling four holes into the copper plates. After about twenty minutes, he had finished. He blew on the holes, brushed away the metal shavings, held the plates up to the light. Nodded in satisfaction. After restacking the plates to one side, he swept up the bits of copper scattered around his workstation and poured them into the recycling bin.

Reseng washed his hands and packed his belongings. After looking around to make sure he hadn't missed anything, he sneaked into the office and removed his résumé from the admin section chief's filing cabinet. Not that it mattered what happened to it. His name and resident registration number were also in the payroll book and on the time sheets. But he took only the résumé. He crumpled it up, shoved it in his pocket, and left. On his way out, he pictured the factory without him in it. What would change if he were not there? Probably nothing. With or without him, the machines would keep on whirring, day in and day out.

Reseng rode home. He opened the door and looked around at the cramped room where he'd lived for the last six months. The time he'd spent there felt like it had happened long, long ago. He started packing the bag he'd brought with him from Seoul, but his belongings had increased since then. There was far too much to fit in the bag. He put everything he'd acquired since moving in with the woman into a garbage bag and threw it away in the next street. Then he put the shirts she'd washed for him, his spare set of work overalls, and his underwear into a black shopping bag and stuck it in a used-clothing donation bin. Back at the room, he inspected every nook and cranny. There had to be something else he should get rid of. He looked around anxiously and started wiping down everything he had ever touched. When he was done, he asked himself why he'd had to erase his fingerprints. But none of the countless faces inside Reseng offered an answer.

He left her no note or explanation. He simply packed his things and went. Halfway down the street, he hid and stared for a long time at the tiny studio where he'd spent half a year of his life. The sun began to set, and he saw her pedaling hard up the hill, her basket filled with bean sprouts, tofu, and green onions. As usual, she parked her bike next to his and went inside. About five minutes later, she came running out. She looked confused. She stood motionless out front until the sun had set and the streetlights came on. Reseng hid in the dark like a rat and watched as she stood there frozen. When she finally tired and went inside, Reseng dragged his bag the rest of the way down the hill. He returned to Seoul and burned the ID card belonging to Jang Yimun.

The rain grew heavier. The sunbeams that had streamed down between the clouds had all disappeared. Reseng finished his beer, crumpled the can, and threw it on the floor next to the hundred or so others. He took a moment to admire the varied shapes of the crushed cans before grabbing a fresh can from the fridge. The one sane voice among the many inside Reseng's head spoke to him: *What are you thinking? Death has crept right up on your ass, and all you're doing is drinking beer?* But Reseng popped the tab anyway. The can sighed, exhaling its carbonation. He smirked. Since when does a can of beer sigh with regret? He took a sip and wondered why he'd bothered to come back. If he'd stayed at the factory ten years ago, he wouldn't have had to tremble in fear at a stupid bomb in his toilet. He would not have had to live this life of constant, compulsory murder.

The night following his first kill after returning to Seoul, he had asked Old Raccoon, "Am I going to end up killing more and more people?"

"No, you'll kill fewer and fewer. But you'll make more and more money."

"How is that possible?"

"The better you get at it, the more valuable the people you kill will be."

But Old Raccoon had been wrong about that. The price of assassinations had fallen. And as their price fell, the value of beautiful, worthy people also fell. The result of which was that great people were dying in larger numbers and more easily than before. It takes countless legends to produce a hero Achilles, but only one idiot prince Paris to kill him. In that case, how many would it take to kill an idiot prince?

Reseng looked at the bomb sitting on the desk. The owner of the hardware shop had warned him, "If this *was* planted by government spooks, you're better off putting it back in your toilet and dying. They don't mess around." He'd said it as a joke, but it wasn't. Once one of them made the list, everyone else hoped for that person to die quietly. Fighting only made things worse for everyone. Detectives would notice something fishy and start sniffing around, which made plotters antsy. If Reseng was on a government hit list, no one would help him. How would you prefer to die? Reseng asked himself. One of the voices inside him murmured mockingly, *At least you know Bear does a good job*. Reseng drained his beer, crushed the can nervously, and tossed it aside.

Don't worry, he thought. No one dies that easily. Some people have lived thirty years with a bullet lodged in their brain. Men have been rescued from desert islands after surviving for a week with a harpoon through their bellies. People have drunk stagnant water from rotten tree trunks, chewed on cactus stalks, drunk their own urine, and eaten the contents of the stomachs of dead animals while crossing deserts. A shipwrecked woman was once rescued after drifting for a month and surviving on her boyfriend's heart, kidneys, liver, and large intestine. There was even a case where a doctor had issued a death certificate, the undertaker had cleaned and shrouded the body, and the coffin lid was being nailed shut, when the person inside suddenly awoke and started pounding like crazy on the coffin lid. Life can be a surprising and cruel and disgusting thing.

Reseng opened the fridge and pulled out the last can of beer. He cracked it open and guzzled it down in one gulp, then crumpled the can and tossed it on the floor. Now he could leave. Beer Week was over.

The next morning, when Reseng stepped into the Doghouse, the cross-eyed librarian was gone. On her desk was a little sign that read

ON VACATION. He assumed it was true, because her stuffed animals and office supplies were still there. But did the Doghouse give librarians vacation days? Maybe the others had simply been fired before they'd had a chance to use them. Reseng went to the study.

Old Raccoon was at his desk, reading out loud, as always. Reseng set the bomb casing in front of him.

"This was in my toilet. It's handmade, and the parts are Belgian."

Old Raccoon peered at the bomb casing through his reading glasses.

"Who do you think put it there?" Old Racoon asked.

"I don't have the slightest idea. Do you?"

"I have too many. Considering how you've lived, it'd be strange if someone *didn't* want you dead."

Old Raccoon sounded like he was talking about somebody else. Reseng hated the way he pretended to be so indifferent. It wasn't as if Reseng was arguing that he didn't deserve to die, nor was he pleading to be saved and claiming how unfair it was. All he'd asked was who might have done this to him.

"Do you know any plotters who use this type of bomb?" he asked, indignant.

For the briefest second, Old Raccoon's expression changed. The look that flashed over his face said that he definitely knew something, and that he was very amused.

"None of the plotters I know plant bombs in toilets. And they're not the type to play practical jokes."

"So it's just a warning?"

He glared. "Why would they waste a warning on the likes of you?"

Reseng didn't know what to say to that. Old Raccoon lit a cigarette and exhaled a long cloud of smoke. Then, to Reseng's consternation, he turned back to his encyclopedia and resumed reading out loud. Reseng stared at him, half-stunned.

What was this pointless form of reading anyway? Reseng had been wondering that ever since he was first brought to the library twenty-eight years ago. Old Raccoon had no interest in anything. Not in politics or power or money or women or marriage or kids.

Those held his attention even less than the tiny blossoms of mold that bloomed between the covers of books. To Old Raccoon, the real world was fiction. The only things that truly engrossed him were the problems raised by books—that is, by the insides and outsides of books. While inside the book, the protagonist trudged across the frozen Siberian wilderness, outside the book, the hot, humid winds of the early summer monsoon ate away at the glue binding the book's pages together. Those worries must have consumed Old Raccoon. So why had he been the leader of a hit squad for the last forty years? It made no sense when you thought about it. He should have owned a secondhand bookshop instead.

Reseng picked up the bomb casing from Old Raccoon's desk and started to leave.

"Go and see Hanja," Old Raccoon said. "If you want to live."

"And if this wasn't Hanja's doing?"

"Doesn't matter who ordered it. You'll live if you talk to Hanja."

"It's that simple?"

"It's that simple."

Old Raccoon went back to his reading. Reseng looked at him for a moment—he looked like he'd shrunk since the last time Reseng had seen him—before closing the door behind him.

THE MEAT MARKET

Dirty, rank, wretched, and revolting. This was the meat market.

Pointless compassion and sorrow, endlessly spawning apathy, and pent-up anger that had nowhere to go, swept around like dead leaves in late autumn until self-combusting. The final destination for fallen lives. Forgery experts, money launderers, murderers for hire, unlicensed physicians, loan sharks, smugglers, cleaners, pimps, insurance fraudsters, drug dealers, organ traffickers, arms dealers, disposers of corpses, assassins, hunters, mercenaries, trackers, fixers, thieves, fencers, hustlers, felons and crooked detectives, whistle-blowers and turncoats—all of them mingled with brokers of every variety, panting like horny dogs on a hot summer day, sniffing around for whatever might make them some money. A home for those who had hit rock bottom so hard that you wished there were a gentle way to say "Hey, maybe in your case suicide *isn't* the worst idea?" but instead they chose to forge ahead and give life one last shot. That was the meat market.

The meat market was the most capitalist of the markets, which meant you could buy anything as long as you had the cash. Nothing there was forbidden by law, justice, or morality. That wouldn't fit with capitalist principles. So products stymied by law, justice, and morality squeezed their way through loopholes into the meat market. You could buy anything here—from a human eyeball, a kidney, a lung, a liver, and other human organs to homemade bombs, poisons, Southeast Asian and Eastern European women, cheap drugs imported from Myanmar and Afghanistan, and guns smuggled off U.S. military bases. If you were lucky, you could even purchase cheap equipment and weapons that former KGB agents had sold to the Russian Mafia for a song. Here you could buy revenge, joy, ruin, resurrection, and rehabilitation. Five hundred bucks slipped into the right hand bought you an illegal immigrant from Vietnam. who would kill whomever you told him to, and the purchase of a corpse—or someone willing to become a corpse—netted you a clean break from your own shitty life. Money launderers could scrub your hidden stash clean of its dirty origins and, surprisingly, even clean up your own dirty past. By purchasing a brand-new face from an unlicensed plastic surgeon and buying a fake name and fake history from a forger, a hideous criminal who ought to have rotted in prison for fifteen years could strut right through downtown Seoul and begin a new life. So, naturally, a married woman with an eye on her soon-to-be accidentally deceased husband's life insurance and a desire to live life to the fullest raised no eyebrows in the meat market. After all, it was the sort of place where a man who'd sold every organ he could spare, only to blow the proceeds on gambling, would drag his barely eleven-year-old daughter there to ask if he could sell her organs, too. This was the meat market.

The only things not bought or sold here were cheap emotions that no one cared about (compassion, sympathy, resentment) and powerless, depressing words *(faith, love, trust, friendship, truth)*. Neither honor nor credit was used as collateral. Far from it. The meat market had no truck with any such beautiful sentiments—not here, among the lowest of the low.

Thanks to the rock-bottom lives drifting in from all over, you could always hear the sound of a life collapsing in the meat market. When you thought about it, few places held as many tears. And yet no one there paid any attention to tears. No one wasted energy on pointless sympathy.

The clueless complained: "Why not just haul them all off to jail?" But that was absurd. The meat market could never be locked up. It was far bigger than any prison, and prison was just another meat market. Like the oases that appear only when rain falls in the desert and that disappear just as quickly, the meat market rose from nothing and flowed forth of its own accord; it was a tumor that formed faster than it could be cut out. The smart prosecutors and detectives took advantage of the meat market. They knew full well that what they were after were the golden eggs, not the goose that laid them. Just as butchering the goose meant no more eggs, if they slaughtered the meat market, they'd be stuck sucking their thumbs, and anyway, the meat market was far too vast ever to be contained.

"He does deserve to die, doesn't he?"

The fifty-something housewife with the short perm was staring pleadingly at Minari Pak. The bruises around her eye and on her cheekbone had not yet faded. Minari stared back at her impatiently.

"Yeah, yeah, of course," he said. "A creep like that is just begging to get knocked off. That's why this is your chance. You can get rid of him and make a fresh start. Find yourself a new husband."

"Sis, he's giving you good advice. You just have to be strong," said the younger woman next to her. Minari's shill.

"He ruined my life!"

The older woman was practically reciting lines from a soap opera. She started sobbing. Fat tears dripped from her eyes as she squeezed her rolled-up handkerchief. She looked like she'd had a rough life. Her forearms were thick, presumably from manual labor, and her skin was rough and darkened from being in the sun. Dressed in a polka-dotted two-piece suit that might have been in style thirty years ago, she looked nothing like the kind of person you'd expect to find in the office of a contract killer, hoping to murder her husband. When she wouldn't stop sobbing, Minari gave the shill a look that said he was going to lose his mind any second. She patted the woman on the back and shot a look right back at him that said, Don't fuck it up now!

"Let it out, sis. There, there. It's okay to cry in front of him. You can trust him," the shill babbled.

Reseng chuckled. He'd been reading a newspaper at Minari's desk the whole time. Were they really telling her to trust a hired killer? The older woman seemed to go along with it, because she started wailing even louder. Minari took out a cigarette and stuck it in his mouth, the look on his face clearly saying, Ah, to hell with this shit.

Reseng put down the newspaper and looked at the three people seated around the coffee table. Minari and his shill looked ridiculous; neither of them had any clue what to do with the woman. Minari let out a long plume of smoke, his eyes fixed on the shopping bag at her feet. It probably held bundles of cash that she'd brought as a down payment. It was a pretty lucrative take, given the small scale of Minari's business. And the job wouldn't be all that hard, either. The shill would already have put in months of work convincing the woman to hire a killer. She would have had to pick a mark, find out everything she could, approach her carefully, and become close friends. Then, when the time was right, she would have had to stealthily plant the idea: "Why do you put up with him? There are options. . . ." Then she would have fallen back on that old chestnut: "Everyone gets one shot to turn their life around." But that's a joke. Life is a tangled knot, years in the making. No one unravels it in one shot.

The woman kept crying, oblivious to Minari's impatience. Why was she crying? Did she feel bad for her husband, now that she was intent on killing him? Or was she feeling bad for herself, having worked her fingers to the bone to support a husband who did nothing but beat her? Was this last-minute guilt? She was sitting in the office of a hired killer with a shopping bag full of cash. She had to prove to Minari how pure and weak she was, like a sprig of baby's breath, and how justified her anger, her tears spilling like the petals of a daisy. Then she had to give her reasons. But there was no need to prove anything to someone like Minari Pak. No need for reasoning. On the scale of hired killers, Minari was a lowly hyena, and he would do anything as long as you paid him. No matter how strong her reasons were or how awful her husband had been to her, none of that made any difference to how Minari did business. The show of waterworks made no difference, either. If her husband were to come in the next day with a bigger bag of cash, then Minari would click his heels and dispose of her instead.

The woman dabbed her eyes with her handkerchief and looked up.

"Couldn't you just reason with him? Killing just seems so . . ."

Minari stared at her as if he'd just been hit in the head with a hammer. He was about two seconds away from flipping the table. But he couldn't blow it now. He took a deep breath.

"'Reason'? Listen, lady, what makes you think it's worth reasoning with him? Need another knock in the head to wake you up? Once a man starts hitting a woman, he doesn't stop. You can't fix him. We looked into him, into all of his gambling, drinking, womanizing. He could be reborn five hundred times and he'd still be a dog. You've handled it so far because you're young and your bones are strong, but as you get older and you start to get that—what's it called?—osteoporosis, after you get osteoporosis, what do you think'll happen when he hits you? If he beats you when your bones are riddled with holes, hot packs won't help. Nope, they sure won't."

Minari stopped mid-rant. His shill was glaring at him. She took the woman's hand.

"Sis, that's not the issue. You're way past the point of reasoning with him. Does that deadbeat have any money in the bank? Any retirement money coming? No! Reasoning with him won't make you rich and it won't make your life any better. Think about what he's put you through. You've suffered so much. He broke your body, and he broke your heart. It's not right! If you keep going like this, your life will be nothing but suffering until the day you die. Sis, you've got the guts for it! He's got *two* insurance policies. You'll get to kick back and relax for the rest of your life. And you don't even have to lift a finger. This gentleman here will take care of everything."

"Listen to your friend," Minari added. "Stop suffering and start enjoying life. This is your chance to make a fresh start."

The woman lowered her head and wept again. Minari's shill patted her on the back. The woman's quiet sobs grew louder. She beat her fist against her chest and pulled at her clothes. Minari let out a long sigh and got up from the couch to join Reseng, murmuring, "Work is a bitch these days."

Just then the woman bolted up from the couch.

"I can't do it! I just can't! No matter what he did, he's still a human being. . . ."

She picked up the shopping bag and bowed repeatedly to Minari. "I'm sorry, I'm sorry, I'm so sorry," she said in her nasal, tear-filled voice, and rushed out of the office. The shill got up in a panic and ran after her.

"I can't believe it! Stubborn idiot," Minari said, staring at Reseng.

Reseng turned back to his newspaper.

"I mean, if she's not going to pay me, why talk my ear off for two hours about her lousy husband? What does she think this is, a domestic violence counseling center? I can't friggin' believe it. Listen to her going on about how that deadbeat husband of hers is a 'human being.' What the fuck are we, then? Does she think they're the only 'human beings' with problems? Goddammit. Can't trust anyone these days."

Minari kicked the wastebasket. Then he sat on the couch and smoked another cigarette. He had nearly finished it when his phone rang. It was the shill.

"Bitch, I thought you said she was ready to sign! How'd you screw it up so bad? You need to be more thorough. . . . What? Are you kidding? . . . Crazy bitch. She didn't seem too worried about money a minute ago. . . . She'll sign if we lower the price? . . . By how much? Son of a . . . What does she think this is, a farmer's market? Does she think killing someone is a game? Just make sure she keeps her mouth shut. Tell her if she talks, we'll kill a bunch of people or whatever."

He hung up. The office grew quiet. He lit another cigarette and slowly sized Reseng up. Reseng put away his newspaper and looked at Minari. Minari stubbed out his cigarette and stood.

"Man, it is tough trying to nail down a job. But what brings Your Majesty to this humble office?"

"Being shut up in the library makes me forget what it's like out here in the real world," Reseng said with a smile. "I thought I'd come and find out what's happening and get some career advice from you."

Minari's face darkened.

"Well, gosh, what sort of advice would I have to offer the great Reseng? I'm struggling just to make ends meet." He pretended to look at his watch. "Actually, to be honest, this isn't a good time for me. I'm supposed to be somewhere."

"Busy, I see. Well then, I'll just ask a few simple questions."

"Sure," Minari said hesitantly. "I hope I can answer them."

"Was there a meeting?"

"What kind of meeting? You mean like a neighbourhood meeting?" Minari joked, feigning nonchalance. But it was obvious the question had caught him off guard.

Reseng looked at him coolly.

"I hear there are a lot of meetings these days. For example, meetings with Hanja but not with Old Raccoon. I want to know if anything important has been said at them."

"There was no meeting. You know those only take place at the library."

"Really? Not a single one?" He narrowed his eyes at Minari.

"If there was, I don't know about it. Why would Hanja summon me? All I do is make a living patting old ladies on the back. He doesn't even see me as human. I'm just—"

Minari stared as Reseng took out a knife and set it on the table. Chu's handkerchief was still knotted around the handle.

"This was Chu's knife. I never understood before why Chu used a kitchen knife. But now that I've tried it out, I can see why."

Minari's gaze shifted back and forth between Reseng and the knife. Was Reseng bluffing, or was he really going to stab him? Reseng could hear the gears shifting inside Minari's head.

Minari forced a smile. "C'mon, this isn't like you."

"No? Then what am I like?" Reseng looked him straight in the eye.

Minari turned away. "You know, it's not news that Hanja's going after Old Raccoon."

"That's not what I asked," Reseng said. "Give me specifics."

"Like I said, why would Hanja tell me anything? Makes no sense."

"Hanja likes you. You never say no to rotten meat."

Minari clenched his teeth. His pride was hurt. He took out another cigarette. His hand shook as he put it between his lips.

He tried to light it but gave up. "Did Old Raccoon send you to kill me because I'm one of Hanja's dogs?"

Reseng stared back at him without responding.

"Well, that hurts my feelings, it really does. Tell Old Raccoon that for me. Tell him he's gone too far this time. He's got me all wrong. I'm not like that. Since when've I ever been that underhanded?"

Minari tried to read Reseng's face, but Reseng was giving nothing away. Minari started chattering away again.

"To tell you the truth, a lot of people have been complaining. How many years has it been now since the library had work for us? Old Raccoon can act like a saint all he wants and pretend to survive on grass and dew, but the rest of us can't. Even when there's no work, we still have to put something in our kids' pockets every month, and pay off the cops, and give a cut of our commissions to brokers and to the men upstairs, which leaves us with barely enough to buy a packet of instant noodles. I'm not eating rotten meat, I'm eating shit! And yet Old Raccoon just keeps a tight hold on that client list of his and won't release the goods."

The look on Minari's face said he wanted Reseng to agree with him, but Reseng didn't budge.

"Do you know how much better things would be right now if Old Raccoon gave up just a few of his big clients? But that stubborn old man refuses. So, of course, the guys bitch about it. Look how hard it is to make ends meet these days. The complaints add up. Of course they do. The moment everyone gets together, all they do is bitch about Old Raccoon. But not me! I'm on Old Raccoon's side. I tell them it's not right to hold a grudge against him just because times are tough, and I remind them of the good he did for us in the past. I tell them there are ups and downs in every life, and we just have to tough it out. I'm serious! Ask anyone! I'm the only one here who takes Old Raccoon's side. Tell me the truth—did anyone else from the market bring Old Raccoon a gift over the holidays? No one, right? I, Minari Pak, was the only one. And I didn't take just any old gift—no, I gave him jukbang anchovies that I purchased myself at the department store. Jukbang anchovies! From Namhae's signature collection!"

The rant seemed to calm Minari's nerves a little. He finally managed to light his cigarette and let out a long cloud of smoke.

"I'll ask another question," Reseng said calmly. "Did Hanja set a date?"

Minari looked at him, dumbfounded. "I'll go crazy trying to talk to you. You still don't get me. Just because I make a living stabbing old ladies in the back doesn't mean I would betray my elders." He shook his head.

A flicker of a smile crossed Reseng's face. He tapped the knife. Minari stared at the tips of Reseng's fingers.

"Would you like to go to Bear's today?" Reseng asked.

"I, Minari Pak, have survived in the meat market for thirty years," he declared, abruptly raising his voice. "I've been through hell and high water. That little kitchen knife of yours is a joke. I'm Minari Pak, dammit!"

He raised a shaking hand to take a drag on his cigarette. Instantly, Reseng picked up the knife and in one swift move sliced off Minari's fingers. The forefinger and middle finger sailed through the air, the cigarette still between them, and landed with a plop on the desk. Minari stared at his right hand then turned to look at his two fingers oozing blood, smoke still rising from the cigarette. As Reseng raised an eyebrow, Minari blanched and took a step back. Reseng calmly set the knife down.

"I'll ask you one last time. Did Hanja set a date?"

Minari's shirt was turning red with blood. He stared half-dazed at the blood pouring out of his hand and looked up at Reseng, who plucked the cigarette from between the severed fingers and stubbed it out in the ashtray before tilting his head to the left to show Minari he was waiting for an answer.

"What the fuck!" Minari started to cry. "What'd you do that for? Fuck, can't we just talk like civilized people? What'd you cut my fingers off for?"

Reseng picked up the knife again.

"Hanja's planning something big, that's all I know, I swear," Minari babbled.

Reseng set the knife down and tapped the handle twice. "What's he planning?" he asked, one eyebrow raised again.

"I'm not sure. I think it's something with the government. The presidential election's coming up, you know."

Reseng frowned to show that wasn't enough.

"I took care of a few small chores for him, but that's it. I'm not the only one. The others are all in on it. But I don't know what it has to do with the library or if he's planning to double-cross Old Raccoon. I swear. I'm telling you, all I did was take out a few old guys who would've died soon anyway."

After rattling this off, Minari grabbed his right hand with his left and grimaced.

"Am I on the list, too?" Reseng asked.

"How would I know?" Minari looked genuinely frustrated. "C'mon, think about it. Why would Hanja share that info with a jerk like me?" His face turned tearful.

Reseng thought it over for a second and picked up the knife. Frightened, Minari scuttled back toward the wall. Reseng grabbed some tissues from the desk and wiped the blade clean. Then he slid the knife back into its leather sheath and put it in his jacket pocket. Minari kept a close eye on him before wrapping his hand in a handkerchief. He started to reach for the fingers lying on his desk but stopped and looked at Reseng, who stared at him for a moment and began to say something, but instead turned to leave. As he walked out the door, he heard Minari bustling around behind him and muttering to himself.

"The fuck just happened? Jesus Christ, what the fuck just happened?"

Reseng was halfway down the wooden stairs when the older woman with the perm who'd run out earlier started coming up the stairs with Minari's shill. When she saw Reseng, she hurriedly covered her face and turned and ran back down. The shill watched her go with a look of irritation.

"That phony. She acts so innocent. As if she isn't a total slut." She looked at Reseng. "Leaving already? You should stay. Hang out with me a little longer . . ."

"I've enjoyed myself for long enough," Reseng said with a smile.

"I can't wait to work a job with *you* sometime, Reseng," she said, making eyes at him.

He gave an indifferent nod.

She glanced back at the bottom of the stairs and muttered, "Why isn't that idiot coming back?"

When Reseng stepped outside, the older woman was standing with her face toward the wall. The bruise glowed on her cheekbone, and scratch marks around her throat showed where she'd been roughed up. Reseng lit a cigarette. The woman glanced over at the sound of his lighter. He exhaled a cloud of smoke and said, "Lady, you'd better consider it. Your husband's never going to change."

The next time Reseng went to the Doghouse, the librarian's desk was still empty, but now the ON VACATION sign was gone. Also gone were the knitting basket that had always sat to her left, the nail polish bottles organized by color, and the dainty mini vanity. The stuffed animals—from Mickey Mouse and Winnie-the-Pooh to the stuffed panda and the maneki-neko—had all been cleared away. The only thing still on her desk was the plastic organizer with the labeled drawers. For no particular reason, Reseng swept his hand across the surface of the desk.

He heard a book fall from the second floor and went upstairs to check it out. Old Raccoon was standing on a ladder, dusting the shelves and tossing books to be discarded down to the first floor. It had been a long time since he'd seen Old Raccoon cleaning the library himself. Back when Reseng was very young, he had sometimes seen Old Raccoon at work, hobbling around the library with a bucket of water and a rag. He would climb a ladder and start at the very top of the shelves, wiping every corner with the damp rag, dusting every book before reshelving it. As he worked, his face, normally blank, would betray the faintest trace of joy. As if he'd returned to a time sixty years in the past, when he'd first started working there as a freshly minted librarian.

Reseng picked the books up from the floor and placed them on a cart. Old Raccoon glanced down at him.

"Are you throwing all of these away?" Reseng asked.

"They didn't stand the test of time."

Reseng looked at the path between the shelves. There were piles of discarded books all over the place, far more than usual. The normally packed shelves now looked sparse.

Old Raccoon came down from the ladder. With his sleeves rolled up to his elbows and the bucket of dirty water and a rag in his left hand, he looked happier and healthier than usual. But his body was leaning at a precarious angle under the weight of the bucket. Reseng reached for it, and Old Raccoon let him take it.

"Seems like Hanja has chosen a date," Reseng said.

"A date for what? Is he getting married?" Old Raccoon joked.

"We should get to him first."

Old Raccoon turned to look at him and said nothing for a moment. Then he grinned. " 'We'?" He tried to give Reseng a look of pity, but his expression was closer to regret and melancholy.

"If we kill Hanja, some other villain will take his place. Will it be you?" Old Raccoon said with a faint smile.

He headed toward a round table and two chairs set between the bookshelves. After wiping down the table, he beckoned Reseng, who joined him and set the bucket on the floor. Old Raccoon offered him a cigarette. Reseng politely declined. Old Raccoon offered it to him again. Reseng hesitated before taking it. Old Raccoon lit Reseng's cigarette first and then his own. He took his time smoking, gazing out the windows in silence.

Dust motes drifted leisurely in the beams of sunlight coming down through the slatted second-floor windows. As a boy, Reseng used to sit in the western corner and watch the dust moving around in the striped light. Even the slightest noise would set the dust in motion. He would watch as the smoke from his cigarette rose to the ceiling like a cirrocumulus cloud, right past Old Raccoon's NO SMOKING sign, and mingled with the dust. He would close the book he was reading and spend hours watching the shapes created by the dust motes and cigarette smoke and light particles colliding with one another, and he'd murmur to himself, "Dust is the true master of this library."

Old Raccoon's eyes were still turned to the western bank of windows as he said, "The oldest human skull in existence has a hole in it from a spear. Prostitution is a much older profession than farming. The first son in the Bible was also a murderer. For thousands of years, human achievements were only possible through war—including civilization, art, religion, and even peace. Do you know what that means? About the human race? It means that from the very beginning human beings have been plotting to kill one another in order to live. Either by killing their opponents or by leaching off the murderer. That's how human beings survive. Humanity has always endured this apoptosis, this programmed cell death. It's the true reality of our world. That's how we began, and it's how we've lived all this time. It's probably how we'll always live. Because no one knows how to stop it yet. And so, in the end, someone ends up playing the role of pimp, prostitute, or hired killer. Funnily enough, that's what has to happen to keep the wheels turning."

Old Raccoon finished his speech and tossed his cigarette into the water bucket.

"What does that have to do with killing Hanja?" Reseng asked. "If his chair is empty, someone else will just take his place."

"The best scenario is for whoever is well suited to sit in the villain's chair to sit in that chair. And Hanja is definitely a wiser villain than I am."

Reseng's eyes widened. "You're just going to take it lying down?"

"What's one dead cripple whose luck ran out? Getting rid of Hanja won't change anything."

Old Raccoon picked up the dust rag and reached down for the

water bucket next to Reseng's feet. Reseng hurried to grab the bucket handle, but Old Raccoon gently tapped the back of his hand. Reseng let go. Old Raccoon picked up the bucket and slowly hobbled toward the bathroom. From behind, he looked as if he were wobbling along a tightrope.

MITO

She was working at a convenience store. After greeting customers with an overly loud "Welcome!" she hit them with a bubbly "Help you find something?" or butted in with a nosy "Ooh, I buy these cookies, too!" Most customers ignored her. But she laughed anyway, indifferent, and kept tossing jokes at them while clacking away at the register, picking up items from the counter with an exaggerated sweep of her arm. When there were no customers, she chattered nonstop on the shop telephone, or cleaned the shelves and reorganized the already perfectly arranged items. Chatting or cleaning, cleaning or chatting. She was like a child with an attention-deficit disorder.

"You're sure she made the bomb?" Reseng asked in disbelief.

"Three of the components were shipped to her," Jeongan, the tracker, said. "So that's pretty much a definite. I mean, what's she going to do? Buy explosives to put on her own fireworks show? And black market explosives at that?"

"I wouldn't put it past *that* woman."

"You got a point. She does look like she'd put on her own fireworks show."

Reseng took out a pill bottle and swallowed an aspirin. He got headaches every time he was out in the city. The streetlight changed and a pizza-delivery boy made an illegal U-turn. The left shoelace of a man in a suit, who was reading a newspaper while waiting for the pedestrian lights to change, was untied. That untied shoelace unnerved Reseng. The lights changed again, and a line of cars made a legal left turn. The pizza-delivery guy drove his scooter down the middle of the crowded footpath as if he were performing a circus trick, then screeched to a stop. The lights changed again and the man looking at the newspaper started to cross, oblivious of the shoelace dragging behind him. These sorts of things grated on Reseng. He blamed his headaches on the overload of useless information. Survival required having long, sensitive feelers, but those sensitive feelers couldn't distinguish between necessary and unnecessary input. Eventually, his overly long feelers, and the anxiety quivering at the tips of them, would be the end of him.

"What's her deal? Is she a device maker?" Reseng asked.

"It's hard to tell. That doesn't seem to be her specialty, and based on her build and the way she moves, she's not an assassin. But she couldn't possibly be a plotter. I don't have a handle on her yet."

"Then what *do* you know?"

"Hey, don't get bitchy at me," Jeongan grumbled. "I've been searching everywhere and getting zero sleep trying to find out who she is. Fact is, I'm the only reason we know this much. No one else would've gotten this far."

He held out a thick manila envelope.

"She is one disturbingly complex woman," Jeongan added. "I can't figure her out, but maybe you can."

Reseng opened the envelope. Inside were hundreds of photos and a file on the woman. He flipped through the photos. In front of her house, in an alley, on the bus, in a library, at a nightclub, at the pool, in a bakery, at a department store, in a café, at a fish market . . . The photos contained a perfect record of her movements over the past week. Reseng pulled one out and showed it to Jeongan.

"What's this?"

The woman was standing in a public square, holding a picket sign that said SAVE THE KOALAS!

Jeongan glanced at it and chuckled.

"Well?"

"There was an international conference on protecting koalas a while back, in front of the National Assembly Building."

"And?"

"That's a picture of her demonstrating. You know, 'Hey, fuckers, lay off the CO_2 already.' Something about how when the amount of carbon dioxide in the atmosphere increases, the nutritional value of eucalyptus leaves, which koalas like to eat, gets destroyed. She was so red in the face from screaming, I was worried she'd drop dead before the koalas do."

Reseng stared at Jeongan, incredulous.

"What a load of bullshit," he said. "She sticks bombs in other people's toilets but doesn't want some stupid koalas to die? What am I? Worth less than a koala?"

"You think you're worth more than a koala?" Jeongan was unperturbed. "So now what? You going to kidnap her?"

Reseng took the kitchen knife in its leather sheath out of his pocket. He unsheathed it, examined the blade, and resheathed it.

Jeongan's jaw dropped. "You're going to stab her? In broad daylight? I don't care how freaked out you are, you can't do that."

"What'm I, a goon?"

"Then why the knife?"

"You know the saying: 'You can get much further with a kind word and a gun than you can with a kind word alone.'"

"Who said that?"

"Al Capone."

"I guess a kind word and a knife will also get you far."

"She started the conversation by planting a bomb in my toilet. I'm just responding in kind."

Reseng lit a cigarette. The woman was still on the phone. When a customer came in, she hurriedly hung up; when they left, she got right back on the phone. Who on earth could she be talking to? Reseng suddenly envied her for having someone who was willing to listen to her chatter for so long.

"What time does she finish?" Reseng asked.

"Three. An hour to go."

Reseng looked at his watch. He took a red ballpoint pen from his pocket and started going over the woman's file. Clearly bored, Jeongan tapped on his saucer with a spoon. Reseng furrowed his brow and stared at the spoon as it struck the saucer and rattled the coffee cup.

"Knock it off, would you."

"Jeez, so sensitive . . . That's life, man. You can't escape noise,"

Jeongan grumbled, and threw his spoon onto the table. It clattered loudly against the saucer. Reseng glared at him. The waitress came out of the shop and walked over to where they were sitting on the terrace.

"Did you need something?"

"Why? You got something we can use?" Jeongan sneered.

The waitress turned pink. She was wearing a black bartender-style vest with a white blouse underneath and a tight-fitting black skirt.

"Would you like some more coffee?" she asked, trying to hide her embarrassment.

"That'd be great!" Jeongan said, laughing nonsensically.

As she took their coffee cups and walked away, Jeongan turned to stare at her.

"She's pretty hot."

"Looks like you're having a relapse of playeritis. What happened to that last girl?"

"Who?"

"The one who talked through her nose."

Jeongan frowned in thought. "Oh! I remember. Yeah, she's old news. You may as well be talking about the Stone Age."

"If three months ago was the Stone Age, then what era is this? The Neolithic? How come you never last more than a month with anyone?"

"That one wasn't my fault. When she kissed me, her nose ran. She got snot all over me." Jeongan made a face, as if genuinely aggrieved.

Reseng gave him a pitying look and went back to the woman's file. "If you continue to treat nice girls like shit, you'll end up alone." Reseng kept his eyes on the file as he spoke. "You're not getting any younger. At some point, you have to stop poking your stick around in the dirt and choose a spot to dig a well."

"Who cares where you poke as long as it's wet? Besides, what's the point? What'm I, digging for oil?"

Reseng underlined a few significant items in red. As he flipped through the file, he shook his head, trying to piece it all together, occasionally glancing up at the woman behind the register. While Reseng silently marked up the file, Jeongan kept grumbling.

"Who said a short relationship means it isn't serious? I've loved every woman I've dated. I mean it. But fate is harsh, man. When I think about it, the path my love life has taken has been steep and treacherous. But how would you know how I feel? You've never sunk into the quagmire of love. You haven't had your heart sliced in two by the razor-sharp blade of a breakup. You don't know what I've been through! You don't know the aching, hungry heart of a man condemned to search for new love to heal the wounds of old love, the painful memories that refuse to go away no matter how hard you drink or pound your chest or—"

"Is she a doctor?" Reseng asked, interrupting.

"Huh? How many times do I have to tell you? The girl I'm dating now is a nurse."

Reseng gave him a dirty look and gestured toward the register with his chin. Jeongan turned to stare.

"Oh, right. Yeah, *she's* a doctor."

"She doesn't look like one. But shouldn't she be working in a hospital? What the hell is a doctor doing at a convenience store?"

"She's actually never worked in a hospital. She was at some sort of lab, but she left a while back."

"Why?"

"I have no idea. How would I know what some messed-up chick is thinking?"

"I heard a lot of plotters are doctors. Do you think she could be one?"

"As far as I know, none of the plotters is that young. It's mostly old guys. The youngest would be, like, in his late forties? Besides, I've never seen or heard of any female plotters."

"As far as you know? How do you know any of this?"

"What, like you and I are the same? Our professional levels are very different. Mine is a high-level job dealing with information. You're a hooligan who pokes at people with sashimi knives. If this were the Joseon dynasty, a lowly butcher like you wouldn't dare hold your head up straight and look me in the eye. If you did, your corpse would be wrapped in a straw mat and left for the vultures to dispose of. You should be eternally grateful and consider it an honor that I deign to be friends with the likes of you. But instead. all you do is pick on me."

"Thanks for being my friend," Reseng scoffed.

Jeongan preened as he lit a cigarette.

Jeongan's father had been a tracker. Before that, he was a career soldier. He'd come back from Vietnam as a much-decorated officer, but he turned out to be pretty lousy at tracking. The funny thing, too, was that he became a tracker only after chasing his runaway wife all over the world. Jeongan's mother had knocked his father out by giving him a beer laced with sleeping pills and then ran off with every last won he'd earned in exchange for risking his life in Vietnam.

"Classy lady, my mother, huh? Abandoned her husband and son for true love. When you're in love, you don't count the cost. Love is all that matters to me—maybe I inherited it from my mother. . . ."

Jeongan's father swore that once he caught up with her, he would tear her and her lover limb from limb and then kill himself. He scoured every inch of the country and then searched abroad, chasing rumors, a packet of cyanide and a knife tucked into his shirt. After five years, he finally found her. She was managing a successful laundry business in the Philippines with the man she'd run away with. But Jeongan's father took one look at her and came home. He did not stab his wife or her lover. He didn't so much as touch the knife that he'd carried next to his heart for five years. Nor did he commit suicide by swallowing cyanide, or even approach the woman he'd spent so long searching for. He did not ask "How could you do this to me?" Jeongan's father merely watched from a distance as Jeongan's mother and her new man hung freshly washed bedsheets out to dry. Then he returned home.

"One day my old man got drunk and explained it to me. He said it was the first time he'd ever seen her look that happy."

Of course there could have been a different reason. Even the most extreme hatred, vengefulness, and anger will eventually, like everything else in the universe, dissolve and fade to nothing. Once, when Jeongan had gone to the Philippines for a job, Reseng asked if he'd met his mother there. Jeongan had given him a forlorn look.

"What's the point?" he'd said. "After all the trouble she went to so she could be happy, why would I butt in and ruin it for her? Whoever we are, we all have to fight our own battles for happiness."

Jeongan's father was only a third-rate tracker, but Jeongan was among the best. He could find any target—anyone at all, assuming they were still alive somewhere on Earth and not on Mars—usually in less than two weeks. But as gifted as he was at finding people, Jeongan was even better at tailing them. In the plotting world, people like him were called "shadows." They followed their targets without being spotted, took pictures, calculated their every movement, and passed that information along to a plotter. Just as the name implied, Jeongan could follow right on his targets' heels all day and never get caught. When Reseng asked him what his secret was, Jeongan had replied, "Being ordinary. No one ever remembers ordinary things."

According to Jeongan, what you needed to be an excellent shadow wasn't agility, skill at camouflage and subterfuge, or fancy disguises. And it wasn't just about being invisible. What really mattered was being someone whom others didn't need to remember, or who had nothing about them worth remembering in the first place.

"To do that, you first have to understand what ordinary means. You have to become the essence of ordinariness. People don't pay attention to things that are ordinary, and even if they do, they quickly forget. But becoming someone unmemorable is really difficult. Blurring your presence. Moving as lightly and indistinctly as vapor until you gradually fade away. Letting people brush right past you, like you're not even there, like you're the air itself. Turning yourself into that person is extremely difficult."

"Hmm," Reseng had said with a nod. "That sounds impossible."

"When you think about it, becoming ordinary is just as difficult as becoming special. I'm constantly thinking about which things are ordinary. Is it being of average height? Having an average face? Behaving in an average way? Having an average personality or job? No, it's not that simple. There is no such thing as an average life.

Whether brilliant or mediocre, everyone's unique. Which is why it's so complicated to love in an ordinary way, be nice in an ordinary way, meet and leave people in an ordinary way. Plus, in that sort of life there is no love, no hate, no betrayal, no hurt, and no memories. It's dry and flavorless, colorless and odorless. But, guess what, I like that kind of life. I can't stand things that are too heavy. That's why I'm learning how to keep people from remembering me. It's tricky. It's not in any book, and no one teaches it. Everyone wants to live a life that makes them special, that makes others remember them. The ordinariness that I'm after is a life that no one remembers. I want a forgotten life. That's what I'm working toward."

Reseng had liked the sound of that. It was why they'd become friends. Jeongan had grown up tagging along with his father, studying in spare moments, and had graduated from high school, gone to university, and majored in geology. Not because his grades weren't good enough to get him into law or economics—geology had been his first choice. He said he chose that major because, whenever he got bored while traveling with his father, he used to suck on small rocks like they were candy, to learn their different flavors.

"Rocks have flavors?"

"Of course. Granite and gneiss are as different as plums and lemons."

"You mean you majored in geology so you could learn more about how rocks taste?"

"In a manner of speaking, yes, but I probably should have studied gastronomy instead."

Reseng couldn't imagine basing a life decision on something so stupid. But Jeongan, the born optimist, didn't seem to care. Jeongan had rolled with the punches in college, maintained perfect attendance, and received his diploma. Though, in keeping with his particular set of skills, none of his classmates remembered him.

Jeongan always had a girlfriend. And his girlfriends changed very frequently. A love life like his would have been a full-time job for any normal person.

"How is it that every girl likes you?" Reseng asked.

"It's not that. They don't actually like me. No girl can love a man who doesn't exist."

"Yeah, right. Look how many girls you've dated."

"They're just lonely. It's a phase they're in. And they need a man to keep them company during it. They could have picked a tree or a houseplant. You know that's my specialty—being as quiet as a houseplant," Jeongan said with a smile.

Every time Reseng saw Jeongan, he thought about his pursuit of ordinariness. It was a very unusual ordinariness. Like a face you'd know anywhere and yet had never seen before. Jeongan's face was reaching the level of ordinariness he was after: You'd feel sure you'd met him somewhere, something about him was so familiar and approachable. And yet he was so ordinary that it was impossible to find the right words to describe him. Reseng imagined that the security and ease women sensed in Jeongan were of a piece with his ordinariness. Which might have been why Jeongan and the women who went for him found it so easy to date, and so easy to break up.

Reseng checked his watch: 2:40 p.m. The woman was still talking on the phone. He turned back to the file.

"Is Mito her real name?" Reseng asked.

"Looks like it. Her younger sister's name is Misa."

"Mito and Misa? As in soil and sand? Their father must have a weird sense of humor."

Reseng held out a photocopy of a newspaper article to Jeongan. It was about a family who had been in a car accident. "What's this doing here?"

Jeongan took the photocopy. "There was a car accident twenty years ago. Her parents were in the front seat. They died instantly. She and her younger sister were in the back. They survived, but her sister's spine was badly injured and she ended up paralyzed from the waist down. The father was driving—it says here the cause of the accident was speeding while under the influence. Based on the tire marks, he was going over one hundred and fifty kph."

"Driving drunk, and at that speed, with his beloved daughters and wife in the car?"

Reseng scanned the article again. The car had been found scorched and totaled at the bottom of an eight-meter-high cliff, near a quiet country town, on a warm day in May. The family had been enjoying a rare day out. There was no reason for the father to have been driving that fast while drunk. It definitely smacked of a plot. And a very hackneyed one, at that. Even worse, the whole thing was sloppy. Why go after the entire family? If the woman's father was the target, they could have taken him out by himself, cleanly.

"What did her father do?"

"High-ranking government official. There's something fishy about him, but I've been too busy chasing after her to look into it."

"Even if a plotter was behind the car accident, why the fuck is she coming after me? She was eleven when that happened. I was barely twelve!" Reseng was suddenly annoyed.

"What are you getting mad at me for? Just go over to her and calmly explain that you were twelve years old at the time. And keep your knife out, you know, to keep things amicable."

Reseng checked the time again: 2:55 p.m. She would leave work any minute now. He put the photos and file back into the envelope, stood up, and straightened his clothes. He could feel the weight of Chu's knife in the inner pocket of his leather jacket. He retied and tightened his shoelaces so he'd be ready to follow her the moment she came out. He could see her laughing inside the shop.

But at the stroke of three, she was still behind the counter. Not only did she not clock out, she was still giggling and chattering into the damn phone ten minutes later. A young woman who looked like a part-timer went into the convenience store, but the woman behind the counter showed no signs of preparing to leave, even though it was already three-thirty by then. Reseng looked at Jeongan.

"I thought you said she got off at three."

"She must've changed her work schedule," Jeongan said, scratching his head. "Every day for the past week, she's left at exactly three. She's just trying to make me look bad."

Things get dicey whenever a target suddenly changes their pattern. It's irritating and nerve-rattling. Because that's when assassins make mistakes. Either the target changes their pattern or the assassin changes his. Both scenarios end poorly. You make mistakes; you leave behind fatal evidence; the plot goes awry. And when plots go awry, assassins die. Why? When you retrace the events, it's always something very minor: a wallet left at home, running out of shampoo that morning, walking down an alley when a kid on a tricycle suddenly shoots out of nowhere.

The woman was still in the shop. No matter. There was no way Reseng was going to kill anyone today. But his heart was racing all the same. Anxiety was running through his nerve endings. She should have come out at 3:00 p.m. Reseng would have followed her. Jeongan would have slowly paced them in his car. A little way ahead was a quiet side street where there were no security cameras for two hundred meters. She always took that side street. Reseng would have tapped her on the shoulder. If Reseng had been her target, she would have recognized him at once. "Shall we go somewhere quiet to talk?" If she'd agreed, that would have been the end of it. No need for long explanations or threatening words, no need for his knife.

Reseng and Jeongan waited another thirty minutes in silence. At 4:00 p.m, Reseng put on his black sunglasses and stomped over to the shop.

"Hey, wait!" Jeongan yelled. "You can't just storm into a convenience store with your knife out. Those places are full of security cameras!"

"Welcome!"

The woman covered the phone with one hand and greeted Reseng loudly. Her voice was cheerful. Reseng stood just inside the door and stared at her. But she turned away, showing no sign of recognizing him, and went right back to her phone call. Everyone in the shop could hear it.

"Oh, you know that song that goes '*Oops! I'm in love with my best friend's girl. What do I do?*' . . . Yeah, that one! He was singing it like he was about to cry! And he kept shaking the tambourine even though it's a ballad! I almost died laughing. . . . Shut up! As if I'd do a duet with that guy! But then he gets to the second part of the song and starts blubbering for real, like his friend's girlfriend has been whacked in the head with a hammer. He's a big guy, too. . . . I swear. . . . What *could* I do? I put my arm around him and patted him on the shoulder. I felt like I had to. He put his head on my chest and tried to act like he was still crying, but I saw the way he looked at my miniskirt. He actually thought that was going to get me in the mood. I was like, Are you kidding me? . . . Well, you know, I couldn't *not* kiss him. But that wasn't enough for this guy. . . . No, it's not that I didn't want to. I just didn't want him to get the wrong idea about me. We'd just started dating. It'd be one thing if we'd gone back to a hotel. But in a karaoke room? The guy was clueless. . . . No, no, he's not that bad. I mean, there's something cute about him, and he seems all right. . . . Exactly. It's important to start off on the right foot. Once they get the wrong idea, there's no going back."

Reseng was still standing in front of the door, staring at her. She glanced over at him. He took off his sunglasses. "Hold on. Don't hang up." She covered the phone again and cocked her head at Reseng.

"Sir, can I help you find something?" she asked in a lilting voice.

Her face bore no hint of fear or suspicion. Plotters always knew their targets' faces. Just as assassins will recognize their targets anywhere. As soon as the plot is issued, you can't help staring at your target's photo every free minute. It's the nerves. The target's face stays with you and continues to float around inside your head for weeks, even after you've killed the person. You see people on the street who look like that person and you nearly jump out of your skin. You have recurring nightmares of running into whoever it was. This woman was no plotter. She was no assassin, either. She was nothing. Who the hell was she? Had Jeongan made a mistake?

"Sir, can I help you?" she asked again.

"What? Oh. Candy bars! Where can I find the candy bars?" Reseng's mouth moved of its own accord.

"Candy bars? Over there to the left, second shelf from the top." Her voice was still friendly.

Why had he said candy bars? He didn't even like candy bars. Reseng went to the shelf and grabbed two. He was thirsty, so he also grabbed a sports drink from the fridge. As he was closing the fridge door, he heard her say into the phone, "Hey, let me call you back. I'll fill you in on the details in person." She'd been on the phone for hours. What details could she possibly have left out? It was crazy. He would never understand women. He placed the candy bars and the sports drink next to the register.

"Big candy bar fan, huh?" she asked.

Reseng gave her a curt nod. He was in no mood for chitchat.

"I like candy bars, too, but I see you're buying two Snickers. Have you tried Hot Break?"

"What?" Reseng stared at her.

"Hot Break. Snickers is made for the American palate, but Hot Break is made for ours, and it doesn't stick to your teeth, either. It offers very high performance for its price, and it's only half the cost of a Snickers, though, of course, they've had to keep shrinking it so they can keep the price the same as it was ten years ago. That's the sad truth, but with everything else getting more and more expensive, I guess that's not so bad. So what do you think? Would you like to exchange one of your Snickers for a Hot Break?"

The woman spoke so fast that Reseng wasn't sure what she'd just said. He gathered that she'd told him she liked Hot Break better. But so what? Who gave a shit whether she liked Hot Break or not, or whether it was half the price of a Snickers or not? Just shut up and take the money.

"How much is this?" he asked, pointing at the Snickers.

"A thousand won. Hot Break is only five hundred won." She held up five fingers.

She gave him a playful smile. Reseng put one of the Snickers back and grabbed a Hot Break. Eager to get it over with, he opened his wallet.

"You won't regret it." The woman held her fist up in the air. "Hot Break!"

"Thank you very much."

"Ha-ha! Ha-ha! No thanks necessary! It's important to share valuable information with your fellow countrymen." She laughed heartily, as if they'd just met in the middle of the Siberian wilderness.

When Reseng left the convenience store, Jeongan was parked in front with the engine running. He looked worried. Reseng opened the door and got in.

"What happened?" Jeongan asked impatiently.

Reseng threw the Hot Break at his face. It bounced off Jeongan's forehead and fell in his lap.

"What's this?"

"What's it look like? It's a candy bar. It'll fill you with brotherly love."

Jeongan frowned and ripped open the wrapper.

"You marched in there like you were going to take down a bull with a kitchen knife, but all you came back with was one candy bar?"

"Two, actually." Reseng opened the sports drink and took a swig. "She's no plotter. Definitely not an assassin, either. She didn't recognize me."

"She didn't?" Jeongan looked incredulous.

Reseng nodded.

Jeongan took out the ceramic bomb casing and examined it.

"We know this was made by an amateur, which means she can't be an expert device maker, either. So who is she?"

"Are you *sure* it was her?" Reseng asked skeptically.

"What'm I, a rookie? I told you, she definitely ordered three of the parts."

Reseng stared at the convenience store. The woman was talking to the younger employee who'd come for the shift change. After a moment, the younger employee looked at her watch, bowed several times to the woman, and left.

"Looks like she's taking that girl's shift," Reseng said. "I swear, she's messing with everyone's schedules today."

"Looks that way, doesn't it? Typical. Why can't people stick to what they're supposed to do? Why do they have to mess up other people's plans? That's why our country's so backward! You need more than freeways and skyscrapers to be a developed country. You have to develop the right mind-set first, dammit!"

"What does *any* of this have to do with being a developed country?" Reseng unwrapped his Snickers and took a bite.

Jeongan's eyes widened. "Hey, how come your bar is different from mine?"

"Mine was made in the USA. Yours was made here. Mine was a thousand won. Yours was five hundred."

"Son of a . . ." Jeongan pouted. "Why'd you buy me the cheap one? You know I prefer American stuff."

Reseng handed him his candy bar. Jeongan grinned like a child as they swapped.

"Dig deeper into her background. Her job, her parents, her younger sister, the lab where she used to work, her bank transactions, anything and everything you can find."

"What? You expect me to do all that in exchange for one lousy candy bar? And with what budget? My prices have gone up, man! There's a little thing called market value, you know."

"Your buddy's in peril, and here you are crowing about market value. . . ."

"Fine. I'll do it as long as you call me 'Elder Brother.' Because I am far too humane to abandon a little brother in danger. And, let's be real, I am two years older than you."

Reseng glared at him. When he didn't look away, Jeongan tapped him on the shoulder and gave him a look that said, Can't you take a joke?

"Please, Elder Brother," Reseng said, his voice flat.

Jeongan looked at him, feigning disgust.

"Holy shit, where's your pride? What a pushover! You really need to man up."

By the time he'd finishing buying cat food and cat snacks at the pet shop and was on his way home, it was nearly dark. Reseng checked his mailbox in the lobby. Bills and junk mail. He turned to go upstairs, but someone was sitting on the bottom step, slumped forward and half-asleep. One hand was wrapped in bandages; the other was holding a department store gift bag. Reseng leaned down to look at the man's face. It was Minari Pak. Reseng shook him by the shoulder. His eyes flew open and he looked around in bewilderment, then let out a big yawn and stood with a grunt.

"What're you doing here?" Reseng asked.

"I came to see you."

"You should've called first."

"I just figured I'd drop by."

"Let's go inside."

"No, no, I'm fine here."

Minari waved his bandaged hand and grimaced.

"How are your fingers?"

"They're okay. Got 'em reattached. Medical technology these days! I didn't think the doctors could do it, even though I ran straight to the hospital with my fingers, but what do you know, they stuck right back on. Like a lizard's tail growing back. Yeah . . . a lizard's tail."

Minari murmured the words *lizard's tail* again under his breath, evidently impressed by his own imagery. He turned his bandaged hand to show Reseng. Then he said, "Oh, yeah, this!" as if he'd nearly forgotten something important, and handed Reseng the bag.

"What is it?"

"Jukbang anchovies. I know how much you like beer. And there's no better snack for a cold beer than dried anchovies. I got them from the department store, just like the set I got Old Raccoon. From Namhae's signature collection! Very expensive!"

Minari looked flustered. Reseng raised an eyebrow. Why had Minari come all this way to bring him a gift?

"You're giving me a present after I cut your fingers off? I didn't even visit you in the hospital. Now I feel really bad."

"Oh, no, no. Don't feel like that. It's the rest of us who should be feeling bad for how we treated Old Raccoon. That wasn't right. In fact, he's the reason we're living as well as we are. I know how kind he's been to me. But little guys like us don't have it easy. Everyone's been tightening their belts down to the first notch, but it's still hard to make ends meet. We haven't forgotten our place or anything. It's just that life keeps closing in on us."

Minari took out a cigarette but struggled to work the lighter with his left hand. Reseng took out his own lighter and lit the cigarette for him. Minari took a deep drag and looked Reseng up and down.

"What did Old Raccoon say?"

"About what? My cutting off your fingers?"

"No, not that. About us going to work for Hanja. I figured Old Raccoon must know about it by now. Of course, we're all independent businessmen with our own gigs, so I can't exactly say that we're completely under Hanja's wing. Even so, I still feel bad about it."

"That's why you're here? To test the winds?"

"Not exactly," Minari said falteringly. "It's only part of the reason."

Minari stared out at the streetlight as he finished his cigarette. Every now and then, he looked like he was about to say something, but then he clammed up. After a long pause, he dropped his cigarette and stubbed it out under his shoe. There was something clownish about his stiffly ironed gray trousers and his shiny, polished red shoes. Minari glanced at Reseng and made a sad face.

"Lately the guys have all been talking about a war brewing between Hanja and the Doghouse. A real war, like in the old days. That'll get messy. Detectives and prosecutors will be crawling all over us and cracking down, while the plotters take out everyone just to save their own asses. Desperate assassins will be roaming around like wild dogs, picking fights with everyone for no reason. The few customers I have left will dry up. I'll be out of business. In the end, only the little guys like us are fucked. Reseng, I am too old to get caught up in this fight. Old Raccoon and Hanja are tough, ambitious. They'll do whatever they have to do to save their pride. But what about us in the middle? If we side with Hanja, we have to watch out for Old Raccoon. If we so much as gesture at the library, we have to watch out for Hanja. We're between a rock and a hard place. And, I tell you, I'm too old for this! I'm scared! You know I'm not the ambitious type. I'm just trying to get by."

"What's your point?"

"Hanja wants to see you. Just meet with him once."

Reseng narrowed his eyes. "And if I do?"

"You know you can't have two tigers on one mountain. Let's be honest; the library doesn't stand a chance against Hanja. It's not like the old days. If war breaks out, we're all dead. Old Raccoon? Definitely dead. You and me, too. And Hanja doesn't stand to gain anything from it, either. We did all the work to build our businesses, but because of this election, someone else will get the credit."

Reseng hurled the jukbang anchovy gift bag at Minari Pak's feet.

"You think a few lousy anchovies can make up for telling me to stab Old Raccoon in the back?"

Minari looked shocked as he scrambled to pick up the bag. "Don't you know how expensive these are?" he muttered. Pouting, he held the bag up to his ear and gave it a shake, stroking it as if handling an antique vase. Then he made the same sad face as before.

"I'm not telling you to sell out Old Raccoon. I'm just saying how things are. It's been a long time since the library had work for us. Businessmen don't wait around. You know that. There's no such thing as loyalty in our line of work. Old times? Favors? That doesn't go far. People always go where the money is. Old Raccoon is getting on in years and he never leaves the library, so he doesn't know how things are changing. If war breaks out, everyone will take Hanja's side. That's what it has come to. There won't be a fight. That's why you need to go and see Hanja. Because you're Old Raccoon's hands and feet. If the conversation goes well between you and Hanja, there'll be no need for war. Old Raccoon can quietly retire to the countryside and live out the rest of his life in peace. And we'll be able to grow our businesses in peace, as well. Everybody wins."

Reseng pictured the general in his mountain cottage, with his old dog, Santa. Someone must've said the same thing to him when he was stepping down: "Move to a quiet place in the country and enjoy your remaining years. It's a win-win all around." What did they mean by that? Growing flowers, planting potatoes, raising a dog, and choosing your final resting place? Basking in the warm afternoon sun, your eyelids the only part of you still moving, like you're some kind of aging, ailing elephant? Or moving into a nursing home, where the only thing to occupy your time is tedious chitchat with old people you have absolutely nothing in common with, or playing endless games of cards and stealing stones from the communal baduk board for your growing collection of useless things. Those days would repeat themselves ad nauseum until death finally came creeping into your room one night like an assassin.

Minari Pak was still holding out the anchovies. Reseng looked at the bag quivering awkwardly in his hand.

"Just take it," Minari said. "Signature collection."

"Give them to your wife. Or to Hanja. I don't care. What makes you think I could stomach those?"

"If you insist on being this stubborn, Hanja will have no choice but to eliminate you."

"Is that a threat?" Reseng glowered at Minari.

"Please don't make things difficult. This fight doesn't have to happen. I'm telling you this as someone twice your age: Kissing ass is better than being an ass."

Minari set the anchovies at Reseng's feet and slowly turned and walked out. Reseng stared down at the bag. All at once, he thought, Old Raccoon must be so lonely. The businessmen who used to take gifts to the library every holiday had all turned their backs on him. This was Hanja's world now. How much longer would Reseng live if he went to see him? Three years? Five? Maybe longer. Maybe he'd even live out his natural years if he got on his knees and started kissing ass like Minari Pak. Sure, nothing wrong with a little ass in your face. Not like honor and dignity had ever mattered to him.

Old Raccoon liked to joke that the only reason he'd brought Reseng home from the orphanage was so he'd have something to lean on when he walked. He said it to ruffle Reseng's feathers, but when Reseng thought about it, there was a certain truth to it. He'd been Old Raccoon's crutch ever since he was eleven. He fetched books from shelves, ran errands in the meat market, delivered letters from a faceless plotter who slipped him envelopes from behind a door. And after the death of Old Raccoon's longtime assassin, Trainer, Reseng did all the assassination work, as well. If Reseng were to turn his back on him now, Old Raccoon would be left to hobble along without a crutch.

"I guess that's not the worst thing that can happen to someone in this line of work," Reseng muttered.

When Trainer was killed, ten years ago, Old Raccoon did nothing. He kept quiet, despite the rumors that Hanja was behind it. Things were different then: Old Raccoon was still on top. And yet there was no retaliation, no punishment, no investigation. Old Raccoon didn't even get angry, even though Trainer had stood by him for three decades. He'd simply washed Trainer's body, with its multiple stab wounds from what had clearly been a vicious battle, and quietly cremated him in Bear's incinerator. It was a gloomy funeral: Reseng had been the only mourner with Old Raccoon, who had silently scattered Trainer's ashes from the top of a windswept hill.

"Aren't you going to do something about it?" Reseng had asked.

"That's how it is for assassins. You can't knock over the chessboard just because you lost a pawn."

That's how it is. Those were Old Raccoon's parting words for the man who'd stood by his side for thirty years.

Reseng had learned everything from Trainer—how to handle firearms, how to use a knife, how to build and defuse bombs, how to set up a booby trap, how to track and hunt prey, even how to throw a boomerang. After the Vietnam War, Trainer found work with a private military company abroad and traveled to war zones all over the world. He had a gentle face, which made it hard to believe his claim of having killed hundreds of people on the battlefield. And he loved housework. Despite his huge body, his hands were deceptively nimble. He made all his own equipment, everything he built was done with care and precision, and he was an excellent cook. He particularly enjoyed doing laundry. On sunny days, without fail, he would hand-wash all the sheets and curtains and hang them on the clothesline in the courtyard. With a cigarette dangling from his lips, his face a picture of contentment, he would watch the sheets billowing in the wind and say, "If only I could get my life that clean."

If only he *could* have scrubbed his life clean. He could've married a nice girl, raised kids, and led a peaceful family life, doing the cooking, cleaning, and laundering he so enjoyed. But unfortunately, life is not a set of sheets. You cannot scrub away your past, your memories, your mistakes, or your regrets. And so you die with them. Like Old Raccoon said, that's how it was for assassins.

Reseng picked up the anchovy gift set and went upstairs. When he opened the door, Desk and Lampshade came running to greet him, rubbing against his calves. Reseng filled their dishes with the chicken soup he'd bought them at the pet shop. The cats purred as they lapped up the soup. He patted their heads.

"Do you know how rough your alley-cat sisters have it? If I toss you out, you scaredy-cats won't last a week. It's hell out there."

The cat café was called Like Cats.

When Reseng sat down, Desk and Lampshade started meowing inside the cat carrier. He opened the latch. But they took one look at the dozens of other cats roaming around the café and refused to budge. The café owner brought him a cup of coffee.

"Ooh, look who's come to visit! Is that Desk and Lampshade?" she asked excitedly.

His cats were clearly happy to meet her. They purred and came right out of the carrier. All cats seemed to love this café owner instantly. What was her secret? After getting married, she'd started raising more than twenty cats at home. But as the number of cats increased, her husband couldn't stand it and told her she had to choose: him or the cats. And just like that, she divorced him and moved out. At gatherings of the cat café members, she would laugh and tell the story again: "Can you believe he asked me to choose? Ha!"

"You finally brought them, after all the times I've asked you to!" the café owner exclaimed as she played with Reseng's cats. "Is it a special occasion?"

Reseng took an envelope from his jacket pocket and handed it to her. Looking at him quizzically, she took out two one-million-won bank checks.

"I'd be really grateful if you would look after them for me," Reseng said. "It might be for a little while, or a very long while. It's also possible I might never come back to get them."

"Are you taking a trip somewhere far away? Are you going abroad?"

"It's not that far, but I'm not sure where this trip will end."

She nodded, as if she understood.

"We all have our dark spells now and then," she said, handing the envelope back to him. "I understand what you're going through, but this isn't necessary. I'll look after your cats anyway until you come back."

"Since you know what I'm going through, please take the money."

He lowered his head in a gesture of pleading. The envelope sat between them in the middle of the table. She looked at it and, after a long pause, nodded.

"When I was your age, I went very far away once, too. I went so far away, I didn't think I'd be able to get back. But when you do finally come back, you realize you weren't nearly as far away as you'd feared."

Reseng patted Desk and Lampshade, who nipped playfully at his hands. They already seemed at home there. He stood and said good-bye to the café owner.

"Good luck," she said.

"Thank you."

Reseng gave Desk and Lampshade one last pat and slowly walked out of Like Cats.

—

Reseng took a cab to the L. Life Insurance building in Gangnam. Hanja's offices were on the seventh, eighth, and ninth floors. Rumor had it that around seventeen different company addresses were registered there. As if it wasn't ironic enough that the country's top assassination provider was brazenly running his business in a building owned by an international life insurance company; the same assassination provider was also simultaneously managing a bodyguard firm and a security firm. But just as a vaccine company facing bankruptcy will ultimately survive *not* by making the world's greatest vaccine but, rather, the world's worst virus, so, too, did bodyguard and security firms need the world's most evil terrorists in order to prosper, not the greatest security experts. That was capitalism. Hanja understood how the world could curl around and bite its own tail like the uroboros serpent. And he knew how to translate that into business and extract the maximum revenue. There was no better business model than owning both the virus and the vaccine. With one hand you parceled out fear and instability, and with the other you guaranteed safety and peace. A business like that would never go under.

Reseng took the elevator to the seventh floor. Hanja's office was on the ninth floor, but to reach it, you had to get off on the seventh floor and pass through the type of metal detector you'd expect to find in an airport. As Reseng walked through, an alarm shrieked. A female employee in a black suit came up to him with a handheld metal detector. She greeted him politely and asked him to raise his arms. He did as he was asked. As soon as the handheld detector came near him, it started beeping. He reached into his inner jacket pocket, pulled out Chu's Henckels in its leather sheath, and placed it in a basket. She looked at him in shock.

"I was cooking just before I left. Must've forgotten to put it away first. I'm so damn absentminded," he said with a smile.

The flustered employee glanced back, and a husky security guard came over, a Taser and a tear-gas gun strapped to his belt.

"What seems to be the problem?"

He narrowed his eyes and looked Reseng up and down. The way his uniform squeezed his rolls of fat reminded Reseng of a pack of hot dogs. He had the build of a nightclub bouncer and his shoulders were tensed. Reseng almost felt sorry for him as he handed over Hanja's gold-embossed business card.

"Do you have an appointment?"

"No."

"Who shall I say is here?"

"Tell him I'm from the Doghouse."

After a brief wait, a woman came up to him and introduced herself as Hanja's secretary. She had a polished, intellectual look about her. She guided him to a separate elevator that served only the three floors leased to Hanja; they got off on the ninth floor and went into a room marked VIP LOUNGE.

As he sat down, the secretary asked in a businesslike voice, "Can I get you a drink? Tea, coffee, water? We also have alcohol if you prefer."

"No, thank you. I had something right before I came here. Is this room nonsmoking?"

He looked around. There were no ashtrays.

"According to the rules, yes. The entire building is a no-smoking zone."

Reseng frowned, and she smiled furtively. Her tone softened as she said, "Well, rules were made to be broken."

"In that case, would you mind bringing me an ashtray?"

"It'll be about thirty minutes before the boss can join you. Do you mind waiting?"

"No, that's fine," he said with a nod.

When the ashtray arrived, Reseng lit a cigarette and took a long look around the spacious room. In keeping with Hanja's preference for the immaculate, there were no decorations apart from a single picture on the wall. Reseng picked up the ashtray and moved to the window so he could look outside. All ten lanes of Teheran Boulevard were jammed with cars. It seemed strange to him: the luxurious digs of an assassination provider bang in the heart of the Republic of Korea. The fact that Hanja's office was on this street, with its sky-high rent, meant that the country's economic hub was desperate for contract killers.

Reseng was on his third cigarette when Hanja finally came in.

"Sorry to keep you waiting. You really should have called first."

Hanja's attempt at an expression of regret came off as more terrifying than apologetic. He took a seat on the couch as his secretary came back in.

"Don't you want anything? I'm having a drink. It's not every day I receive such a special guest."

Hanja sounded more buoyant than usual. His secretary looked at Reseng, who hesitated. This strange hospitality made him uncomfortable.

"Do you have Jack Daniel's?" Reseng asked the secretary.

She nodded.

"I'll have the same," Hanja said. "On the rocks."

After the secretary left, Hanja kept glancing nervously around the room, as if expecting someone else to be there. He was trying to pass it off as excitement from being in a good mood, but it wasn't working. Considering that they were on his turf, where he called the shots, who or what could possibly have been after him? Reseng was suddenly dying to know. The two of them sat in awkward silence until the secretary came back with their drinks.

"I'm really glad you're here. I was worried you wouldn't come."

Hanja raised his glass in a toast, but Reseng didn't reciprocate. Hanja looked at his lone glass held aloft and took an embarrassed sip.

"What're you after?" Reseng asked bluntly. "The Doghouse? Old Raccoon's life?"

Hanja leaned his head back and laughed.

"What would I want with a musty library full of secondhand books, or some decrepit old man's life, for that matter?"

"That's what everyone's saying."

"Damn those rumors."

Hanja raised his glass and took a sip, then said, "You know, Old Raccoon was the one who taught me never to kill anyone unless I was paid fairly. That's the sort of wisdom all contractors should carve into their brains. Honor, faith, friendship, loyalty, revenge, love, saving face—none of those reasons matter, because no decent contractor will kill someone unless there's profit to be made. So what sort of profit would be coming to me if I killed Old Raccoon? I mean, sure, some *good* would come of it. Fewer headaches, for one. But on the whole, when you crunch the numbers, there's nothing in it for me. Old Raccoon might wish that on me, but I'm not stupid."

"I don't care about your number crunching."

"You should care about it. Killing you would net me quite a profit. As would killing your mate Jeongan." Hanja drained his glass.

"I had no idea I was so valuable," Reseng said as he took a sip. The distinctive aroma of Jack Daniel's filled his sinuses.

Hanja sneered at him. "Don't get the wrong idea. You're not. You simply occupy a unique position."

"What about my position?"

"The big money is in politics. But the old geezers who pull those strings refuse to trust anyone but Old Raccoon. They have some sort of nostalgia for the library. Or maybe they don't trust anything that's less than a hundred years old. Either way, it's a joke. Since when does tradition matter to a contractor? But that's how old men are. They're suspicious and they hate change. It's frustrating, but what can you do? That's reality. So what I need is a dead Zhuge Liang."

Reseng gave him a quizzical look.

"In the Battle of Wuzhang Plains," Hanja explained. "After General Zhuge died, his army carved a wooden statue that looked just like him and used it to trick Sima Yi's army into thinking he was still alive, which scared them off. But a living Zhuge Liang is too much—there's no telling what he'll do. If Old Raccoon just stayed nice and quiet in that Doghouse of his, I wouldn't have any complaints. Since you and I grew up in the library, too, it makes sense for us to continue the old fart's legacy. And it's a nice little business. But the problem is that you're not letting him rest in peace."

"Rest . . . in peace." Reseng slowly echoed Hanja's choice of words.

"You're his hands and feet. And that drip Jeongan is his eyes and ears. Jeongan is always bringing the old man information—he's like a mother sparrow feeding worms to a baby sparrow—while you run around wiping his ass for him. I'll be honest. I was pretty annoyed with you for bringing the old general back in an urn."

"So?" Reseng glowered.

"'So?'" Hanja sneered. "So, killing Old Raccoon won't make for more business, but at the same time, I can't *not* finish what I started. What to do? It's really tragic, but I have to ax something. Sometimes, to keep the body alive, you have to chop off part of it. Like a hand, or a foot . . . or an ear."

"Is that why you killed Trainer?"

Hanja's face flushed. He was quiet for a moment, stroking his chin.

"Seems you still don't know the difference between what's okay to talk about and what isn't."

Hanja was about to say something more but stopped himself. He picked up the phone and asked his secretary to bring him another glass of whiskey. She came in, put down the new glass, and took away the empty one. Hanja took a sip.

"I know you have it in for me because of that. He was like a father to you and an older brother to me. I learned everything I know from Trainer, too. But the world is much more complicated than you think. We have to do what we can to survive in this incomprehensible place."

"I don't care what kind of world this is. What's the benefit of killing family members? So you can afford a fancy office?"

Hanja glared at him.

"Don't tell me you think we're actually family. Who's related? You and Old Raccoon? Me and Old Raccoon? That's a big fucking joke. You know as well as I do that we were just his crutches—to be used and then thrown away. You seem confused, so I'll try to make things clear for you: If you were knifed right now and got carted off to Bear's, Old Raccoon wouldn't even blink an eye. He'd simply find himself a new crutch. I learned that twenty years ago. But you, boy wonder, still don't get it."

Hanja took another sip. Reseng scowled at him. Hanja turned to the window. He looked annoyed; the conversation was apparently not going the way he'd hoped it would. The phone buzzed.

"All right. Tell him I'll be there in ten minutes."

He hung up. Reseng lit a cigarette. Hanja checked his watch.

"It's B., from the National Assembly. His idiot son is constantly in trouble, but the kid got what he deserved this time. He trapped a girl in his hotel room, tried to force his dick into her mouth, but she bit it. Sank her teeth in so hard, he said it was barely hanging on by the skin. Good for her." Hanja gave Reseng a mischievous look. "I'm guessing a dick is not as easy to reattach as fingers, huh? A few days ago, B. came to see me, crying about how his darling boy, the apple of his eye, the only son born to an only son of an only son, had his dick bitten off, and with it all hope of his carrying on the family name. He grabbed my hand and said I was the only one who could make things right. It was so embarrassing! Like you said, I built this fancy office right in the heart of Gangnam and I seem to be living well. But the truth is, what can I do? If I want to make ends meet, I have to help lick his wounds. If a national assemblyman of the Republic of Korea can air his dirty laundry in front of me, then how dare a lowly contractor like myself say, 'Oh, no, I could never stoop so low'? I'd be too afraid! My life is no different from everyone else's. That's why you should put away your pride and join me. You'll live, and your friend Jeongan will live, and, thankfully, I'll live, too. I'm not asking you to do much. Just stay at the library, but give me a call whenever work comes in."

Hanja's eyes were fixed on Reseng's. Reseng puffed on his cigarette and said nothing. Hanja's smile slowly disappeared and his face hardened.

"Election's right around the corner," he said. "This is a sensitive time. Everyone's running around trying to get their share. Lethal mistakes can happen. Did you know that the D Group had over twenty subsidiaries, but it took the government prosecutors less than six months to dismantle all of it? Their only crime was refusing to help fund a political party during the elections. If people like us make a mistake, we'll be dead and dismembered before we hit the ground. Just thinking about it makes my head hurt. So don't complicate things. I don't want to kill you, but if you keep resisting me, I'll have no choice."

"We still don't know who'll end up with a knife in the stomach," Reseng said weakly.

"You're right. We don't. But you can't be in this business if you're not prepared to get knifed at some point. Are *you* prepared?"

The phone rang again. "Be right there," Hanja said, and hung up. "I have to go. Behave yourself. And tell your friend Jeongan what I said."

"Did you put a bomb in my toilet?"

Reseng asked the question as Hanja was walking away. Hanja turned, a confused look on his face. After a second, he caught on and assumed a look of wounded pride.

"Do I look like I have time to be sticking my hand in your filthy toilet?"

Hanja shut the door behind him. Reseng sat down and finished his cigarette. His mind was filled with too many thoughts at once. He stubbed out the cigarette and took the elevator back down to the seventh floor. The woman in the black suit took Chu's Henckels out of its cubbyhole and gave it back to him. The pack of hot dogs stared at him and tried to look tough. As Reseng looked down at Chu's knife, a sense of shame settled over his shoulders. He put the knife in his pocket. Then he took the elevator the rest of the way down and rushed out of the building. He couldn't get away fast enough.

Reseng returned home. But Desk and Lampshade were no longer there to rub against his leg as he came in. He stood in the doorway for a moment and stared blankly around at his apartment. The only things missing were the two cats, and yet the whole place felt empty. He took off his shoes and went in. The empty cat dishes were sitting under the table. He stared at them for a moment and then opened the cabinet, took out the cat food, and filled the bowls to the top.

He decided to run a hot bath. Though he hadn't done much,

he felt exhausted, and his body ached as if he'd been beaten with a hammer. As he watched steam rise from the tub, he felt helpless, useless. As if he were a cog that had been spit out of a clock, a cog that had once been an integral working part, only to find itself now staring at the complex inner mechanism that kept right on ticking without it.

Every time Reseng came home from a kill, he was filled with inertia. He had no idea why. It wasn't guilt, nor was it displeasure or self-loathing. It was inertia, pure and simple. An overpowering sense that he could no longer be responsible for anyone, let alone himself. Everything seemed too hard—chatting and laughing with others, meeting women and going on dates, having a hobby, building a model boat, even cooking dinner. The only life he could manage was one of drinking can after can of beer until he was drunk, staring out the window through unfocused eyes, or lying in bed, staring at the patterns on the ceiling and wallpaper, until he couldn't take the hunger anymore and grabbed whatever he found in the fridge, before falling back to sleep. "It was only natural." What would be really strange, he thought, was if someone who earned their living by killing others felt revitalized by it.

As he lay in the hot bath and watched condensation form on the ceiling, Reseng pondered Hanja's, Old Raccoon's, and Minari Pak's math. Everyone had their own particular way of keeping accounts. Even the small-time businessmen of the meat market, the disposables, and the washed-up assassins who'd sunk as low as they could go all walked around doing their own private calculations. Whether they got the numbers right or wrong in the end, they based their ambitions, their movements, their fears, and their kills on their own math. As he picked up a handful of soap bubbles floating in the tub, Reseng wondered about Old Raccoon's math. It made no sense to him at all.

He dunked his head under the water and started adding up the number of people he'd killed so far. As he did so, he was overcome with a sense of ruin.

—

Jeongan showed up around midnight. The doorbell woke Reseng from a deep sleep. He opened the door with his eyes half-closed. Jeongan looked annoyed.

"You're sleeping? Must be nice. Meanwhile, I've been hopping all over the place in the middle of the night like a frog in a frying pan."

He looked around as he stepped into the apartment.

"Desk! Lampshade! Get out here with those stupid names of yours. I know you've been pining away to see Mr. Handsome, and now here I am!"

Jeongan looked inside the cat tower, under the couch, and behind the curtains.

"Where are those girls? Why are they so shy all of a sudden?"

"I sent them away."

"Where?"

"Somewhere better than here."

"What place could possibly be better than their master's loving arms?"

"If I get knifed in the street, they'll starve to death."

Jeongan stared at Reseng in shock, then laughed.

"You idiot! No one's going to . . . Don't worry. Elder Brother just finished a very thorough investigation."

He pulled a thick manila envelope from his bag and put it on the table.

"You've heard of Dr. Kang Jigyeong?" Jeongan asked.

"The forensic pathologist?"

"Yeah, he worked at the National Forensic Service for a long time. Turns out, he was a plotter. I'd always wondered about him. Every time I saw his picture in the paper, I got this funny feeling."

"Why is that?"

"That place had a disturbing history. Back when all those meathead military guys were in power, they didn't need any fancy plots, only signatures."

"Signatures?"

"They didn't hire any fancy plotters because they could just sweet-talk medical examiners into signing falsified death certificates for them. The Agency for National Security Planning could beat the shit out of people all they wanted, but as long as the medical examiner wrote that the cause of death was suicide, and signed it—case closed! They had it pretty sweet compared to plotters nowadays, who freak out about leaving even the slightest bit of evidence behind. Anyway, that's how those guys got into the business. At first, the medical examiners had no choice but to sign the paperwork, because they had their wives and children to think about, and the military had so much power. But once they got sucked into it, they sank deeper and deeper. You think the contractors would let them just walk away? You know what they're like."

"But what's the deal with this Dr. Kang?"

"Mito, that woman from the convenience store, was his lab assistant."

Reseng nodded. "I get the idea."

"Just the idea? The answer's right there. Who do you think a hotshot like Dr. Kang would work with? Minari Pak? Yeah, right. He would work with Hanja or Old Raccoon. But now that Old Raccoon has practically retired, it's very likely that he was Hanja's plotter."

Reseng lit a cigarette. He wasn't convinced about Hanja or Old Raccoon. Besides, he and this Dr. Kang had never crossed paths. And even if they had, why would a plotter of his stature bother to plant a bomb in the toilet of some lowly assassin?

"What does Dr. Kang do these days?" Reseng asked.

"He died recently."

"Died?"

"Yeah, and they say it was suicide. Can you believe it? Someone who spent his whole life officially passing off murder as suicide turns around and commits suicide himself. Suspicious, right?"

"How'd he die?"

"Jumped off a roof. Or someone dropped him off a roof. He weighed over a hundred kilograms, so it had to be a pretty strong someone."

Jeongan handed him a stack of photos taken at the scene of the accident. An overweight man was sprawled on the ground like a lump of wet clay. His skull was crushed, and his right shoulder and neck were broken so badly that his head was twisted all the way around. The pool of blood around him was a dark cherry red against the stark white of the lab coat he was still wearing when he died. Stranger still, lying on top of the dried blood was a single slipper.

"He only fell five stories, but what a mess," Jeongan said. "The bigger they are, you know. He had a good appetite for someone who did autopsies all day. He wasn't that tall, so he must've really been packing it in. He should've watched what he ate."

"Where'd you get these photos?"

"Where do you think? From the cops. Cops nowadays are nice to people."

"He killed himself in his slippers." Reseng tilted his head. "The official cause of death was suicide?"

"You know how cops are. They'll do whatever it takes to lighten their caseload. Also, he left a will, and there were no signs of homicide."

"What did the will say?"

Jeongan flipped through the papers and extracted a single photocopied sheet.

"'I'm sorry for all the lives I ruined and the people I hurt. I am ashamed of myself,'" he read.

"A crisis of conscience?" Reseng said.

"Ha! That guy never had a conscience. The people at his funeral looked like they were celebrating. Might as well have been a wedding."

Reseng took a drag on his cigarette. Plotters sometimes became targets. They made mistakes, too, just like assassins. They left clues, they got caught. But they were always eliminated quietly. Because, unlike assassins, who never had information to give no matter how far you dug, once a plotter surfaced, the past he'd buried surfaced right along with him. Plotters had to be killed more carefully, more covertly, and more quietly than any other target. That was the unwritten law of this world.

"Who killed him?" Reseng asked.

"I think it was her."

Jeongan held up a photograph of Mito. Reseng laughed.

"Oh, sure, that tiny chatterbox would have no problem killing a guy that size. Let me guess. She knocked him out with a Hot Break to the head, then called up her gorilla of a boyfriend to toss him off the roof? Fine. Let's say it was her. Why'd she do it?"

"I don't know, but there's something very, very fishy about her. You and I both know plotters never use their own names. And they keep everything separate—the address where their mail goes, the secret hideout where they hatch their plots, their secret rendezvous with brokers—different places, so it won't all blow up in their face at once. Plus, they use a different name in each place. But this woman ordered bomb parts in her own name."

"Maybe Dr. Kang used her address?"

"Why bother when there are more than enough fake names and registration numbers to go around?"

Reseng stared at the photograph of Mito, her face turned to the sky, smiling. She looked naïve, almost simple. The sort of girl who'd shriek at the sight of a cockroach. He couldn't believe she was behind any of this. Even if Jeongan was right, none of it added up. Given Dr. Kang's life, he would've had plenty of enemies. Mito could have been one of them. And she might have killed him because of it. But what did that have to do with Reseng and her planting a bomb in his toilet? It made no sense.

"I think you've just got the hots for her," Reseng said, tossing the photos on the table. "You're barking up the wrong tree."

Jeongan looked exasperated.

"You don't know her. She's scary. According to the people who work in the marketplace where she grew up, she worked nonstop— delivering milk, newspapers, doing odd jobs for everyone, from the fish shop to the greengrocer—in order to support her sister, who's in a wheelchair, and put herself through school. All while maintaining a perfect GPA. Everyone I met kept praising her and saying she was sent from heaven. They said she was so smart and pretty and nice and honest and hardworking that they all chipped in a bit of money each month to help pay for her education. And even though she was up at dawn every morning to work at the market, she still graduated top of her class in medical school, too. That's scary!"

Jeongan looked positively enamoured.

"Girls with perfect GPAs are scary?"

"Oh, c'mon, that's not what I mean. What I'm saying is, why work as a plotter's assistant after all that? Her hard times were behind her. She got into Korea's best medical school."

"Medical school's expensive. And plotting is an easy way to make a good pile of cash."

"But this woman, Mito, isn't that simple. I've shadowed hundreds of people. Dated dozens of women. I basically have a Ph.D. in women. Why don't you get me?"

"Fine. Then why would such an honest, hardworking woman kill a doctor and plant a bomb in my toilet? That makes no sense."

"We don't have the whole picture yet. But we will soon. I can feel it."

Jeongan rummaged in his bag and pulled out a map. He handed it to Reseng.

"What's this?"

"I've circled the most likely locations of Dr. Kang's and Mito's secret hideouts. You should check them out."

"What about you?"

"I have plans. I'll be back in a week."

"What plans?"

"It's a secret." Jeongan grinned.

"You're going on vacation with some girl while your friend's life hangs in the balance? Who is it this time?"

"It's no fun hanging out here now that your cats are gone. You know I get along better with females," Jeongan joked as he packed up his bag and put on his shoes. The sneakers weren't that old, but the backs were already worn down.

"Are you doing a job for Old Raccoon?" Reseng asked.

"What if I am?"

"I saw Hanja today. I don't know if it's the upcoming election, but he was an even bigger prick than usual. He said if we don't stop, he would have to kill us. Something about how I'm Old Raccoon's hands and feet and you're his eyes and ears. What a joke. Anyway, after what happened with the old general, Hanja is pretty angry and wants us to lie low until the election is over."

"Aw, is our little Reseng scared? If you fall for every bluff in this line of work, how will you get by?"

"It's worse this time. He'll cool off once the election's over, so don't do anything until then."

"You know how bored Old Raccoon gets when I don't deliver his newspaper. Besides, that old fox Hanja isn't going to start anything now. He's bluffing. He just wants to scare you. So stop worrying and bring those kitties back. It's not the same here without the ladies. I can't believe the great Reseng evacuated his cats because of an itty-bitty bomb in his toilet. Don't you think you're overreacting?"

Halfway out the door, Jeongan stopped and turned, as if he'd just remembered something. He undid his belt and pulled his jeans down.

"Hey, check this out. Scorpion-brand virility underwear! I got them for one hundred and seventy thousand won. See here— crystallized jade and yellow clay that emit infrared rays to maximize stamina. It's like I'm wearing Superman's underwear."

Reseng watched, dumbfounded, then said, "The guy who owns the corner shop wears those."

"Yeah? I bet he says they're amazing, right?"

"They worked so well, he had a stroke."

Jeongan pouted as he pulled his jeans back up. "I don't know why I expected to have a productive conversation with someone whose goal in life is to die a virgin. I'm out of here."

Reseng grinned as he watched Jeongan walk away wiggling his butt.

KNITTING

Reseng had been casing the front of the knitting-supply shop for an hour. The sign MISA'S KNITTING ROOM looked like a child had written it. The shop was on the first floor of a two-story building on the corner of a quiet residential street. The building itself was old and run-down, but Misa's Knitting Room had been renovated, decked out with hardwoods and fabrics to look quaint and charming, like something out of a Disney movie. Printed on the shop window were various advertisements, including KNITTING, QUILTING, NATURAL DYES, AND CROCHETING and GREAT HOBBY FOR HOUSEWIVES!

At exactly 11:00 a.m., Misa wheeled up to the shop. A lunch bag dangled from one armrest, and a canvas bag stuffed with fabric and skeins of wool dangled from the other. She dusted off her hands and took out a handkerchief to blot the beads of sweat from her forehead. Mito and Misa's apartment was a brisk ten-minute walk from the shop, with several low hills along the way. Not the easiest of distances for someone in a wheelchair. It had probably taken Misa a good thirty minutes to get to the shop. No wonder she was perspiring. Misa took out her key and unlocked the security gate. She leaned down to retrieve the newspaper and mail sitting in the entrance, flipping through the envelopes before setting them on her lap. She turned her head and gazed briefly at a large one-cubic-meter box a delivery person had left outside the shop. It was clearly too big for her to pick up without the use of her legs. She left the box where it was and went inside.

Reseng had spent the last several days visiting the suspicious locations Jeongan had circled on the map. But none of them looked like a secret hideout. Dr. Kang's laboratory was no different from any other faculty office crammed with musty old books and papers, and the spot that Jeongan had indicated as his potential hideout was empty. That was to be expected. If Dr. Kang had indeed been Hanja's plotter, then the moment Kang was dead, fixers would have been sent in to sweep up every last file. Hanja would never let so much dangerous evidence just sit there.

The sisters' apartment was likewise unremarkable, except that, while Misa's bedroom was spotlessly clean and well organized, Mito's room looked like a chimpanzee lived there. The windowsill was covered in panties left to dry, bras dangled from coat hangers outside the open window, a pair of elephant-print pajamas lay crumpled on the bed, and ankle socks, their soles blackened with dirt, were strewn everywhere. Underneath the bed was a pair of old-fashioned boxer shorts, the kind only someone's dad would wear, and a torn condom. Reseng picked up the boxers, covered in dust and hair, and thought, What kind of idiot takes off so fast that he leaves his underwear behind? On the desk were medical books and a notepad. Reseng flipped through the notepad, but it contained no evidence that Mito was a plotter.

Craziest of all, Jeongan's claim that Mito was Dr. Kang's assistant had turned out to be nothing more than speculation. Everyone at the university and the research center had looked puzzled by Reseng's questions.

"Mito and Dr. Kang? I thought she was Professor Kim Seonil's research assistant."

Officially, then, it was impossible to say whether Mito and Dr. Kang had been involved with each other. Jeongan had jumped to conclusions about their relationship simply because Mito had ordered bomb parts and had at some point worked in the same lab as he had.

Reseng took out a cigarette. Just as he was about to light it, Misa came back out. She stared grimly at the oversize box and leaned forward to try to lift it. After a few groans, she gave up and tried dragging it. That didn't work, either. Each time she tugged on the box, her wheelchair rolled and threatened to tip her out. After wrestling with it for a while, she paused to wipe her forehead.

Reseng tucked the unlit cigarette back into the pack and walked over to her.

"Would you like some help?" he asked.

Misa raised her head and stared at him. Her skin was as clean and pure as a baby's and her eyes as big and innocent-looking as a calf's. She looked at him in surprise, then smiled radiantly, less a smile of gratitude for his kind gesture and more like she was stifling laughter. What was so funny?

"Why, thank you!" she said finally.

Reseng picked up the box. It was definitely too heavy for anyone to manage without using their legs. He waited for instructions from her, but she was still staring at him in blatant amusement.

"So . . . am I supposed to just stand here all day holding this?" he asked.

Finally, Misa burst out laughing.

What was so funny? Reseng was seriously confused. Now Misa was laughing so hard, she was crying.

"I'm sorry. So sorry! Once I start laughing, I can't stop. Oh my. Wow. I don't know what came over me. Please come in."

She wiped her eyes and opened the door, then skillfully guided the wheelchair between a chair and a sewing machine and pointed to a round wooden table.

Reseng set the box on it.

"You're Reseng, right?" Misa asked, the laughter not yet faded from her face.

Shocked, Reseng said, "You know my name?"

"Of course I do! You're my sister's boyfriend—how could I *not* know your name? We talk about you every day up in the attic."

The words *boyfriend, every day,* and *attic* swirled around inside Reseng's head. What on earth was going on?

"Your sister said I'm her boyfriend?" he asked.

"What? You're not? Are you another of my sister's crushes?" Misa now looked like she was going to burst into tears at any second. "I knew it. I knew she was turning into a stalker again."

Misa picked up a piece of yarn from the table and twisted it

around the tip of her finger, then let it drift to the floor. She looked
so crestfallen that Reseng almost felt bad.

"No, I, uh . . . I only said that because I thought I was the one
with the crush."

"Really?" Misa's eyes widened.

"Of course."

He smiled at her. Her face immediately lit up like a child's.

"Oh, where are my manners? Please have a seat!"

She offered him the chair next to her. He sat down, still confused.

"Would you like some coffee?"

"If it's not too much trouble."

"Trouble? Don't be silly."

Misa gave him another big smile and wheeled over to a small
kitchenette that had been added to the corner of the shop. The sink
and counter were set low to accommodate her. While she prepared
the coffee, he took a quick look around.

Though you might expect a place where people worked with
fabric and yarn to be messy, the inside of the shop was as neat and
charming as Misa herself. A cabinet along one wall held tidy stacks
of cloth, quilting supplies, knitting needles and yarn, and fabric
samples. Displayed on another wall were tablecloths, aprons, dolls,
bags, and other quilted objects. The items all had little labels in
pretty handwriting—either *For Display* or *For Sale*. The center shelf,
which had a sign that read PETTING ZOO, was lined with various
stuffed animals. There was pantsless Winnie-the-Pooh, his stomach
sticking out, and Chester Cheetah giving the thumbs-up, with a
speech bubble that read *You are Zeus, god of the sky. I am Cheetos,
god of the snacks.* Staring blankly at Reseng were Tom and Jerry,
Papa Smurf, and a whole gaggle of his Smurf buddies, as well as
all the Teletubbies, their arms in the air, as if they were about to
lead everyone in a round of calisthenics. Reseng caught himself
wondering nonsensically, Do they belong in a petting zoo? Another
shelf, with a sign that said THE GARDEN, held a display of quilted
cacti, carrots, watermelons, and strawberries. A pair of Brother
sewing machines sat next to each other facing the window, and two
mannequins dressed in a hand-knit sweater and vest appeared to be

having a friendly chat in the corner. But there was no sign of any staircase leading to an attic room.

"What brings you to our shop? Are you meeting my sister here?" Misa asked while washing fruit.

"Yes," Reseng said absentmindedly.

"When did she say she's coming?"

"Soon."

Another sign said BATHROOM, in front of a curtain over a doorway. Reseng pretended he was having a look around and drew the curtain back. At the end of a hallway no more than five meters long was a bathroom. He walked down the hallway and opened the door. Other than the stainless-steel handrails on each side of the toilet and the low sink for wheelchair access, there was nothing out of the ordinary. He closed the door and walked back. Just before the doorway back to the shop, he stopped in front of a large built-in wardrobe. Wondering why anyone would install a wardrobe there, Reseng opened the door and found it stuffed with clothes. He pushed the clothes to one side and rapped his knuckles against the back wall. It sounded like an empty wooden barrel. He ran his fingers along the edge and at the very bottom discovered a handle for a sliding door. It slid open, revealing a steep, narrow set of wooden stairs. He stuck his head out of the curtain and checked the shop. The sound of running water was still coming from the sink.

"Do you mind if I use your bathroom?" he called.

"Go ahead!" Misa said cheerfully.

Reseng slipped off his shoes and held them in his hand as he closed the cupboard door and crept up the stairs. It was pitch-black inside. He slid his hand along the wall until he found a light switch. Other than the lack of windows, there was nothing remarkable about the room. A Japanese-style tatami mat lined the floor, and the only furnishings were a low desk and a single mattress. The desk held a lamp and a laptop computer, and the mattress had a single blanket and pillow.

Reseng turned to look at the wall behind him. He froze. The wall was covered with hundreds of photos of him. Not just photos but also X-rays, medical records, online order receipts, copies of his bankbook, his resident registration card, his medical insurance card, his driver's licence, and even photocopies of his utility bills. Each photo had the date, time, and place written on it in permanent marker. There was so much data on him that he felt as if he were looking at his very existence, cut up and pinned to the wall.

Reseng stared at the photos of himself. Those who didn't know him would have thought they were of his everyday life, but in fact there was nothing everyday about them. Several had been taken just before Reseng had committed an assassination, and several just after. Not only that, the black Samsonite attaché case that Mito had zoomed in on in some of the photos was the same briefcase that plotters used to send him dossiers. The briefcase also held any weapons, drugs, or other items he needed to complete an assignment, and was always returned to the plotter once the job was done. Mixed in with the photos of Reseng were photos of targets he'd taken out.

Mito was a plotter after all.

Reseng checked the time. Five minutes had already passed since he'd told Misa he was going to the bathroom. He took out his Swiss Army knife and used it to remove the hard drive from the laptop, then slipped the drive into his pocket and screwed the laptop casing back on. After one last look around the room, he turned off the light and crept back down the stairs. He closed the cupboard door and stole a peek inside the shop. Misa was sitting at the table, which was set with coffee and fruit, waiting for him. Reseng slipped into the bathroom, flushed the toilet, and washed his hands. Then he shut the door noisily as he left.

"Must've been something I ate. How embarrassing, getting the runs right after meeting someone for the first time!" Reseng babbled as he rubbed his stomach.

Misa covered her mouth, laughing. He couldn't help thinking that her smile lit up the room.

"The coffee got cold. It tastes better when it's hot," she said.

"That's okay. I've always been a lukewarm sort of guy anyway."

Reseng took a sip. It was good, rich, with a bold flavor and aroma.

"It's delicious! Kenyan?"

"Ethiopian."

"Ah, you're supposed to be able to guess the beans' country of origin from the taste alone, but I'm still not hip enough."

Misa laughed again.

"You laugh no matter what I say." Reseng's face turned serious. "Am I that clownish?"

Misa looked flustered. "Oh, no! I've always laughed easily. You're not clownish or anything. I just like to laugh."

"Actually, I am a clown. Everyone says so."

Misa stared at him for a long moment, until he finally asked, "What is it?"

"What do you like about my sister?" Her expression was serious now.

Reseng stared up at the ceiling. *What did he like about her?* What on earth was he supposed to say?

"Hmm, well, first of all, Mito is pretty and smart. And she knows everything about me. She knows me so well, it's almost shocking. And she always tells me what to do, even when *I* don't know what I'm supposed to be doing."

Misa looked satisfied with his answer.

Just then, someone burst into the shop, calling out in a loud, giddy voice, "Oh, darling Miiisa! I finally finished that oversize sweater!"

Reseng looked up and stared in surprise. Waltzing into the shop was none other than the cross-eyed librarian. She froze and stared right back at him.

"This is Reseng!" Misa was like a little kid eager to show off her new prize. "Mito's boyfriend! She wasn't making it up this time!"

The librarian nodded almost imperceptibly in response. Reseng slowly stood and glared at the librarian. Her eyes filled with fear and she looked away. The door opened again, and this time it was Mito. She quickly took in the librarian frozen on the spot, Misa smiling brightly, and Reseng standing between them with a deadly serious expression. She seemed taken aback but not the least bit scared.

"Reseng! Nice to see that cute ass of yours is still in one piece," she said with a grin.

He stared at her, flabbergasted. "You. Crazy. Bitch."

The words sprang out of his mouth of their own accord. Misa gasped.

For a moment, they all just stood there. No one spoke, no one moved. He couldn't piece it together. Plotter, librarian, knitting-shop owner—what on earth were these three mismatched women doing together? And in this ridiculous shop, of all places, watched over by Papa Smurf and Winnie-the-Pooh and all the Teletubbies? He felt like a ball of yarn that had been slowly unraveling, only to tighten suddenly into a tangled knot. The librarian let out a tense sigh. Reseng couldn't get over it. As surprised as he was by Mito, he could not grasp why the cross-eyed woman, the same docile librarian who'd been cooped up in the Doghouse all that time, was here. Had she gone over to Mito, or to Hanja? No, that wasn't it. Now that he thought about it, the librarian had been knitting up a storm ever since she first arrived at the library five years ago. That meant she'd been in cahoots with Mito from the start.

Mito was the first to speak. "Let's talk somewhere else." It was a voice meant to soothe an angry child.

"I prefer it in here. Misa and I were in the middle of a conversation, it's a pretty shop, and, you know, there's just something special about this place." Reseng mimicked knitting with his fingers and looked up in the direction of the attic room.

"Besides," he added, smiling at Misa, "our sweet Misa went to all this trouble to serve coffee and fruit. It'd be a shame to leave now."

Misa gave him an anxious, confused look as she chewed on her bottom lip. The librarian kept looking fearfully back and forth between him and Mito.

"That's right," Misa said, making an effort to keep her voice light. "I don't know what's going on, but you two should stay and work it out over a cup of coffee."

Mito slowly walked over to the table, as if she had no choice.

The librarian stayed where she was but kept a careful eye on Mito, who pulled her over by the arm.

"Misa, would you mind making us some coffee, too?" Mito asked with a smile.

As soon as Misa went to the kitchenette to make more coffee, Mito leaned in close to Reseng and hissed, "My sister is not a part of this. Let's go somewhere else."

"We're all a part of this." Reseng said, his eyes locked on the librarian's. "Because we're all connected by the most amazing coincidences."

The librarian turned to avoid his gaze. Mito pushed her face right up to Reseng's ear. "Mess with my sister and you're *dead*."

Reseng glared back at Mito's face, which was far too close to his own, then leaned back, his nose in the air. "*Oh-ho,* aren't you scary! I thought you two were like those singing, dancing Silver Bell Sisters, but it turns out you're just a couple of goons. Guess I should call you the Silver Bell Goon Squad instead."

Reseng stared at the two of them. Misa paused in the middle of taking a coffee cup from the cupboard and turned to call out, "Sis, you didn't eat breakfast! Would you like some toast?"

"No, we're leaving now."

"I'll have some!" Reseng said cheerfully. "Some delicious toast made by Miss Misa!"

Mito looked daggers at him. The librarian sent her some sort of signal, and Mito winked back, as if telling her not to worry. After a moment, Misa returned to the table, carrying a tray with toast and two cups of coffee in one hand and steering her wheelchair with the other.

"Reseng, you work at a library, right? Sumin works at a library, too," Misa said, trying valiantly to break the tension.

"Yes, I know. Sumin." Reseng kept his eyes on the librarian as he spoke. "We used to work at the same library, in fact. Back then, our jobs were different, but now it seems Sumin and I are doing the same thing. It's nice to see her here. There's always so much to talk about when you meet someone in the same line of work as you."

The librarian looked sheepishly at Misa and nodded. Reseng picked up the toast and took a huge bite.

"Wow, now that is delicious! If I'm in the area again, can I come back for more toast?"

"Of course!" Misa said with a smile. "Drop by anytime."

Mito glared at him. An awkward silence descended over the table. Misa kept glancing around at the others. She looked like she wanted to change the subject but couldn't think of what to say. The librarian was no less tense than when she'd first arrived. Mito, who was sitting across from Reseng, drummed her fingers on the table. After a moment, she spoke.

"Whenever two people date, misunderstandings are bound to occur. The man does something, thinking it's no big deal, but it hurts the woman's feelings. Or a single careless word from the woman hurts the man's pride. That message I sent you wasn't because I wanted to end it for good. I just meant that we should take a break and think things over, decide what we want in the future. But I guess you couldn't wait and decided to come running back? And to my little sister's shop, of all places? Aren't you embarrassed?"

Reseng stared at her. What the hell was she talking about?

"What? You dumped him? Of all things!" Misa looked at Reseng in shock.

Reseng shook his head. Mito continued.

"But since you came all this way, let's go get a drink. If there's been a misunderstanding, we'll hash it out. And if there are things you need to get off your chest, I'll listen. Or if there are things you've been wanting to ask me, you can ask."

"'Misunderstanding'?" Reseng glowered at her.

"She's right, Reseng." Misa squeezed his arm. "Have a drink with her and let all your feelings out."

Mito stood and grabbed her bag. The librarian stood, too.

"Stay here," Mito said. "Why interfere in someone else's relationship?"

"Yes, Sumin! Stay and make Pikachu dolls with me." For some

reason, Misa sounded overly excited about that idea. The librarian sat back down hesitantly.

"Shall we?" Mito said to Reseng.

Reseng crossed his arms, tipped his head back, then let out a deep sigh and stood up. The librarian sat hunched over, her eyes fixed on the floor. He stared at her for a moment before turning to Misa and smiling.

"Thank you so much for the delicious coffee and delicious toast. Oh, and the fruit, too."

"Come by again, Reseng."

"I definitely will. Besides, I have to talk to Sumin, too."

Misa smiled brightly at him.

Mito took Reseng to a place in the market that specialized in soup made with blood sausage and rice. Mito seemed to be a regular. The owner greeted her by name as she came in. Mito headed for a corner table and called out her order.

"Auntie, could we get two orders of spicy stir-fried tripe with a side of liver and blood sausage, and two bottles of soju?"

The owner brought over the two bottles of soju, two beer glasses, and a small bowl of sliced onions and peppers marinated in soy sauce.

"Drinking in the middle of the day?" she asked.

"This guy says he's in love with me and won't leave me alone," Mito said, feigning arrogance. "So I decided to throw him a bone and let him have a drink with me just this once."

The owner gave Reseng the once-over.

"A handsome boy like this begging for a date? Better watch yourself, girl. Don't come sobbing to me like you did last time."

When she returned to the kitchen, Mito filled her beer glass two-thirds full of soju and knocked it back. She picked up a slice of onion and chewed on it noisily.

"Acting tough for my benefit?" Reseng asked.

"I always drink fast. I don't live a life of leisure like you. I have to work, and study, and love, and because life is sad, I have to drink. But I don't have all the time in the world to get drunk."

"You must be busy. Because on top of all that, you've got people to kill."

Mito snickered.

"Let's get to the point," he said. "Why'd you put a bomb in my toilet? That's the part I don't understand."

"To tell you to think about your life. You don't seem to give a shit."

Mito sounded flippant. She chomped on another slice of onion, then poured half a glass of soju for them both.

"Are you trying to get revenge for your dead parents?" Reseng asked. "Are you so full of hatred that you're going on a killing spree and taking out anyone who has anything to do with plotting?"

Mito stared at him speechlessly for a moment, then burst into laughter. "See, what'd I tell you? You don't think. Pull that pea-size brain out of your ass for once and think outside the box. Look at the big picture. Like world peace, or the future of humanity."

Reseng wondered what made her so cocksure. She'd been caught in the act of plotting by one of her targets. And by a trained assassin, no less. She was small, maybe 160 centimeters, and couldn't have weighed much more than fifty kilograms—clearly no match for him. She could be dead anytime between leaving this restaurant and returning home. But she looked perfectly calm. And not fake calm, either. Where did this unfounded confidence come from?

"It seems to me you should be feeling pretty nervous right about now," he said.

"Why, are you going to pull a knife on me?" Mito snickered again. Laughing every time someone spoke seemed to be a genetic trait shared by the sisters.

"And if I do?"

"You're not the type to stab a woman to death."

"You think you know everything about me because you taped a few photos to your wall?"

"That woman Chu let live. That pretty, pathetic woman who

weighed no more than thirty-eight kilograms. We gave you crystal clear instructions to break her neck, but instead you gave her pills. I'll never understand why assassins think they're smarter than plotters. If a forensic scientist *specifically* tells you not to give someone pills but to break their neck instead, then you can bet they've got a damn good reason."

"How did you know?"

"I'm the one who put that bottle of barbiturates in your briefcase. It came back empty."

"Then why put it there in the first place if I wasn't supposed to use it?" he said, his face changing color.

Mito looked him in the eye as she said, "I wanted to see what choice you'd make."

She took a sip of soju. Her hands looked rough and calloused; Jeongan must have been right about all the work she did in the marketplace. Reseng picked up his glass and drained it in one swig. Mito gave a faint smile.

"I guess you're not going to kill me today. You never drink on assassination days."

"You're my plotter?"

"No, Dr. Kang was your plotter. I was his assistant."

"I thought Dr. Kang was Hanja's plotter."

"Ultimately, there's no difference between Hanja and Old Raccoon. They look like they're at each other's throats, but the truth is they need each other. They're like the crocodile and the crocodile bird. If one of them gets a big kill, the other picks over the bones. But once this election is over, Hanja is going to take out Old Raccoon. Then he'll kill you, as well."

The owner came out of the kitchen with a platter of tripe. This time, she inspected Reseng at length.

"Wow, you are one handsome, sturdy-looking fellow! Eat up!" She set a bottle of Chilsung Cider on the table. "On the house," she said. "Our Mito might act like a donkey in heat, but once you get to know her, she's a good girl with a lot of heart. She suffered a lot at a young age. So take good care of her."

Reseng nodded bashfully.

"Auntie," Mito grumbled, "I told you, he's the one chasing after me."

"Who the hell would want to chase after your crazy ass?" The woman gave Mito a rap on the head with her knuckles. She bowed at Reseng, who found himself automatically rising from his chair to bow back. As the woman turned to leave, Mito picked up a large piece of tripe with her chopsticks and shoved the whole thing in her mouth.

"Taste it. It's delicious. Don't let her mouth fool you—she's a great cook."

Mito pushed the platter closer to him. The food looked like someone had sliced up a rubber hose and slapped on some hot-pepper paste. That unmistakable tripe smell wafted up from the platter. He frowned, while Mito's chopsticks never stopped moving.

"Every time I eat tripe here," she gushed, "I can't help picturing God's intestines. The intestines of a God that human beings have never seen and can't imagine. The dirty, smelly, and disgusting things hidden inside the holy, sacred, and divine. Shame hiding behind grace. Ugliness hidden behind beauty. The complex web of lies lurking behind what we think is truth. And yet human beings try to deny that every living thing has to have intestines."

"Snap out of it," Reseng said. "It's just pig guts."

"The closest thing to human organs are pig organs, and since the Bible says humans were made in God's image, then these intestines must resemble God's intestines."

Mito blew on a piece of God's intestines to cool it off before putting it in her mouth.

"Did you kill Dr. Kang?"

"Maybe," Mito said flatly.

"By yourself?"

"How many people does it take to get rid of one fat guy? It's not hard."

Mito swallowed the bite of tripe she'd been chewing on and took a sip of soju.

"You're stronger than you look. He weighed over a hundred kilos."

"Cranes were invented five thousand years ago. The wheel was invented six thousand years ago."

Reseng lit a cigarette.

"You planted a mole, Sumin, in Old Raccoon's library, killed Hanja's plotter, Dr. Kang, and made it look like suicide, stuck a bomb inside my toilet . . ." Reseng mumbled to himself, then added, "What the fuck were you thinking? Are you declaring war on all the contractors?"

"Maybe I am," Mito said innocently, as if she were talking about someone else.

"War on Hanja? Or on Old Raccoon?"

"Both."

Reseng stared at her, incredulous. She still had the same innocent look on her face. He smiled stiffly.

"A girl like you going to war with those monsters? You've got to be kidding."

Mito put down her chopsticks and wiped her mouth with a napkin.

"What do you mean by 'a girl like you,' and what is so funny about it?" She glared at him.

"Hanja and Old Raccoon aren't going to fall for your tricks like Dr. Kang did. They won't let you toss them off a roof. You seem to think you know this business just because you helped out a plotter a few times. But you are no match for someone like Hanja. You'll be cremated before you even begin. Stop before this goes any further. In fact, if you stop now, I'll keep my mouth shut about these little games of yours—for nice, sweet Misa's sake. As a bonus, I'll forgive you for the bomb in my toilet."

"It's too late. And I know Hanja and Old Raccoon just as well as you do."

Reseng took a drag and exhaled slowly.

"Do you know how long it took me to find you? Less than a week. Hanja will find you much faster. Then you'll have every single creep from the meat market coming after you with their knives out. Obviously, Misa's knitting shop won't be safe. So I'm warning you. Those guys won't be as nice as I am."

"You didn't find me. I summoned you."

Reseng raised his eyebrows and stared at her. She stared straight back at him. She looked serious and determined. Reseng stubbed out his cigarette, filled his glass a third full of soju, and swigged it. The soju was hot and bitter in his empty stomach. He grimaced, and Mito tapped the plate of tripe with her forefinger. He stared at her for a second before taking a bite. He'd never tried tripe before. Just as she'd said, it tasted much better than it looked. He took another sip of soju.

"You're a funny woman."

"Thanks. I'll take that as a compliment. You're a funny guy."

"But why me? You could've had your pick of assassins in the meat market."

"You're cute."

She gave him the same innocent look as before. He returned it with a look of supreme irritation. But Mito didn't seem bothered in the slightest, as she took another sip of soju and another bite of tripe. Much to his aggravation, she kept chewing slowly and mechanically before finally swallowing and speaking again.

"I need someone who can go back and forth between Old Raccoon and Hanja. Someone who can put them on edge, shake them up, egg them on. You're perfect for that because you're Old Raccoon's son and Hanja's brother."

"I am not Old Raccoon's son! And I'm definitely not Hanja's brother," Reseng yelled, before he could stop himself. The owner paused in the middle of chopping green onions to stare at him. Embarrassed, Reseng lit another cigarette. Mito laughed, shook her head, and took another sip of soju and another bite of tripe.

"You're not eating? We have to finish all the meat so she can make us fried rice with the leftover sauce."

Reseng stared at her. How could she talk about fried rice at a time like this? Seriously, what planet was she from? As he watched her talk around a mouthful of pig intestine, he felt like planting his fist in it.

"So, what makes you think I would help you?"

"Because you're not going to survive this without me. I've prepared the most wonderful plot just for you."

"Well, isn't that something. Lately, I'm surrounded by people telling me I can't survive without them."

"Plotters keep a preroster, a list of information on people who are likely to become targets, so we can move quickly once an assassination date is set. And you're on it."

"Did Hanja put me on it?"

"Maybe. Though it could just as easily have been someone else."

Reseng inhaled deeply on his cigarette, then slowly exhaled.

"Thank goodness I'm only on the preroster," he said. "But even if I were on the main list, I still wouldn't dream of crawling under some chick's skirt and begging for my life."

Mito sneered at him. "Why, because you're a man? Your problem is that damn Y chromosome of yours. Women have two lovely, flexible X chromosomes that balance each other out, but the only thing your stupid Y chromosome is good for is getting hard-ons and flying off the handle."

"I'll figure my life out on my own, so worry about yourself. From what I see, you won't last long. To say nothing of your little sister, Misa, in that wheelchair of hers. How is she going to run away in that thing?"

Mito gave him a look. "Don't you dare joke about my sister with that filthy mouth of yours."

Her eyes were like daggers. Reseng suddenly pictured Misa's bright, innocent smile as she'd laughed at his jokes and patted his shoulder. He held his hand up to show he was sorry. Mito picked up her glass and drank the rest of the soju.

"Why are you so fixated on Hanja and Old Raccoon anyway? Is it revenge for your parents? Or for Misa's legs—" Reseng stopped himself before he went any further.

"I did start this initially because of them." Mito refilled her glass. "But I don't know who killed my parents, and I don't care anymore who was behind it. I'm not looking to get personal revenge on the dogs who paralyzed my sister. They're probably dead already—

killed by people like us. People who kill human beings and go home afterward to shovel dinner in their faces and take hot baths and tuck themselves into bed and fall asleep peacefully, as if the things they do mean nothing at all. Dirty, ugly, revolting people like us. Cowardly, weakest-of-the-weak people who say, 'We had no choice because that's how the world is and because life is hard and because we have no power.'"

Mito took a swig of soju.

"So you're going to change the world by getting rid of all the hit men?"

Mito stared at her glass and didn't answer.

"Will killing Hanja and Old Raccoon change the world?" Reseng continued. "It's just an empty chair spinning in circles. The moment the chair is empty, someone else will rush to sit in it. Killing them won't make a difference."

"You're right. Getting rid of a few measly hit men won't change anything. That's why I'm planning to get rid of the chair. So that no one can sit in it."

Reseng stared at her. Her face didn't change.

"I thought you were a smart girl, but you're actually just a crazy bitch."

"Did you think I was a sane bitch? How could I do this work if I were sane?"

"You plan to enact justice all on your own? What a joke. Not even the movies are that unrealistic anymore."

"Do you know why the world is like this? Because of villains like Old Raccoon and Hanja? Because of the puppet masters giving them assignments? No. A handful of villains isn't enough to affect the world. The world is like this because we're too meek. Because of people like you who believe in resigning yourselves to apathy, who believe that nothing you do can change anything. You dismiss it all as an empty chair spinning in circles. You think that makes you sound cool? It's because of people like you—who obediently do whatever Hanja or Old Raccoon tell you to do without so much as a peep, worrying only about whether there'll be food in your bowl, cursing and grumbling over booze, and acting like you know everything—that the world is the way it is. You're worse than Hanja. While you help turn him into an infamous villain, you try to convince yourself that you're still better than he is. You commit every sin in the book and then claim you had no choice. But Hanja *is* better than you. Because he, at least, is willing to take the blame."

"Brilliant Miss Mito came up with an awesome plot to save the world, but she still needs an idiot like me to pull it off?"

Mito stared at him without answering.

"If you'd like to know my answer now," he continued, "it's *no*. I don't care what you're thinking or what plot you came up with. I will live my ugly, cowardly, disgusting life, just as you said, until the day someone sticks a knife in me and I'm dead. But I don't care. Because I've lived like a worm and I will die like a worm."

Reseng stood up. He directed his next words at the top of Mito's head.

"If you mess with me again, I'll fucking kill you. That's your final warning."

She looked up at him. Her expression was as arrogant as ever. "Better grab a Hot Break," she said. "You're going to need the energy."

With that, she took another gulp of soju and ate another mouthful of tripe. The owner was looking over at them, disappointment written all over her face. Reseng stared at Mito for another three seconds and then walked over to the register.

"How much is the bill?" he asked.

"Eighteen thousand."

He pulled two ten-thousand-won notes from his wallet and handed them to the owner. She looked sad as she handed him his change.

"I know she's a lot to handle, but please give her another chance. . . ."

"Thank you for the food," Reseng said, and left.

He wasn't sure if it was from drinking in the middle of the day, but the sun beating down on the marketplace made him dizzy.

FROG EAT FROG

Jeongan's body arrived at the library over the weekend. It wasn't Hanja, but Hanja's lawyer, who stepped out of the car. Two men dressed in black suits pulled Jeongan's body from the trunk, where it had been shoved in carelessly, and carried it into Old Raccoon's study. Hanja's lawyer followed them in. As the men in suits stepped back outside, the lawyer greeted Old Raccoon, bowing a full ninety degrees from the waist.

"We are just as upset about this as you are," the lawyer said. "Jeongan crossed a line that shouldn't have been crossed. We ought to have consulted you first, of course, but the situation became all too urgent. . . ."

Old Raccoon unzipped the body bag just far enough to identify Jeongan, whose face was bluish, frozen in a look of terror.

"A line that shouldn't have been crossed, huh?" Old Raccoon said, speaking slowly and calmly, as if he were admonishing a child. "Maybe I'm getting senile, but nowadays whenever young people beat around the bush, I cannot work out what they're saying. Just give it to me straight, prosecutor. What line was crossed?"

Hanja's lawyer had started out as a government prosecutor. People still addressed him by his old job title, even though he no longer did anything of the sort.

"Jeongan had a list of the names and locations of our plotters—a good five of them. We think he was planning to make a deal with another company. As you know, that type of information is extremely sensitive, so we . . ." His voice trailed off.

"Which company?"

"Some guys from China. They were going to pay him three billion won."

Old Raccoon scowled. "You expect me to believe that? How could Jeongan have had a list of your plotters when even I don't know who they are? I'm sure you don't store classified information like that between the pages of a phone book."

The lawyer hesitated before responding.

"We don't yet have all the details on how he got his hands on it. Once we do, the boss will come in person to give you a full report."

Old Raccoon unzipped the body bag the rest of the way. There were seven knife marks in Jeongan's throat, chest, and stomach.

"Did Hanja give the order?"

"The boss is currently abroad."

"Then who did?"

"I gave the order to subdue him and bring him in, but Jeongan is not an easy person to catch. I guess our guy slipped up."

"Slipped up . . ."

The lawyer snuck a glance at Old Raccoon's face and said, "He will be soundly punished for it."

Old Raccoon gave him a contemptuous look. " 'Soundly'? Meaning you're going to kill him?"

The lawyer covered his mouth with his fist and pretended to cough as a look of embarrassment crossed his face.

"Or was it your plan all along to swap my knight for one of your pawns?" asked Old Raccoon.

Reseng gritted his teeth at the mention of chess. The lawyer still had his fist over his mouth and the same awkward look on his face.

"We've lost three of our plotters in the last two months alone," he said courteously. "We don't know for sure whether Jeongan had anything to do with it, but this is a very sensitive time for us. And it's election season. We trust that you understand our position."

Old Raccoon cocked his head at the mention of three dead plotters. He rolled up his sleeves and examined the stab marks on Jeongan's body with his bare hands. The predator had taken his prey down slowly, starting on the outside of the torso and working his way to the center as the prey lost strength. Both Trainer and Chu had been dispatched the same way.

"The Barber?" Old Raccoon said.

"No, sir. It was a young knifeman. Former yakuza . . ."

The lawyer was quick with a lie. Old Raccoon snorted. He felt the spot where the knife had pierced Jeongan's heart, almost certainly the fatal stab.

"Impressive knife work for a young guy. What's his name?"

The lawyer hesitated, obviously trying to make up a name on the spot.

"He calls himself Dalja."

"How old?"

"Twenty-five."

"Very young. All right, bring me his body and we're square. We can't let him think it's okay to threaten the library and get away with it. It'll go to his head."

Reseng stared at Old Raccoon in surprise, but Old Raccoon's expression didn't change. The lawyer thought it over and nodded.

"It's a deal. Once it's taken care of, I'll compile a situation report and have it delivered to you."

"I don't need any goddamn report!" Old Raccoon suddenly yelled. "What do you think this is? The government?"

"Forgive me." The lawyer hung his head.

"You can go. We'll deal with Jeongan's body."

The lawyer gave him another polite ninety-degree bow before exiting.

When he was gone, Old Raccoon finally allowed himself to reveal his grief. His ramrod-straight body seemed to collapse in on itself. He braced his hands against the table and stared at Jeongan's face for a long time before resting his palm against the young man's forehead.

With his eyes still fixed on Jeongan, he asked Reseng, "How did Jeongan get the list of Hanja's plotters?"

"I have no idea."

"No guesses?"

"None."

Jeongan might have stumbled upon it when he found Dr. Kang's hideout. But were the plotters likely to have left a list of names and addresses lying around for anyone to stumble upon? Not a chance.

Mito must have planted some bait in Jeongan's path. And he'd taken it. Like an idiot. Had he really thought he could sell a list of plotters without getting caught? It was a fool's errand.

"What the hell is going on?" Old Raccoon asked.

"If *you* don't know, then I don't know," Reseng said.

"Was Jeongan taking orders from someone else?"

"He was tracking bomb components, but it had nothing to do with the plotters."

"Three plotters are dead, Jeongan was attacked, everyone's got their swords drawn like all hell is about to break loose, and I know nothing?" Old Raccoon yelled, his eyes bloodshot.

"That's what you're angry about?"

"What?" Old Raccoon glared at him.

"You're not angry about Jeongan. Your pride is hurt simply because you weren't kept in the loop, right? Jeongan is dead! Don't you see?" Reseng cradled Jeongan's head in his hands and turned it to face Old Raccoon. "Who cares about your pride? Being informed won't bring Jeongan back to life, so why do you care whether you knew what was going on or not? It's obvious the Barber killed him, but you're settling it by having some other guy killed? What kind of justice is that? I guess we're all the same to you. We're all just pieces on your chessboard, so why should you care whether your knight or your rook or whatever goes down? As long as you keep playing, we're all dead anyway."

Old Raccoon's hands shook. Tears fell from Reseng's eyes.

"Move him down to the basement," Old Raccoon said gently. "We need to have the body cleaned and readied."

"Is that really Jeongan?" Bear looked shocked.

Reseng stayed silent.

"Poor Jeongan! Poor little Jeongan! So young! I cremated your father, and now I'm cremating you. What has the world come to?"

Bear stroked Jeongan's cheek inside the body bag. Reseng lit a cigarette. Old Raccoon had stayed in the car. Bear collapsed on the ground and wept for a long time before getting up again. He brushed off his pants and checked the surroundings out of habit before going over to the car and tapping on the back window. Old Raccoon unrolled the window a crack.

Bear wiped his eyes with the back of his hand as he said, "Shall I get started, Mr. Raccoon? It won't be long before the sun comes up."

Old Raccoon nodded. Bear got the cart from the shed and nodded to Reseng, who flicked away his cigarette and went over to the trunk. Together, they lifted Jeongan's body onto the cart. It must have been true what they said about the dead weighing more than the living, because Jeongan weighed a ton.

Bear stopped the cart in front of the incinerator and spread out a mat. He placed a small table on top and set it with a candle, incense, a bottle of rice wine, and wine cups. Reseng stood to one side and watched. Bear lit the incense, checked that nothing was missing, then walked back to Old Raccoon's car.

"Mr. Raccoon, everything's ready."

Old Raccoon stared blankly out the car window without saying anything.

After about ten seconds, Bear said, "All right, I guess we'll get started without you."

Old Raccoon gave an almost imperceptible nod. Bear bowed and returned to the mat.

He lit another stick of incense, poured wine into the cup, and raised it in offering before drinking it, then bowed twice. He glanced over at Reseng, who got up, lit some more incense, and picked up a wine cup. Bear filled it. Reseng raised it in offering and bowed twice, as well. Then he stood there as if in a trance until Bear tapped him on the shoulder and cleared away the table and mat. Reseng was still in a daze, so Bear lifted Jeongan onto the tray by himself. Before closing the incinerator door, Bear looked at Reseng once more. Reseng's face remained blank. Bear slid Jeongan into the oven and closed the door.

As the flames rose, Bear brought out a bottle of soju and sat next to Reseng. He took a swig of the soju and offered it to him. Reseng took a swig and handed it back. Bear stared at the oven wordlessly with the bottle in his hand.

Jeongan the Shadow was dead. Jeongan, who'd sworn to live a life no one would remember, who'd vowed to become as light and indefinite as vapor, to live without love or hate or betrayal or hurt or memory, to be a nonpresence, like the air itself, was dead. Why kill him? No one would've known the difference if they'd let him live. Reseng pictured a shadowless man standing at the top of a tall hill in the desert with the sun beating down on him, and thought, How am I supposed to live without a shadow now?

If he hadn't called Jeongan, Reseng might have been the next to die. He wouldn't have bothered calling if Jeongan had been on another job. Jeongan had had nothing to do with this business of the bomb until Reseng involved him. Reseng should have dealt with it on his own. But instead, he'd called, and now Jeongan was dead. He'd become a shadow, just like his father, and was being cremated in Bear's oven, just like his father. Reseng pictured Jeongan's blood and bones turning to smoke and ash in the searing flames of Bear's incinerator. Once his ashes were scattered on the wind, he would be forgotten, just as he'd wanted all along.

The sun was rising. Bear looked at his watch, then checked to see if anyone was coming up the mountain. He opened the oven door and, using a long metal hook, pulled out the tray even before the heat had fully dissipated. Fresh from the flames, Jeongan's white bones looked fragile, ready to crumble in an instant. Bear fished out the bones with a cheap pair of tongs sold at any hardware shop. He checked his watch again and peered down the hill. Then he placed what remained of Jeongan into the iron mortar and got to work, clearly flustered by the thought of customers suddenly showing up.

He stopped after less than five minutes and quickly transferred the ashes to a maple box and wrapped it in a white cloth. He looked contrite as he handed the box to Reseng.

"You should've come earlier. I wanted to do a better job for him, but there isn't enough time."

Reseng took the urn and handed Bear an envelope in exchange.

"It's okay," Reseng said flatly. "It's not like grinding the bones any finer will bring the dead back to life."

Bear's eyes reddened as he took the envelope. "That Jeongan was a good kid," he said between tears.

"Thank you for your help. I'll see you later."

As Reseng put the urn on the passenger seat and started the engine, Bear went to the back window to say good-bye to Old Raccoon.

"Good-bye, Mr. Raccoon. And good luck."

Old Raccoon looked at him for a moment and nodded.

On the way back to Seoul, Reseng parked the car on a hilltop. Old Raccoon watched in silence as he picked up Jeongan's box from the passenger seat.

"I'll be right back," Reseng said without looking at him.

The short mountain path ended at a cliff. The wind blew hard; it was a good spot for scattering ashes. Reseng pulled on a pair of white gloves, unsealed the box, and took a handful. As he opened his hand, a gust of air moving up the face of the cliff caught the ashes and sent them soaring. Reseng suddenly remembered a dumb joke Jeongan had once made.

"I wonder if my ability not to be remembered is hereditary. Like a gene for obscurity that I got from my father, etched into my DNA. That would be why my mother never felt sad about leaving him. If you don't remember someone, there's no reason to be sad. Pretty cool gene, right?"

"What's so cool about that kind of stupid DNA?" Reseng had asked.

Jeongan had laughed and said, "I can con someone I've already conned, or hit on a girl I broke up with, then dump her again and not feel bad about it. Because they're not going to remember my face anyway."

The morning after scattering Jeongan's ashes, Reseng took a long, hot bath. Afterward, he opened his wardrobe and stared at his clothes for a while before selecting a white button-down shirt, a black leather jacket, and blue jeans. As he toned and moisturized his skin and combed his hair back, he thought about how long it'd been since he'd had such a peaceful morning. The anxiety that normally plagued him had momentarily vanished. He looked at himself in the mirror and grinned.

"Damn, you're handsome," he told his reflection.

He opened a drawer. Inside were Chu's Henckels and a Russian PB/6P9 handgun fitted with a silencer. He tapped the grip with his finger. After a quick glance out the window, he took the knife and left the gun.

The first place Reseng headed was the M. Beef Market. An eccentric old man named Heesu worked there. People called Old Heesu "the king of the meat market." Everyone who worked in the market had to pay him a monthly fee. Drug dealers, gang members, organ traffickers, con men, middlemen for contract killers, fencers, pimps—no one was exempt. Even Hanja and Old Raccoon had to pay Old Heesu in order to do business in the market. But Old Heesu's fees were no more than fifty thousand won per month. He never took more just because someone made more, and he never let anyone off just because they made less. As long as they paid, he didn't care what they did. What was the point of collecting only fifty thousand? Did he use it to change the burned-out bulbs in the marketplace? No one knew.

When Reseng opened the door to Old Heesu's shop, two men— one in his late fifties with a wrinkled face, and one in his early twenties who looked like an adolescent—were gutting a cow. The baby-faced man was lifting entrails out of a red bucket, and the older man was carving out the cow's liver and lungs with a small curved knife. Each organ went into a separate bucket. As Reseng stepped in front of one of the buckets, the older man paused to look up at him.

"I'm here to see Mr. Heesu," Reseng said politely.

"Who're you?"

"I'm from the Doghouse."

The older man looked him over and turned to the younger man.

"Drop that and go tell Mr. Heesu he's got a visitor. From the library."

The younger man lowered the entrails back into the bucket and hurried inside. The older man took off his rubber gloves and sat on a bench, then shoveled a spoonful of rice soup into his mouth and followed it with a swig of soju. The sour smell of blood wafted up from the bucket of intestines. The smell was everywhere, but he kept slurping away at the soup, as if it didn't bother him one bit. After a moment, the baby-faced man returned.

"He says to go on in."

Old Heesu was sitting at a low table, reading a newspaper. Next to a cup of black coffee, a half-empty bottle of soju, a saucer of sesame oil, and an ashtray with a lit cigarette sticking out of it was a raw liver that looked like it'd just come out of the cow, and a small knife. Reseng bowed.

"Long time, no see. Everything okay with Old Raccoon?" Old Heesu asked as he lowered the newspaper.

"Yes, sir."

"From what I hear, things haven't been too peaceful for him lately."

"Well, from what I see," Reseng said, "he's pretty much always at peace. Or maybe he's losing interest in peace these days."

"Yeah? Of course, most of the rumors floating around the meat market are horseshit."

Old Heesu chuckled and took a sip of coffee, then relit the cigarette butt in the ashtray.

"So, what brings you to this smelly place?"

"I was hoping to ask you something."

"Ask away."

"I'm looking for the Barber. You'll know where I can find him, right?"

Old Heesu raised his eyebrows and stared at Reseng.

"Why come all the way here to ask me something Old Raccoon could've answered for you? He may stay cooped up in that library of his, but there's nothing he doesn't know."

"There's no way he'd tell me."

"Is the Barber on a plotter's list?"

"No, this is personal."

A mischievous look came over Old Heesu's face.

"Don't tell me you're looking to get a haircut."

"As a matter of fact, I am."

Old Heesu smiled and scrupulously stubbed his cigarette out again. There wasn't much left of it, but it was clear he planned to relight it later.

"How? You're not as smart as those pen-twirling plotters. And I assume you're not going to use a gun or plant an explosive."

"I'll use a knife."

Old Heesu leaned back against the couch. "Reseng versus the Barber . . ." He closed his eyes tight and murmured, "How would that end?"

Just then, the baby-faced man rushed into the office.

"Grandpa, Gukmangbong is refusing to leave until we give him an order of tripe."

"We're sold out. Tell him to come back on Thursday. We'll have more then."

"You know what he's like. He won't listen."

Old Heesu laughed. "What's old Mangbong doing out there?"

"He's thrown himself on the floor and won't stop crying and yelling. He did the same thing for two hours last time. We couldn't get any work done. He's such a pain in the ass!" The baby-faced man was at his wit's end.

Old Heesu laughed again and shook his head. "Ah, that Mangbong. He was so much happier when he was knifing people. Retiring has given him nothing but grief. Tell you what, boy. Skim a little off Kim's order and tell Mangbong to do what he can with that for now. And tell him to come in early Thursday morning, when the good stuff arrives."

"Yes, sir." The young man looked relieved as he left.

Old Heesu kept chuckling—no doubt at the thought of old Mangbong sobbing on the floor—as he poured himself a glass of soju. He cut a piece of raw liver, dipped it in the oil, and ate it.

"Funny how the older you get, the better you are at fending off knives, but I still have no knack for fending off tears. I swear, tears are mightier than swords."

He cut another slice of raw liver, dipped it in the oil, and offered it to Reseng, who took a hesitant bite.

"Fresh, huh?" Old Heesu asked.

"Yes, it's delicious. Looks terrible, though."

Old Heesu nodded and offered him a glass of soju, as well.

Reseng took the glass.

"That's life. Not much to it. Just one big stinking, filthy, squalid mess. But once you get a taste of it—ah! Then it's not so bad. Sometimes it's even delicious. So how about it? I think you should go home now and not do anything. And you should drop by more often, have a drink with me."

"I've already unsheathed my blade," Reseng said grimly.

"What, that? That's nothing. You just slip it back in its sheath and go on home."

"First Trainer, then Chu, and now Jeongan. It sure feels like the Barber is throwing down the gauntlet." Reseng sneered. "I could have lived with losing the first two, but all three? That's just too much. And I assume I'm next in line. I'm sure you've heard the rumors. But even if things were different, I'm still not exactly fated to live a long life."

Reseng drank the soju. Old Heesu cut off another slice of liver and offered it to him. Reseng ate it and poured a glass of soju for Old Heesu.

"What'll you give me?" Old Heesu asked.

"I was thinking we'd keep it simple with cash. I know cash is what makes the meat market go round."

"Four big ones."

Reseng took out his wallet, but Old Heesu waved his hands.

"Pay me later. If you come back alive."

"And if I die, I get to keep it?" Reseng asked with a laugh.

"Consider it travel expenses for the underworld. I can't be too stingy. It's bad for the soul."

Old Heesu gave him a pitying smile and tossed back the glass of soju. Then he wrote the Barber's address on a scrap of paper and showed it to Reseng, who nodded. Old Heesu set the paper on fire and placed it in the ashtray. Once the paper had burned down to ash, Reseng stood. He bowed politely to Old Heesu and left the shop.

The taxi pulled up in front of the convenience store, but Mito wasn't there. A young woman in her early twenties was at the register instead.

Reseng went inside and glanced around the shop. It looked as if Mito hadn't reported for work. He took a canned coffee from the fridge and two Hot Break bars from the shelf.

"The woman who worked here before—did she quit?" he asked.

"You mean Mito? Yes, she quit a few days ago," she replied flatly as she scanned his items.

"Right." Reseng nodded.

He sat at a table outside the shop and took a sip of the canned coffee. Then he smoked a cigarette. It was a clear November day. He might be dead in a few hours at the hands of the Barber, but, strangely enough, he wasn't nervous or afraid. It was a peaceful morning, perfect weather for taking a stroll. He took one of the Hot Breaks from his pocket, unwrapped it, and took a bite. It struck him as odd that candy could still taste sweet even when his friend was dead.

The hard drive that Reseng had stolen from Mito contained countless technical diagrams of elevators, sensors, closed-circuit cameras, monitors, and lights. He felt like he'd stolen an engineering student's homework. But when he examined them more closely, he found a single plotting file cleverly buried among the hundreds of other files. It contained a photo of a balding forty-five-year-old engineer who'd died in an elevator shaft. He had to have been one of the three of Hanja's plotters Mito had killed.

It was a simple plot. The man pushes the button for the elevator. He reads the paper as he waits. He always reads the paper while waiting for an elevator; he's a busy man. The elevator climbs to the seventeenth floor. But the only things actually climbing are the numbers on the digital display, not the elevator. The doors open with a friendly *ding!* A light turns on. His eyes still fixed on the newspaper, the man steps into thin air. Fade to black.

If someone were to have looked up "elevator accident" online, they would have found an article on a man who fell to his death about a month earlier due to a faulty elevator sensor. According to the article, the elevator company claimed there was nothing wrong with the equipment. The apartment building manager said that the elevator in question had been inspected regularly, and that nothing had been amiss at the most recent inspection; nothing unusual had been recorded on the security cameras, either. One member of the dead engineer's family had sobbed and said, "A perfectly healthy man is dead, and no one takes any responsibility?"

Reseng ate the rest of the Hot Break and left. When he reached the intersection, he debated whether he should head toward Mito's apartment or Misa's knitting shop, then slowly made his way to the knitting shop.

Fortunately, Misa wasn't there. Mito was by herself, knitting in the rocking chair. Just knitting away, like a farmer's wife who'd finished the day's work and had nothing else to do with her evening. She glanced at him and finished a row before getting up. She walked over and held the nearly finished garment to his shoulders to measure it.

"Hey, it's just right. I'm knitting this for you."

With a satisfied look, she went back to the rocking chair and resumed knitting. Reseng smirked and pulled a chair over to her.

"I heard Jeongan died," she said without looking up.

"Yeah, thanks to you," he said with a scowl.

"So now you're here to kill me?"

Reseng picked up the ball of yarn from the table and rolled it around on his palm.

"I haven't decided yet. Whether to kill you, then Hanja, then the Barber, or first the Barber, then Hanja, then you."

"In that case, kill me last, please. I have a lot to do. I need to finish knitting this before winter. And I need to find a home for Misa, somewhere safe. Then take out Hanja and Old Raccoon along with the rest of the garbage, and then . . ."

"You think you're funny." Reseng's voice was frosty.

Mito looked up from her knitting.

"Don't worry," she said. "Even if you don't kill me when it's over, I'll take care of it myself."

"You're going to commit suicide?"

"Yeah."

Reseng stared at her. She was giving him her naïve, no-big-deal look.

"No wonder you're so fearless. You've been planning to die all along."

Mito resumed knitting. There was something resolute about the skillful, practiced way she worked the needles.

"Why?" Reseng asked. "Just come up with a great plot with that smart brain of yours. Kill all the plotters, then kill all the assassins as a bonus, and after you've purged the world to your liking, you can escape overseas with Misa and cross-eyed Sumin and live happily ever after."

"I'd love to, but at some point little ol' Mito here turned into a monster, too."

Her expression hardened. She put the yarn and knitting needles back in the basket and set it to one side, then laced her fingers together and stretched her arms overhead.

"You know the story," she said. "The sad story of the hero who hunts down a monster, only to become a monster herself in the end. I am that tragic hero. So what can I do? Once my job is done, this poor, gruesome monster will have to finish off the good Mito, as well. But hey, if you're still angry at me then, you're welcome to do the job yourself."

"Do you enjoy planning people's deaths?"

"Not at all." She laughed weakly. "Jeongan's death hurt you, right? It hurt me, too. It hurts every time—always has. Every person you and I killed and all the people they left behind hurt just as much."

Reseng glared at her. She took the brunt of it head-on. He

dropped his gaze. On the toe of his shoe was a splotch of dried blood that must have come from Old Heesu's shop. Reseng stood up.

"The Barber, Hanja, then you. Better get all your knitting done before then."

Mito's eyes widened. "The Barber will kill you!"

"Wow, I guess I've been a pretty terrible assassin," he said with a chuckle. "No one wants to bet on me."

"Don't do anything yet." She looked panicked. "I have a plan. I'll kill the Barber and Hanja and little ol' Mito, just the way you wanted it."

"Didn't I tell you last time?" he scoffed. "I'm not hiding under your skirt. I'm not saying I wouldn't get up in there for other reasons, but to be honest, mean, skinny girls like you have never been my type."

Reseng took the other Hot Break bar from his pocket and put it on the table.

"Here. A present."

Mito stared at him, dumbfounded. He smiled at her, then slowly headed for the door.

"You dumb fuck! If you go to the Barber, you're a dead man!" Mito's shouts followed him as he stepped outside.

THE BARBER AND HIS WIFE

"You seem like a distinguished gentleman. I can tell you live a fine, distinguished life," the Barber said as he cut Reseng's hair.

Snip, snip went the scissors as they danced around Reseng's ears. The barbershop was old, with outdated white tiles lining the sink area. It looked like something you'd see in a black-and-white photo, like the kind of place Reseng had seen when he was twelve or thirteen, running errands for Old Raccoon, where boys went to get their compulsory buzz cuts before starting middle school, shyly rubbing their scalps as they walked out the door in front of him, identical to the one Reseng had gone to for the same buzz cut, even though he wasn't a student, while the other boys were in class.

"You strike me as far more distinguished," Reseng said.

"Me? Not at all. I'm just scraping by one day at a time with my scissors here. But you, on the other hand, seem like a successful man. I've been cutting hair for thirty years now, and I can always tell what a man is like just from the back of his head. I have a sixth sense about these things."

"Oh yeah?" Reseng cocked his head dubiously.

"Absolutely. Trust me. You'll be an important person one day."

The Barber smiled. His was an ordinary face. The face of a friendly neighborhood uncle you'd see anywhere. He wasn't especially tall, hovering somewhere around 170 centimeters, and he was extremely lean, almost devoid of muscle except for the bare minimum he needed to cut hair. How could someone who was just skin and bones have killed elite assassins like Trainer and Chu? Reseng was starting to wonder if he'd come to the wrong barbershop.

The Barber placed a finger below each of Reseng's ears and

examined his face in the mirror. Then he picked up his scissors again and snipped off a tiny bit of hair on the right-hand side.

"You have a long forehead, so you probably don't want it too short in the front. . . ."

"Do whatever you think is best, as long as it's nice and neat."

" 'Nice and neat,' " the Barber said, echoing his words. "I take it you have an important occasion? Blind date, perhaps?"

Reseng laughed and said, "More like a solemn occasion."

The Barber nodded. He combed down the front of Reseng's hair, scooped the ends up between his fingers, and took small snips. Then he combed it again and checked that the hair was straight. He looked satisfied.

"How's that? Look all right?" he asked.

Reseng inspected himself in the mirror. "You're talented."

"That's kind of you to say so."

The Barber looked pleased. He used a sponge to wipe away the strands of hair from Reseng's head and the front of the cape, and from his own arms. Then he lathered up the back of Reseng's neck and shaved off the stray hairs.

"All done!"

The Barber carefully removed the cape and guided Reseng over to the sink. He placed a showerhead in a plastic basin and filled it with hot water. When it was half-full, he mixed in several scoops of cold water from a barrel and checked the temperature. He added some more cold water and felt it again, repeating the process several times. When the temperature seemed just right, he handed Reseng a plastic dipper instead of the showerhead.

"Sometimes the water turns scalding and startles customers. I know it's a little awkward, but you'll be better off using this."

Reseng nodded and used the dipper to pour water over his head. Thanks to the Barber's careful work, the temperature was perfect. The tiny snippets of hair spilling into the white sink looked like ellipses on the blank page of a book. While Reseng shampooed his hair, the Barber put two clean towels on the counter and hummed as he swept the floor.

Reseng filled the dipper again, this time with cold water to splash his face, and dried his hair with one of the towels. A chest of drawers next to the mirror was piled high with unopened envelopes. Reseng slipped one of the envelopes out of the pile while pretending to towel his hair. It was an urgent reminder of overdue hospital bills.

"You don't see many barbershops like these nowadays. I'm guessing business is good here?" Reseng asked as he dried his ears with the towel.

"Hardly. Nowadays, young people prefer to get their hair cut in salons by pretty stylists. Why would they come to an old-timer like me? But since we're on the outskirts of the city and there's an army base nearby, the officers drop by now and then, and the old guys in the neighborhood come here to play chess and get a shave. So I manage to make ends meet."

He discarded the hair he'd swept up, placing it in a blue plastic trash can. Reseng sat back down while the Barber brought out a hair dryer and began to dry his hair for him.

"Would you like a shave today?"

Reseng stroked his chin. Three freshly sharpened straight razors sat side by side on the counter, as spick-and-span as the Barber himself.

"I just shaved this morning," Reseng said.

The Barber nodded and handed him a comb. Reseng combed his hair and studied himself in the mirror. The Barber wasn't lying about his thirty years of experience; it was a flawless haircut.

"Are you from here originally?" Reseng asked.

"Yes, born and raised. Did my army training here, too."

"The HID base is here, right? Where they used to train secret agents to send into North Korea?" Reseng continued to arrange the front of his hair.

The Barber's hands skipped a beat in the middle of folding the cape.

"That was a long time ago. Not that I would know anything about it. I was just an ordinary infantryman."

"It must be hard living way out here."

Reseng poured some aftershave into his hands and patted it onto his face. It smelled the same as whatever the Barber had used on his own skin.

"It's a little boring at times, but it's not bad. Once a month, my wife and I visit a retirement home in the mountains of Gangwon Province and give haircuts to the old people there. It's a chance for us to enjoy the fresh country air."

"Do you have any other side jobs?"

"You mean like driving a taxi?"

"No, more like assassinations and contract killings."

The Barber's face hardened.

"You have an odd sense of humor. How could a weak old barber do those terrible things you only see in movies?"

"You look pretty trim and agile to me." Reseng looked the Barber up and down. "Not an ounce of flab on you."

"I wouldn't call it trim. More like scrawny." The Barber lowered his gaze to the floor.

"Is that so?"

"That is so."

"How much for the haircut?"

"Seven thousand won."

"That's cheap."

"Country prices."

Reseng walked over to the coatrack and reached into the inside pocket of his leather jacket. He felt the weight of Chu's knife. The Barber tossed Reseng's used towel into the laundry bin and started washing his hands in the sink.

With his back to Reseng, he said, "Let's leave that knife where it is. Take it out and you're dead."

Reseng put the jacket on. The Barber dried his hands on a fresh towel. Reseng walked over to the front door and locked it. Slowly, he pulled Chu's Henckels from its leather sheath. Chu's handkerchief was still tied around the top of the handle. The Barber put the towel on a chair and shook his head at Reseng.

"Pretty sure I already fought that knife's owner. What's your name?"

"Reseng."

"Then you're from the library." The Barber's voice was hollow.

He placed his left hand on the headrest of the chair. There was no trace of fear in his face, despite the knife in front of him.

"Am I on the library's list?" he asked.

"There's no list. This is personal."

"Personal . . ."

The Barber gazed off into space, his eyes fixed on some distant point. He might have been recalling past events; occasionally his eyes glazed over. A faint shadow appeared over his melancholy upturned face and then vanished. Reseng gauged the distance between them. About four meters. One step, and then another quick step, and then a leap, and he could sink his knife into the Barber's throat. An antique grandfather clock on the wall ticked loudly. The silence continued. Reseng had been holding the knife up in front of his solar plexus and it was getting heavy. He lowered it. The Barber tore his eyes away from whatever spot he'd been contemplating and looked at Reseng.

"Is this because of the boy I killed a few days ago?"

"It might be. And it might not be."

Reseng looked down at the Henckels. A single loose thread was sticking out of the knot in the handkerchief. Reseng plucked it and let the thread drop to the floor. The Barber stared hard at the knot.

"To be honest, I don't really know why I'm doing this," Reseng said with a smile.

"Then you can still walk away."

Reseng smirked. "I don't know about that. I'm already here— how can I walk away now?"

"It takes more courage to put a knife back in its sheath and walk away than it does to take a knife out."

"I guess I'm a coward, then. Sorry."

The Barber lifted his hand from the chair and started to say something, then stopped himself. He let out a deep sigh. His shoulders drooping, he looked old and frail, like one of those elderly men who sit on park benches in the sun. Bits of black hair were stuck to the front of his white smock.

"I feel bad about the knife's owner. And bad about the boy. But I had no choice. You and I are both assassins, so you know what I mean."

"Yes, I do know what you mean."

"Since I'm not on your list, and you're not on my list, we have no reason to fight. We're not the type to settle things this way. We're just assassins for hire."

"Yes, we are just assassins for hire."

"Are you going to put the knife down and walk away?"

The Barber was staring him straight in the eye.

"No."

"Why not?"

"Boredom. All kinds of boredom. Boredom that slowly eats us up, like rust, on both sides of the knife. Since we're both assassins, I think you know what I mean." Reseng mimicked the Barber's voice.

The Barber's face fell. He looked at the three freshly sharpened razors sitting side by side on a towel. They were not what he'd used on Trainer and Chu.

"Mind waiting a second?" the Barber asked.

Reseng nodded. The Barber took off the white smock and hung it up, then went into another room farther inside the shop. Reseng moved the Henckels from his right hand to his left and wiped the sweat from his palm onto his jeans. The checkerboard pattern on the floor, which would soon be slick with someone's blood, made him dizzy. The ticking of the grandfather clock paused for a moment, and a chime rang out, signaling that it was 3:00 p.m. The Barber came back in. He opened a black bag and peered inside before pulling out a knife. It was a Mad Dog SEAL ATAK, the kind Trainer had used. It had a serrated back, and was the same brand that Reseng had used when Trainer first taught him how to use a knife. Mercenaries from the special forces loved those knives. Simple design, excellent cutting power, and a superior grip, which made it easy to grab even in the dark. Sharp and strong. But also very expensive and difficult to find nowadays.

"Nice knife," Reseng said.

"Better than yours."

The Barber was watching Reseng in the mirror. He looked forlorn. He glanced back and forth between Reseng's reflection and his own and let out a short sigh, then closed the bag. He walked to the center of the barbershop and stood in front of Reseng.

"Good timing," he said, gesturing at the grandfather clock with his chin. "My wife's not home. She still thinks I'm an ordinary barber."

"Good for her. For never figuring it out."

"Is that a good thing?"

"Not knowing is better than pretending not to know. Especially when it comes to people like us."

"I suppose you're right," he said, lowering his head as he echoed Reseng. "It's much better not to know people like us."

The Barber raised his head and locked eyes with Reseng. It seemed there was nothing left for them to say. Reseng switched to a reverse grip and dropped into a fighting stance. The Barber didn't move. He just stood there, relaxed, his arms behind his back and the knife hidden. Reseng gauged the distance between them again. Two meters? If he took a step forward and swung the knife, he might be able to graze the Barber's throat or chest with the tip of the blade. But the Barber just stood there. There wasn't an ounce of tension in his shoulders or neck or arms. He was waiting for Reseng, inviting him in, all stance and no strength.

Reseng realized he was making the wrong move. He straightened up and turned the knife around so the blade was pointing in front of him. Then he very slowly leaned his body forward half a step. The tip of the knife nearly reached the Barber's throat. But the Barber, apparently unconcerned, did not move at all.

The ticking of the grandfather clock was unusually loud. The Barber blinked. Reseng used that moment to lunge for his throat. The Barber pivoted his shoulders a fraction of an inch to dodge the blade, while the knife he'd hidden behind his back darted out and sliced Reseng's forearm. Then he feinted to the left, slicing Reseng in the side as he went. Before Reseng could turn all the way around to face the Barber, who was now behind him, the Barber stabbed him in the thigh, released the knife with a twist, and stabbed him again in the left armpit. Reseng swung his knife wide, but the Barber skipped backward a few steps. The distance between them opened to about two and a half meters. The Barber flicked the blood from his knife. Then he put his arms behind his back again and looked at Reseng. He wasn't the slightest bit winded.

Blood dripped onto the checkered linoleum. It trailed down Reseng's forearm and over the back of his hand, soaking Chu's handkerchief. The blood was warm. Reseng slowly looked down at himself. The blood pouring from his side and under his arm had already soaked his white shirt and was dripping from his belt. He reached inside his leather jacket to feel the wound. It wasn't as deep as he'd feared. If he hadn't been wearing the jacket, the blade might have gone much deeper.

The Barber was keeping his knife hidden behind his back. Now that he'd exposed Reseng's weaknesses, he looked carefree, even arrogant, inviting Reseng in again. But that would be the wrong move. If Reseng went at him, he'd get cut again. It was hard to tell where the Barber's weight was centered, and, without seeing his knife, Reseng couldn't tell where the next slash would come from. The knife wouldn't move until Reseng did. He couldn't read anything from the Barber—not from his face, his eyes, or his feet. He wasn't even completely sure where the Barber's feet were planted. It struck him then that he was not going to win. He was going to die there.

Reseng switched the knife to his left hand. The Barber cocked his head at this. Reseng took a step forward, the blade aimed at the Barber's throat. The Barber didn't move. Reseng took another half step forward. The Barber still did not move. His eyes invited him in again. Reseng slid his left foot forward and simultaneously lunged at the Barber's throat with his left hand. The Barber took the knife out from behind his back and sliced Reseng's left forearm just as Reseng's right hand jabbed the Barber hard in the throat. The Barber staggered backward. Reseng switched the knife to his right hand and lunged at the Barber's face. The Barber threw his head back to dodge it. But his face wasn't Reseng's actual target. The Henckels sank deep into the Barber's inner left thigh. Reseng pulled it out and turned the blade so it was facing skyward and aimed for the Barber's abdomen. The Barber regained his footing and blocked the knife with the back of his hand, simultaneously sticking his own knife into Reseng's side as Reseng lunged toward him. The blade plunged deep into Reseng's body, then withdrew. Reseng fell to his knees.

The Barber took several steps back to catch his breath. Blood was gushing out of Reseng's side. He felt dizzy. He stuck the tip of his knife into the floor and struggled to keep from collapsing. The Barber stood there looking down at the top of Reseng's head.

"Using your left hand as bait," the Barber said as he flicked away the blood dripping down the back of his hand. "You learn fast. Much faster than the knife's owner."

Drops of blood fell from the tip of his Mad Dog. Blood was gushing from his thigh and soaking the leg of his pants. But Reseng realized that was as far as it would go. His knife would not reach the Barber's heart. Reseng leaned on his knife and staggered up to a standing position. The Barber shook his head. Reseng tried to grip Chu's knife again, but he had no strength in his right hand.

"The nice thing about *this* job is that I don't have to disinfect my knives," the Barber said.

"Hilarious," Reseng said with a weak laugh.

"I guess I can't ask you to stop now."

"I'm nearly there."

Reseng swung the knife at him uselessly. The Barber grabbed Reseng's right wrist with his left hand and twisted it, then sank the Mad Dog deep into Reseng's right side. Reseng slumped to his knees again. The Barber knelt in front of him and pulled the knife out. Then he placed his hand on Reseng's chest. He seemed to be catching his breath, because he paused there for a moment with his head down and his eyes fixed on the floor.

"I'm sorry," he said. "This old barber is so ashamed of himself."

Reseng lost his balance and leaned his head on the Barber's shoulder. With Reseng's head resting against him, the Barber pressed the tip of his finger between Reseng's ribs, looking for the right spot to insert his knife. Then he aimed for Reseng's heart.

A soft, pale hand came out of nowhere and wrapped around the blade. The sharp edge sank into the delicate skin. Blood dripped. The Barber did not move or turn his head.

"Honey, you can stop now. Our daughter wouldn't want this, either."

Reseng lifted his forehead from the Barber's shoulder and looked up. A woman, fifty-something, with a gentle-looking face, was standing behind the Barber, crying silently.

"It's time for us to say good-bye to our daughter and let her go," she said. "We've lived long enough, too."

The Barber's hand shook violently on the knife's grip. Reseng was dizzy; he had lost too much blood. He rested his forehead on the Barber's shoulder again. Blood continued to drip from the Barber's wife's lovely pale hand, which was still squeezing the blade. The sound of the Barber's wife's stifled tears was as cold as the winter wind seeping in through a crack in the door. His head resting on the Barber's shoulder, Reseng passed out.

THE DOOR TO THE LEFT

He heard laughter.

Laughter like a flower garden in May. Laughter like the wings of tiny birds flying low and fast, like the buzzing of honeybees busily cruising the tops of flowers. Endless chatter followed by firecracker bursts of laughter. What was so funny? The sound made Reseng laugh along in his sleep, although he had no idea what he was laughing at.

Where was he? He heard running water. Was there a stream nearby? Not likely. There were no streams. It was just the sound, ringing in his ears for no reason. Ever since becoming an assassin, he had sometimes heard this sound in his dreams, and each time he thought to himself that this must be death: lying still in a place with the sound of water in the background. A place just like this one. Where he could hear water. Where he could not move any part of his body. Where he lay stretched on a cold gravel bed, looking up at the sky for an eternity. It occurred to him suddenly that death must be very close. He fell back to sleep.

Reseng walked slowly into a forest carpeted in fog. His feet sank deep into its plush vapor, his pace as slow and plodding as that of an ox carrying a child on its back. Leaves weighted with ice-cold dew licked his cheeks as he passed. There, under the trees, was the nunnery's garbage can, where Reseng was born. He looked inside. It was filled with baby's breath. His cradle wasn't as bad as he'd thought. He turned his face to the sky and laughed. The leaves of a thousand-year-old gingko tree laughed with him. He threw his head back and looked up at the countless gingko leaves hanging from the heavy canopy. As the wind blew, the leaves all tipped in the same direction and laughed in chorus. What's so funny? he wondered. He cupped his hands around his mouth and shouted at the leaves, "Tell me what's so funny! Let me in on the joke!" But they just kept laughing and did not answer. *Teeheeheehee. Teeheeheehee.* The tittering of the gingko leaves sounded like the laughter of factory girls. Laughing girls brightening an alley at lunchtime. Walking along the beautiful forest path beneath a tunnel of tall trees were four factory girls, giggling as they went. A girl with a cute round face clutched her belly, as if she'd been laughing too hard, and said, "Oh, that's too funny, that's hilarious!" Reseng was delighted to see them.

"What are you doing here so deep in the forest?" he asked, blocking their path. "Don't you have to get back to work?"

The factory girls shook their heads. "Who are you?"

"Don't you know me? I did chrome plating, on Work Team Three. I rode the bicycle with the pink basket!"

They shook their heads again. They did not know him. They tried to walk past. He blocked the way. They cowered and looked scared. But the round-faced girl was brave.

"Get out of our way!" she said.

He grinned and pointed at her.

"I know you well."

"How do you know me?" Her eyes widened.

"You have a birthmark on your left butt cheek. In the shape of a rabbit. And two birthmarks next to your right nipple. One big, one little. Like a snowman. Like the sun and the moon. And . . . uh . . . you hate men who throw away pairs of underwear after wearing them only once. You say it's a waste of money. That's why you wash underwear hundreds of times before throwing them out. You squat on the bathroom floor and hum happy songs while scrubbing pairs of underwear, until they eventually fall apart. And . . . uh . . . when you get angry, your ears turn red."

The furious factory girl's earlobes had indeed turned red.

"Ha! See! They're turning red right now," he said excitedly.

She slapped him hard across the cheek. His eyes filled with tears as he stared at her. But she was still angry. She raised her hand again. Scared, Reseng turned away.

"You really don't know me? You don't remember?" he asked between tears.

"No! I don't know you!" A look of irritation crossed her face as she said, "What a weirdo, I swear."

The four girls continued along the beautiful forest path, leaving him behind. He could still hear their chattering voices in the distance. "What's with that guy? Is he crazy?" "I don't know how you can be so brave. I thought I was going to die of fright." "Seriously. He didn't look like a creep, so maybe he's just stupid." Their nonstop chattering could be heard all the way from the end of that long forest path. Then, more bubbles of laughter. Why didn't she remember him? He stared down the path where the girls had gone.

He heard water again. Ice-cold water running over gravel. "Am I dead?" he asked himself in his dream. The gingko leaves rattled in the wind as they answered him. *You're dead. Long dead. Long, long dead.* The ancient trees nodded, as if it must be true.

When Reseng came to, the first thing he saw was a skinny blond Barbie standing on his chest. Misa was holding the doll and poking its legs into his collarbone. Pooh Bear was sitting alongside Barbie, and a stuffed Dalmatian stared dumbly at him from his solar plexus. Misa picked up the Dalmatian and shook it. "Booooring! Oh my god, I'm so bored!" The dog wagged its tail and scampered across Reseng's stomach. Misa grabbed the Barbie again.

"Ooh, he's so muscular!" Barbie exclaimed.

"You have a thing for muscles, don't you?" said pantsless Pooh. "But this is a hill we're standing on. Who ever heard of a muscular hill?"

"Shut up, Potbelly Pooh," said Barbie. "Go put on some under-wear."

Misa walked the Barbie doll down Reseng's chest and onto his stomach. Each time the doll's legs pressed into him, his knife wounds ached so much, it felt like they were reopening.

"Misa, that hurts," Reseng whispered.

She jumped in surprise, then smiled brightly and called out toward the living room.

"Mito! Sumin! Reseng is awake!"

Mito and the cross-eyed librarian ran into the room and stared at Reseng. They looked as if they were staring down into a well. Mito held one finger up in front of his eyes and moved it slowly from left to right and right to left. He frowned and ignored her finger. Mito's eyes bored into his for a moment, and she laughed.

"Hey there, Mr. Frankenstein," she said.

Reseng looked around. They were in a cabin. Outside the window was a persimmon tree that had shed its leaves, and beyond that was a high mountain.

"Where are we?" he asked.

"The house where Mito was conceived," Mito said, referring to herself in the third person, as if Reseng were a child. "The weekend farm where my father tricked my naïve mother into coming with him to pick tomatoes so he could jump her. Though fortunately, that's how Mito was born."

"Sis!" Misa gave her an angry look.

"Oh, sorry! Our darling Misa was conceived in love, with consent. But her big sister's birth wasn't so nice. Whenever our mother was angry with our father, she told me, 'That man jumped me. He grabbed me from behind when I was picking tomatoes. That's where you came from. And that's why my life turned out this way.' Each time she told me that, our dad's face turned bright red and he didn't know what to do with himself." Mito burst into laughter.

Misa and the librarian stared dumbly at her.

"How long was I out for?" Reseng asked.

Misa held up five fingers. Reseng's face fell.

"Are you hungry?" Misa asked.

Was he? This was his body, but he couldn't seem to feel anything.

"I can't tell," he said.

"You must be starving. You haven't eaten for five days, after all."

"Why would he be starving? He's been gulping up all that expensive dextrose solution," the librarian said with a pout.

"You know that's not the same as food," said Misa. "I'll make him some delicious rice porridge."

She wheeled over to the kitchen. Reseng raised his head to check his body. His arm, shoulder, and stomach were bandaged.

"Did you do this?" Reseng asked Mito.

"Yes, at my friend's animal hospital. You lost a lot of blood. You almost died."

The cross-eyed librarian was looking at him with the same sour face as always. At least he assumed she was looking at him; he was never quite sure. What he was sure of was that she thought he was pathetic.

"Next time, use a gun," she said quietly, so Misa wouldn't hear. "Don't go rushing into battle if you're not up for it. You just end up making trouble for everyone else."

"The Barber knows who I am now, thanks to you," Mito said. "Sumin's been exposed, too. All three of us are in danger because of what you did. It's also thrown a small wrench in the plot I came up with for bringing down Hanja. But that's okay. It just means I'll have to put things in motion now rather than later. It's important that we continue to think positive."

She glanced over at the librarian, who smiled back at her. Reseng could not figure out what was going through those crazy girls' heads. "You saved me from the Barber. I don't suppose you managed to grab my knife, too?" Reseng asked somewhat bashfully.

Mito gave him a frosty look. What did he want with Chu's knife? Reseng was surprised at himself for asking.

"I'll take care of the Barber," she said firmly. "You have a different job to do."

Mito left the room, followed by the librarian. Reseng could hear the three of them laughing and chatting in the kitchen. Most of it was about how to cook rice porridge. After a moment, Misa appeared with a bowl. Mito and the librarian put on their coats and prepared to leave. While the librarian laced up her shoes at the front door, Mito came over to Reseng and whispered in his ear.

"Don't get any stupid ideas in that empty head of yours. You'll only make things worse. Just eat your porridge and get lots of sleep until I summon you." She dragged out the word *lots*.

She and the librarian left. Misa dipped a spoon into the bowl, blew on it to cool it, then offered the spoon to Reseng. He gazed blankly for a moment at Misa's face and at the steam rising from the spoon. Misa held it closer. He opened his mouth. Her porridge, the first warm food he'd eaten in five days, was delicious. Reseng ate the whole bowl and fell back to sleep.

Reseng slept, just as Mito had told him to. He fell asleep and dreamed, and when he awoke, he ate more of Misa's porridge, then fell asleep again. No matter how much he slept, an endless drowsiness kept washing over him. He couldn't help wondering if Misa had added sleeping pills to the porridge. Or maybe there were sleeping pills in his water cup, or in the flowers in the vase, or in the warm sunlight spilling through the window and over his bed. He ate porridge and slept, and even in his dreams he slept.

In the evenings, Mito returned and undid Reseng's bandages to disinfect the wounds. Then she gave him an injection. On the nights Mito didn't come, the librarian changed his bandages for him instead. "How did you get involved in all this?" Reseng asked the librarian as she wordlessly wrapped a clean bandage around him.

She didn't answer.

"This isn't a game," he said. "You could die."

She pulled hard on the bandage as she tied it off. It was agony. Reseng felt as if the wound was going to burst. He groaned.

"You're not the only one with a story," she said, gathering up the scissors and the old bandages. "So stop acting as if you know everything, as if you're the only tragic one here."

She was right. Everyone had a story. Old Raccoon, Chu, Bear, Mito, the Barber, even Hanja. They fed their anger, hated one another, and even killed one another because of their particular story. They all believed their injuries justified their actions. But did they? What a load of crap, Reseng thought, then said to himself, And you're as big a prick as the rest of them.

Now and then Reseng awoke, to find Misa playing with her Winnie-the-Pooh on his stomach. It reminded him of how Desk and Lampshade used to fall asleep on his back or with their tails draped across his thigh.

"Aren't you a little old to play with stuffed animals?" Reseng asked. "Why not try something else?"

"Something else?" she asked, stroking the loose seams on the doll.

"Yeah. For instance, you could get a cat. Cats make people happy."

Misa raised an eyebrow, considered the idea. But she shook her head.

"I don't want a cat or a dog. It'll die before I do, and I can't get close to anything that will die before me. My stuffed animals will outlive me as long as I mend them." She gave the old Winnie-the-Pooh a shake.

"How come you never ask any questions?"

"About what?"

"About anything."

"Because even if I knew what was going on, I couldn't do anything about it. So I pretend not to know anything about the things I can't control. The more I pretend not to know, the more I actually don't know." She smiled.

Pooh shook his head on Reseng's stomach.

"Have you ever read a book called *The Doubting Polar Bear*, by G. Y. Gumdory?" he asked.

"Is that a famous writer?"

"Not at all. The book is about a polar bear who questions whether he's really a polar bear."

"Why would a polar bear question whether he's a polar bear?"

"Well, it's a funny story about a polar bear who wonders why he's a 'polar' bear, specifically, and not any other kind of bear. Is it simply because he was born at the North Pole? He hates the fact that where he was born determines what he is, and he hates that he had no choice in the matter. He could've been a grizzly bear instead, or a panda bear, for instance. He agonizes for a long time over why he had to be born a polar bear."

"Sounds more like a stupid bear to me."

"No, for a bear to be asking that sort of question, it means he's a very philosophical bear. Anyway, the doubting bear decides that he has to leave the North Pole in order to find out what kind of bear he really is. He opens up a map to look for a place that's completely different from the North Pole and chooses California."

"A bear does that?"

"Yes, a bear does that."

She shook her head in disbelief.

"Wouldn't he need a boat or something to get all the way to California from there?"

"Sure. But sadly for him, the polar bear doesn't have a boat. So he saws off a piece of iceberg. He climbs onto it and sets sail for California. The wind blows hard, and the tides push him farther and farther away into the huge ocean. But the farther he gets from the North Pole, the faster his iceberg melts. His raft is disappearing beneath him, with no new land in sight, let alone California. When the enormous iceberg he started with is barely an ice cube, the doubting polar bear finally figures it out. "Aha!" he says. "This is why I'm a polar bear. Because I can never leave the North Pole." Then the last of the ice melts and dumps him in the water, and the doubting polar bear has to swim all the way back home. The end."

"Does the polar bear drown?"

"I don't know. The story ends with him still swimming."

"I hope that bear was a good swimmer," Misa said worriedly.

"Don't you think we're the same?"

"Same as what? That stupid polar bear?"

"We were all born at the North Pole and we hate it at the North Pole, but no matter how hard we try, we can't leave."

Misa stared at him.

"I don't mind the North Pole," she said, smiling brightly. "California's too hot. And besides, who ever heard of a California bear? That just sounds weird. If I'm born at the North Pole, then I'll stick with being a polar bear."

With December, the frost arrived in the forest. By morning, the grass and leaves were pale, frozen, and covered with icy powder. The birdsong died, as if all the birds had left for warmer places. On the second day of December, Sumin, the librarian, chopped down a pine tree; that evening, the three women trimmed it with tiny lights, colorful balls, and ornaments shaped like presents, stars, bells, Santa Claus and Rudolph, magic wands, and sweets. Misa turned bits of cotton into snowflakes and stuck them on the branches. Their laughter never stopped. They seemed intent on laughing until Christmas Day. But there was something anxious about their merriment. Their laughter had a nervous edge; it sounded at times like dogs howling at the dark. Their movements were exaggerated, their joy bordering on desperate, as if they were bracing for a coming sadness.

Reseng's wounds healed. He was able to walk around more easily, although he still had trouble standing up straight. Misa seemed entertained by the way he shuffled around with his bottom sticking out. She laughed her head off each time he went for a walk.

Mito checked his scars and reminded him, "You need to move around as much as possible."

So Reseng went for walks in the forest around the cabin. The garden was wreathed with peach, pine, apricot, and chestnut trees. If no one had died and no one had been hurt, Reseng thought, weekends at the cabin would have been peaceful and beautiful. As long as no one died or got hurt.

The cabin had been built on a mountain slope. A single paved road led to the front, and out the back was a steep, narrow path inaccessible to cars. Reseng examined the path. It was unpaved, with tree roots jutting out here and there. It didn't look as if a wheelchair could negotiate it. If assassins found them, the three women would never make it out alive. Already rumors would have spread about Reseng's fighting the Barber, about a woman disappearing with Reseng. The rumors might have even reached Hanja's ears. Trackers could already be on the move. How long did they have?

Mito and the librarian were coming and going constantly. Each night, after Misa went to bed, the two of them sat in the attic and had long, heated discussions. Some of the discussions dragged on so long that Reseng could still hear their murmuring voices when the sun came up. But neither Mito nor the librarian told him anything. They didn't tell him how they planned to fight Hanja or Old Raccoon, or how the whole foolhardy lot of them intended to make a living later.

Reseng passed the time reading books and sleeping and gazing out the window at the wintry mountainscape. Sometimes he stared up at the roof beams and pictured the way the Barber had moved. There one second, gone the next. Light, easy, fluid, and lightning-fast. If I fight him again, can I win? he wondered. No sooner did he ask himself that than an icy terror gripped him; he felt as if he were standing on the tip of a knife. It would be too difficult. If he went up against the Barber again, he really would be a dead man.

Reseng awoke, to find Mito standing over him. He had no idea how long she'd been there. Her expression was grim.

"What time is it?" he asked.

"Three a.m."

"What are you doing?"

"I have instructions for you."

"I don't need your plans. Just a gun and a knife."

"Don't get any stupid ideas. Now is not the time for another of your childish tantrums."

"When assassins come bursting in here, what're we going to fight them off with? Pots and pans?"

"The election is less than twenty days away. Hanja doesn't have time to worry about us, and frankly, he doesn't have any reason to yet. We're going to hit him before he hits us."

"Fine. What the hell is your plan?"

"So you'll help?"

"Don't know. Can't make any guarantees."

She gave him a long, quiet look before continuing.

"I have all of Dr. Kang's data. Information on plots dating back twenty years, of people who died without a trace. And Hanja keeps ledgers in his safe. They contain records of every transaction he's ever made with politicians, businessmen, the library, contract kill brokers, and assassins. He's landed himself a big account for the election, so that information will also be in the ledgers. Also, there's Old Raccoon's book."

"What book?"

"The book that describes in detail every major assassination in South Korea's modern history over the last ninety years. The previous library directors wrote the chapters for the first fifty years, and Old Raccoon wrote the last forty."

"Old Raccoon wrote a book? You certainly know a lot about it, considering you've never set foot in the library. Meanwhile, I've been there for twenty-eight years and have never heard of it."

Mito glanced toward the librarian's bedroom. "There's definitely a book. And I know where it is."

"Are you telling me that this book that will overturn everything we think we know about contemporary Korean history, and throw the entire country into turmoil, is sitting right out in the open alongside the other two hundred thousand books in the library? Where? Next to *Crime and Punishment*? Or no, wait, I know. It's next to *The Grace and Drama of Japanese Baseball,* isn't it?"

"It's under Old Raccoon's study," she said calmly.

"In the basement?"

She nodded. "It's a thick book with a leather cover. Looks like a Bible. You'll know it when you see it."

"How did you find it?"

"Men like Old Raccoon think all women are airheads. Especially when those women are cross-eyed."

Reseng burst out laughing. To think that the dopey-looking cross-eyed librarian had been screwing over Old Raccoon the whole time. Reseng tried to imagine the look on proud Old Raccoon's face when he found out.

"Hanja doesn't keep his ledgers at work," continued Mito. "They're in a safe house, and only Hanja and his lawyer have access to them. Hanja won't respond to threats, but his lawyer will. He has two pretty daughters and a wife, and he's a weak, sniveling coward. If you poke him a few times with your knife, he'll start talking. As for the library basement, two people have access: Old Raccoon and you. If you can bring me both Old Raccoon's book and Hanja's ledgers, your work is done. Whatever you do after that is up to you. Once I have all three, including Dr. Kang's data, I'll be holding all the cards."

Reseng stared at her.

"You really think you can pull it off? Even if you do get your hands on all those documents, you'll have every assassin in the country out for your blood. And not just them. The government, the military, the police, the prosecutors—everyone will be after you. Because everyone in this country who's ever held even the slightest bit of power is connected to a plotter."

"Aren't elections fun? It's like one big party. Ambition, greed, and vanity, all gathered together in the same spot, all sticking their necks out. And everyone's eyes are fixed on the spectacle, hoping to see the lies exposed. It's perfect timing for something to explode. And everyone's hoping something will explode. I have a plan. What do you say? Will you help me?"

Reseng thought it over.

"If you succeed," he said, "then everyone I know dies. I'll die, too. But the plotters behind the scenes, who control us like puppets? They'll come out of it alive. That's what history tells me."

Mito laughed.

"Maybe, maybe not. I haven't gone into battle yet. But at least you won't die a cowardly polar bear."

The next day, the first snow of the year fell. Misa couldn't keep away from the window. She was completely entranced. But for Reseng, the heavy blanket of snow made him feel cut off, as if he'd come too far and was in greater danger because of it. He added coal to the stove and topped up the kettle. The muscles in his side were still stiff, but he could move more easily now. Mito and the librarian were gone. He felt relieved. If they'd been home, the three of them would've driven him crazy, prattling on all day, no doubt, about the snow.

"Isn't the world just so beautiful when it snows?" Misa said as she gazed out the window.

"Beautiful?" Reseng muttered. "Two centimeters of snow is all it takes to make the dirt and filth underneath beautiful?"

Misa frowned at him. "Why are you so negative? It's just snow."

Reseng laughed. "I guess you're right. It's just snow."

"Ah, I wish I could go out in it," she said, stretching her arms overhead.

Reseng immediately put on a hat and went out to sweep the snow. Snowdrifts filled the garden and forest path. He liked the feeling of the cold flakes that stuck to his face and melted there. As a child, he used to spend hours sweeping up the cherry blossoms that swirled around the courtyard every spring. The broom had been taller than he was. He would sweep the ground clean and turn around, only to discover more fallen blossoms piled up behind him. Distraught by the dying flowers that never stopped falling, he had spent whole afternoons sweeping up blossoms. He finished clearing a path from the garden out to the main road, and returned to the cabin. He got a blanket and tucked it around Misa's lap.

"Put on a hat, or you're not going out," he said.

Misa obediently pulled on a knit cap. He lifted her onto the wheelchair and took her outside. The wheels made a funny crunching sound as they rolled over the snow.

"Isn't my chair too heavy in the snow?" she asked.

"It's not heavy."

Each time the wheels rattled over a rock or a root, Misa giggled. She stuck out her hand and caught a snowflake, then tilted her head back and let the flakes fall on her closed eyes.

"What kind of life do you want to have?" Reseng asked.

"I like this one," she said without opening her eyes. "Just like this."

Mito returned in the middle of the night. The gears ground and the car engine sounded unnatural as it came toward the cabin over the snow-covered road. The headlights illuminated the front window; then there was darkness. But Mito did not come in. Reseng got out of bed and looked through the window. Mito had both hands on the steering wheel with her head down, and her shoulders were shaking. She sat in the car for half an hour before finally coming in. Reseng got back into bed and pretended to be asleep. He heard the refrigerator door open and close, followed by the sound of Mito slumping onto the floor. Then, for a long time, he heard nothing at all. Reseng stared up at the ceiling in the dark for another twenty minutes before getting out of bed and going to the kitchen. He turned on the light and found Mito curled up next to the fridge, crying. He looked at her for a moment and got a bottle of water from the fridge. He drank a glass himself, then poured a glass for Mito.

"I didn't know tough bitches like you ever cried," he said.

Her smile was more of a sneer. She took a sip. Reseng sat at the table. Mito wiped her tears away with her sleeve.

"Aren't you going to ask why a tough bitch like me is crying?" she asked playfully, her eyes still welling with tears.

"No, women cry for as many reasons as there are stars in the sky."

She nodded in agreement.

"If I let you live, could you look after Misa?" The look in her eyes was mournful and earnest. "For five—no, just the next three years."

Reseng looked at her quizzically.

She added, "I'm not saying that's what'll happen, but just in case."

"What about you?" he asked.

"I'm not going to live that long."

"Why should you die, while I get to live? Because of that stupid morality of yours about monsters or whatever? Your dying won't change the world. So just live. What's the point of single-handedly saving the world, and then being the only one who dies? What kind of bullshit is that? Who do you think you are, Jesus?"

"I killed a little girl today. I gave her an injection. A little girl who's been in a coma since she was nine. A little girl with no sins and no power. And I killed her. With an injection."

Mito sounded drunk.

"Who was she?"

"The Barber's daughter."

Reseng stood up. He'd seen a pack of cigarettes somewhere in that kitchen. As he was opening the empty coffee jar on the shelf and peeking inside, Mito pulled a pack from her pocket and offered him one. He took it and lit it. On his second inhale, a wave of dizziness hit him; it was his first cigarette in a month.

"Why her?" he asked.

"Because she was what kept him working, not Hanja."

His left eye was suddenly throbbing. He rubbed it with his palm. Had he ever killed before out of faith or justice or anything like that? Never. He hadn't believed in those things. He'd killed because he was told to kill. Because the person he killed was on a list, and because he was an assassin. What was Mito killing for? The idea that you could kill someone for something you believed in suddenly filled him with fear. When he thought about it, that might have been what made plotters tick. Reseng took another drag.

"People hide their true motivations even from themselves," he said. "And they have to invent fake motivations in order to keep on fooling themselves. You don't know what your true motivation is, do you? You don't actually know *what* you're doing, do you? From what I see, you're no different from the rest of us. You're just like the Barber. And just like Hanja. You're exactly like all the other plotters out there. This new world you're imagining will end up being no different from the old world. The way cats still catch mice, no matter what color they are."

He stubbed his cigarette out in the water pooled at the bottom of the sink and tossed it in the garbage bin. Mito was still slumped on the floor, a look of devastation on her face.

"I'll get Hanja's ledgers for you," he said, aiming the words at the top of her head. "But not Old Raccoon's book. That's the best I can do."

The next afternoon, Reseng packed his things. Misa brought out winter clothes from the wardrobe and put them in his bag. The clothes had belonged to the sisters' deceased father. Most were slightly too big for Reseng.

"Your father was tall?"

"Tall and handsome," she said with a smile.

"I'll drop you off at the station," Mito said, standing next to him.

He could tell she wanted to say something to him in private.

"No, thanks," he said. "I want to walk alone."

With one eye on Misa, she offered him an envelope. He looked at it. He assumed it contained the location of Hanja's safe house and the room with the safe, the method for bypassing the security system, the date and time the lawyer would be there, and the list of ledgers he needed to retrieve. He put the envelope in his bag.

"Don't be late," she said.

"I won't," he said firmly.

Reseng smiled at Misa. She looked sad. He patted her on the shoulder and turned to leave, then walked slowly down the now-slushy road. Misa waved until he was out of sight.

Hanja's safe house was in a quiet residential area. It was an ordinary two-story home with a well-tended garden. The neighboring house was so close, the eaves were nearly touching. It was the kind of home where Reseng half-expected to see a family man walking up to the front door with a giant birthday cake for his twin daughters. Following Mito's instructions, Reseng climbed onto the neighbor's roof first and jumped over to the roof of Hanja's safe house. Next to a water tank was a boiler cabinet with a thirty-centimeters-square ventilation window. He gave the window frame a shake. It was shoddy quality; he was certain he could lift the frame out without breaking the glass. This is her big idea for getting me inside? Some plotter she is, he thought with a laugh.

Hanja's lawyer still hadn't arrived. Reseng checked his watch: 8:00 p.m. With his back against the water tank, he took the PB/6P9 out of the holster and looked at it in the glow of the streetlight. He unscrewed the silencer and reattached it, then took out the magazine, pulled back the empty slide, and released the trigger. Not bad, he thought. He liked Russian handguns because they were quiet. So quiet that the gun seemed to have been designed for the silencer, rather than the other way around. When was the last time he'd used a handgun? Several years ago at least. If they had to get close enough to a target to need a handgun, then most professionals preferred knives. Handguns were sloppy and left behind gunpowder residue and bullet casings. Not that he had to concern himself with that anymore.

He started to take out a cigarette from the pack in his pocket, but hesitated. Then he took one out anyway and lit it. One more thing to stop worrying about. When he was halfway through the cigarette, his cell phone vibrated. Mito was calling.

"Hanja's lawyer just left the office. He'll be there in twenty," she said.

"Don't do anything stupid like try to tail him. Just get over here and wait."

"When you get the ledgers, tell him you'll give them back for seven hundred and fifty million won. Otherwise, Hanja will get suspicious."

"Why's it got to be seven fifty?" Reseng grumbled. "Why not an even seven hundred or eight hundred?"

"The lawyer will have two bodyguards with him. Be careful. I'll be in the alley across the street."

She hung up. Reseng stubbed out his cigarette and slipped the butt into his pocket out of habit. Then he removed the ventilation window, slowly lowered it to the floor, and stuck his head inside. The space was tight, but if he wiggled his shoulders, he wouldn't have too much trouble getting in and out.

Just as Mito had said, the lawyer arrived almost twenty minutes later. Reseng stuck his head out over the roof and watched. A heavy-set man came running out to open the car door. The lawyer got out of the backseat, followed by a tall, slender man who appeared to be a bodyguard. He looked strong and deadly. The engine shut off, and a man who looked nothing like a chauffeur got out from behind the wheel. One fat guy, two bodyguards, and a lawyer. If things went sideways, this could get complicated.

As the lawyer went into the house, Reseng slipped through the ventilation window. He cracked open the door to the boiler cabinet and waited. He heard the men talking on the first floor. After a moment, the lawyer came up to the second floor alone, unlocked one of the rooms, and went inside. That room would have the safe. Reseng quietly crept out into the hallway and checked the first floor. The other three men were eating in the kitchen and cracking jokes. Reseng came back and tested the knob to the door of the lawyer's room. It was locked from the inside. He glanced downstairs again. The three men were laughing loudly. Reseng knocked on the door. He heard the lawyer say, "What is it?" He waited and didn't answer. More laughter from the kitchen. He knocked again. He heard a chair squeak and the lawyer's irritable-sounding voice. Reseng squeezed a wet handkerchief in his left hand and gripped the gun with his right.

"What the hell is it?" the lawyer asked as he opened the door.

Instantly, Reseng shoved the wet handkerchief into the lawyer's mouth as he pushed him backward into the room, then fired a bullet into his left thigh. The lawyer looked bewildered as he gazed down at his bleeding leg. Reseng turned to check downstairs. The sound of raucous laughter was still coming from the kitchen. He closed the door and locked it.

"Make a sound and I shoot you in the head. Got it?"

The lawyer nodded. Reseng took the handkerchief out of the lawyer's mouth. Then he shot him in the left knee. The lawyer shrieked. Reseng raised one eyebrow.

"What're you, deaf? I just said two seconds ago that I would shoot you in the head if you made a sound."

He aimed the gun. The lawyer closed his mouth, his eyes welling with tears.

"Think you can follow directions now?"

The lawyer nodded repeatedly. Reseng shot him again in the left knee. The lawyer gritted his teeth and fell to the floor. He rolled from side to side, smearing the carpet with blood. After a moment, he seemed to adjust to the pain, and his groans subsided. Reseng nodded at him.

"That's a very painful place to get shot, but you're handling it like a champ. I guess that's how you were able to pass the bar exam."

Reseng sat down at the table in the middle of the room. The

lawyer had his face to the floor, grinding his teeth. Reseng lit a cigarette.

"You won't be able to use that knee anymore. The knee joint's a tricky thing. Once it's broken, it's very difficult to repair. But there's a big difference between limping on one leg and limping on two legs. You could say it's the difference between a cane and a wheelchair."

Reseng exhaled a long puff of smoke.

"So what do you think? Would you like to keep your right knee?"

The lawyer nodded.

"I need Hanja's ledgers. I know they're here, and I know you know how to open the safe. So open it. If you drag your feet, you'll spend the rest of your life in a wheelchair. If you don't open it, you're dead."

The lawyer looked up at him. "What do you need the ledgers for?"

"I'm planning to retire, but no one's offering me a pension."

"There's money in that suitcase. Around three hundred million. You can have it."

Under the desk was a black wheeled suitcase. Reseng walked over, the cigarette in his mouth, and opened it. It was filled with cash.

"Three hundred million?"

The lawyer nodded.

"Three hundred . . . That's an awful lot of cash. I guess because it's election time? Anyway, thanks."

Reseng picked up the suitcase and walked back to the lawyer. He stared down at him. The lawyer raised his head and stared back. Reseng raised his gun and shot the lawyer in the right thigh. The lawyer stifled a shriek.

"The next bullet's going in your knee. So out with it: Where are Hanja's ledgers?"

The lawyer's face twisted in pain. "If I give them to you, I'm dead anyway."

"I hate lawyers. You guys are always so sharply dressed, so calculating, so smooth with your logic, and so slippery, you think you can worm your way out of anything. But how're you going to get out of this one? I think today is the day you're going to have to apply the same impeccable logic as when you waltzed into the library with Jeongan's body. Do you prefer to die at my hands, after I've run out of bullets shooting you in every single one of your joints? Or at Hanja's hands? Think fast, now. I don't have a lot of time."

Reseng aimed the gun again.

"The safe is under the desk."

Reseng grabbed him by the back of the collar and dragged him over. The lawyer balked. Reseng pressed the gun to his head. The lawyer pulled back the carpet underneath the desk, took a remote control out of his pocket, and keyed in a number. The floor opened, revealing a safe. The lawyer keyed in another number and the safe opened. Inside were several ledgers and CDs. Reseng stuffed them all into his backpack. The lawyer stared at him dumbly.

"This is what you tell Hanja: All I need is money. Two billion in bearer bonds, one billion in cash. Split the cash evenly into two leather bags."

The lawyer nodded. He looked relieved. Just then, there was an urgent knocking at the door. Reseng turned to the lawyer, who looked panicked.

"What'd you push?" Reseng asked.

"I forgot to cancel the alarm when I opened the safe. . . ."

A lame excuse. Reseng zipped the backpack shut and looked at the lawyer, who was now shaking uncontrollably. Reseng frowned and shot him in the right knee. This time, the lawyer screamed at the top of his voice.

The knocking changed to pounding, and then someone started kicking the door. Reseng pressed himself to the wall next to it. He slowed his breathing and cracked the door open just as the man outside was in mid-kick. The man fell into the room. It was the driver. Reseng shot him in both legs. Then he shot at the slender man standing in the hallway. The slender man did a front somersault, dodging the muzzle of the gun, and grabbed Reseng by the arm into a shoulder throw. It was a smooth, skillful move. Reseng dropped his gun as he was hurled to the hallway floor, and the slender man grabbed it. Reseng stood, massaging his shoulder. The man pointed the gun at him. He looked at ease with the weapon. From his shoulder holster, Reseng took a brand-new Henckels that he'd bought at a department store on the way there. The man sneered.

"What're you, stupid? I've got a gun," the slender man said.

"You're out of bullets. Your boss wasn't very cooperative."

The man pointed the gun at the wall and pulled the trigger. It clicked. He tossed the gun to the floor. There was another in his jacket, but it looked like a tear-gas gun. He pulled a knife from his belt—a military knife used in the special forces.

"Have we met?" Reseng asked.

"Yeah, at Chu's funeral."

Indeed, it was the same beanpole of a man who had accompanied Hanja the day they cremated Chu.

"You don't look like an assassin. I'm guessing you're a soldier?" Reseng said.

"I was for a long time."

"Then keep being one. Defend your country and your family—with honor."

"Honor doesn't put food on the table," the slender man said, raising his knife.

Reseng lowered his knife and walked closer. His stride was easy, as if he were out on a stroll. The man lunged at Reseng's face. Reseng pivoted left to dodge the blade, and slashed the other man from shoulder to armpit. The man dropped his knife. Reseng moved to the right and slipped his knife gently into the man's side. The man fell to his knees. He lowered his head but didn't groan. Reseng pulled the knife out. Then he picked up the fallen gun, put it back in the holster, took out a handkerchief, and wiped the blood from his knife. When he went back into the room, the lawyer was flailing in a pool of blood and talking to someone on his cell phone.

"It's that asshole from the library. He's taking the ledgers. Yes. Yes. They're right next to me. I've been shot. . . . No, not bought, *shot*."

Reseng looked down at the lawyer in amusement. The lawyer glanced up at him and put the phone down, terrified.

"You work too hard," Reseng said.

He took his backpack off the desk, picked up the suitcase full of cash, and headed downstairs. Halfway down, the fat man appeared with a baseball bat. Despite his size, the man's hands were trembling violently. Reseng looked more closely. It was the same security guard from Hanja's office, the pack of hot dogs. Reseng sneered as he glanced up at the bat.

"You counting on hitting me with that?"

The pack of hot dogs looked up at the bat, too, fear spelled out clearly on his face. Reseng shook his head.

"C'mon, don't use that on people," he said.

The pack of hot dogs collapsed on the floor.

Reseng opened the front door and walked outside. When he reached the alley, he saw Mito's car. He tapped on the window. She rolled it down. He took his backpack off and handed it to her.

"This should settle my debt," he said.

Mito unzipped the bag, pulled out one of the ledgers, and checked the contents. Reseng held up the suitcase he'd taken from the lawyer. "I'll give you this if you promise to stop now and leave the country with Misa. There's three hundred million in here."

"You think you can buy me?"

"Maybe."

"Get in."

He shook his head. She stared at him.

"Get out of here," he said. "Hanja's people will be all over this place any minute now."

Mito reluctantly started the engine.

"We'll meet again. Stay safe until then. And remember," she said with a smile, "the only person who can save you is Mito."

Reseng watched as she drove away. An absurd sense of loneliness washed over him. He lit a cigarette. Although he'd been away for only a month, the city lights felt strange, dizzying. Soon, Hanja would be releasing his trackers and assassins. Reseng suddenly had no idea which way he should go.

He headed down the street. The suitcase was heavy. The tiny wheels crunched loudly over the asphalt. He could leave the country. He had a bag filled with three hundred million won. It wasn't a huge amount, but it was nothing to sneeze at, either. He could get a fake passport, smuggle aboard a ship in Incheon or Busan, sail around the world to Mexico, swig tequila and grow old peacefully. He could go somewhere far, far away, where no one knew him and his past could not follow him, where he would stutter his way through learning the language, come up with a new name, marry an exotic woman, make babies with her and a new life for himself doing honest physical labor.

"Could I really?" he asked out loud, his voice weak. When he looked up, the city lights were like knives slashing at his pupils. Fatigue descended over him all at once, and his legs grew weak. The black suitcase dragging behind him and the gun and knife hanging from his shoulders all felt so heavy. But maybe the weight he felt wasn't actually from the suitcase or the gun or the knife. . . . He hailed a taxi. The gray-haired driver asked where he was headed. "Seoul Station," said Reseng.

At the station, Reseng perused the endless list of city names posted above the ticket booth. He spent close to an hour staring at the timetable with its unfamiliar destinations, but he could not for the life of him decide where to go or why he was standing there in the first place. He walked outside. People running for trains rushed across the station plaza. Christmas carols were playing on a loop through loudspeakers. Reseng went down the stairs into the underground passageway and put the suitcase in a coin locker.

At the other end of the passageway, two drunken homeless men were shoving each other and swearing. Others were asleep behind windbreaks they'd fashioned out of cardboard, while a few were eating dried ramen noodle crumbs and drinking soju. Reseng sat down on the cardboard next to the sleeping bodies. One of the men who'd been drinking glanced at him and sidled over. He poured soju into a paper cup and offered it to Reseng. Reseng read the expression on the man's face: Fuck my life. Bleary-eyed from alcohol, Fuck My Life kept holding out the paper cup. Reseng took it and drank, then handed the cup back. The man offered him another, but Reseng waved his hand. Fuck My Life stumbled back to his seat. The alcohol spread quickly from Reseng's empty stomach to warm the rest of his body. He lay down on an empty sheet of cardboard. A cold wind blew in through the entrance. In the distance he heard the faint ringing of a Salvation Army bell. Neatly dressed women walked past, giggling. I like the sound of women's laughter, he thought. Women's laughter all sounds the same. Those women, Mito, that cross-eyed librarian—he bet even women from Swaziland to Sweden laughed the same. Reseng laughed, too. He pulled his knees up to his chest, rested his head on the inside of his arm, and fell asleep alongside the homeless men.

In the morning, Reseng took the first train to D Town, back to the Barber's shop. He tested the doorknob. He'd assumed the barbershop would be locked, but the door swung right open. He stepped inside. The Barber was sitting there with the lights off. Reseng sat next to him. The Barber looked at him in the mirror. His eyes were vacant. No surprise or anger. Just the tired face of an elderly barber overcome with loss.

"Oh, good, you're in one piece," the Barber said quietly.

Reseng nodded. An urn wrapped in white cloth sat on the shelf.

"Is that your daughter?" he asked politely.

"My wife. Funeral was yesterday." The Barber's voice was flat.

Reseng nodded again. They sat side by side for a while without speaking. The Barber's eyes were fixed on his hands in his lap, while Reseng stared back at his own reflection in the mirror. He took a pack of cigarettes from his pocket and offered one to the Barber. Reseng lit it for him and then lit his own.

"Mind if I ask what brings you here? I assume you're not just looking to avenge your friend," the Barber said.

Reseng took a long drag before speaking.

"If your daughter hadn't been sick, would you still have worked as a cleaner?"

In turn, the Barber took a drag and slowly exhaled.

"Hard to say." His voice was calm. "What would you have done if you were me?" He turned to look at Reseng.

"I made a huge mistake when I was twenty-two," Reseng said. "I was just a kid, young and awkward and full of fear. But that's no excuse in this line of work. As you know, assassins who mess up have to die. Otherwise, someone else dies in their place. Just like that kid Dalja who died instead of you."

The Barber's lip twitched.

"In my case, Trainer died instead of me. He was a million times better than I am. And you know what I did? I ran away. To a factory. Something inside me just flickered out." Reseng let out a bitter laugh. "I've been running ever since. From my mistakes, from Trainer's death, from an opportunity to live a normal, honest life, from the woman I loved. Trainer told me once, 'The second you close your eyes, you never open them again.' Well, I closed my eyes. I've been terrified of going up against the brutal Barber, whom not even Trainer or Chu could beat."

"That's why you came looking for me?" the Barber asked, a mocking edge to his voice.

Reseng nodded. The Barber looked up at the ceiling. Ash fell from the cigarette dangling between his fingers.

"Did that woman kill my daughter?" he asked.

"She's a doctor, so it would've been painless."

The Barber stubbed his cigarette out in an ashtray and got up from the chair.

"Wait here a second."

He went into the inner room and came out with a bag. He opened it, took out Chu's knife, and offered it to Reseng. Reseng took it. The blade had been cleaned. The Barber pulled out the same Mad Dog knife as before.

"Have you ever killed someone without being paid to?" the Barber asked.

"Nope, never. I shot and stabbed a few people last night, but they should still be alive."

"You're the last assassin I'll ever kill. And the first one I'm killing for free."

Reseng took off his jacket and leather holster and hung them on the coatrack. The Barber looked at the gun in Reseng's holster and ran his forefinger along the tip of the Mad Dog. Reseng moved first to the middle of the barbershop. The Barber walked slowly over and stood in front of him. Reseng raised his knife. The Barber nodded once, then lunged at Reseng's face. Reseng pivoted to avoid the blade. The Barber swung again for Reseng's throat. Reseng blocked the incoming knife and nicked the Barber's forearm with his own knife. The Barber's blade twisted around and cut Reseng's right cheek. Both took a step back from each other. Blood dripped from the Barber's forearm. Reseng felt his right cheek with his left hand. Blood came away on his fingers.

"You've gotten much better," the Barber said, wiping away the blood dripping down his forearm to his wrist.

"I lay in bed and thought about you thousands of times a day."

"In bed, huh?"

Reseng resumed his fighting stance. Just like the last time, the Barber hid his knife behind him and stood there looking relaxed. The old grandfather clock ticked off the seconds. The soles of Reseng's shoes squeaked against the tiled floor. He thought he could hear running water. Cool water flowing over gravel. It occurred to him that he didn't care anymore whether he ended up lying next to that stream. The Barber's body swayed slowly from left to right and right to left again, like a tree stirring in a breeze, saying, *Come on, come on over.*

Reseng lunged hard at the Barber's throat. As if he'd been waiting for exactly that, the Barber stepped back, whipped the knife around in his left hand, and stuck it in Reseng's side. Reseng grabbed the Barber's hand and pulled the knife even deeper into his own body. The Barber stared at him in shock and confusion. With one strong slash of Chu's knife, Reseng sliced the Barber's throat open. The Barber stood there, stunned. Reseng leaned against the chair next to him. The Barber lifted his hand to feel his throat. Blood gushed from the wound. He gazed at his wife's urn for a moment, then smiled at Reseng and slumped to the floor, his head dropping to his chest.

—

Reseng sat in the barber's chair and leaned back. The pain had finally hit him. He looked down at the knife buried deep in his side. Blood was seeping out along the blade and soaking his shirt. Pulling the knife out would only speed the blood loss. He lit a cigarette and exhaled a cloud of smoke at the mirror. The Barber was reflected in the glass, still on his knees, with his head down, as if repenting his sins. The clock on the wall pointed to 8:40. Reseng smoked half his cigarette, then took his phone out of his pocket and made a call. After about ten rings, Bear answered in a sleepy voice.

"Eight a.m. is the middle of the night for Bear," Bear grumbled.

"You're going to have to make a pickup. The barbershop across from the post office in D. It's a small town, so you can't miss it. You'll find one dead body and one urn. After you cremate the body, please mix the ashes with the ones in the urn and scatter them together. With great care, please."

"Who is it?" Bear still sounded a little groggy.

"The Barber."

Bear swallowed hard—Reseng could hear it over the phone.

"Will you be there?" Bear asked.

"No, I have to go. The door will be locked, so you'll have to find a way in."

Reseng hung up and checked his face in the mirror. Blood dripped from the cut on his right cheek. He wiped it away with his palm. "There's something different about you," he said to his reflection. The face in the mirror smirked and the head shook slowly. He gave his reflection a halfhearted grin, then took another drag on his cigarette. When he stood up, blood ran along the back of the knife and dripped onto the floor. He crushed his cigarette out in the ashtray and grabbed two towels from the shelf. He wet one of the towels in the sink and used it to wipe the blood from his side, then rolled up the dry towel and stuck it inside his shirt to stanch the bleeding. He tilted his head back, a grimace on his face, and let out a deep groan. Then he sat down again, took Hanja's business card out of his wallet, and dialed.

"I assume your lawyer gave you my message. Three billion. Better start counting those bills," Reseng said.

Hanja was quiet for a moment before responding. "Ever seen an anaconda swallow an alligator? It can't digest it. Ends up dead of a ruptured stomach." He sounded furious.

"Don't worry, I won't get a tummy ache. I'll give you three days. After that, I'm selling the ledgers to someone else for less. So be a good boy and get that cash ready. Don't get overzealous and release the hounds too soon."

Reseng hung up. The Barber's blood had pooled on the floor and was spreading toward the sink. He went to the coatrack and put the gun holster and jacket back on. But the jacket wouldn't close around the knife sticking out of his side. The Barber's old winter coat was hanging on the rack. He hesitated and then put on the coat, as well.

Reseng locked the barbershop's door behind him. He took five steps and glanced back to see whether he was leaving drops of blood. There were none. With one hand pressed firmly on the towel inside his shirt, Reseng slowly headed out of D. But before he could reach the town limits, he was hit by a wave of dizziness. His side was screaming with each step. What was worse, each time he flinched from the pain, blood dripped from the knife onto the dirt road. He hurriedly scuffed the dirt to erase the blood. He wouldn't get far at this rate. He stopped and looked around. An old two-story building on the edge of town had a medical clinic. Reseng headed toward it.

The clinic was small and very old. There was only one other patient, an elderly woman. The nurse seemed to have stepped away from the front desk. He peeked inside the half-opened door of the office and saw an old man, around seventy, playing the card game Go-Stop online and cursing at the computer. "You idiot, why'd you take that card? Well, you ate shit, so now you better shit it out." Reseng walked into the doctor's office with his gun drawn.

"I'll leave once you stop the bleeding," Reseng said, making an effort to sound polite. "As long as you don't call the police, no one will get hurt."

The elderly doctor slid his reading glasses to the tip of his nose and looked Reseng up and down. Reseng pulled back one side of the coat to show him the knife. The doctor got up and walked over slowly. He eyed the coat for a moment, then pulled it back to study the wound.

"Take off the coat and sit there."

He gestured with his chin to an examination table at one end of the office. Reseng took off the Barber's coat and hung it on the coatrack.

"You'll have to take that off, too."

The doctor was looking at the leather holster slung around Reseng's shoulder. Reseng took off the holster and hung it next to the Barber's coat. The doctor tossed a syringe, several bottles of medicine, a pair of scissors, antiseptic, gauze, and bandages onto a tray and pulled on a pair of surgical gloves. The equipment looked a little meager for treating such a deep knife wound. But Reseng didn't have much choice in the matter. He lay down on the table.

"You going to point that gun at me the whole time?" the doctor asked as he cut off Reseng's shirt.

Reseng lowered the gun. The doctor soaked a piece of gauze in alcohol and disinfected the skin around the wound. Then he inserted the syringe into one of the medicine bottles.

"I don't need anesthetic."

"It's going to hurt."

The doctor pressed the plunger to clear the syringe of air bubbles and tried to inject it next to the wound. Reseng raised his gun and aimed it at the doctor.

"I said I don't need anesthetic. Or painkillers."

The doctor stared at him.

"This is an antibiotic."

Reseng sheepishly lowered the gun. The doctor gave him the injection, then stared at Reseng for a couple of minutes without moving. Reseng gave him an incredulous look.

"That wasn't an antibiotic, was it?"

"Hard to say. I might've mixed up the bottles."

The doctor's voice sounded surprisingly similar to Old Raccoon's. Reseng let out a hollow laugh before he passed out.

The December sun beamed down into the hospital room. Reseng startled awake at the sunlight warming his face. An IV solution dripped slowly out of a bottle hanging above him. It took all of his strength to get out of bed. His shirt and pants were gone, and he was dressed in old-fashioned blue-striped hospital pajamas. Blood showed through the bandage around his stomach. Reseng pulled the IV needle out of his wrist and put on the Barber's old coat, which was still hanging on the rack. When he came out into the hallway, he heard women's laughter from another room. The doctor was still playing online Go-Stop in his office. Reseng went inside. The doctor looked up from the computer screen and stared at Reseng.

"Woke up, huh?" the doctor said.

Reseng bowed and asked, "Why didn't you call the cops?"

"What's the point? They'd just be a headache, and I am too old for that kind of headache. You leaving now?"

Reseng nodded.

"You know insurance won't cover this."

Reseng smiled. It was nice to meet someone with a sense of humor.

"Thank you for your help. I'd like to say that I'll repay your kindness next time, but to be honest, I don't know if I'll get that chance."

The doctor took a shopping bag out from under his desk and handed it to Reseng. Inside were Reseng's knife and gun, the leather holster, and the Barber's Mad Dog.

"I know the owner of that coat. I was one of his regulars," the doctor said.

Reseng's hand paused while taking hold of the shopping bag.

"Was he a good friend of yours?" he asked.

"Not really. Sophisticated intellectuals like me don't have much reason to rub shoulders with that world. I got a haircut from him now and then, and sometimes we played baduk. At any rate, judging by the shit knife he used, I'd say he wasn't planning to kill you."

Reseng stared at him, dumbfounded, and nodded slowly. The

doctor turned his gaze back to the computer. Reseng said good-bye. At the front desk, the nurse was explaining something to the elderly woman. After the woman left, Reseng took out his wallet.

"Checking out already?" the nurse asked.

He nodded. The nurse tapped at the keyboard to calculate his bill. He took out ten hundred-thousand-won bank checks and put them on the counter. The nurse stopped typing and stared at them.

"This is for the hospital fee and these ugly pajamas, and for forgetting you ever saw me. Will that cover it?" he asked.

The nurse's jaw was hanging open. Reseng took five more hundred-thousand-won checks from his wallet and added them to the stack. Then he left the hospital.

It was night when he reached Seoul Station. Reseng opened the coin locker and stared at the suitcase of money inside. If he took that money and left right now, would he make it? India, Brazil, Mexico, Papua New Guinea, Venezuela, the Philippines, New Zealand, Czech Republic . . . Names of countries he'd never been to scrolled through his mind. "I hear there are a lot of beautiful women in Venezuela," he babbled nonsensically. This was his last chance to leave. In three more days, every assassin and tracker from the meat market would catch up with him.

A loud shout came from the corner of the underground passageway. Reseng turned to look. Two homeless men were shoving each other, arguing. Sitting next to them, guzzling alcohol just like last time, was Fuck My Life, who'd given Reseng a paper cup of soju. His only worldly possessions appeared to be his mismatched layers of dirty clothes, the pieces of cardboard on the ground to insulate him from the cold, and the bottle of soju. Was it a terrible life? Probably. And yet his face, with its look of complete and total resignation, struck Reseng as somehow serene.

Reseng opened the suitcase and transferred ten bundles of one million won each to a shopping bag. He zipped the suitcase shut and took it out, then switched it from the day locker to a long-term storage locker and closed the door. On his way out of the underground passageway, the locker key in his hand, he paused to look at Fuck My Life.

"Can you spare a thousand won for ramen?" the man asked bluntly.

Reseng looked him straight in the eye, but the man didn't seem to remember him.

"If you're not giving me anything, then go. Don't just stare at someone when he's talking to you, goddammit. I'm not a bum."

What a joker. Begging for money but swearing he wasn't a bum. What did that mean? Probably nothing at all. It was just meaningless prattle, to match his meaningless life.

"What? What?" the homeless man yelled. "Goddammit, what's your problem? Why're you being a dick? You mad? If you're mad, hit me. Hit me!"

Reseng dropped his eyes from the man's face and scraped his shoe against the ground to dislodge a piece of gum stuck to the sole. Fuck My Life babbled to himself about "fuckers looking down on him" and took a swig of soju. Reseng took five bundles of cash out of the shopping bag and placed them in front of the man, who looked up at him in shock.

"Use that to start over. Before you drink yourself stupid and freeze to death on the street."

The man stared wide-eyed at the money but didn't touch it, as if dubious it was really his. Would he be able to make a fresh start? Probably not. He'd live it up for a while without having to worry about how to afford his next drink. Eventually, the money would run out. He'd end up back here, get drunk, and freeze to death. Right in the same cold, miserable, stinking, familiar spot. Reseng walked away. From behind him, he heard the man saying, "Thank you, sir! Thank you! People like you are going straight to heaven, sir!"

Reseng went up to the Seoul Station plaza to have a cigarette. The smoke felt like shards of broken china going down his throat. The painkiller seemed to have worn off; the knife wound in his side was throbbing. The cold December air sharpened the pain.

Clutching his side with his left hand, Reseng squatted in the corner of the plaza to catch his breath. People eyed him as they walked by. A Salvation Army volunteer was ringing a bell in the middle of the plaza. Reseng used his cigarette butt to trace the Chinese characters for his name in the dirt: 來生, "Next Life." Then he wrote *Venezuela*. He wondered where Venezuela was. He spun a globe inside his head to try to find it and laughed out loud at himself. "Idiot," he muttered as he flicked the cigarette butt away. He got up, walked over to the taxi stand, and got into a cab.

The library looked like a bomb had gone off inside: The floor was strewn with thousands of books, shelves had toppled over, and the librarian's desk was littered with boxes and drawers. Reseng headed for Old Raccoon's study. The hidden door in the back that led down to the basement was wide open. Old Raccoon was picking up fallen encyclopedias and reshelving them.

"Did Hanja do this?" Reseng asked.

"Who else? You think a pack of wild boars tore through here?" Old Raccoon said, straining to feign humor.

Being attacked by boars would have been better. No one had ever done anything like this to the library. For ninety years, it had been lady-in-waiting to the country's highest powers, the truth behind every major assassination, and the inner sanctum for contract kill brokers, plotters, and assassins. Hanja had panicked. Or maybe he'd finally gotten sick of showing his perfunctory respect for the Doghouse.

"When did he come?"

"Last night. You must've done something pretty spectacular. He was out of his damn mind. He threatened, then pleaded, then threatened again," Old Raccoon said with a chuckle.

Reseng picked up an encyclopedia from the floor.

"What're you doing here anyway?" Old Raccoon asked. "Hanja's people will be out there hunting you down."

Behind his cynical tone was a hint of anxiety.

"I thought I should say good-bye before I go."

"Before you go? Don't you mean before you die?"

Reseng didn't answer. He put the encyclopedia back in its proper spot on the shelf. Old Raccoon sat on the couch and lit a cigarette. He gestured for Reseng to sit with him. Reseng took the chair opposite.

"Is this because of that girl?"

"Who said that? Did Hanja say that?" Reseng asked angrily.

"Jeongan told me a few days before he died. Said you were hung up on some amazing girl."

"No, I'm not," Reseng said, flustered. "Jeongan was full of shit and talked too damn much about things he didn't understand."

"And yet I miss that mouth full of shit that talked too damn much. Without him, I have no idea what's happening anymore."

Old Raccoon smiled glumly as he took a long drag on the cigarette.

Glancing over Old Raccoon's shoulder, Reseng spotted an open gun case sitting on the desk. Inside was a .38 Smith & Wesson, practically an antique. When he was little, Reseng had gotten the scolding of his life from Old Raccoon for playing with the revolver. He hadn't seen the case since. All at once, the events of the past few days, which had been hanging in his head like a thick fog, sharpened into focus. A cold, distressing sensation pierced Reseng right through the heart, as if he'd stepped on a trip wire and set off a booby trap. He felt like a fish with a torn fin that had drifted too far and could never return home. Old Raccoon read the look in Reseng's eyes.

"People think villains like me are going to hell," Old Raccoon said. "But that's not true. Villains are already in hell. Living every moment in darkness, without so much as a single ray of light in your heart, that's hell. Shivering in terror, wondering when you'll become a target, when the assassins will appear. True hell is living in a constant state of fear, without even knowing that you're in hell."

Old Raccoon took another drag. Reseng lowered his head. They sat in silence for a moment. Old Raccoon finished his cigarette and lit another.

"Aren't you here for the book?"

"No, I'm not," Reseng said firmly.

Old Raccoon nodded to show he didn't care either way, and said, "Come with me."

He stood and walked out of the study. Reseng jumped up and followed him. Old Raccoon stopped in the middle of the bookshelves near the western wall and pulled out a book. The shelf was the same as all the other shelves in the Doghouse, accessible to anyone, even a certain nine-year-old boy who could have reached out his hand and grabbed it at any time. Contrary to what Mito had said, there was no leather cover and it did not resemble a Bible. It was simply a book, hardly any different from the countless other books in the library. Old Raccoon looked around at the shelves, the book clutched in his hand.

"Will this book make the world a happier place? Hard to say, but I doubt it. Nothing good ever came out of a book."

Old Raccoon held the book out to Reseng, who stared back at him in confusion.

"What do you want me to do with it?"

"Do with it what you will. You can give it to the girl, burn it, sell it, or fill the rest of the pages yourself. It's just a book, after all."

Old Raccoon's hand shook. The book looked heavy. Reseng hesitated to take it from him.

"There's one thing I've always wondered," Reseng said. "The name you gave me. Does it mean that since this life is already messed up, I should try harder in my next one?"

Old Raccoon laughed.

"I had no idea your name had such a clever meaning behind it." The laughter still showing in his face, Old Raccoon held the book under Reseng's chin. Reseng accepted it with trembling hands.

"Don't come back. It takes tremendous courage to run away. I could never escape this hell. You know, coming here for the first time as a clueless young librarian was heaven for a cripple like me. But it never was for you."

Old Raccoon hobbled away between the shelves and closed the study door behind him. Reseng stared at it for a long time. That door was always shut tight, but today it looked more solid, impenetrable. He headed for the exit, glancing back as he went. Bracing for the sound of a gunshot.

Snow fell as he made his way up through the forest, heavy flakes turning the narrow path into cotton candy. The wound in his side throbbed each time his foot slipped. Reseng checked his watch: 3:00 a.m. The dead of night. The snow-covered path was luminescent against the dark, and the shadows of trees cast across the snow looked like spilled blood.

When he reached the garden gate, Reseng stopped to smoke a cigarette. Mito's attic window was the only one with a light on. It looked warm and inviting, like a lighthouse on a hometown coast. Though he hadn't knocked, the door to the cabin swung open, as if it had been waiting just for him. Mito looked out at him, one hand on the doorknob. Reseng stubbed out his cigarette and went inside. Mito closed the door behind them without a word.

In the bed under the living room window—the bed in which Reseng had recuperated—Misa was asleep, the tattered Winnie-the-Pooh clutched in her arms. Her elephant-print pajamas looked baggy; either they'd always been too big for her or she kept getting smaller.

"Was that Misa's bed to begin with?" he asked.

"No, that's the guest bed. But she's been sleeping there ever since you left."

Reseng looked down at Misa's sleeping face. A few tiny capillaries were visible through her pale skin. Reseng placed his hand lightly on her forehead. At the touch of his cold hand, she tossed in her sleep.

"Why are you touching my little sister?" Mito whispered.

"She's so pretty."

Mito smiled and nodded, as if that were obvious.

"I guess that means I'm pretty, too. Since we're from the same parents."

Reseng stared at her in astonishment.

"What, you don't own a mirror?" he said.

Mito grinned, then pointed toward the attic room.

"Wait up there for me," she said. "I'll bring us something to drink."

Reseng tiptoed up the stairs. The table in the attic was piled high with documents. There were more boxes of documents under the table. Reseng was rifling through files when Mito returned with a pot of persimmon-leaf tea.

"What is all this? Preparation for fighting Hanja?"

"Hanja?" Mito scoffed. "Hanja fights in the sandbox with the little kids like you. Mito is after much bigger adversaries."

"You're not planning to kill Hanja?"

"Not with a knife."

"Then?"

"I'll send him to prison."

Reseng gave her a disappointed look.

"How naïve of you. Do you seriously think the law will judge him?"

"No, not at all."

"Then . . ."

"They'll have to go through the motions at least. It's election season. They won't be able to just cover it up. There's the money, and the ledgers, and too many watching eyes. Once the dam breaks, there'll be no stopping it. I'll keep backing them into a corner, little by little, and then right at the end, *pow!*" Mito glanced over the pile of documents as she spoke.

"How do you plan to have him arrested?"

"As loudly as possible. In front of as many people as possible. Ideally, with lots of cameras and all of it broadcast live," she said cheerfully.

"Dream on. A fox like Hanja will never come out of his den."

"He has no choice. Without his ledgers, he's dead anyway. And he doesn't have time to pull any stunts right now. With everything that's going on, even a nine-tailed fox would have to come out of its hole."

"What about you? How do you plan to get away after making your deal with Hanja? His people will be all over you like a swarm of bees. Dealing with them is not like twirling a pen and scribbling down schemes. They're highly trained."

"I won't get away," she said nonchalantly.

"You won't get away?" Reseng cocked his head.

Mito sat down at the table.

"The only way to fight is to go into the tiger's den. For both Hanja and me. The prosecution will be investigating a suitcase full of cash, Hanja's ledgers, Dr. Kang's data, and me: Dr. Kang's assistant and South Korea's greatest contract kill broker and plotter. Can you imagine how many people that will put on edge?"

Mito was smiling. She was clearly amused. But what on earth was so funny about this?

"You plan to die there."

"Not without a fight."

"You could just smoke him out. That's your specialty."

"That only works for catching rabbits."

"If you go in, then who'll take care of the rest?"

"Sumin will. She'll control the flow of information, release it at the right times. She's better at that than I am. Information management is her specialty, after all."

"That's true. That cross-eyed librarian really does have a knack for keeping things organized. You two are a good fit." He sneered. "Like Tweedledum and Tweedledee. But I doubt you two could even catch a rabbit."

"If I get caught, Sumin will start feeding out information. She'll do it gradually, just enough to keep everyone on their toes. She'll send it to newspapers and TV stations, or post it online. She could even e-mail it to hundreds or thousands of people. When they open it, the e-mail will automatically forward to everyone else in their address books. After a few days, millions of people could have their hands on the information."

"You don't seriously think an e-mail virus is enough to protect you, do you?"

"They won't be able to kill me right away. Not until they track down the host."

Mito looked serious. Reseng leaned back and lit a cigarette.

"Then I inflated the ransom to three billion won for no reason," he said. "The prosecution will just keep it for themselves."

"Three billion?"

"Of course. Seven hundred and fifty million split between four people isn't much."

"So you demanded three *billion* instead?"

Mito glared at him. She looked genuinely upset. Reseng gave her a chastened nod. After a moment, her face softened.

"You were really planning to split it with us?" she asked.

"Of course."

"That's pretty quick thinking for that empty head of yours."

She smiled and took a sip of tea, then reached over for one of Reseng's cigarettes. As she smoked, she picked up a paper from the table at random and put it down again.

"I scanned every single one of these. They explain all the secret stuff that takes place behind the scenes. All the ugly, low-down fights that have happened. So many people died, and no one knew the truth behind their deaths. Not their friends or family or even the victims themselves. I think half the battle will be won simply by releasing this information to the world. Even if I die, it will still reach thousands upon thousands of people. Some of those people will be brave or reckless enough to rise up, and some among those will be willing to fight."

"You seriously think there's another crazy bitch out there like you who'll rise up?"

Mito sat deep in thought, without answering. Then she asked, "Did you bring the book?"

"Nope."

"You didn't look for it? Or you couldn't find it?"

"It's not in the basement. It'll be hard to find as long as Old Raccoon's alive. Actually, it'll be hard to find after he's dead, too. At any rate, I don't think there ever was a leather-bound book as you described."

Mito looked disappointed. But she shrugged it off and went over to the desk, took an envelope from the drawer, and offered it to him.

"What is that?"

"A plot that will keep you alive, just as I promised. Since you're in this deep, you can't just brazenly go on living. You'll have to die and come back to life."

"When did you come up with it?"

"*In the beginning was the Plot.* . . . I've had it since I first laid eyes on you."

She handed him the envelope. It looked like all the other envelopes plotters used to send to the library. Reseng pulled out the paper inside and skimmed it. It was a car-accident plot.

"All you have to do is exactly what's written there," she said. "Just do what it says to the letter, and don't get cocky. You'll need to make a few changes to your car and put a body in it. You know how to get a dead body, right?"

"This is a pretty clichéd plot."

"All good plots are. Special cases call for special plots; ordinary cases, ordinary plots."

"Will they fall for it?"

"So you do want to live!"

She was making fun of him.

"Well, if there's no reason I have to die," he said self-consciously. "But what about you?"

"What about me?"

"Do you have to die?"

"If I'm not doing this, then I have no reason to live."

"What about Misa?"

Mito hesitated before answering.

"I'm not like the Barber. He used his daughter to justify his actions, but it's not the same for me with Misa. This world isn't a mess because people are evil. It's because everyone has their own stories and excuses for doing bad things. But I'm not stupid or insensitive enough to use my sister to fool myself. To put it simply, I can't live like that. I'm wired differently."

"I've only met one other person like you in my whole life. Cold as a reptile. He's cold because he hates himself more than he hates the world, and he can never truly accept anyone, because he doesn't know how to accept himself. That person is Old Raccoon."

Mito considered this for a moment and nodded.

"Get some sleep," she said. "Misa's bed is empty." Her face as she rose from the chair suddenly looked very tired. "If I get caught and you survive, will you look after Misa? Just until the coast is clear. Three years will do."

"You would trust your angelic little sister to an assassin like me? Are you crazy?"

"Besides my sister, I know you better than anyone. I've been watching you and researching you for a long time. But more than that, my sister likes you."

Reseng didn't say anything. She waited a moment for his answer and then went into her room. Halfheartedly, he skimmed the document she'd given him and shoved it back into the envelope. Then he went downstairs and lay on the bed in Misa's room. The pillow, the blanket, and the sheets all smelled like Misa. They were as soft as freshly laundered baby clothes hanging in the sun. The moment he closed his eyes, he fell asleep. He slept deeply for the first time in a very long while.

Reseng was wakened by a warm sensation against his cheek. Misa was looking down at him.

"Sorry to wake you," she said.

"That's okay, I should get up anyway. What time is it?"

"Two in the afternoon. I'm leaving now."

"Where are you going?"

"Japan. One of our distant relatives owns an onsen spa."

Reseng got out of bed. Outside the window, Mito was loading Misa's bags into the car. The cross-eyed librarian came into the room.

"Misa, you don't want to miss your plane," Sumin said.

"You should visit me sometime. Come with Mito and Sumin. It's a really nice place."

Reseng nodded. Misa smiled brightly. The librarian looked at her watch again. Misa waved good-bye to Reseng and wheeled out of the cabin. He followed her. The car was packed with far too much luggage for a short trip. Mito picked up Misa and put her in the car, then folded the wheelchair. Misa rolled down the window and looked at Reseng and the librarian.

"Sumin, bring him with you when you visit me!" she said with a wave.

The librarian waved back. Reseng waved, too. Mito gave the librarian a look and turned to Reseng.

"Will you be here when I get back?" she asked.

"Yeah, I'll be here," he said.

Mito got in the car and left. Misa waved her hand out the window until they were out of sight. The car made its way down the forest road, leaving Reseng and the librarian alone. They looked at each other awkwardly.

"Now that Misa's gone, all that's left is for you and Mito to die, right?" he asked sarcastically.

Sumin gazed off down the road, her face imperturbable.

"You won't succeed," he added. "Mito will die, and so will you."

She turned to glare at him.

"Better to die than to live like a dead person," she said. "I've had enough of that."

His watch read 5:00 a.m. Reseng got out of bed, dressed, and went into the bathroom to wash the face looking back at him from the mirror. The face had a dark cloud hanging over it. Reseng recognized the cloud as fear. He dried his face on a towel and went into the other room, where he packed his belongings and put the bag on the table. He went over to Mito's room, steadied his breath, and quietly crept inside. Mito was lying in bed. Her face looked haggard, no doubt from all her long days and late nights. Reseng opened the chloroform bottle and tipped some onto a handkerchief, then held it over Mito's nose and mouth. Her eyes flew open and she stared at him for three long seconds. Her eyes held no fear or surprise, only disappointment bordering on despair. After a moment, she passed out.

Reseng pulled two bags from under Mito's bed. One contained Hanja's ledgers, and the other contained guns, explosives, and all the other items Mito had prepared for her meeting with Hanja. Reseng took a quick inventory of the second bag and zipped it shut. Then he took it with him, grabbing the bag he'd left on the table, as well. After a quick glance at the librarian's room, he left the cabin.

Reseng called Hanja as soon as he arrived in Seoul.

"You got the money?" Reseng asked.

"It's ready. What do you plan to do?" Hanja sounded exasperated.

"Leave the country. You know I have no other choice."

Hanja fumed. "Watch yourself. I assure you, you will never pull this off."

"Wait for my next call, and don't do anything stupid. The moment you do, you'll be stepping on thin ice."

Reseng hung up and turned off his phone.

He got in a cab and headed for G World. Around a central plaza was a hotel, a shopping mall, and a small theme park. Reseng surveyed the shopping mall. Two glass elevators went up and down the outside of the eleven-story building. A sky bridge connected the mall to the hotel on the seventh floor. Reseng got into one of the elevators and pressed all the buttons. A middle-aged woman in the elevator gave him a look of supreme annoyance.

"Sorry, ma'am. Routine inspection."

She nodded apologetically. Each time the door opened, Reseng got out to look around before getting back in and riding up to the next floor. For almost an hour, he alternated between the two elevators before heading back down to the middle of the plaza, where he sat on a bench and smoked a cigarette. Two pigeons flapped giddily around the plaza, snatching bread and cookie crumbs from the ground. They've got wings. Why don't they fly out of this miserable old city? he thought with a smile. He finished his cigarette and headed for a high-end boutique in the mall, where he bought a new suit and a button-down shirt. The salesgirl offered him a shopping bag for his old clothes.

"You can just throw them away," he said.

Reseng went next to a shoe shop across from the boutique and bought a pair of shoes he liked. He threw away the shoes he'd been wearing. After buying a pair of underwear, some socks, and toiletries, he took the glass elevator to the seventh floor and walked slowly across the sky bridge to the hotel. He crossed back and forth three times before heading to the restaurant in the hotel's sky lounge. A stately waiter in his early fifties greeted Reseng and told him the day's special was dry-aged Hanwoo sirloin.

"Dry-aged? What is that?" Reseng asked with a smile.

While the waiter explained the difference between wet and dry aging, Reseng studied the shopping mall on the other side of the sky bridge.

"So, would you like to try the special?" the waiter asked.

"Sure, I'll have that."

The steak turned out to be delicious. Steak was the most re-quested final meal for Americans on death row. The carnivorous desire for raw flesh lurking behind the veil of cooked meat. The taste of blood bursting in your mouth as you chew on another mammal's flesh. Mourners at a funeral eat meat together because that is the privilege of the survivors, and proof of their strong desire to go on living. Reseng savored his food as if he were a death-row inmate, gazing at the glass of red wine that came with the special. He didn't usually drink while working. He picked it up and took a sip. Meat and blood. That's why people love steak, he thought, that cannibalistic instinct hidden inside their neatly pressed suits.

When he had finished eating, Reseng went down to the hotel lobby and booked a room on the seventh floor with a view of the plaza. He took a long bath, washed and combed his hair, and applied toner and lotion to his face. He looked at himself in the mirror. The scar from the Barber's knife stood out vividly on his right cheek.

"You handsome son of a bitch," Reseng said to his reflection. "That scar only makes you sexier."

Reseng put on his new underwear, shirt, and suit. He strapped the holster over his shoulder, the PB/6P9 fitted with the silencer on his right side and Chu's Henckels on his left. He took a .38 revolver from Mito's bag and tucked it into the back of his waistband, then put three PB/6P9 cartridges in his right jacket pocket and thirty bullets for the revolver in his left jacket pocket. His preparations complete, Reseng sat on the edge of the bed and waited for the sun to set.

After darkness had fallen and all the lights had come on in the glass-fronted shopping mall, Reseng called Hanja.

"G World. Shopping Mall. Gate One. Come alone."

He hung up and turned off the phone. After half an hour, Hanja arrived at Gate 1. At first glance, he appeared to be alone. He was dragging two wheeled suitcases. Presumably the larger bag was for the billion won in notes, and the smaller one for the bearer bonds. Reseng took out his binoculars and inspected the east and west ends of the plaza, the mall entrances, and the emergency stairwell on each floor. He turned his phone back on.

"Go to the seventh-floor elevator."

Hanja dragged the suitcases onto the elevator and got off at the seventh floor. Reseng called him again.

"Emergency stairs, eleventh floor." He hung up.

When Hanja was in front of the eleventh-floor emergency stairs, Reseng called again.

"Third-floor elevator."

"Sixth-floor bag department."

"First-floor convenience store."

By the tenth call, Hanja was losing his patience. "What the fuck is this? Obedience school?"

"You're pretty well trained for a mutt. Take a break in the second glass elevator. You've earned it."

Reseng hung up. Hanja dragged the bags back over to the elevator. Each time Hanja moved, Reseng checked the mall entrances, the elevators, and the emergency stairwells through the binoculars. Hanja had brought seventeen assassins with him. Two were posted at each of the mall's four entrances, two were to the left and right of the emergency stairs, one was near the front of the elevator on the first floor, one was near the elevator on the eleventh floor, two were on the sky bridge, and the guy directing all the action was standing in the middle of the plaza. There were probably more in the parking lot and on the roof, and there would also be a car waiting at the curb outside. Reseng grabbed his bag, put on his sunglasses, and headed out of the hotel room. Two brawny men in suits were standing at the end of the sky bridge, examining everyone as they walked by. When Reseng was about to pass them, one of the men raised his hand.

"Hey, you in the glasses."

Reseng pulled out the gun with the silencer and shot both men in the leg. As they fell, Reseng shot the bigger of the two twice more in the thigh, and the smaller guy once more in the thigh. He pulled out the cartridge and slid in a new one. When he'd gone a few more steps, he heard screams behind him. He walked briskly over to the second of the glass elevators and stood in front, pushing the buttons for both. The few seconds it took for the elevator to descend from the ninth floor to the seventh felt like an eternity.

The door opened. Hanja was inside. Reseng pulled the .38 from the back of his pants and fired two shots into the ceiling of the elevator. Everyone screamed and dashed out. Hanja stared at him in shock. Reseng fired two bullets into Hanja's right knee. Hanja shrieked and collapsed against the back wall. A portly middle-aged gentleman was cowering in the corner; he hadn't escaped with the others. Reseng pressed the emergency stop and tapped the man on the shoulder.

"Mister? Everyone's gone. Sure you want to stay?" he asked.

The man looked up at him and rushed out of the elevator. Hanja used the distraction to try to pull a gun from inside his jacket, but Reseng shot him in the right arm and shoulder. He took Hanja's gun and stashed it in his bag, then emptied the revolver's spent casings onto the floor and quickly reloaded it with the bullets in his pocket. He took explosives and duct tape out of Mito's bag and taped a small flash bomb to the outside of the elevator, then lit a Molotov cocktail and waited for the first elevator to reach the seventh floor. When the door opened, he fired bullets into the ceiling again to drive everyone off, then threw the Molotov cocktail and a small can of paint thinner into the first elevator. The inside was quickly engulfed in flames. Reseng got back in the second elevator and shut the door. Hanja groaned and stared at Reseng.

"What the fuck are you doing?" Hanja said.

Reseng shot him in the thigh. "You get another bullet each time you speak."

The car next to them climbed several floors and stopped. Reseng lit a cigarette and smoked it while watching the other elevator burn. People were gathering in the plaza.

"Not quite the box-office smash I was hoping for," Reseng muttered.

He opened one of the suitcases Hanja had brought. It was filled with ten-thousand-won bills. Reseng fired four shots at the glass wall of the elevator and smashed it open with the butt of the revolver, then grabbed handfuls of cash and tossed them out. The bills fluttered down onto the plaza. With a satisfied look, he emptied the rest of the suitcase out of the elevator. Hanja watched, stupefied. Dozens of police cars and fire engines were pulling up. Between them and the hordes of shoppers scrambling to grab the cash, it was instant pandemonium.

Reseng pulled another Molotov cocktail and can of paint thinner from the bag, shook them at the elevator's security camera, lit the rag, and set the bottle in the middle of the elevator. Hanja's face darkened with terror. He opened his mouth to say something, but Reseng pointed the gun at his face and slowly shook his head. Hanja closed his mouth.

Reseng took out his cell phone and called Mito. She answered.

"I'm sorry I didn't get to see you change the world," he said. "To be honest, I don't really believe it's possible . . . but you'll find a book and a locker key in the second drawer anyway. Please tell Misa I'm sorry I couldn't join her."

Mito started to ask what he was talking about, but he hung up on her. He took out his mobile phone's USIM chip, burned it with his lighter, and tossed it outside. Then he lit a cigarette and took a drag. Everyone in the plaza was staring up at him. Were they watching the fire? Or were they waiting for more money to rain down? Maybe they're waiting for me to die, or for me to kill someone, he thought. A police officer was yelling something at him through a megaphone. But Reseng could not make out a word; the sound was lost in the cacophony of all the spectators. Maybe the cop was asking what he wanted. What do I want? he asked himself.

It had been a very long time since he'd last asked himself what he really wanted from life. Why was that? It's not like it cost anything to ask. Maybe he had figured there was no point. The life of an assassin was like cigarette smoke—too hazy and indistinct to settle anywhere. It was a life spent sucking strong tobacco smoke down into the deepest reaches of your lungs and expelling it, staring blankly at the cloud of lethargy and nausea as it floated up into the air, and rushing to take another deep drag on your cigarette for fear of that lethargy and nausea. It was a cowardly life. Any life spent not asking yourself what you truly loved was a cowardly one.

Reseng pictured a very tall house with vaulted ceilings. If only he had lived in a place like that, he could have installed an enormous cat tower the size of Jack's beanstalk and watched Desk and Lampshade play like squirrels leaping from branch to branch. He and Trainer could have opened a pizza or a pasta cart across from a high school. He could've grown delicious potatoes for Old Raccoon, forever reading his encyclopedias, and ditched that damned Doghouse Library once and for all. That would have been something. Trainer was a great cook, and the laughter of high school students was as loud and cheerful as nightingale song. If neighborhood thugs had come around to pick a fight, demanding to know who'd given them permission to set up shop on their turf, Trainer and Reseng would have bent the knee and pretended to beg for forgiveness only to turn on those punks and beat them to a pulp. Then they would have looked at each other's bruised faces and laughed their asses off.

Reseng pictured the bicycle with the pink basket from his factory worker days. At the time, he would have preferred a green basket—

emerald green, like the Mediterranean Sea. But looking back on it now, he decided the pink basket wasn't so bad. After all, the factory girl had loved that basket. He wished he could fill the basket to the brim with fish and fruit and vegetables and ride it uphill with her again, or better still, go for a ride along the river. He would feel the breeze blowing off of the river and catch the scent of freshly washed baby clothes drying in the afternoon sun that she always seemed to carry somehow on her body. If only he could have worked hard at learning a skill on Work Team Three, earned his lathe technician certificate, and spent his days paring iron into splendid machine parts. If only he'd been lucky enough to father a beautiful daughter the spitting image of the factory girl and tickled those tiny baby toes with calloused hands. How wonderful that would have been. His heart would have been so full, as if there were no better life than that one.

"Put down your gun and let's talk. That's the only way we can give you what you want."

The cop with the megaphone was standing right below the elevator and was shouting up at him. Reseng snickered. *Now* they offer to give me what I want, he thought. He fired two shots at a car parked below the elevator. The cop cowered in fear and scuttled behind the car. The other officers and spectators standing nearby scattered in a wide circle. Reseng took out another Molotov cocktail and chucked it at the parked car. It burst into flames. Snipers were being deployed to the hotel side. One on the roof, one in the hotel room across from the elevator, and one on the sky bridge. Though he saw only three, he figured there were more hiding elsewhere. Outside the plaza, TV crews had finally arrived and were setting up their cameras. Cameramen were edging through the crowd to get a shot of Reseng. The police officer who'd moved back in fear was still yelling through his megaphone. Reseng took out a stun grenade, held it aloft in his left hand, and shook it at the crowd as if he were waving hello.

Suddenly, Hanja started chuckling. Reseng turned to look at him. He didn't stop. Reseng cocked his head, raised the revolver, and shot

Hanja in the left thigh. At the sound of the gun, the commotion in the plaza grew louder. Hanja groaned, but he started talking anyway.

"I guess you want to be like Chu. But can people like us ever live up to him?"

"People like us?" Reseng said, keeping the revolver pointed at Hanja.

Hanja wiped the blood dripping from his mouth with the back of his hand.

"Do you know why you hate me?" Hanja asked. "It's because you and I are like twins. You're furious because you're so much like the thing you hate most. But what can you do about it? This is just how we turned out."

Hanja didn't seem to care that talking meant taking another bullet. Even while grimacing in pain, he never lost his mocking gaze.

"How the hell are we alike?"

"People always end up resembling that which they hate the most. Just as a son always ends up taking after his father." Hanja took a deep breath, his body contorting like it was difficult to draw in air. He spat out a mouthful of blood. "But what I really want to know is which of us is more like Old Raccoon. You or me?"

Hanja or him? Him or Hanja? Which one? The sniper wondered. The sniper on the roof was staring at Reseng through the telescopic sight on his rifle. Someone was always being put in the crosshairs; triggers were always being pulled. This time around, it was Reseng's face or chest in death's crosshairs. He wanted to ask the sniper, What face am I making now? He thought about the old man's face as he'd talked to the flowers in his garden. He even pictured old Santa chasing after the deflated soccer ball. It had been a beautiful, clear autumn day, as perfect as a day can get. The old man had smiled brightly in Reseng's crosshairs. The old man living such a lonely life deep in the woods with no refrigerator, no salt, and no visitors had smiled brightly at the end. As if he had finally been able to strip off the carved wooden mask and reveal his true smile.

Reseng lowered the revolver.

"What face am I making now?" he asked.

Hanja stopped laughing and cocked his head.

"What's that supposed to mean?"

"If I could go on living, then starting tomorrow I'd do it all so much better."

"What the fuck are you talking about?"

Reseng didn't answer. Hanja furrowed his brow in confusion. Reseng looked up at the sniper staring down at him from the hotel roof. The sniper raised his head and looked back at Reseng for a moment and then looked through the lens again. The cop on the ground floor was still bellowing something into the megaphone. The television crews were scrambling to get a tighter shot of Reseng. He turned his head up to the sky. The night sky was dark and blurry, the stars drowned out by the city lights. It looked like the entrance to a cave leading to another world, or like the gaping jaws of an enormous fish about to swallow something. Reseng drank in his fill of the night sky and then nodded, as if to say that all was good now. Hanja was staring at him, his face anxious and his breath coming fast as he lay back against the corner of the elevator. Reseng took a step toward Hanja. Then he raised the revolver and pointed it at Hanja's face.

"I'm saying that I feel like I've finally escaped hell. What about you?"

Hanja stared down the barrel of the revolver through unfocused eyes. Reseng glanced down at the plaza and then back at Hanja. He pressed the muzzle of the gun against Hanja's forehead. He could feel Hanja's throat clenching. Hanja closed his eyes.

A shot rang out. Reseng looked down at his chest. There was a hole in it. He felt the hole with his finger. The blood was dark. The bullet must have pierced his liver. When Reseng was turning his head to see where the bullet had exited, a second bullet passed through his lung. He stumbled backward and grabbed the handrail inside the elevator. Blood poured from the bullet holes. His legs shook. He could feel so many things rapidly escaping his body. What were they? Water and blood? Piss and shit and other filth? Or maybe the countless parasites that had been living off of him, using him as a host? Maybe, Reseng thought, this thing leaving his body right now was his soul. And leaving with it were all of the thoughts that he had had during his stay on Earth, all of his sorrow, rage, resignation, and other emotions, and all of his warm and painful and mushy and aching senses. But having dragged this heavy, cumbersome body and soul around for a lifetime, Reseng thought that it wasn't so bad, this losing of something, this growing lighter. If he were to spill all of his blood, have his flesh fall away, decomposed by tiny insects, his bones dried and pared down by the sun and wind like an ancient camel skeleton in the middle of the desert, if he were to grow infinitely light, how fine would that be? If only he could grow smaller and smaller, lighter and lighter, and travel freely on the wind.

His ears filled with the sound of running water. Cool water rolling over a bed of gravel. Water as ice-cold as it had always been. But now he thought it wasn't such a bad place after all. He would become a stone at the bottom of that stream. Or some flat moss. Or a butterfly dodging drops of water as it fluttered away.

Reseng fell to his knees and aimed his trademark smirk at the sky.